The Lady in Question

Books by
Victoria Alexander

VICTORIA ALEXANDER

The LADY IN QUESTION

AVON BOOKS

An Imprint of HarperCollins*Publishers*

This is a work of fiction. Names, characters, places, and incidents are products of the author's imagination or are used fictitiously and are not to be construed as real. Any resemblance to actual events, locales, organizations, or persons, living or dead, is entirely coincidental.

AVON BOOKS
An Imprint of HarperCollins*Publishers*
10 East 53rd Street
New York, New York 10022-5299

This book is dedicated
to Tory
with love from Mom.
Giving you roots was easy,
giving you wings was
the hardest thing we've ever done.
In spite of your wacko parents,
you've grown up beautifully
and your dad and I are so proud.
Stretch your wings, sweet baby girl,
and know we will always be here for you.

Prologue

January 1820

Could he indeed change his life?

He stared into the dark night and the darker water, his senses alert to any odd sound, any movement out of place in this secluded section of the Dover docks. Tonight, as always, his life depended on it. A man who was not vigilant every moment could find himself a failure and a dead failure, at that.

He leaned against a stack of crates, well out of the lit areas of the docks, as much a part of the shadows as any creature of the night. He'd always rather liked this part, this waiting for the unknown. There was an odd sort of solitude, even comfort, offered by the dark. He was truly alone at moments like this, accompanied only by his own instincts and his private thoughts.

Or had she already changed it?

Even now, when he could ill afford any distraction, the question demanded attention. He hadn't planned on allowing her into his life. Hadn't planned on anything past using her to get the information he needed. And he certainly hadn't planned on marriage.

But the blasted woman had touched something within him he thought long dead and buried. She'd looked beyond the carefully cultivated image of rakish scoundrel and womanizing rogue, tolerated in society only because of parentage and title, to what he'd once been. Perhaps what he could be again.

No.

What he *would* be again, one way or another. Much depended on what happened tonight. He'd never before considered what he would have to do to leave the work he'd done, and done well, for more than a decade. Ending his relationship with the clandestine department that had quietly evolved after the war would not be easy. But who else among the brave fools he'd worked with could accomplish such a coup as well as he? St. Stephens, perhaps.

"I assume you brought the money."

She emerged from the darkness like a specter made of nothing more substantial than the fog. He was hard-pressed to hide his shock at the sight of her. Of course, he should have realized the truth of her nature years ago. It was annoying that he hadn't. And annoying as well that he hadn't noted her approach. His mind was not where it should be, and that was as dangerous as the woman before him.

"I should have suspected your lovely hand in this." His voice was cool, casual, as if they were meeting one another during an afternoon stroll in a park and not on a Dover dock late in the night.

"I am surprised you didn't." The tone of her response matched his. Even in the faint light, he could see the slight, familiar curve of her smile. "No doubt your mind was far too occupied with thoughts of your new wife."

He shrugged, refusing to show so much as a twinge of emotion at her charge.

"I was surprised as well you had taken such a step." Genuine curiosity sounded in her voice. "I did not think you were the type of man ever to wed."

"Perhaps you did not know me as well as you thought."

"Perhaps." She paused. "Nor did I think she was the sort of woman you would choose to warm your bed."

He bit back a satisfied smile. A voice in his head warned him to watch his step. He ignored it. "The sort of woman one chooses to warm one's bed is rarely the same sort one marries."

He sensed more than heard her sharp intake of breath. It was foolish of him to bait her this way. But she'd known, as well as he, their times together had been little more than an enjoyable diversion on either side. Odd, then, her reaction to his marriage.

"I believe you have something that belongs to me." Her voice was brisk and businesslike but carried a sharp edge that did not bode well.

Again, he hid his surprise. If indeed she knew what he had found, this meeting was far more treacherous than he had expected. He chose his words carefully. "I brought the money."

"Excellent. And I'm more than willing to give you the documents." Her voice hardened. "But I want the notebook."

He should have paid closer attention to the contents of the notebook, but there'd scarcely been enough time to do more than glance at it and find a hiding place where it would be safe until all this was resolved.

"I don't know what you're talking about." He shrugged.

"I don't believe you."

Her gaze slipped past him and at once he realized she was not alone. Without warning, strong hands gripped him on either side. It was pointless to struggle. Only his wits would get him out of this now.

"I'm here for the documents, nothing more. Now." He glanced at the men on either side of him. Both outweighed him and were no doubt armed. Escape would be a challenge. "If you will have these gentlemen release me, the money is in my carriage."

She studied him for a moment. "I don't believe that either."

Still, she nodded at the man to his right, who released him and headed off. The other pulled his arms behind his back and held him securely. At least the odds were better now. And his carriage was some distance away. It would take time for her other henchman to return. She was right, of course. He had the money on him.

"Now I want the notebook."

"I have no idea—" The man behind him jerked his arms back harder and he winced. "Well, that's scarcely polite."

"I am not in the mood to be polite." She stepped closer, and the moonlight glinted off a knife in her hand. Yet another thing he should have expected. She'd always been good with a knife.

"I cannot give you what I don't have." He stared down at her and wondered if there was a better way to get out of this than confrontation. He softened his tone. "But we have always given one another pleasure. We have been good together. Have you forgotten that?"

"I have forgotten nothing."

"And nothing needs to change between us simply because I am now married."

"And what of your wife?"

"My wife has a great deal of money." He forced an

offhand note to his voice. "She is a necessity. A man in my position needs a respectable wife and an heir. My marriage means nothing more than that."

She moved closer, close enough to kiss. "Once again, I don't believe you."

But the tone in her voice said she wanted to believe him. It was at once a good sign and far and away more dangerous. Emotions always raised the stakes.

"Believe me, my dear. There has only ever been one woman for me." He lowered his head to meet her lips.

Her lips whispered against his. "Do you love her?"

He hesitated for no more than a heartbeat, but it was enough.

"No," he said in tandem with the plunge of her knife deep into his gut and the sharp pain that ripped away his breath and buckled his knees.

"Get rid of him." Her voice was hard, cold, unyielding.

"But the money—" her cohort said.

"I don't care," she snapped.

The man released him and he realized his ploy for freedom had worked. Even as he tumbled into the cold water and unconsciousness enveloped him, confidence in his own abilities, his own invulnerability, never wavered.

He would not die like this. Not here and not tonight. He had survived before and he would survive again. Now he had far too much to live for.

Now he had her.

Chapter 1

June 1820

Dearest Cassie,

I have at last returned to London to take up residence in my husband's house. I am all too aware that Mother has yet to forgive me for my transgressions and continues to forbid you to so much as speak to me, but if it is at all possible could you pay me a call this afternoon? I have missed you terribly, dear sister. I arrived three days ago and there is no one here to talk to save the servants, and they are an odd lot indeed. . . .

"Given the circumstances, that is, all things considered, and the time that has passed . . ." Lady Wilmont, Philadelphia—Delia to her dearest friends, and, up until a scant six months ago, Miss Effington—picked at an odd thread on the arm of the far-too-masculine sofa in the parlor of her late husband's town house and forced a casual note to her voice. "Do you think Mother will ever speak to me again?"

"I certainly wouldn't wager on it at the moment. She's already gone on far longer than I would have expected." Cassandra Effington, Delia's younger sister by no more than two minutes, drew her brows together thoughtfully. "You know how Mother is. She has taken all of this as an affront to the stars, a defiance of destiny, that sort of thing."

"Yes, she would, wouldn't she?" Delia heaved a resigned sigh.

"Mother will come around eventually." Cassie leaned closer and patted her twin's hand. "In truth, I think now that you have returned from exile—"

"It wasn't exile, Cassie, it was the Lake District."

Cassie scoffed. "The Lake District in winter sounds very much like exile to me."

"Not at all. Besides, each of our brothers visited and Father sent letters."

"Even so, for the most part you were ensconced with a relative so distant we have scarcely heard of her."

"Great-Aunt Cecily. She was quite nice—if rather private—which was well and good, because what I needed was time and distance," Delia said firmly. "Away from London and gossip and scandal."

"Perhaps we should send Mother to the Lake District. It's taking her rather a long time to get over her—"

"Anger? Outrage? Embarrassment?"

"Yes, of course, all of that." Cassie waved away her sister's words as if they were of no importance. "I believe Mother could manage anger, outrage, embarrassment, humiliation, disgrace, dishonor—"

"I don't think I actually used the words *humiliation, disgrace* or *dishonor,*" Delia murmured.

"Use them or not, they are present nonetheless," Cassie said firmly. "However, my point is that Mother could cope with all that and more. She is, even if merely by marriage, an Effington. And Effingtons are well used to dealing with the petty problems brought on by the occasional minor scandal."

"You think this was minor, then?" Delia sat up a bit straighter.

"Oh, dear Lord, no. Not at the time anyway." Cassie shook her head with far more enthusiasm than was necessary. "No, an Effington running off with a scoundrel of Lord Wilmont's reputation was quite the *biggest* scandal of the year."

"I suppose so." Delia sank back in her seat, an odd rational portion of her mind chastising her for such posture. Miss Philadelphia Effington never slouched. Apparently, however, Lady Wilmont did.

"This may well be the biggest scandal of the last few years," Cassie added. "In fact, I am hard-pressed to recall a bigger scandal ever. Although I do suppose—"

"That's quite enough, thank you." Delia sighed again and slumped deeper into the sofa. The perfect carriage expected of a properly bred young woman of two-and-twenty scarcely seemed of significance when one was the center of the biggest scandal of the last few years. Or ever.

"Oh, dear, I haven't been any help at all, have I? Very well. Perhaps I have exaggerated somewhat. It probably only seemed so huge because it occurred in December and there was little else for everyone to talk about." Cassie cast her sister a sympathetic look. "I do apologize, dearest, it's simply odd for me to be in this position. And frankly, that's why I think Mother has had such a difficult time with it all."

Delia raised a brow. "Because it isn't you?"

"Exactly." Cassie nodded firmly. "She and everyone else have always thought if one of us were ever to be embroiled in a scandal of this magnitude—"

"It could have been far worse. I did *marry* him, after all," Delia pointed out.

"In this particular case, I daresay that *does* make it worse," Cassie said. "I still do not understand why you did it."

"Nor do I," Delia said under her breath.

She had no idea how to explain what she could only call the madness that had inflicted her in weeks surrounding Christmas and ultimately led to scandal and her current odd position of barely wed widow.

Six months. It scarcely seemed long enough for a life to change so completely. Six months ago she hadn't a care in the world save for the usual questions about whether or not she or her sister would find a suitable match in the coming year.

"Your letters were not at all informative, at least not about anything of significance. We have had no chance to talk since it all happened." Cassie shrugged casually. "You fled so quickly—"

"I didn't flee. I"—Delia wrinkled her nose—"escaped. It was cowardly of me, I know, but I was hard-pressed at the time to accept that I lost my mind, ran off and ruined my life."

"It's not entirely ruined. You did marry him."

"You just said in this case that might well have made it worse."

"I did, didn't I? Well, I might have been wrong."

Delia snorted in a disdainful and unladylike manner most unbecoming for Miss Philadelphia Effington but quite appropriate for the widowed Lady Wilmont.

Cassie studied her sister carefully. "I have been most patient, but it's past time you told me everything."

"Everything?"

Cassie nodded. "Absolutely. Every detail. Do not leave a single thing out. It's the very least you can do."

She crossed her arms over her chest, settled back in her chair and stared at her sister. "You have no idea what it feels like to discover one morning your sister, your *twin sister,* has run off with some man—"

"Charles," Delia murmured.

Cassie ignored her. "—and you knew nothing about it. You hadn't so much as a hint of what she'd been up to. I can tell you right now it's quite distressing. In addition, not one soul in the entire household believed I was completely innocent and no more aware of your intentions than anyone else."

Delia winced. "I am sorry about that."

"Mother and Father questioned me as if I were a traitor to the crown."

"I can imagine."

"No, Delia, I don't believe you can. You've never been in this position because we have never had secrets between us. At least I have never kept secrets from you."

"Nor have I," Delia said quickly. "Until now."

Cassie sniffed. "I'm still not certain I shall ever forgive you."

"But I do apologize. Really, I do." Delia couldn't blame her sister for being overset, even angry, over Delia's failure to confide in her.

"You can begin making up for it by telling me everything. However, I don't have much time. Mother doesn't know I'm here."

"It's absurd the way she's separating us, as if we were still children." Delia studied her sister. "I must say, your willingness to abide by her edict is somewhat surprising."

Cassie laughed, the dimple in her left cheek a mirror image of Delia's own. "I'm rather surprised by it myself. But, as I've always been the sister expected to totter off the edge of respectability, and therefore you've always been something of a favorite—"

"I most certainly have not!"

"Perhaps." Cassie shrugged. "Nonetheless, I have quite enjoyed being the proper sister in your absence. It's really quite pleasant, although not entirely fair. I've always maintained the differences between us were minimal and nothing more than superficial at best." She grinned. "And I must say I do appreciate your proving me right."

"So glad I could be of assistance," Delia said wryly.

Cassie might indeed be right, although Delia had never thought so before now.

The sisters were as alike in appearance as two peas in a pod, save that Delia favored her right hand and Cassie her left. Cassie had long believed it was the same for their temperaments and had always insisted the difference between them was no more than a matter of degree. Shading, if you will. She considered herself a bit more impulsive, outspoken and adventurous than her barely older sister, but only a bit. Delia rarely disagreed with this assessment aloud but privately thought it was a great deal more than a bit. She saw herself as far quieter, much more reserved and entirely more cautious than her sister.

"Now, you may begin by telling me exactly when you met Wilmont." Cassie settled back in her chair. "Go on."

"Very well." Delia blew a resigned breath. "Do you remember Lady Stanley's Christmas ball? How frightfully overcrowded and stuffy it was?"

"It's overcrowded and stuffy at every ball."

"It was particularly so that night. I felt the need for a breath of fresh air, so I slipped out to the terrace."

She'd since thought there must have been something in the air that crisp winter night, in the glow cast by the stars, in the promise of the spring to come. A promise of something new and unknown and exciting. Some kind of magic spell, perhaps, or more, something she had always yearned for but hadn't recognized she'd wanted until that very moment.

"And that's when you met Wilmont?"

"Yes." Lord Wilmont. Baron Wilmont. *Charles.*

"And?"

"And . . . we exchanged pleasantries." He'd appeared out of the shadows, almost as if he had been waiting just for her.

"Pleasantries?"

"One might call it something of a flirtation, I suppose." He'd been outrageous. Totally improper and far and away too intimate. He'd taken off his jacket and wrapped it around her shoulders. Completely scandalous. And utterly, utterly charming.

Cassie raised a brow. "Oh? And were you flirtatious in return?"

"I might have been." Delia shrugged offhandedly. She'd responded in kind that night with a confident, teasing demeanor not at all like her usual reserved nature. In the back of her mind, she'd wondered what on earth had possessed her, but enjoyed it nonetheless. "A bit, perhaps."

"I see." Cassie considered her sister for a long moment. Delia resisted the urge to squirm in her seat. "And then what?"

"Then?"

"Yes, *then.* Unless you decided that very moment on the terrace at Lady Stanley's that you would run off with him, there was obviously a *then.* When did you next see him?"

"The next day. At a bookseller's, Hatchard's, I think." He'd scarce acknowledged her acquaintance save to tip his hat and politely recommend a book of poetry, handing it to her as he left. Inside, she'd found a scrap of paper with his signature and the words *until we meet again*. Later, he'd given her the same book. "And again at Lady Concord-Smythe's soiree. . . ."

Lord Wilmont, *Charles,* was not the type of man who was generally attracted to Miss Philadelphia Effington, which she could see now made him all the more attractive. His reputation as an irresponsible spendthrift and gambler rivaled only his reputation with women. Gossip had it that he had been the ruination of more than one young woman and no respectable lady should so much as favor him with a dance. His frequent absences from London for long periods during the last decade only fueled the rumors about him.

Still, when Wilmont did deign to make an appearance, his impeccable family ties allowed him entrée into the tight-knit and somewhat hypocritical world of London society. Of course, the ladies could not fail to notice that he was exceedingly handsome, with hair the color of spun gold, a wicked twinkle in his eye and a smile that told a woman it was for her and her alone. And the gentlemen were quite aware that regardless of whatever else he may be, he always paid his debts. In addition, he was possessed of a significant fortune and bore an old and honorable title, if perhaps a bit tarnished.

As for his reputation, it was all rumor and innuendo. Why, Delia had never actually met anyone who had been ruined by the man. The stories she'd heard about him might well be little more than fabrications spun by those jealous of his appearance or his wealth or his name.

Not knowing had made him all the more mysterious and dangerous and exciting.

And *he* wanted *her*. From the moment they'd met, that simple fact had made her reckless and daring, entirely different from her usual nature. She'd reveled in the difference, in who she was with him and only with him, and reveled as well in the certain knowledge that this dangerous rake wanted her not because she was an excellent match but because she was very much a woman and he was every inch a man. It was the most intoxicating sensation she'd ever known. And completely irresistible.

"And at Lady Bradbourne's New Year's ball, and . . ." Delia smiled weakly. "I met him quite a bit, actually."

"Good Lord." Cassie sank back in her chair and stared. "I can't believe no one noticed."

"You'd be amazed at how easy it is to slip away from a crowded ballroom to a secluded library or empty parlor." Delia drummed her fingers nervously on the armrest of the sofa. This had been her secret and hers alone for so long, it was surprisingly awkward to reveal it now, even to Cassie, the one person Delia had never kept anything from.

"Indeed I would. I suspect you can teach me a great deal, dear sister." Grudging admiration shone in Cassie's eyes.

"This is surprisingly difficult to talk about." Delia rose to her feet and paced the room, wringing her hands absently with every step. "I had thought, given the passage of time, that it would be easy to tell you, but I find I am not at all good at confession."

"It is good for the soul, they say," Cassie said primly.

"I doubt that. My soul doesn't feel the least bit good. Only quite, quite foolish."

"Nonsense. Oh, not that it wasn't foolish," Cassie said quickly, "every bit of it, but you probably couldn't help falling in love with the man."

Delia stopped and stared at her sister, her words coming before she could stop them. "Oh, but you see, I didn't."

Cassie's brows drew together in confusion. "But I thought—"

"Oh, I know." Delia waved her sister quiet. "I would have thought exactly the same thing: that someone in my position would have gotten in my position in the first place because she had quite fallen head over heels and therefore lost all sense of proper behavior. But it wasn't like that at all."

"I'm afraid to ask precisely what it was like."

"It was . . ." Delia clasped her hands together and screwed up her courage. "Quite the most exciting thing I have ever imagined. The adventure I had always dreamed of."

"Adventure?"

"I'm not certain how else to explain it." Delia groped for the right words. "It was very much like riding a horse entirely too fast. You know it's dangerous and will more than likely end badly, but it's so exhilarating, you don't really care."

Delia returned to perch on the edge of the sofa. "I know this makes absolutely no sense whatsoever, but Charles was not at all the kind of man who is usually interested in me. Even you must admit my suitors were inevitably somber in character, serious in demeanor and bent on the altogether critical quest of finding a suitable wife. And to a man they were one and all deadly dull."

"Well, yes, they were rather—"

"Whereas gentlemen who seek your favors are typically dashing and exciting and often have an air of danger about them."

"I have never understood it myself." Cassie shook her head. "We are both precisely the same in appearance—"

"Yes, but there is something about you." Delia studied her sister, trying to put her observations into words. "As much as staring at you is like staring at a mirror, there is a difference. In the look in your eye or the tilt of your smile, perhaps. Something that says you could be terribly improper given the slightest provocation." She sighed and settled back on the sofa. "I obviously look like I would never so much as have an improper thought."

"Looks indeed can be quite deceiving, as I have never particularly done anything improper save speak my mind. However, you managed to make yourself the center of scandal."

"I did marry him."

"And everyone asked why. Good Lord, Delia, people wondered if Wilmont married you for the respectability of your family or your family's money—"

"Actually, his solicitor wrote me about that. I am apparently quite well off," Delia murmured.

"—or to save your honor. Of course, that would make him a much better man than anyone suspected and would make you . . ."

Heat flashed up Delia's face.

"Delia?"

Delia jumped up and crossed the room in a futile attempt to avoid the inevitable.

"Philadelphia Effington!" Shock sounded in Cassie's voice. "I can't believe—"

Delia whirled to face her sister. "Did I fail to mention the excitement of riding entirely too fast?"

"You were speaking about a feeling! And blast it all, you were talking about a horse! At least, I thought you were talking about a horse." Cassie stared, her eyes wide with shock. "You didn't, Delia, I know you. You couldn't. You wouldn't."

"I might have." Delia pretended to study her fingernails. "Once."

For a moment silence hung in the room. Delia held her breath.

"How?" Cassie asked at last.

Delia's gaze snapped to hers. "What do you mean, *how*?"

"How did you manage it?" Cassie's eyes narrowed. "Surely you didn't take that little horseback ride—"

"Cassie!"

Cassie ignored her. "—in a library or an empty parlor."

"Of course not." A touch of indignation sounded in Delia's voice. "That would be most improper."

Cassie raised a disbelieving brow.

Delia ignored her. "Do you remember the night I feigned illness and you and the rest of the family went off to whatever party it was you attended?"

"Vaguely."

"I had a hired carriage waiting to take me here. To Charles's house."

"Oh, nothing improper there." Sarcasm colored Cassie's words.

Delia raised her hands in front of her in a helpless gesture. "And Charles insisted afterwards on marrying me."

"I see." Cassie's expression was annoyingly noncommittal.

"And I do wish you wouldn't refer to it as a horseback ride." Delia drew her brows together. "It makes it all so . . . unseemly."

"And we wouldn't want that." Cassie got to her feet. "I was wrong, though. It was a good thing that he married you. Pity he had to get himself killed within the week."

"Yes, it was." There was a familiar pang when Delia said the words. Of regret for what might have been and of guilt as well that he was gone and she hadn't truly cared for him the way she'd always wished she would one day care for the man she married.

"However"—Cassie put on her hat and adjusted it to the proper angle—"his death has been of some benefit."

"I scarcely see—"

"Actually, you needn't see, because I do." Cassie pulled on her gloves in a slow and deliberate manner. "No one knows this was not a love match, indeed I didn't know myself until a few minutes ago." She pinned her sister with an accusing look. "Did I mention how lacking in anything of substance your letters were?"

"You may have."

"I knew your return would renew discussion of the scandal, which had died down nicely, I might add. So, I am taking it upon myself to rectify the situation."

"What do you mean, *rectify*?" Delia said slowly.

"Nothing much, really. A few carefully placed words here and there and the way the world sees this incident will change dramatically. You will no longer be the subject of scandal and curiosity, but sympathy."

"Cassie, what are you—"

"It's obvious you were swept off your feet by this rake and obvious as well that he felt the same. Why would a man with as unsavory a reputation as Wilmont's marry you otherwise?" Smug satisfaction sounded in Cassie's voice. "I wish I had thought of it months ago, but it didn't occur to me until I learned you were on your way home.

"You reformed this rake into becoming an honorable man, but before either of you could enjoy your new-found love, he was tragically killed. In your grief, you exiled yourself—"

"The Lake District is not exile."

"—until you could once again face the world."

"That part, at least, is true, although it was embarrassment more than grief—"

"Yes, but my version is perfect and too, too romantic. Tragedy combined with love is irresistible."

"I don't think—"

"It might even alleviate any speculation that Wilmont

was leaving you, so soon after your marriage, which was why he was on the packet to France alone."

"That's absurd," Delia said staunchly. "Charles had pressing business interests in France and did not think it was appropriate for me to accompany him." Delia hated to admit that she did not know her husband well enough to truly know if indeed what he had told her as to the purpose of his trip was true. Given his behavior after their marriage, she too had wondered if he was leaving her. Whatever the purpose of his trip, it cost him his life when the packet wrecked during a storm in the channel.

"Regardless, my idea is brilliant and you may thank me for it later. It might even hasten Mother's forgiveness. I daresay she would much rather be the mother of a tragic, bereaved widow who sacrificed all for love than the mother of a—"

"Very well, then," Delia said quickly. "I suppose it's worth a try, at any rate."

Cassie flashed a grin. "I shall do more than try, dear sister, I shall rally the Effington women, except for Mother, of course, in a valiant effort to twist the flow of gossip to your advantage. I haven't the least doubt of what we can accomplish."

For the first time in a long time Delia laughed. "It is indeed a formidable force."

The ladies of the Effington family were well known for strength of character and other qualities considered either sterling or troublesome depending on one's point of view. They'd long understood the power wielded by their family had as much to do with the tenacity of its female members as its men.

Cassie pulled on her gloves and started toward the door.

"You're not leaving, are you?" A sliver of panic shot

through Delia. "You've scarcely been here any time at all and it's so dreadfully lonely."

"I don't want to, but," Cassie sighed, "Mother is keeping a closer eye on me than usual. She firmly believes if she had been as watchful when it came to you, all of this would have been avoided." She considered her sister for a moment. "You could come with me, you know. Father would welcome you and Mother can just as easily not speak to you at home as she can if you remain here."

"I should like that, but . . ." The idea was exceedingly tempting. To return home and pretend nothing had ever happened. But among all else she had realized during her months of relative solitude, she understood and accepted that her life had changed forever and no amount of pretense would undo what was done. Besides, she had the blood of generations of Effington women in her veins and it was past time she behaved with the courage that was her birthright. "I have chosen my path and now I must live with it."

"I knew you would say that; I would have been quite shocked if you hadn't." Cassie shook her head and smiled. "I must say I rather envy you."

"Why on earth would you envy me?"

"As a widow you are no longer subject to the limitations that govern my life. You may not realize it at the moment, dear sister, but you are free."

"Free?" Delia folded her arms over her chest. "I'd scarcely call the restrictions of mourning free. I have simply traded one set of rules for another."

"But there is an end in sight for you and then you may do precisely as you wish." Cassie's eyes sparkled with amusement. "Perhaps I can find myself a wealthy rake to marry who will then conveniently die. Someone quite old, I think, barely tottering, to ensure I would become a widow as quickly as possible."

"Cassie!" Delia tried and failed to hold back a laugh.

"It was just a thought and at least I have made you laugh." Cassie gave her sister a quick hug. "I don't know when I'll be able to visit again, but I suspect I can manage to write and dispatch a servant to deliver my notes. Every day, if you wish."

"That would be wonderful," Delia said with relief. "I feel quite isolated here. This house is not overly large, but it's rather empty."

"Surely Wilmont had servants?"

"Only a housekeeper, who also served as cook, and a butler, and they up and quit right after I was informed of Charles's death. Father had this house closed up for me when I left. As for my own maid . . . you remember Martha?"

Cassie nodded.

"She met a farmer while we were gone and stayed to marry him when I returned to London, so I shall need to replace her. Did I tell you the house had been broken into while I was away?"

Cassie gasped. "Good Lord."

"The thieves left quite a mess and, I confess, it was most unnerving. There wasn't a single room left untouched. All the books in the library were torn from the shelves, every drawer pulled from every chest, furniture upended. The picture of chaos, really."

"Delia, are you certain you're safe here?"

Delia waved away the question. "Of course. Such things are bound to happen when a house is left empty for so long. Fortunately, the very day I returned, a new butler, sent by an employment service, I assume, arrived. I hired him at once, and he promptly hired a housekeeper and a footman. They have spent the last few days setting everything to rights while I have tried to determine if anything was taken."

"It's fortunate that you have help, but isn't it a little odd that these servants just magically appeared on your doorstep?"

"There was nothing magical about it. No doubt the previous servants notified the service and they were simply waiting to send anyone until I had returned." Delia shook her head. "And I don't mind in the least, given the state of the house. Besides, their references were excellent."

"I met the butler when I arrived. He seems rather old."

"And therefore has a great deal of experience. He will serve for the moment," Delia said firmly. The last thing she wanted or needed to worry about was hiring servants. "Besides, he came highly recommended."

"Well, that's something, I suppose." Cassie started to open the door, then paused and met her sister's gaze. "Delia, what was it like?"

"It?"

"*It*. You know exactly what I mean by *it*." Cassie studied her cautiously. "With him."

Realization struck Delia and her face burned. "Oh, that *it*."

"Well?"

"It was"—Delia struggled to find the right words— "interesting. Rather enjoyable, really. . . ."

"Was it as painful as they say?" Cassie's tone was casual, but curiosity shone on her face. "The first time, that is?"

"Not really. It was odd and a bit uncomfortable, but . . ."

"And after that?"

Delia was not about to admit, even to Cassie, that

there had been nothing beyond a first time. Nor would she ever tell her it was not quite as wild and glorious as she had expected. She drew a deep breath. "All in all, I'd say the experience had a great deal of potential."

"Potential?" Cassie raised a brow.

"Potential," Delia said firmly.

"Potential," Cassie murmured. "That is interesting." A few moments later she kissed her sister on the cheek and took her leave.

Delia lingered at the parlor door long enough to watch the new butler, Gordon, see her sister out, then closed the door and slumped against it.

It was exceedingly hard to be an outcast in one's own family. She regretted that, but little else.

Even now, Delia knew if she could indeed turn back the clock and live once again the days that had led to to-day, she would make the same choices. Oh, she would do what she could to prevent Charles's death and do what she could as well to build affection from what started as nothing more than passion, but she would not change her actions.

For all of her twenty-two years, she'd known it was her lot in life, as well as her sister's, to look as lovely as possible, to learn those skills that would serve them well as the proper hostess and mistress of a household and, of course, to make excellent matches. What real choice was there other than marriage for the daughters of Lord William, William Effington, the brother of the Duke of Roxborough?

The sisters had on occasion through the years discussed, or rather bemoaned, whatever quirk of fate that had decreed them female with no true purpose in life save to wed and breed well. They quite envied their brothers and male cousins, who were free to explore the world and have grand adventures and lead exciting lives.

With age, they'd discovered there was a certain amount of adventure offered in the flirtatious smile cast by a handsome lord, the promise of excitement to be found in the meeting of the admiring gaze thrown by a roguish gentleman across a crowded ballroom. Adventure and excitement that had not truly tempted Delia before Charles.

In hindsight, she wondered if rebellion had always simmered unacknowledged beneath her calm exterior, some reckless unknown need for excitement or adventure, and wondered as well if the realization that she fast approached an age when she could no longer avoid a suitable marriage, with or without affection, had simply brought forth that part of her nature. Charles had offered the excitement and adventure and, yes, danger she didn't know she yearned for until she met him.

Regardless of the outcome, this had been the grandest adventure of her life.

Now she simply had to live with it.

Chapter 2

The door closed behind the Effington woman and he breathed a silent sigh of relief.

Blast it all. What did he know about being a bloody butler save that he should be at once completely indispensable and virtually invisible?

Anthony Artemis Gordon St. Stephens, the new Viscount St. Stephens, had been in countless awkward and dangerous situations through the years, but none quite as irritating as this one. He could handle himself under the most dire of conditions, but the behavior of a properly trained butler was not in his repertoire. Perhaps if the servants of his childhood in his father's house had not been quite so well trained he would at least have been more aware of their activities, although he doubted it. He had not been overly perceptive as a child.

He stepped away from the door and started toward the back hall. At least Miss Effington—no, Lady Wilmont—was not experienced enough as the mistress of a household to note his lack of training. At least not yet. Surely his purpose here would be accomplished by the time she realized there was something distinctly odd about this particular servant.

Without thinking, he scratched the back of his head, then remembered to brush from his jacket the dusting of power the action had dislodged. Powdering his hair to achieve the impression of age was almost as annoying as the false mustache, eyebrows and spectacles he sported to complete the illusion of age, or the small wads of cotton stuffed between upper teeth and jaw to distort his face and remind him constantly to alter the pitch of his voice. Besides, the blasted powder itched.

It was, in truth, Wilmont's fault. If he had stuck to the plan and followed proper procedures, Tony would not be in this position in the first place. Not only had Wilmont unexpectedly wed Philadelphia Effington, but he'd uncovered valuable information far and above his current investigation. Pity, both his reasons for marrying as well as this newfound information, allegedly detailed in a notebook, were lost with him when he died.

Tony pushed aside the regret that stabbed him every time he thought of Wilmont's death. One would think he would have become used to death during the war. Or perhaps it was a sign of humanity that one never became used to death, especially the death of friends.

"Gordon?" Lady Wilmont called from the parlor door.

Tony adjusted his spectacles, nearly as annoying as the mustache, gritted his teeth and turned back to her. "Yes, my lady?"

"Would you join me in the library for a moment?"

"Certainly, ma'am."

She swept across the foyer and opened the library door a step before him. Damnation. He should have done that. He'd never realized servants had to be quite so quick on their feet, especially necessary in a household like this, where the staff, besides himself, consisted of Mrs. Miller, who served as both housekeeper and cook, and John MacPherson, the footman, neither of whom was any more servant than Tony. Tony could certainly see where an additional footman or two and one or more maids would come in handy, especially given the chaos in the house upon Lady Wilmont's return. The place had definitely been searched. Still, for now, Tony, Mac and Mrs. Miller would have to serve.

However, Tony would have to do much better. It would not serve to be dismissed before he was ready. Of course, Lady Wilmont should have known better as well. Still, what could he expect from a woman who'd married a man she'd known less than a month? A woman who obviously had no sense of proper behavior. Such a woman was either incredibly stupid, unbelievably naïve or impossibly romantic. Probably all three.

Lady Wilmont seated herself at her husband's desk, folded her hands nervously on top of an untidy stack of papers and drew a deep breath. Tony stopped before the desk, clasped his hands behind his back in his best butler stance and waited. Finally she glanced up at him with a tentative smile, her eyes wide and a rather seductive shade of blue. Odd, he hadn't thought of her eyes as seductive before now. It was probably no more than a strange quirk of the late afternoon light in the library. The same light that was responsible for turning her fair hair into a golden halo around her head. Ironic, as he had no doubt she was a far cry from anything approaching angelic.

"Gordon, I have a confession to make."

His muscles tensed. "Yes, my lady?"

"I don't quite know how to say this." A look of helplessness crossed her face and he knew, with an instinct that had served him well in the past, this confession had nothing to do with his purpose here. He steeled himself against a surprising stab of sympathy. Whatever else she might be, she had lost her husband, and one could only assume she would not have married Wilmont if she had not harbored some affection for him.

"Yes?"

"It's just . . ."—she waved her hand over the papers—"all of this. I haven't the faintest idea what to do about it."

"Forgive me, my lady, but I'm not certain I understand," he said slowly.

"This has all been awaiting my return and must be dealt with at once. There are bills and statements of banking accounts and documents about interests Lord Wilmont held and property he owned and heaven knows what else, and"—panic sounded in her voice—"I don't even know where to begin."

"Perhaps Lord Wilmont's solicitor could—"

"No, no." She brushed off his suggestion with an impatient gesture. "I met with him yesterday and, well, I didn't like him. No, that's not entirely accurate. I didn't"— she thought for a moment—"trust him, I suppose. I know it sounds foolish, obviously Lord Wilmont trusted him, but there was something about him. . . ."

Whatever else the woman's failings might be, she had excellent instincts. About this, at least. For reasons of security, Wilmont's solicitor, Mr. Edmund Danvers, handled Tony's financial affairs as well as those of the other men he worked with. In truth, the man was as much a part of the department as Tony himself, but Danvers was a strange sort and Tony had never quite gotten over his own discomfort with him. He didn't entirely trust him either.

"Perhaps your family could—"

"No." Her chin lifted slightly and there was a spark of defiance in her eye. "I would much prefer not to involve them in anything regarding my late husband." Her gaze dropped to the papers on the desk and her voice was resigned. "Besides, they are not especially fond of me at the moment."

The tone in her voice softened something within him and he had the strangest impulse to offer her comfort. He pushed the thought aside. He was here to protect her and, with luck, learn what she knew, if anything, of her husband's work and what he had found—nothing else. Besides, he was to be her servant, not her friend.

"Surely under the proper—"

"Gordon." Her gaze caught his. "Are you aware of my circumstances?"

Of course he was aware of her circumstances. Who in London was not? Even disregarding his own connection to Wilmont and his personal knowledge of the events of six months ago and the past few weeks that went well beyond the woman's own, he would have to have lived on a deserted island in the South Seas not to have heard of the scandalous marriage of this particular member of the Effington family.

Even so, he chose his words carefully. "I am aware that you recently lost your husband."

She scoffed. "Come, now, Gordon. I may know little about putting the finances of a household in order, although I daresay I can plan a proper dinner party or musical evening or arrange flowers effectively. Admittedly, relatively worthless skills." She smiled wryly. "But I do know servants talk and they usually have as much information as to what goes on in the world as everyone else, if not far more."

"I have heard rumors, my lady. I paid them no heed."

"Then you are the only one. Unfortunately, while the

tale has probably grown in the telling, the facts are indisputable. My marriage was somewhat abrupt and . . . incautious on my part. On his too, no doubt. And unfortunately he lost his life soon afterwards." She paused for a moment as if remembering, or perhaps regretting, the events that had brought her to this point. Then she drew a deep breath. "I find myself quite alone, Gordon. My family has not precisely disowned me, but it may well be some time before their attitude, or more precisely my *mother's* attitude, eases and I am once more welcomed into their bosom." She smiled again and he wondered idly how that smile might light her eyes when it wasn't so wry. "I must pay the piper for my sins, you see.

"And I must deal with my situation as well." She shuffled the papers before her and selected one. "I have been reviewing your references."

"Is there something amiss, my lady?" There shouldn't be. His references were perfect. Totally false, but perfect. Wrought from the skillful hand of Mr. Alistair Pribble, there was not a man alive who could tell one of Pribble's fabrications from the genuine article.

"Not at all. However this one, from the manager of a Lord Marchant's estate . . ." She looked up. "I don't believe I recognize the name."

"He was exceedingly old, my lady, and without issue." The lie rolled smoothly off his tongue. "Nor was he active in society. As such, it is not surprising that his name is unknown to you." Particularly as Lord Marchant did not now exist, nor had he ever.

"I see." She studied the paper. "This notes you are exceptionally good with figures and managed the household accounts when in his lordship's employ. It says his lordship trusted you implicitly."

"Does it?" he said without thinking. Damn Pribble

anyway. The man was a genius when it came to forging documents or producing facsimiles of important papers, but he had a nasty sense of humor. It was well known in the department that Tony had no head for numbers. With a great deal of effort, he was competent but nothing more. This was his own fault, though. He'd never thought it necessary to actually read the references Pribble had provided. Then again, Tony had never realized the duties of a butler were quite so complicated

"Yes, it does," she murmured, still perusing his references.

"That was some time ago, ma'am," he said quickly. "I daresay my faculties are not as astute now. I'm certain I have forgotten any number of things."

"Nonsense, Gordon," she said firmly, and looked up at him. "Numbers are one of the few things in life that are immune to change. One plus one always has been, and always will be, two."

"I understand that, my lady, but—"

"I realize you are not as young as you once were," she said in a kindly manner, "and I know you have not long been in my employ, but I have not noticed anything that would lead me to believe your hiring was a mistake in any way."

"You haven't?" Apparently she was not especially observant.

"You seem entirely competent in your position."

"I do?" Not observant in the least.

She nodded. "Indeed you do. Furthermore, I believe your age and, more importantly, your experience will be a great asset to me as I adjust to running a household and, in truth indeed, a new life, completely on my own."

"Surely your family—"

"As I said, they cannot be counted on at the moment,"

she said briskly. "So we shall carry on on our own. Now then, Gordon, I do not plan on turning over the finances completely to you."

"You don't?" He fought to keep the relief from his voice.

"No, I too am good with figures. However, this is all quite complicated and I need assistance in the sorting of it." Her brows drew together in frustration. "I find it terribly confusing and the more I try to instill some semblance of organization, the more I seem to flounder. I need your help in making sense of this, putting everything in some reasonable order. Once that is accomplished, I'm certain I can manage alone."

Impertinent creature. She had a great deal of nerve taking over Wilmont's affairs. It was most annoying to watch this interloper, this *female,* take over his friend's life. Still, a small voice in the back of his head noted, it was very much her right to do so. She might well be an interloping female, but she was also, for whatever reason, Wilmont's wife.

That too was a question without an answer at the moment.

"Gordon?" She tilted her head and gazed up at him, a tenuous smile playing on her lips. Again, he thought it must have been nothing more than the light that made her lips look so red and rich and inviting. "I realize this is not part of the duties you expected to—"

"I shall lend whatever meager assistance it is within my power to provide."

He really had no choice, given Pribble's references. Besides, this perusal of Wilmont's personal and financial papers might turn up something of benefit, although that was unlikely. Whatever else Danvers might be, he was an excellent solicitor and unquestionably loyal to the department. If there was something amiss, Danvers would have reported Wilmont without so much as the blink of an eye.

"Excellent." Relief rang in her voice. "I shall be eternally grateful, Gordon. Now then, I think we can begin—"

"I beg your pardon, ma'am, but you wish to begin now?" Years of training kept the panic from his voice. "It's late into the afternoon and I should think a task like this would best be started in the morning."

"Perhaps under other circumstances, but . . ." For no more than a instant, that annoying helpless note crept into her voice. Then her tone hardened. "This will just grow more confusing the longer I put it off. I would much prefer to deal with it now. Besides, I have little else to occupy my time.

"But you're right: it is growing late and I anticipate working well into the evening. Could you ask Mrs. Miller to prepare a light meal"—she glanced at the clock on the mantel—"in a few hours or so, say around seven, and serve it in here?"

"Very well, ma'am." He turned and started toward the door.

Fortunately, he was fairly skilled at tasks that called for a certain amount of organization. He had, in the past, often compiled pieces of information that made no sense until he arranged them in a logical order either on paper or within his own mind. He'd viewed such matters as a sort of puzzle and it had always been quite satisfying to see the pieces fall into place. And if his ability with numbers was poor, it was not nonexistent. It simply took him some time and, in this case, he could blame that on advanced age.

"Gordon."

He turned back. "Yes, my lady?"

"Do have her prepare a plate for you as well." She

paused and grimaced apologetically. "If you don't mind, that is. I realize it's highly unusual for me to ask you to join me, but I suspect ours will be a rather unusual household, especially as it is so small. However, if you feel at all uncomfortable, I shall quite understand if you prefer to eat alone."

"I shall be delighted to join you, ma'am."

"And I shall be most grateful." She cast him a relieved smile and he was oddly touched by the gratitude on her face.

He strode from the room and headed toward the back stairs, then belowground to the kitchens. It was a fair-sized house, not overly large but perfect for an unmarried man with little need for more than a place to sleep on those occasions when he chanced to reside in London.

Wilmont's butler and maid had quit not merely because of his reported death but because they too were in the employ of the department. They were servants, but with training that went beyond that of mere household skills, and upon Wilmont's death, received new assignments. Men in Wilmont's and Tony's line of work needed to be surrounded by those who were alert for any unusual occurrence. Those who could be trusted unconditionally, whose loyalty was unquestioned.

The house, of course, had been thoroughly searched after Wilmont's death, simply standard department procedure. Nothing of significance was found, although it wasn't until last week that the department learned precisely what it was looking for. And it had no idea who else might be looking.

He pushed open the door to the kitchen. "Mrs. Miller?"

The woman was seated at the table and glanced up at him with a slight smile. "Yes?"

Mrs. Miller was one of those rare women who could become whatever she wished with a minimal amount of effort. She'd been with the department as long as Tony had, and when it came to altering her appearance, she was as good, possibly even better, than he. He'd seen her range from seductively stunning to plain and nondescript.

For this assignment, she had the look of a woman who could blend into a crowd without notice, without attracting so much as a second glance, without anyone remembering her presence. Her age was indeterminable, somewhere between thirty and sixty. Her hair was dull, her form dumpy, her clothes ill-fitting. All in all, she was quite unmemorable and, as always, Tony was both impressed and envious of her skill.

"Lady Wilmont requests a light supper be served in the library later. I shall be joining her."

Mrs. Miller raised a brow. "Oh, you will, will you? I daresay that was a bit quicker than expected."

"She wants to go over Wilmont's papers and wishes to begin at once." Tony blew an annoyed breath. "In my references, Pribble claimed I was excellent at matters of finance."

Mrs. Miller laughed. "Pribble does enjoy a good joke." She studied Tony thoughtfully. "And, you never know what you might uncover."

Tony's gaze met hers. "I don't expect to uncover anything."

Certainly there was a moment last week when the idea that Wilmont might still be alive raised its head. And there was a great deal of money missing, enough to tempt even the most trustworthy of men. It was discarded at once, of course. Regardless of what he'd been working on, Wilmont would have made his existence known well before now if indeed he was alive. His loyalty to the crown had never been questioned.

"Still," Mrs. Miller said slowly, "things aren't always what they seem."

"I know Wilmont would never betray his country," Tony said firmly.

Charles Wilmont had been his closest friend, indeed his only friend. They had worked together during the war and continued to work together in the years since, saving each other's lives on more than one occasion. Wilmont was gregarious and sociable while Tony was reserved and solitary, and the two had found a good counterpoint in each other's characters.

"Have Mac bring in supper when it's ready." Tony smiled ruefully. "Any chance it will be so much as mildly edible?"

Mrs. Miller grinned. "Probably not."

There had been talk in the department of instructing Mrs. Miller in the finer points of the culinary arts, but the woman had balked every time the subject came up. If her cooking improved at all, she knew she would be forever trapped in the role of servant when such occasions arose. She had avoided domesticity up to this point and such activity was certainly not why she had joined the department in the first place, nor were such skills why the department valued her.

"Perhaps we can get someone a bit more skilled to join us," Tony said hopefully.

He would have preferred an adequate cook in the first place, but it was thought there should be another woman in the house aside from Lady Wilmont and, budgets being what they were in the department, Mrs. Miller was the only female available.

"A man needs to be able to count on a decent meal, after all, in work like this." John MacPherson sidled into the room. "It seems to me a competent cook is a reasonable expenditure." Mac winked at Mrs. Miller. "Not that you don't have other qualities that make up for it."

"I'm assuming you're not talking about her skills as a housekeeper either." Tony grinned.

"If I'd wanted to spend my life cooking and cleaning," she said in an overly sweet manner, "Mr. Miller would still be with us."

Tony and Mac traded glances. It had long been a question as to the fate of the mythical Mr. Miller, and even whether he had existed at all. Indeed, no one knew much about Mrs. Miller's background either in the days before she had worked for the English, brilliantly spiriting information across enemy lines. She spoke several languages fluently, hadn't a single drop of domestic blood in her veins and exuded a seductive presence that made most men in the department envy the long-gone Mr. Miller.

Tony cleared his throat. "Just do the best you can."

Mrs. Miller laughed. "You needn't look that way, St. Stephens, I daresay, I've yet to kill anyone with my cooking."

"There's always a first time," Mac said under his breath.

Tony stifled a laugh. If Mrs. Miller was a mystery, John MacPherson was an open book. Tony and Mac had served together during the war and afterward, and Mac was one of the few people Tony ever had or ever would trust with his life.

Tony started back to the library. At once his thoughts returned to the situation at hand and, more, how it had gotten so horribly out of control.

Wilmont had originally been charged with uncovering the truth regarding allegations leveled against senior members of the Effington family, specifically the duke himself and one or more of his brothers. The proof of those allegations was reputedly contained in correspondence currently in the hands of persons unknown who had offered them to the government for a hefty price. The political influence and power of the Effington family was such that, whether true or false, the information contained in what the department had dubbed the Effington Papers would cause a scandal of immense proportions, threatening the very stability of the government itself. There was no question as to payment, but Wilmont and Tony's superior, Lord Kimberly, and the man he reported to in this most secret branch of the Foreign Office, were determined to find out if indeed the charges were true.

Wilmont was simply supposed to pay court to one of the unmarried Effington chits with an eye toward being a welcome guest at upcoming family gatherings. A gentleman in active pursuit of an unmarried Effington female could count on being asked to any number of family entertainments, even perhaps a visit to Effington Hall, the country seat of the Duke of Roxborough. And if said gentleman was of questionable reputation, the odds were excellent that more than one member of that powerful family would want to meet—no, scrutinize— the suitor. In Wilmont's case, the scrutiny would be on both sides.

It was decided that one of the twin nieces of the Duke of Roxborough would best suit this purpose. They were, after all, at an age when they might well be getting anxious over their prospects for marriage and bored by the possibilities presented them. A man like Wilmont, regardless of his reputation, could appeal to such young women.

Tony was surprised when Wilmont focused his attention on Miss Philadelphia Effington, reputed to be more levelheaded than her sister and, one would think, more skeptical regarding the attentions of a well-known rake. More than one coin changed hands among members of the department the day Wilmont's choice was made known. But he was never supposed to marry her. His attentions were not to go anywhere near that far.

Matters spiraled quickly out of control after that. Wilmont claimed to have been contacted directly regarding the sale of the Effington Papers, possibly because he was now an Effington by marriage, and insisted on being allowed to handle the purchase. He was given the princely sum of fifty thousand pounds in banknotes for that purpose. The exchange was to take place aboard the packet to France, but neither money nor the papers were recovered after Wilmont's death. Nor was there any further contact from the parties involved, who in spite of the department's best efforts remained unidentified. It was assumed they, along with Wilmont, had gone down in the channel and the entire incident was believed at an end.

It was not until an unrelated investigation just last week had turned up the information that Wilmont was seen on the docks at Dover with a woman and furthermore never boarded the ill-fated boat. Now attention had turned toward his widow and his house. And the question arose as to whether he was dead at all.

Men were sent at once to the small village near Grasmere where Lady Wilmont was residing, to ascertain if her husband had visited or perhaps even joined her. Nothing untoward was discovered. Indeed, it appeared Lady Wilmont had spent these last months in solitude broken only by long walks to the village and rare visits from her brothers.

However, her return to London coincided with a report that the woman seen with Wilmont might also be in

London. Sources indicated, as well, that she did not have the notebook and was determined to recover it. Whatever was in that notebook had already cost Wilmont his life and the department had no doubt his wife's life could be at risk as well. As it was entirely the government's fault she was in this position, and given she was the niece of a powerful duke, it was decided to employ every resource necessary to protect her. The most discreet way to do that—as well as determine what, if anything, she knew, and possibly trap whoever was seeking the notebook and who, more than likely, was responsible for Wilmont's death—was to have trusted agents pose as her staff. Without her knowledge, of course.

The lady in question was studying Wilmont's papers when Tony quietly reentered the room. He had to admit she was lovely, and so was her sister. Neither was a great beauty, yet they were indeed well above average. The sister, Cassandra, was said to be the most impulsive and outspoken of the two, but from what Tony had observed thus far, that well might be a mistaken perception. Lady Wilmont had a spark in her eye and a firm set to her chin that indicated she was made of far sterner stuff than anyone had suspected.

"Now then, Gordon," she said without looking up, "if you would be so kind as to join me, we can begin."

He stepped to the desk and hesitated. Anthony St. Stephens had never in his life been at a loss as to suitable behavior, but at this particular moment he had no idea what to do. Should he stand? Sit? Lean over her shoulder? And wouldn't that be presumptuous? Not merely for a servant, but for any man?

He tried to tell himself this ruse was no different than any other he'd perpetrated in the course of his work, but the simple fact of the matter was that it was indeed entirely different. Those he had fooled in the past in the service of national security were criminals or in the traitorous employ of foreign powers, not simply the misguided daughter of one of Britain's most prestigious families. At once his masquerade seemed not merely dishonorable but somehow morally wrong.

"Do sit down, Gordon, and stop hovering," Lady Wilmont said under her breath. "I cannot abide people hovering over me."

"Yes, ma'am." He drew a deep breath, pulled up a nearby chair and settled himself on the side of the desk to her right, a respectable distance from her, yet close enough to examine the papers now spread out before her.

She glanced at him and smiled. "Excellent." Her gaze returned to the myriad of documents. "I wish to start with these. They appear to detail property holdings of some sort, but I don't quite understand . . ."

It was all far more complicated than he had anticipated, and within moments he was immersed in the intricacies of unraveling Wilmont's finances. Wilmont's interests were more varied and extensive than Tony had imagined and fully captured his attention. He almost managed to ignore the vague floral scent of Lady Wilmont's fragrance that drifted toward him whenever she gestured and the startling blue of her eyes when her puzzled gaze would meet his and the most intriguing dimple that appeared in her right cheek on those rare occasions when she smiled.

Almost, but not quite.

In a corner of his mind not taken up with the complicated documents and legal papers, he wondered if there wasn't far more to Lady Wilmont than appeared on the surface.

And wondered as well why he found it so intriguing.

Chapter 3

"Well"—Delia studied the piece of cheese she held between her fingers ruefully—"this is one meal she couldn't muck up."

Gordon snorted in agreement, then started. "I beg your pardon, ma'am."

"Nonsense, Gordon. Your reaction was perfectly acceptable, given Mrs. Miller's complete lack of culinary skills." She popped the cheese into her mouth, then settled back in her chair and considered the platters the housekeeper had prepared. Cold meats and cheese and breads were not precisely what Delia had had in mind when she had requested a light supper. Why, at home, Cook would have prepared a savory capon in the lightest of cream sauces flavored expertly with delicate spices. Delia sighed at the memory.

"Forgive me for mentioning it, ma'am, but perhaps it would be best if you gave me leave to hire someone to assist Mrs. Miller with the cooking." Gordon's expression was noncommittal. "While we still have the strength to do so."

She stared at him for a moment, then laughed and noted how delightful it was to laugh over something totally inconsequential. "I daresay our strength will hold out for a bit longer, but she's not particularly competent, is she?"

"Not in the kitchen, no, ma'am."

"It's quite disappointing, as you said her references were excellent."

"References can be misleading, my lady," he said firmly.

"Yes, well, I imagine you are the expert on that."

A bushy brow twitched above his spectacles. "Ma'am?"

"You were charged with the hiring of other servants in your previous position, were you not?"

"Yes, of course." There was a subtle note of relief in his voice.

Delia considered him thoughtfully. Poor old soul. Perhaps his faculties really were fading, but she'd seen no evidence of it in the work they'd done thus far this evening. His mind seemed as sharp as a much younger man's. Still, since his arrival, she'd noticed he'd seemed vaguely confused about the performance of his duties. Nothing truly significant, it just appeared he was never quite certain what to do next.

She stifled a sigh. This was indeed an unusual household she'd amassed: a cook and housekeeper who could neither cook nor clean adequately, a Scot with a twinkle in his eye who was rather too forward for a footman and a doddering old man. She'd allow him—no, encourage him—to find someone to take over culinary duties for Mrs. Miller but the woman could keep her position as housekeeper, at least for now. Mrs. Miller did seem a pleasant sort, and if she was not overly competent, a friendly nature was adequate recompense. It could be the woman simply needed time to settle into the household, as, in truth, did they all, and her skills would surely improve.

As for Gordon, he too could remain in Delia's employ for as long as he wished. He was kind and well meaning and obviously needed this position. Given his age, it would no doubt be his last. Perhaps they could find an underbutler or another footman to assist him. In hiring him, as well as Mrs. Miller and MacPherson, Delia had made a commitment and she would honor it. One had a certain responsibility to those in one's employ. In many ways, they became not merely part of one's household but members of the family. While she did not know any of her staff well as of yet, already she didn't doubt for a moment that all three would feel a similar allegiance toward her.

Delia leaned back in her chair. "May I ask you a question of a personal nature, Gordon?"

For a fraction of a moment he hesitated. "As you wish, ma'am."

"Why do you powder your hair? It's rather old-fashioned and makes you seem much older than you are, as does the mustache. Besides, you have rather an abundance of hair. Many men, my own father included"—she grinned—"would give a great deal for your head of hair."

"Thank you, my lady." He paused, gathering his thoughts, no doubt. "I am of an age, ma'am, where the wearing of wigs or powdering of hair was required of men in my position. I suspect I am simply set in my ways. As for the mustache, nothing more than a personal preference and no doubt vanity on my part."

"How old are you?" She winced. "Is that too personal a question?"

"Not at all, ma'am," he said without hesitation. "I am one and sixty."

"That old," she murmured. The admission surprised her. In spite of his display of some characteristics she associated with age, she'd noticed he moved with the grace of a much younger man.

"I can still perform my duties, ma'am," he said staunchly.

Regret stabbed her. "Of course you can. I didn't mean to imply otherwise." Impulsively she reached forward and placed her hand over his. "You will have a position here for as long as you wish."

He withdrew his hand politely. "I am most grateful, my lady."

"When things are more settled, you can see about a cook to take over those duties from Mrs. Miller. In the meantime, we shall have to make do." She shook her head. "It will not be easy, but I am certain we shall weather her tenure."

"As you wish." There was a distinct grim note in Gordon's voice and Delia fought back a grin. This butler of hers would not be overt in expressing his opinion, but she had no doubt he would indicate exactly what his thoughts were on any given subject.

It struck her that Gordon may well be the only person she could count on right now.

He stood and collected the plates and platters, stacking them precariously, and in an altogether dangerous manner, on the tray MacPherson had left. Delia had spent her life thus far surrounded by servants who were unquestionably efficient. Those days were obviously over.

Delia jumped to her feet. "Here, let me help you." She

circled the desk and reached to help steady the tray, brushing against him in the process.

He yanked it out of her hands and stepped back, the dishes tottering threateningly. "I appreciate your assistance, ma'am, but I can well manage this."

He swiveled and stepped toward the door, balancing the tray awkwardly in one hand, pulling open the door with the other and ramming his foot against it to prop it open. Before she could say a word, he was gone, and she stared after him in surprise.

He certainly moved quickly for a man his age. And he'd seemed surprisingly solid when she'd inadvertently brushed against him. Regardless of the effect of the years on his mind, he was apparently quite physically fit. At least she wouldn't have to worry about his duties being too strenuous or him keeling over in the middle of serving tea. There was something else odd about Gordon, but she could not quite put her finger on it. It was probably of no significance at any rate.

She returned to her chair and blew a tired breath. Thus far she and Gordon had managed to sort through the papers regarding Charles's assets. There was more work to be done, of course, but she had a basic understanding of Charles's worth—of *her* worth. And it was considerably greater than she had imagined. Nowhere near the respective Effington fortunes, of course, but impressive nonetheless. In truth, she was a very wealthy, woman. A very wealthy independent woman.

A very wealthy *widow*, with all the freedoms widowhood and wealth offered.

Still, she'd trade it in a moment for the opportunity to have her husband back and make right whatever had gone horribly wrong.

Oh, certainly he was not the love of her life, and she had no doubt he did not love her either, but she had quite liked him. And thought he had liked her as well. Until after they were wed.

Charles had procured a special license and they were quietly married early on the morning two days after she'd shared his bed. Then he'd insisted on going to her family. There was a great deal of hell to pay through the rest of that interminably long day. Her father and brothers grim-faced and threatening, and her mother weeping and throwing herself about in fits of despair over the impending scandal of a spur-of-the-moment marriage between an Effington and that . . . that . . . *man*. How said marriage was in total opposition to the order of things, and how it could not end in anything but disaster. Then there was Cassie's obvious hurt at having been excluded from any knowledge of her sister's ruinous adventure. Charles had been cool and collected and Delia was rather proud of the way he presented himself to her family.

It was not until Delia and Charles were once again alone that his character seemed to change and she'd realized just what a mistake she had made. Oh, not in sacrificing her virtue. The significance of that was probably of far more concern to others than to herself. She'd long accepted that most of the men who wished to marry her did so primarily because of her family and position and dowry and would not be entirely offset by her ruined status.

No, the magnitude of her mistake lay in not truly knowing the nature of the man she'd tied herself to for the rest of her life. Charles grew more and more preoccupied and withdrawn, in the manner of a man with pressing matters on his mind. Matters he refused to share. He was gone much of the time, and when he was near her, his manner was brusque, even cold. He'd been reticent to speak with her, reluctant to so much as be in her presence. It was as if, having married her, he no longer wished to have anything to do with her. As if he regretted ever meeting her in the first place. And she slept alone.

His demeanor was confusing and painful and more than a bit frightening. Any hope she'd harbored that affection, even love, between them might grow vanished. A heavy weight hung in her chest and she'd considered means of escaping the dreadful mess she found herself in. She dismissed the idea of returning to her family; that was an admission not merely of her mistake but of failure. Effingtons, even female Effingtons, did not fail. No, she would stay with Charles, and if that meant a marriage that consisted of nothing more than two strangers living in the same house, so be it. Still, she had hoped, with time, the friendly affection and passion they'd shared could be found again.

She'd never dreamed there would be no time.

She would not have wished him dead, ever, but his untimely death released her from vows they never should have taken. In marrying her, he had changed her life completely. In widowing her, his gift was her freedom and an entirely new life that could hold anything she wished. And if the price for that gift was guilt and a heart heavy with regret for what might have been, she could live with that. She had no choice.

"Lady Wilmont." Gordon's voice sounded from the doorway and her gaze jerked to his. "I do not mean to be presumptuous, ma'am, and I do realize you were only trying to be helpful, but you must allow me to perform my duties, and . . ." His brow furrowed over his spectacles and he stepped closer. "I beg your pardon, ma'am, but is something amiss?"

Abruptly she realized her cheeks were wet from tears that had fallen unnoticed. She dashed them away with the back of her hand. "Regrets, Gordon, nothing more than regrets." Her gaze dropped to the papers on the desk and she rearranged them aimlessly. "And, as there is little one can do about regrets, they are pointless."

"I see." His voice was so soft she wasn't sure he had actually spoken.

For several moments she shuffled through the documents in an attempt to recover her composure. She hadn't cried since the day she'd been told of Charles's death and even then had wondered if those tears were for him or for herself. Damnation, she had made a terrible mess of things. And now she felt so blasted guilty about it all, as if his death were somehow her fault. As if the simple fact that she had married him without loving him had somehow led to his demise. If she had loved him, would he have left her for some absurd trip to France? It was ridiculous, of course, nothing more than her own sense of right and wrong raising its ugly head. Charles hadn't loved her either. And, in fact, didn't most people she know marry for reasons that had nothing to do with love?

She pulled a deep, steadying breath and her tone was brisk. "You're quite right, Gordon, I should let you get on with your work without my assistance. You are extremely competent and I shouldn't—"

"Beg pardon, my lady."

She looked up. Gordon stood before the desk, his expression contrite and concerned.

"My apologies, ma'am. I am perhaps too cognizant of my years to be as gracious as I should. You attempted to assist me, and for that you have my gratitude."

"Accepted." He really was a very dear man, and if he was a bit confused at times or sensitive about his age, it was to be expected and overlooked. "Now then—"

"Forgive me, my lady but . . ." He paused as if looking for the right words. "I realize you find yourself in a difficult position, with no guidance forthcoming from your family, and I should like to offer my assistance in any manner you might require."

She smiled in appreciation. "That's very kind of you, Gordon. You have already been a great help and I am most appreciative."

"Should you find yourself in need of"—he straightened his shoulders slightly—"someone to talk to, I would be honored should you wish to confide in me. I am nothing if not discreet." He paused. "Lord Marchant considered me his closest confidant.

She studied him for a moment. It must have taken a great deal for a man like Gordon to make such a suggestion. In her experience, servants of a certain age and position were not given to offers of a personal nature. Obviously the kindness of his character superseded the restrictions of his training.

Or perhaps she was such a pathetic creature even the hardest of hearts could not resist her. And if this sweet elderly man could make such an offer, she could certainly do no less than accept it. She'd rather enjoyed his company tonight and would wager he was a font of knowledge and wisdom about the ways of the world.

Besides, between mourning and scandal, she was virtually isolated from the rest of society and quite at a loss as to how to spend her time. She had no particular interest in needlework and had yet to find anything of interest in the library. She had her sketchbook, but the long months in the scenic Lake District had reminded her she was not nearly as skilled with pen and pencil as her sister. She had somehow managed to fill the endless hours of her exile—or perhaps *drift* was a more appropriate word than *fill*—but had no idea as to what she would do with her time now. It was punishment of a sort, she supposed, her own personal purgatory for marrying a man she did not love and for now mourning not really the man himself but the promise of the man.

She cast the butler her brightest smile. "I shall keep that in mind, Gordon. Now"—she nodded at his chair—"perhaps we should get back to work."

"Of course, ma'am." Gordon retook his seat and began sorting the accounts due into stacks of those regarding household expense, those of a personal nature and those that didn't fit into either category.

She watched him with a sense of satisfaction. In a year in which she'd made no end of foolish decisions, hiring Gordon may well have been the only intelligent thing she'd done. In spite of his age, the bit of confusion he displayed and his obvious vanity when it came to his appearance, he certainly understood the art of organizing finances. Beyond that, he was a good sort if a bit odd. Still, she had no doubt they'd get on famously. And if indeed she felt a need for a compassionate confidant, she would not hesitate to turn to him.

At the moment, he was the only untarnished spot in her life.

He was a cad. A beast. The vilest sort of creature.

Lady Wilmont's head bowed over the papers before her, and she was intent upon the work at hand just as she had been since they had started this chore three nights ago. The lamplight caught the strands of hair that tenaciously escaped a rather untidy, but utterly charming, coiffure. She did indeed look angelic at the moment.

Tony, however, was a villain, a fiend, the devil incarnate.

His self-loathing was emphasized by the thunder outside and the sound of the rain striking against the window, the violence of nature in stark contrast to the warmth of the scene in Wilmont's library.

Lady Wilmont was vulnerable and alone, with no one to turn to. From what he'd overheard, even visits from her sister would be rare and, indeed, since they'd begun their work sorting Wilmont's finances, had that insensitive twin appeared even once? There had been a note or two but nothing else.

For that matter, had anyone from her family paid so much as a single visit? Certainly she had been the center of scandal, but that had been months ago. The woman had also lost her husband, and one would think that alone would be cause for her family to forgive and unite around her. Obviously, each and every Effington in existence was inconsiderate and thoughtless.

And was he any better? Wasn't he taking advantage of her plight for his own miserable purposes, no matter how legitimate they may be?

Oh, he was indeed a scoundrel, a bounder, a nasty piece of work to be sure. The Effingtons had nothing on him.

He never imagined his opinion of her could change so dramatically and so quickly, never imagined he could have been so wrong and never dreamed he'd feel so wretched about deceiving her. In the days that Tony and Lady Wilmont had worked side by side sorting her husband's papers, Tony had gained a much clearer picture of this woman his friend had married. She wasn't at all as he'd thought, although she was substantially less willing to share confidences with him than he'd expected. Indeed, she was fairly reserved and prone to long stretches of silence when he was certain her thoughts turned to Wilmont.

Blast the man anyway. It was now obvious to Tony that Wilmont had gone too far in his courtship and had probably seduced the woman. There was no other reason he could see for their marriage, although Wilmont had certainly never before wed a woman he'd seduced, and their numbers were legion.

Still, if nothing else, Tony had learned a great deal about Lady Wilmont's character. She was unfailingly kind and pleasant. As she considered him an elderly servant who was well meaning but not as sharp as he once was, a perception he turned to his advantage, her behavior displayed a good heart and a caring nature.

Damnation, the woman was bloody nice. And surprisingly intelligent, which meant her involvement with Wilmont made absolutely no sense at all. She was not the type to run off impetuously with any man, let alone a rake like Wilmont. She certainly did not deserve whatever game he had played with her.

Was Tony any better?

"That's it, then, isn't it?" She slapped the pencil down on the desk firmly and leaned back in her chair.

"It, my lady?"

"As near as I can tell." She rubbed her hand across her forehead in a decidedly tired manner. "We have managed to sort out Charles's assets from his debts and all the odds and ends that entails. The accounts are in order, outstanding bills paid, investments and property identified. All in all, yes, I'd say that's it." She smiled wearily. "I could not have done it without your help, Gordon. I am most appreciative."

"It has been my pleasure, ma'am." As soon as he said the words, he realized how true they were. He had quite enjoyed these long hours in her company. Tony had always preferred women who could think over those who merely fluttered and simpered. Clever women were a challenge that fired his blood. If they were pretty as well, so much the better.

The rare woman who could engage his mind as well as

his body was precisely the type of woman he would one day marry.

Pity this one was unavailable and unsuitable. The acknowledgment brought an odd, disquieting sensation to the pit of his stomach.

"I cannot believe how exhausting this has all been." She closed her eyes and rubbed the back of her neck, her head dropping forward, her blond hair tousled.

He resisted the urge to reach out and let the silken strands run through his fingers.

"I feel as if I have walked from Great-Aunt Cecily's to the village and back," she murmured. "Over and over again."

Caress the warm flesh of her porcelain neck.

"Still, it's not as if we've done any real physical labor, after all."

Feel the muscles of her shoulders relax under the gentle pressure of his hands.

"And what of you, Gordon?"

"Me?" The word was more a startled squeak than anything else. He cleared his throat and hoped she hadn't noticed. "What do you mean, ma'am?"

She lifted her head and cast him a fatigued smile. "Are you tired as well?"

"Not at all."

She raised a brow. "You have an amazing amount of stamina for a man your age, Gordon. Do you attribute it to anything in particular?"

He said the first thing that popped into his mind. "An honorable life, my lady."

"An honorable life? How very interesting." She fell silent, a thoughtful expression on her face. Abruptly her gaze met his. "Gordon, do you know if there is anything approximating a good brandy in the house? I daresay Lord Wilmont would have had some kind of spirits around and there is an impressive selection of wine in the cellars, but I have not yet had the opportunity to peruse every nook and cranny of this place and I was wondering if you had stumbled across anything of interest." She blew a long breath. "As tired as I am, I am rather too restless to retire. I feel not unlike a tightly wound spring. Brandy has always helped me sleep and I have not slept at all well of late."

"Permit me, my lady." He rose to his feet, crossed the narrow library and opened one of the small cabinets that ran in a row encircling the room and divided the upper bookshelves from the lower. He grabbed a decanter with one hand and a glass with the other.

"Well done." She cast him an admiring look. "And do join me. This is as much your accomplishment as mine."

"As you wish, ma'am." A second glass awkwardly joined the first and he returned to place brandy and glasses on the desk. She glanced at them and bit back a smile. Damnation. A proper butler would have used a tray. Thank God she attributed his incompetence to advanced age and not simply to, well, incompetence. And thank God as well she didn't question how he knew precisely where to find the brandy. He had shared many bottles with Wilmont in this very room.

He carefully filled both glasses, then resumed his seat.

She took a sip and sighed. "Excellent, but then I knew it would be. If I knew nothing else about my husband, I knew his taste in fine liquor would be exceptional." For a long moment she stared at the amber liquid in the glass as if it held the answer to any number of unanswered questions about the man she had married. "What makes an honorable life, Gordon?"

"Honesty, above all else, I should think." Unless, he amended silently, pure honesty conflicts with a higher purpose such as service to one's king and one's country.

"Being true to one's self, one's principles." And such principles should always be guided by the interests of king and country.

"Do you think Lord Wilmont lived an honorable life, Gordon?"

He chose his words carefully. "It's not my place to say, ma'am."

"Nonetheless, you have helped me set the leavings of his life in order. Surely you have formed some impression of the man?"

"I would not venture—"

"Nonsense." Impatience rang in her voice. She rested her elbows on the desk, cradled her glass between her hands and studied him. "You are a man with a vast amount of experience and, I suspect, an acute observer of those around you. Is there anything you have seen in all this that indicates to you that my husband lived a dishonorable life?"

"No, my lady. Not at all." It was the truest thing he'd said all night and came as something of a shock. Tony had had no idea what to expect from Wilmont's papers, but he certainly hadn't anticipated a total lack of questionable activity. Why, even some of Tony's own personal transactions were, on occasion, not entirely aboveboard.

"He had a dreadful reputation, you know. Regarding gaming and wild living and drinking and"—she shrugged matter-of-factly—"women."

"Reputations are not always as they appear, ma'am," Tony said firmly. He couldn't defend Wilmont at the moment and, even if he hadn't been in disguise, would have been hard-pressed to do so at any rate. Some of Wilmont's reputation was indeed exaggerated to hide his true activities, but much of it was well earned. Still,

Tony wondered if perhaps he had judged his friend too harshly.

"He did marry me." There was a cool note in her voice. "And that probably speaks well of him." Without warning she rose to her feet and paced the room.

Tony jumped up a beat behind her.

"Oh, do sit down, Gordon." She gestured impatiently. "I cannot seem to sit still, but there is no need for you to be uncomfortable as well."

"I couldn't possibly, ma'am." The shocked note in his voice wasn't entirely feigned.

She rolled her gaze toward the ceiling. "Very well."

Lady Wilmont circled the room casually, brandy still in hand, and perused the shelves as if searching for something of interest, but there was a tension in the line of her body and edge of her step that indicated she had far more on her mind than reading. She stopped and peered at the shelves, then selected a book and glanced at him. "Do you like Lord Byron's works?"

"I wouldn't presume to say, my lady." In truth, he thought both the man and his poems overpraised and overrated.

She chuckled. "No, you wouldn't, would you?" She took another swallow of the brandy, set the glass on a shelf, then flipped the book open. "I myself am not overly fond of his more political offerings, but some of his poetry is rather evocative." She paged through the book and stopped to read aloud. "*She walks in beauty like the night, of cloudless climes and starry skies . . .*"

And all that's best of dark and bright meet in her aspect and her eyes.

"It's quite nice, ma'am." It was one of the few works of Byron he did indeed like, and suspected it appealed to a romantic aspect of his nature usually hidden.

"Do you think so?" She continued to study the page, a frown creasing her brow. "*The smiles that win, the tints that glow but tell of days in goodness spent. A mind at peace with all below, a heart whose love is innocent.*" She glanced at him. "Is there such a thing as a heart whose love is innocent, do you think, Gordon? Is there, in truth, such a thing as love?"

"I fear you have me at an disadvantage, ma'am," he said cautiously. "I am not entirely certain what you are asking."

She laughed in a humorless manner. "Nor am I, Gordon." She snapped the book closed and offered it to him. "Why don't you take this? You might find it enjoyable. I have another copy."

He moved to her and accepted the book. "Thank you, my lady, I shall treasure it."

"You shall have to tell me how you like it. I know I could certainly use something interesting to read. To occupy my mind." She plucked her glass from the shelf and sighed. "I daresay my odd mood is due to nothing more than weariness and being in this house and the storm raging about us. Or perhaps it's the realization that with the end of sorting Charles's papers we have come to the end of my grand adventure."

At once he was alert for any hidden meaning in her words. "Grand adventure, ma'am?"

"I . . ." She shook her head. "I am rambling, Gordon, which in and of itself is unusual. I never ramble. Or at least, I never used to. I find myself doing any number of things I never used to do." She sipped the brandy thoughtfully. "I'm sure you noted, as did I, that I am now possessed of a significant fortune."

"I am aware of that, my lady." Between Wilmont's family fortune and a number of shrewd investments, the

man was astoundingly well off. The missing fifty thou-
sands pounds was something of a pittance to such a
man, and as such would have played no role, for good or
ill, in his actions.

"Perhaps I shall use it to travel. I have never been beyond England's shores and there is an enormous world
out there more than willing to show a wealthy widow its
offerings. And I have always wanted to see the canals of
Venice and the ruins of Rome.

"Did your Lord Marchant travel, Gordon? Did he
take you with him to see castles and cathedrals, great
mountains and grand oceans? Have you had adventures
abroad?"

"No, my lady," he said without hesitation.

In truth, he had had far too many adventures in far
too many places during the long years of the war. He had
ventured into the grim back alleys and dark, disreputable sections of Paris and Marseilles, where information was bought and sold and a man took his life in his
hands just to pass there. He had seen the battlefields of
Spain and Portugal and the hidden lairs of partisans and
mercenaries eager to provide assistance for a price, paid
in coin or blood.

Even after the war, when official military intelligence
was deemed unnecessary, he'd become part of a newly
formed arm of the Foreign Office innocuously titled the
Department of Domestic and International Affairs. Together with men like Wilmont and Mac whom he'd
trusted with his life in the effort to defeat Napoleon, it
was a unique intelligence service intent on protecting national interests from threats within the country and
without.

"Time enough tomorrow, I suppose, to think about
what I shall do with the rest of my life." She stepped

back to the desk and tucked the now-neatly-arranged documents into a large ledger. "It seems I have a great deal of time stretching ahead of me."

There was a resigned dignity about her that clutched at something deep inside him. He was seized with an urgent desire to take her in his arms and comfort her. Tell her that her life would turn out well. Assure her, promise her, that he and he alone would make it all right. And if his lips met hers in the process . . .

He couldn't, of course. Couldn't pull her into his arms and kiss her lips still tasting of brandy or bask in the heat of her body next to his or feel the beat of her heart against his own. She was part of his job, nothing more. As distasteful as it was, she was bait of a sort, to lure whoever might be lurking out there. And no matter how tempting he might find her, she was still a new widow and the wife of his best friend. Dead or not, Wilmont deserved better from Tony.

Yet, in this room, with the storm raging about them and the resigned look in her blue eyes, it was easy to forget who he was and why he was here.

An agent of His Majesty's government, posing as an elderly butler, whose sole purpose was to keep her safe.

Except he wasn't old, he wasn't a servant and the one person he might truly need to keep her safe from could well be himself.

Chapter 4

Delia bolted upright in the night. She gasped for breath. Her heart thudded in her chest, her blood pounded in her ears. The dark engulfed her, surrounded her, overwhelmed her. For a moment, she had no knowledge of where she was or what she was or who she was, existing only in the terror of being totally and completely alone.

She clenched her fists, breathed deeply and willed herself to calm. She should be getting better at this: unidentified, unreasonable emotion akin to fear had jerked her from her sleep every night since Charles's death. And every night she'd lain awake for long hours struggling to determine exactly why this awful feeling gripped her.

In a rational part of her mind, she knew there was nothing to fear here save the dreadful loneliness of being without the people, the family, who had always surrounded her. Indeed, she'd decided it wasn't fear so much as an overwhelming sense of guilt that she could ignore during the day but had no defense for during the helplessness of sleep. Still, identifying the problem had done nothing to vanquish it.

Tonight was different. Tonight, with the slowing of her pulse and the ease of her breath came determination. And anger. Sharp, unreasonable, unrelenting anger. It was past time to settle accounts that had nothing to do with banks and bills and property.

She threw off the covers and stalked across the small bedroom that adjoined Charles's through a dressing room. She flung open the door of the dressing room, hesitated for no more than a heartbeat, then slammed open the door leading to Charles's room.

The storm had passed, the sky had cleared and enough moonlight streaked in through the tall windows to turn the masculine room, with its costly, massive furnishings and heavy, expensive, damask hangings, into a faded watercolor in varying shades of silver-grays and blue-blacks. She hadn't been in this room—his room—since the one night she had shared his bed.

Fury drove her to the very center of the chamber. "Enough, Charles, I have had quite enough."

The words came of their own accord. "I will not continue to play this game. I have given you six months in return for one mere night. My debt is paid. You are dead and I am sorry for it, but I am not to blame. I shall not feel guilty for one moment more because of your death. Nor shall I continue to berate myself because there was no love between us. I, apparently alone among us, thought at least there was affection.

"I would have made you an excellent wife. I would have done everything in my power to make our lives together good and happy." She wrapped her arms around herself and stared into the darkness. "Why did you marry me? I didn't demand it. I didn't even expect it. I realized full well what I was doing when I came here to your bed. I am not a fool, I knew what the consequences would be. And for that acknowledgment, I credit you.

"You made me see a side of myself I had never known. From the very beginning, I was a different person with you. You drew something out of me I never suspected existed." Her anger rose with her voice. "I was confident and flirtatious and, blast it all, Charles, I was passionate with you. Not just in your bed but in my life. You made me feel as if I had never lived before, and I liked it. I liked the secrecy and the adventure and the illicitness of it all. I liked making my own decisions, choosing my own path regardless of the restrictions of propriety. It was glorious. I shall not give it up now and I shall not let you take it back from me. I shall not be the quiet, reserved creature I was before you. Never!

"You tried to take it away, though, didn't you? Why?" Her voice lowered. "When we married, you treated me as if I were of no consequence. As if you didn't care in the least. I did not expect love, Charles, but I did expect"— she searched for the words—"something beyond polite tolerance. Something akin to the charm and desire you had shown me up until then. I didn't understand at the time and I do not understand now. Did you regret our marriage the very moment we said our vows? Did you know what a horrendous mistake it was? Did you dislike me so intensely then that you could not bear to be in my presence? Did you leave me?"

She paused to catch her breath. Maybe it was anger as much as guilt that drove her from her sleep every night.

She forced a note of calm to her voice. "You have left me a great fortune, Charles, substantial enough to live a life of independence. I shall not have to marry some deadly dull gentleman now. You have given me choices and for that I shall be forever thankful. I shall mourn you, of course, but not for a man I now realize I did not know at all. But for what you and I never shared, never had the chance to share. And for that loss, my errant husband, I blame you. We could have had so much together. We might have loved in time. I liked you a great deal, and I thought you liked me."

Her chin jerked up defiantly. "You are gone and I will tell you here and now for the last time, I am sorry for your death. But I have an entire lifetime stretching before me. And I shall not hesitate to live it."

A sense of urgency to act rushed through her and without thinking she stepped to the bed, grabbed the draperies hanging from the cornice and yanked hard. The fabric resisted for a moment, then ripped free with a satisfying sound that echoed in the night. Delia tore at the bed hangings until they piled on the floor. She pulled the coverlet and pillows off the bed and tossed them aside, then moved to the windows and pulled down the draperies. She wanted to tear the very paper from the walls with her bare fingers. And with every act, with every shred of material that floated to the floor with a slow ease that bespoke more of a dream than reality, the weight that had settled on her six long months ago lessened.

She paused in the middle of the room to catch her breath and survey her handiwork. This was all ridiculous, of course. She had no idea what had come over her. She'd never been prone to displays of violence or anger. But she had changed and Charles had changed her and, no matter what happened from here on, for that she would be eternally grateful.

Fabric lay in soft drifts around the room, illuminated by the starlight, a strangely peaceful scene. A peace that invaded her soul.

Somewhere in the distance, or possibly only in her mind, she heard the sound of amused laughter. Charles's laughter. Not the cold, remote husband he became but the rake who had charmed her in private parlors and teased her in discreet meetings and introduced her to secrets in this very room and captured, if not her heart, then at least her desire. And the oddest belief seized her that he approved. That, regardless of his behavior at the end, he would want her to carry on with her life.

The very idea that her dead husband wanted her to destroy his room was absurd. Yet, what about the two of them from the first moment to the last was not absurd?

"Charles . . ." She shook her head and smiled. "I will never know what was real with you and what was a pretense, will I?"

She started slowly toward her room. In the morning, she would begin a new life and, for the first time since her marriage, she looked forward to the new day.

She reached the dressing room door and glanced back at her husband's chamber. Tomorrow, she would make it hers.

"Thank you, Charles," she said softly, and closed the door firmly behind her.

She looked dreadful in black.

Delia studied her reflection in the long mirror in Charles's—no—her room. Or at least it would be, once she had the walls repapered and the fabrics replaced and installed new furniture as well.

Regardless of the cause for her behavior last night, this morning she was a new woman. A woman prepared to face the forbidding world of London society. *Lady* Wilmont. And while Miss Philadelphia Effington would have hesitated to flout the conventions she had abided by much of her life, Lady Wilmont had no such reservations.

She flashed a wicked grin at her reflection, then winced. Black was not at all her color. It drained the color from her face and turned her pale complexion a stark white. She looked, well, dead. Why hadn't she noticed this before? She'd been wearing black for months. Indeed, there had not even been time to unpack her clothes sent from her parents' house after her marriage before she'd had to change her wardrobe to mourning. The dresses she'd worn before her marriage and her widowhood were still packed away in the trunks still stacked in her room. She sighed with resignation. And would have to remain packed for the rest of the year.

Of course, she was already the subject of scandal and gossip. How much worse could it be if she flouted convention altogether and wore colors? She wrinkled her nose. Much worse and scarcely worth the effort. In spite of her resolve, she wasn't entirely certain she was ready to face the world as the scandalous Lady Wilmont. Although, as she had destroyed her reputation, she might as well enjoy it. Precisely how to enjoy it was still a question.

A discreet knock sounded on the door.

"Come in," she called.

The door swung open and she watched Gordon in the mirror. He stepped into the room and paused. His gaze darted around the room, a look of concern flashing across his face, to be replaced almost at once by his usual noncommittal expression. She stifled a grin. Charles's room looked as though it had been ransacked, the disarray appearing far worse in the light of day than it had last night.

"I fear it's a bit of a mess in here, Gordon." She turned toward him and waved at the chamber. "I had something of a revelation last night."

"This is a revelation, my lady?" he said skeptically.

"Indeed it is." She nodded firmly. "My life has changed dramatically in recent months, although I believe I needed to return here to truly face that fact." She paced the room in an erratic path, avoiding the piles of linens scattered over the floor. "Entirely my fault, of course, and I make no excuses for it. However, the time has now come to move on. I am a widow with wealth and property and an entire life ahead of me. It is time I begin to live it."

"And how do you propose to"—he cleared his throat—"live it, ma'am?"

"First of all . . ." She paused and glanced around the overly masculine room. "This is my home now and I intend to make it mine. Each and every room. I have made a list." She stepped to the bed, picked up her sketchpad and scanned the neatly written words. "I want you to send for cabinet makers. While the furniture in here is of excellent quality, it is far too heavy and entirely too ancient for modern sensibilities. I also wish to see fabrics for bedcoverings and drapes and curtains and upholstery and carpets and, oh, yes, selections of wallpapers and paint." She looked up at him. "Have I forgotten anything?"

He had the oddest look in his eye, like that of a cornered woodland creature, but his expression was unruffled. "It does not appear so, ma'am."

"Come along, then, Gordon, we have a great deal to do." She beamed at him and started toward the door.

"We shall go room to room and make notes on changes I want made. I want this to be my house, but I don't wish to turn it into an overly feminine enclave. I have never been keen on flourishes and florals, although I have frankly never had much say in my surroundings. I daresay you shall be of great assistance to me, from a masculine perspective, that is, and I shall greatly value your opinion." She pulled up short and whirled around. He paused in midstep a few paces behind her. "I do hope you won't hesitate to be completely honest with me."

"I shall do my best, ma'am." His voice was collected, but behind his spectacles, the look in his eyes was distinctly uneasy.

"Come, now, Gordon." She grinned. "It shan't be that bad. In truth, I see it as great fun. Oh, not an actual adventure, of course, but something to occupy my time in the coming months." She turned and again started toward the door. "I shall have a great deal of time on my hands and I think it's best to put it to productive use."

"I take it your revelation involves household furnishings, my lady?"

"That's just the beginning, Gordon." Again she stopped and swiveled toward him, turning so quickly he nearly walked into her. At once she noted the butler was substantially taller than she'd realized and the oddest thought flashed through her mind that he must have been quite an attractive man in his youth. He immediately stepped back and she pushed the disquieting idea away.

"No, Gordon, my revelation has to do with the nature of my new life as well as the nature of my late husband." She pulled her brows together. "You see, I did not know Lord Wilmont well enough to have married him and in that I have already admitted my mistake. Much of his character was known to me only through his reputation and, in truth, I disregarded that as nothing more than rumor and gossip. He was dashing and charming and I quite thought we shared a certain amount of affection. At least before we were wed. Afterwards . . ." She shook her head and thrust the memories of her brief marriage aside.

"Suffice it to say, the man I knew before we married is the memory I will retain, and *that* gentleman would not have wanted me to pine away through mourning that is more a show for propriety's sake than anything else. The Charles who captured my"—she searched for the right word—"*hand* was known for reckless behavior and squandering his fortune and his exploits with women. While I have no intention of following the example he set entirely, I shall spend his money—my money—in whatever manner I see fit. I am quite certain he would approve, and until he comes back from the grave to tell me otherwise I shall conduct myself under that assumption."

"I see." Gordon studied her for a moment. "May I speak freely?"

"Please do."

"I wish to inquire, then, ma'am, as to precisely how closely do you intend to follow his example? This refurbishing you propose strikes me as neither improper nor scandalous, although there may well be talk about a newly wealthy widow freely spending her deceased husband's wealth—"

"Do you know what they call women who marry for money in this day and age, Gordon?"

"I wouldn't hazard to say," he said in a lofty manner.

"They call her clever." She cast him a quick grin, then shrugged. "Although I had no idea of my husband's worth. And, between my dowry and my own expectations from my family, I had no need of his wealth. Given that, I doubt if anyone would consider me especially clever, but his money has made me independent." She tilted her head and narrowed her eyes. "You have more to say, don't you, Gordon?"

"I was merely wondering, ma'am, do your intentions toward your new life involve activity of a more scandalous nature? I should point out there are certain rules regarding mourning and the behavior of widows, indeed of all women, that society does not take the breaking of lightly."

"I am well aware of that and I'm not entirely certain

that I care. I have lived my life thus far according to the rules of propriety, at least until recently. It seems rather a pity to turn back now." She hugged the sketchpad to her chest and leaned against the open doorframe. "However, honesty demands I confess that my thoughts have not gone considerably beyond this house. I have been a widow far longer than I was a wife and I plan on fulfilling the latter role considerably better than I did the former. But I shall do that according to no one's standards save my own."

She straightened and met his gaze head-on. "At the moment, I don't know precisely what I intend, but if I have learned nothing else in the past months or so, I have learned I have a longing for adventure and excitement I never suspected. Charles has given me the means to pursue both.

"I am embarking on a grand adventure, Gordon, the adventure of the rest of my life." She paused. "At the very least I shall need a stable household in order to do that. If I have offended your sensibilities, if indeed you do not feel at ease with what might well be a rather unusual circumstance, I will certainly accept your resignation and send you on your way with a sizable severance and excellent recommendations."

Gordon stared, obviously shocked, and Delia pushed aside a twinge of guilt. She had no desire to sack the elderly servant. In truth, she found his presence a comfort, his quiet dignity reassuring. Yet from this moment forth, she would accept whatever criticism came from without, but she would not tolerate disapproval within her own home.

"I shall remain here as long as you wish, my lady," he said staunchly. "On one condition."

She raised a brow. "A condition, Gordon?"

"You said I may speak freely."

"And I meant it. Go on."

"Since I have been in your employ, you have on occasion mentioned that you value my experience and counsel and whatever wisdom I may have accrued during my long years."

"Indeed, I meant that as well."

"Very well. My condition is simply that you continue to allow me to speak my mind, and furthermore that you heed any advice I may offer in your best interests."

She laughed. "I accept wholeheartedly the first part of your condition. As for the second, I will agree to listen to your advice and give it my complete consideration, but I will not promise to blindly follow it." She leaned toward him and met his gaze directly. "I must live my life as I see fit, Gordon, and I daresay I shall make any number of mistakes, but I must be free to make them. Would you deny me that?"

"I would deny you anything that would make you unhappy or cause you harm, my lady," he said without hesitation.

A flush of warm affection for this old man surged through her. What a dear he was. "Thank you, Gordon. Will you stay in my employ, then?"

"For as long as I can be of service." There was an odd intensity in his tone she attributed to loyalty. She had indeed done well to hire him.

"Excellent. Now then, if there is nothing else—"

"There is, my lady." He held a note in his hand she hadn't noticed. "This arrived a few minutes ago."

She handed him the sketchpad, took the note eagerly and unfolded it. "It's from my sister."

My Dear Delia,

The tide is turning quite nicely. Yesterday, while driving in the park, Lady Heaton and her daughter approached me and requested that I convey their sympathies upon the death of your husband. The younger lady remarked as to how tragically romantic your current circumstances are and her mother was quite sympathetic as well, saying the course of true love can be sadly cut short. These were not the only comments I received during my ride.

I must say I was hard-pressed not to chortle with satisfaction. My plan is working far better and far more quickly than I had hoped. You, dear sister, are fast becoming the symbol of lost love and shall soon surpass Juliet herself. Even Mother seems to be softening, although that may be more attributable to a change in the stars, father's annoyance at her unyielding attitude and the fact that, while she refuses to admit it, she has missed you.

There is more good news as well. We received a letter from Grandmother insisting you present yourself at Effington Hall by week's end. The Ride is two days hence and Grandmother's ball, as always, the next evening. Mother protested, of course—all that mourning business, you know— but she cannot go against Grandmother's wishes. Grandmother wrote that this is not the time for you to be estranged from your family, and furthermore she wishes to speak to you personally. She is sending her private carriage for you.

I am off to the country today and I shall be eagerly awaiting your arrival.

Until then, I remain affectionately yours,

Cassandra

"Wonderful news, Gordon." She beamed at the butler. "I am going to the country for a few days at my grandmother's request."

"Then all is well with your family, ma'am," he said cautiously.

"It will be." A determined note sounded in her voice. Effington Hall was the perfect place to confront her mother. Right or wrong, it was past time Lady William, Georgina, accept that her daughter's life was her own to live. Or ruin. And the stars be damned. "It most certainly will be.

"The Roxborough Ride is in a few days, Gordon." She started down the hall, addressing him over her shoulder. "It's an equestrian competition that my family holds every year. The Ride is quite a test of both horse and rider and as much fun as my grandmother's ball, always held the next night. I doubt if I'll compete this year, although perhaps I will." She swiveled back to him. "Yesterday, I would not even have considered such a thing, but today, I am in a glorious mood and the world is full of possibilities. How is your mood?"

"Cautious, ma'am."

She laughed. "Of course, it would be." Once more, she started off. "While I am gone, I should like for you to begin arranging appointments regarding the refurbishing and, oh, yes, we must hire additional servants. I am in dire need of a lady's maid and I should like an additional maid as well and a footman or two. And do start looking for a good cook. I am frankly desperate for something with flavor."

She marched to the next room, Gordon a step behind her, jotting notes on her pad or making a quick sketch of a window or piece of furniture, but her thoughts were distracted. Gordon's question lingered in the back of her mind and she couldn't quite ignore it.

Do your intentions toward your new life involve activity of a more scandalous nature?

Did they indeed?

She'd meant it when she'd said she hadn't thought

that far. But she'd also meant it when she'd said she would live her life by no one's standards but her own. And weren't those standards already questionable? Why, hadn't she come to Charles's bed entirely of her own accord? With no expectation of marriage and knowing full well the repercussions of her ruination?

Delia had no desire to marry again. She'd only just tasted independence and quite liked it thus far. She suspected it would only get better.

Precisely how closely do you intend to follow his example?

How closely indeed?

The answer was at once wicked and delicious.

Independence wasn't the only thing she'd had a taste of. She had rather liked relations with her husband, brief as they had been, and suspected that too could only get better. As she had told her sister, the act of lovemaking had had potential. Great potential. She was fortunate enough not to have become with child from that and she was certain there were ways an experienced woman could avoid such complications. Certainly she was not an experienced woman yet, but in the eyes of the world, her status as a widow assumed her experience.

Perhaps the best way to begin the grand adventure of the rest of her life was to become what the world assumed she already was.

An experienced woman.

Chapter 5

"Blue in here, I should think."

"Blue would be exceptionally nice, my lady," Tony murmured, then winced to himself. *Blue would be exceptionally nice*, indeed. This entire charade was absurd. Ridiculous. And he was in it up to his ass.

"A deep blue, perhaps." Lady Wilmont stood in the middle of the bedchamber one door down from her husband's and considered the room thoughtfully. "Not so deep as the night sky, nor as light as the morning, but something more akin to a . . . a what, Gordon?"

Your eyes, my lady. "The sea, perhaps?"

"The sea, exactly what I was thinking of. Thank you." She sighed wistfully. "Oh, I do love a nice sea-blue."

It complements the color of your hair. "May I suggest, ma'am, that you then employ blue in the room you intend to make your own and in here use a pleasant"—he forced the words out—"sunny yellow?"

"Yellow? I hadn't thought of yellow." She nodded at

the window. "Although there is but one window in here and yellow would brighten it up a great deal. Yellow it is, then." She flashed him a smile that lit her face as much as any color could ever light a room, then scribbled a note on her pad.

What was he thinking? This sort of thing would only get him deeper in trouble and he was already off his stride.

He'd berated himself ever since he walked into Wilmont's room and saw the disarray. He should have heard her last night, but his own quarters were in the back of the house on the ground floor. And blast it all, after the long days and nights of sorting Wilmont's finances he was exhausted. No excuse, really. He should have been on his guard.

"The furniture in this room as well is horribly out of date and . . ."

Anyone could slip in here unnoticed in the middle of the night. Starting tonight, after she was abed, he would sleep in one of the rooms on this floor.

". . . the carpet is quite worn and really unserviceable . . ."

There had been no incidents, nothing at all unusual since Lady Wilmont had moved in, and it was entirely possibly whoever had searched the house before her return had already found the notebook.

". . . and I daresay there is no longer a need for . . ."

However, if indeed the notebook was still missing, there was also a distinct possibility whoever wanted it would assume she had knowledge of it.

"I think that will do in here for the moment." She glanced at him. "Have I missed anything?"

"I cannot think of a thing, ma'am."

She grinned and shook her head. "You are not enjoying this, are you?"

"I can think of nothing I would rather do, my lady," he said staunchly.

It was only a partial lie. He didn't find it the least bit taxing to follow her from room to room, her dark skirts swishing provocatively with her walk, although it was difficult to keep his mind on questions regarding anything other than the lush figure those skirts concealed.

"You are not a very good liar, Gordon." She laughed, laid her hand on his arm and lowered her voice confidentially. "However, I am most appreciative that you are willing to placate me."

He'd never been particularly enamored of women in black, but black quite suited her. Her pale complexion contrasted with the stark shade and made her appear fragile and vulnerable and altogether exquisite. Her blue eyes were even more intense against the canvas of her porcelain skin and her blond hair glowed with a light of its own. She was far lovelier than he had first thought. Was this what Wilmont had seen? Had the man married her for a reason other than honor? Had he been so enamored of her charms and her unsuspected wit that he'd lost his head?

Nonsense. Wilmont was not the type of man to be lured into marriage by a pretty face and clever manner.

She removed her hand and headed out of the room. "Once we finish this floor, we will go downstairs and see what can be done about the public rooms. I think in the future I shall wish to do a great deal of entertaining and we will need . . ."

He watched her walk down the hallway, her hips swaying seductively, invitingly beneath the black fabric. His arm was warm where her hand had rested and his stomach clenched. He drew a deep breath. He might as well face it.

She had charmed him utterly and completely. And he

wanted her as he had rarely wanted another woman before. But he'd never dallied with the wife of a friend before, regardless of whether said friend was alive or dead, and he had no intention of doing so now. Still, with Lady Wilmont, Philadelphia, *Delia,* he suspected it would not be a mere dalliance. It would be something better, richer, deeper. Something forever.

Was this what Wilmont had thought?

"Any suggestions for this room, Gordon?" Delia stood in the doorway of the next chamber and inclined her head toward the room.

"Red," he said without hesitation.

"Red?" She drew her brows together and studied the room. "Red. What an interesting idea."

"Red would make a . . . statement, my lady," he murmured. He didn't give a fig whether she used red or purple or tartan plaid in this or any other room, it was simply the first thing that had popped into a mind occupied with more pertinent questions.

"It would indeed. I quite like the idea," she said thoughtfully. "I wonder if I can persuade my sister to assist me in all this. Her sense of artistry has always been much better than mine."

At the moment, it was his duty to watch over this woman but nothing more. Surely Tony's desire for her was due only to their close proximity. He would probably feel precisely the same way toward any other moderately attractive woman whose constant company he shared. He could not, would not, allow the waters to be muddied with irresponsible desire. He would not let his loins rule his head no matter how delightful he found Delia, Philadelphia, *Lady* Wilmont.

"I shall ask her when I see her." Lady Wilmont nodded firmly. "Of course, it will mean going against my mother's edict, but I daresay in another week or so

Cassie will have had quite enough of being the perfect daughter. Besides, I have high hopes for my visit to Effington Hall. With any luck at all, I shall be at least partially back in my family's good graces by the time I return."

She turned toward him. "I shall make a list for you of the appointments I should like arranged while I am gone. I trust you will have no difficulties with that?"

Bloody hell. He'd forgotten all about her trip to the country. He couldn't possibly let her out of his sight, yet there was no way he could accompany her. Or, at least, her butler could not accompany her.

"None at all, ma'am."

Of course, the dowager duchess was sending her private coach for Lady Wilmont and she would travel by day. She should be safe enough. Still, he would have the department arrange for men to follow her and others to pose as servants during the duration of her stay at Effington Hall. Surely serving as footmen or stable hands wouldn't be nearly as taxing as masquerading as a butler. As for the dowager duchess's ball . . .

Gordon could not attend, but Lord St. Stephens certainly could. It should be fairly easy to procure an invitation. Tony had never particularly had much use for society. He'd started in service to the crown well before his majority and had had no expectations of a title. Not until the recent death of his older brother had he even considered the possibility that he would one day be Viscount St. Stephens. The thought struck him that he did need to do something about his inheritance and everything that accompanied it. But it had all happened so blasted quickly and he simply hadn't had time. When this business was over, perhaps.

The department could arrange for his invitation and, while he was gone, handle this nonsense about meetings with cabinetmakers and whoever else Lady Wilmont wished to see. From Lord Kimberly to Mr. Pribble to the department secretary, they were seasoned and hand-picked. A professional lot, dependable and competent, each and every one of them. They could certainly manage the details involved with the mere refurbishing of a house.

He wondered how Wilmont might have felt about what his wife was doing to his house. For the first time since Wilmont's death, the thought of his old friend brought a smile to his face.

"Did I say something amusing?" She cast him a puzzled look.

"Not at all, ma'am." He groped for an acceptable excuse. "I was merely thinking how charming the house will be when you are finished."

She burst into laughter. "I'll say it again, Gordon, you are a poor liar. However, I shall let you keep your thoughts to yourself, as amusing as they may well be."

"Thank you, my lady," he said with a genuine sigh of relief.

"We have a great deal to accomplish and I would like to at least have an idea of what I am doing before I leave."

She crossed the hall and entered another room, chattering all the while about colors and fabrics and God knows what else. He followed and feigned attention, nodding at appropriate moments, murmuring an inane suggestion now and then.

This refurbishing was, to his way of thinking, a complete waste of time and money. Was there really a significant difference between shades of green? And indeed, who particularly cared or noticed?

She did. And in this absurdly female undertaking, she exuded a passion that was nothing short of intoxicating.

If indeed he allowed himself to be intoxicated, which he did not. Still, he couldn't help thinking what might happen when they met at the duchess's ball. He was confident she had not seen through his disguise thus far. She didn't suspect for a moment that he was not exactly who he claimed to be.

And he couldn't help thinking as well about the passion she exhibited in the simple choosing of fabric.

And what other forms her passion might take.

Delia hated eating alone.

She idly ran her finger around the rim of her glass of Madeira. Indeed, she hated *being* alone and even after all these months she wasn't at all used to it.

At her family's house she'd been rarely alone. Her parents or her sister or one of her three brothers had been a constant presence and there'd been a full staff of servants in attendance as well. She'd always considered herself something of a solitary person and quite valued her rare moments of privacy, but those moments had been by choice. Here, there was no choice. Here, the emptiness of this place fairly echoed. That would change somewhat, of course, when Gordon hired more help, but right now, she could almost hear herself think.

For now, she had the trip to Effington Hall to look forward to. The annual visit to the country for the festivities surrounding the Roxborough Ride was always a great deal of fun. It was the one time in the year when nearly every Effington in existence gathered under one roof. There would be no opportunity to be lonely or alone at Effington Hall.

Delia could mark her life by happenings at the Ride. There was the year her cousin Thomas fell trying to climb the ivy that covered one wall of the hall and everyone thought he might well be dead. And the year she and Cassie had seen how tragic life could be when it was learned their cousin Gillian's first husband had been killed fighting Napoleon. And more recently, the year her cousin Pandora had played a ridiculous game with a charming earl and lost. Or won, as she did marry the dashing lord.

Delia sighed with resignation. This would be the year she, and everyone else, would remember as the year of Delia's disgraceful marriage.

And afterward, she would still have to return here. To her own house. And her new life. Whatever that might consist of.

She stared at the wine in her glass, the crystal humming under the stroke of her finger. Her resolve to become a woman of experience was both exciting and daunting. How on earth did one do such a thing? She was not about to throw herself at the first man who presented himself, although she was fairly confident there would indeed be men interested in a young, wealthy widow. She did hope they were not as dull as those who had courted her before her marriage. No, surely such respectable, boring gentlemen would honor the restrictions of mourning and give her a wide berth. She brightened at the thought. The type of man she wished to become experienced with would not give such things as the rules of convention a second thought.

"Will that be all for tonight, ma'am?"

She looked up. Gordon stood towering over her. He had already cleared the plates from what could only optimistically be called supper. Again, she noted his height. He did seem to tower rather a lot.

"I believe so." She sighed again and got to her feet.

It had been a very long day. She and Gordon had evaluated each and every room in the house save for Mrs.

Miller's, MacPherson's and the other servants' quarters on the upper floor, Gordon's room on the main floor and the kitchens belowstairs. She was certain those would all need, at the very least, a fresh coat of paint. She had no idea how he'd managed, but Charles had had only the two servants when they'd married. The furniture she was getting rid of elsewhere in the house was still more than serviceable and perhaps could be employed for use in the servants' rooms. When she had servants, that is.

She picked up her glass and started toward the library. She'd already replaced the book of poetry she'd given Gordon with the copy Charles had given her, the only thing she'd thus far removed from her trunks. Beyond that, and a handful of other books she'd already read, she'd yet to find anything of interest on the shelves. Still, there were a great number of books and surely there was something that might strike her fancy. She was too restless to retire and hoped that the later she put off bed, the more soundly she would sleep. She did not want to ever again awake in the middle of the night gripped by nameless fears and apprehensions.

"If there is nothing else, then, my lady . . ."

"Not a thing." She would spend an hour or so perusing the library's offerings until she was tired enough to sleep. A thought struck her and she paused. "Gordon, do you play backgammon?"

"On occasion, ma'am."

"Would you care for a game?"

He hesitated.

"I know that once again I am wandering past traditional boundaries of our respective stations and, well"—she drew a deep breath—"damn it to hell, Gordon, I am bored and lonely and I cannot sleep and I shall go starkraving mad if I have to talk to no one but myself for one more minute, and . . . and—"

"Then I shall consider it my duty to join you." He paused. "On one condition."

"Another condition, Gordon?" She shook her head in amusement. "And I thought I was the one overstepping my bounds."

"You are, my lady," he said in his all-too-proper butler manner. "However, as you are, I should like to request you refrain from the use of expressions such as *damn it to hell*. I find it most distressing and not at all becoming in a woman of your position."

"You are absolutely right." She stifled a smile. It was obviously her newfound sense of independence that provoked such language, even if both she and her sister had on occasion employed less-than-proper language and had discovered a wicked sense of satisfaction in doing so. Still, given his age and experience and sense of propriety, she could not fault him for chastising her. "I shall contain myself in the future." She turned again toward the library, glancing back at him. "I should warn you, however, while I do understand the game and have played now and again, I am by no means very accomplished at it."

"Excellent, my lady." He skillfully stepped around her, opening the library door before she reached it. His speed and agility never failed to amaze her. "As I am really quite good."

The corners of his mouth under his mustache quirked upward slightly in what just might have been a smile.

"Could that possibly be a joke, Gordon?"

"Possibly."

A few minutes later they were seated across from one another at the backgammon table at the near end of the small library. It was an exceptionally fine set: the markers made of ebony and ivory, the table inlaid with mahogany and rosewood. She would expect no less from

Charles. Indeed, while she planned on changing much of the furnishings in the house, she had to admit everything was of excellent quality. Apparently, Charles had spent his money on more than wild living.

They played silently for a few minutes, the game moving quickly and rather more evenly matched than she'd let on.

"You have lied to me, my lady," he murmured, not raising his gaze from the board.

"Have I?" She smiled to herself.

"You are far better at this than you led me to believe."

"I too enjoy a good joke, Gordon."

"Indeed." He rolled the dice. "However," he said, and moved a marker, sending one of hers out of play, "this is a game of both chance and skill. There is a certain amount of luck involved. The skill is in best knowing how to take advantage of it."

She put the dice in the cup, rolled them out, then replaced her marker on the board and tried not to smirk. "You mean like that?"

"Exactly." The butler's concentration was firmly on the lay of the board.

"You should know Effingtons refuse to lose. It is in our blood."

"Then this shall be a new experience for you, my lady."

A few moves more and it was clear he did indeed know how best to take advantage of the luck of the dice. And clear, as well, luck was on his side. She took scant comfort in the fact that he had not trounced her in his victory.

"Another round, my lady?" Innocence sounded in his voice and once more she thought she noted at least a hint of a smile.

"Most definitely," she said firmly. She had never been

especially good at losing. She didn't know an Effington who was.

They replaced the markers and began again. He was good, but so was she. She watched him move his markers without hesitation, his hands strong and sure and not at all the hands of an elderly man. She had played any number of times with her father, and his hands had a much more aged look to them than Gordon's did, even though her father was a younger man. Odd, how people showed age in various ways. Her grandmother had seen eighty years and her mind was sharp and clear as was Gordon's when it came to games and finances; but Gordon did seem a bit muddled when it came to the position he had held for much of his life.

"Do you have family, Gordon?" she asked idly.

"I am alone in the world, ma'am," he murmured, his attention firmly on the game.

"Oh, dear, I am sorry." Even now, she couldn't imagine being without any family at all.

"It is simply a fact of my life."

"Did you always wish to be a butler?"

"My father was a butler, as was his father before him." He studied the board. "I never considered anything else."

"Do you like it?"

"I find great satisfaction in service, my lady. My years with Lord Marchant were quite fulfilling." His manner was offhand, his voice had the cadence of a recitation, no doubt because he was intent upon the game. "I am quite content with my life."

"But if you could have done something else, what would it have been?" she pressed.

"I should have liked to sail the seas and explore undiscovered parts of the world," he said without pause.

She stared in surprise. "Really?"

He looked up, startled, as if he weren't aware he had said it aloud.

"Why didn't you, then?"

"I . . ." For a moment he seemed befuddled, as if searching for memories so old he could no longer recall them. "It was merely a boyhood desire for adventure, my lady, with no more substance to it than that."

"But you didn't pursue it?"

"I grew out of it," he said firmly, as if to put an end to the subject.

"My sister and I used to long for adventure. We thought it quite unfair that only boys have such opportunities." She paused. "Why didn't you do what you wanted with your life?"

He stared at her as if she were at least slightly insane. "One has responsibilities. To one's family and employers particularly. I feel I *have* done as I wanted with my life." His gaze returned to the board. "It is your turn."

She rolled the dice and moved her piece.

"And what shall I do with my life, Gordon?" she said under her breath.

"I thought you were refurbishing the house." His tone was mild.

"I shall have a few good years remaining when the house is completed. I am not in my dotage yet." The man was being nothing less than obstinate. From what she knew of her butler thus far, he had definite opinions. The trick was in getting him to state them. "It's not an especially large house and won't take more than a few months to finish. What shall I do after that?"

"It is not for me to say, ma'am."

"Surely you have some thoughts on the matter?" She huffed in exasperation. "I should very much like to hear them."

"Your roll."

She shook the cup rather more violently than necessary and threw the dice on the table, then moved a marker.

"Are you certain you wish to do that?"

"Yes," she snapped.

He glanced at her and raised a brow. "Is something amiss?

She glared silently.

"If I may say so, my lady, you are a stubborn sort. Very well." He sat back in his chair, folded his hands together and rested them on the table. "I admit your pronouncement this morning that you will live a grand adventure from this moment forth strikes me as being fraught with all manner of dangers you have yet to consider. Setting that aside, I have always believed one should live one's life in the manner that nature and tradition intended. I was intended to follow in the footsteps of my father and his father."

"And what I am intended for?"

"To be a good wife and, God willing, mother. It's what your family, your heritage and nature has prepared you for. If indeed you wish to know what I think you should do with the rest of your life, I would advise you to marry again. A lady should not live her life alone. She needs a husband's council and guidance."

At once, Delia had an overwhelming urge to shake this dear old man until his teeth rattled. She would never do that, of course, yet the annoyingly sanctimonious tone in his voice set her own teeth on edge. "I suspected you were opinionated, but I had no idea you were stuffy and narrow-minded as well."

"I commend you on your astute assessment of my character, my lady."

She stared at him, then laughed. "I am exceedingly glad I have encouraged you to speak freely."

"And I am glad I have said nothing to offend you."

"Not at all. I quite enjoy a good debate." She paused to gather her thoughts. "What if I do not wish to marry again? What if I wish to follow the course you desired as a boy?"

"Balderdash. Utter nonsense." He snorted in disdain. "You said it yourself: Adventure is not for women. Far too dangerous and uncertain for the fairer sex. No, marriage is the only true purpose in life for women."

She studied him for a long moment. "Have you ever been married, Gordon?"

"No indeed."

"I see. So you have denied some poor woman from fulfilling her *true* purpose in life," she said innocently.

"Perhaps." He raised a brow. "Or I have saved her from a long life with an opinionated, stuffy and narrow-minded husband."

She laughed. "Have you never wished to marry at all?"

He shook his head. "Never."

"You have never been in love then either?"

"No, my lady."

"Surely there was a comely parlormaid in your past?"

"There have been several, ma'am," he said coolly. "But none that have captured by heart."

She grinned. "To their regret, no doubt."

"No doubt."

"I can scarce believe you have not succumbed to some woman's charms. An entrancing housekeeper, perhaps? Or a buxom cook?"

"We could certainly use a cook of any form or figure at this point," he muttered.

She laughed, any annoyance with him now gone; he was far too much fun to tease. "I think you protest too much, Gordon. I cannot believe there is not a lost love somewhere in your past." She leaned her elbows on the table and propped her chin in her hands. "Possibly a farmer's daughter?"

"No."

"I know." She grinned wickedly. "A vicar's sister?"

He paused and the corners of his mouth twitched as if he were fighting a smile. "Not that I recall."

"A governess, then?"

"Not one."

"A merchant's widow?"

"No."

"A shepherdess?"

"No."

"A lady of the house?"

His gaze shot to hers. For a moment, his controlled butler facade disappeared and the years seemed to drop away. For a moment, his gaze locked with hers and there was an intensity in his eyes that stole her breath. For a moment, she glimpsed the man he might once have been. It vanished as quickly as it had appeared.

"No." His gaze dropped to the table. He rolled the dice and played as if nothing of consequence had passed between them.

But it had.

She had overstepped the barrier between mistress and servant. No, she had bounded over it. The poor man had inadvertently revealed his soul to her. Thanks to her prying, his most private secret was exposed.

From the look in his eye she knew full well he had once lost his heart to a woman above his station. A woman who had obviously broken his heart. Anger on his behalf surged through her.

She rolled the dice and forced a casual note to her voice. "Did she care for you as well?"

His tone was clipped. "Her affections were otherwise engaged."

"I see." She moved a marker seven spaces. She was in an excellent position, but it scarcely mattered. Her attention was firmly on the man across from her. "She was in love with someone else, then?"

"Lady Wilmont." Gordon flattened his hands on the table and met her gaze firmly. "This was a very, very long time ago and I can scarce remember the details. My life is in the past where it belongs and I prefer it that way."

"Of course," she murmured and fell silent. She should let it rest. Gordon did not wish to discuss this. Still . . .

"So she *was* in love with someone else, then?"

He moved his men without looking up at her. "She was a widow still in love with her deceased husband."

"I see." She tried to hold her tongue and failed. "And you gave up on any possibility that with time—"

"The circumstances were unusual. I did not give up, I accepted the situation for what it was. There is a difference." He set the dice cup firmly in front of her. "If we are quite done examining the foibles of my past, I feel I should tell you I have always enjoyed the playing of backgammon in a certain amount of peace. And silence."

"How very interesting." She picked up the cup and rolled, her tone light. "As I have always found conversation to be as stimulating as the game."

"Imagine my surprise, my lady," he murmured.

She bit back a grin. Whether he realized it or not, he was most amusing. What a strange turn her life had taken. Her butler was fast becoming her dearest friend.

Perhaps it was the lateness of the hour or the intimacy of the cozy library or the banter that accompanied their play, but it struck her that the candid relationship she and the elderly man had forged was very much the kind of relaxed comradeship she'd hoped to have with a man someday, albeit a much younger man. In her mind's eye, she could see herself playing backgammon late into the night, talking and laughing and teasing this as-yet-unknown gentleman. There was no face, as he did not, in truth, exist in her life at this time, but she could see his hands: strong and sure and confident.

Very much like Gordon's hands, except, of course, these would belong to the man she loved.

Chapter 6

Delia stepped into the entry at Effington Hall and drew a deep breath. The scents of childhood memories surrounded her. The odd, comforting aromas of ancient houses, vague hints of cinnamon and clove, of lemon oils and waxes, of days gone by and affection lingering always.

As good as it was to be here again, she could not dismiss a nagging sense of trepidation. It was to be expected, of course; this would be the first time she had seen most of the members of her family since her marriage and she had no idea how she would be received. Certainly her grandmother wished her presence here, but what of the others?

It would be something of a test, she supposed. As appealing as the whole idea of flouting convention and defying the rules of mourning was, Delia wasn't entirely sure she had the courage to go through with it.

"I cannot believe it took you so long to get here."

Cassie sailed into the entry and threw her arms around her sister. "I've been watching for you for two days now and I very much feared you would not come at all."

"Grandmother requested my presence and I could scarce ignore that. Regardless of my other crimes, that would be unforgivable." Delia untangled herself from her sister's embrace and stepped back. "I assume Mother is here as well?"

"Of course." Cassie's gaze skimmed over her sister and her brows drew together. "Gad, you look awful in black. I noticed the other day, but I hated to say anything."

"Thank you for your restraint."

"Now, now, you needn't take that tone." Cassie grinned. "I'm simply surprised, as I look rather nice in black."

Delia returned the smile sweetly. "Then *you* can be the widow."

"Precisely what I had in mind," Cassie murmured with a wicked look in her eye.

"Exactly what do you mean by that?" Delia had seen that look before and didn't like it one bit.

"Time enough for explanations later." Cassie hooked her arm through her sister's and steered her toward the stairs. "Your room is ready, the one connected to mine so that we may catch up on everything that has happened."

"That should take all of a moment or two." Delia sighed and started up the stairs beside her sister. "Nothing at all has happened in my life since we last spoke. Other than that, I have decided to spend Charles's money on the refurbishing of the house and I should like your help."

"What fun. I should be delighted. From the little I've seen of your house, it certainly needs something. It is far too dark and heavy for my taste. Yours too, I would imagine. Besides, it is your house now and you have every right to make it your own."

"I do feel a touch guilty about it, though."

Cassie stopped and stared. "Why on earth would you feel guilty? Charles ruined you and then had the nerve to get himself killed. I should think spending his fortune in whatever way you please is the very least you should get out of all this."

"Cassie!"

"Oh, dear, that did sound rather mercenary and quite unsympathetic, didn't it?"

"Indeed it did."

"I am sorry, dearest, but that's how I feel about it all. You were ill-treated by this man—"

"He *did* marry me."

"And by doing so, enabled you to inherit his fortune. Damnably decent of him and, being quite blunt, the only favor he did you." Cassie continued up the stairs. "You do want me to be honest, don't you?"

"Not really," Delia muttered.

Her sister laughed. "We shall get you settled and refreshed from the journey and, oh, before I forget"—her tone was deceptively casual—"Grandmother is waiting to see you."

"What?" Delia stopped and stared in disbelief. "Now?"

"Well, not this very minute, but"—Cassie wrinkled her nose—"as soon as possible. The moment your carriage was seen in the distance, Grandmother sent me to watch for you and gathered everyone else—"

"Everyone else?" Delia's voice rose. "What do you mean, everyone else?"

"Not really everyone. Not Father or the duke or any of the other uncles or Cousin Thomas or—"

"Who, then?" Delia asked, even though she already knew the answer.

"Aunt Katherine, of course; she is the current duchess, after all. And Aunt Abigail and Aunt Grace and—"

"Mother?"

Cassie nodded.

"Good heavens." A heavy weight settled in the pit of Delia's stomach. She should have known this was coming. Should have suspected the moment she learned the dowager duchess had insisted on her presence at Effington Hall, where the entire family would be in residence. Most notably its female members.

"And Gillian and Pandora and Marianne as well."

"Of course, they would be included, wouldn't they?" A grim note sounded in Delia's voice. "They are the newest members of that exclusive club of Effington matrons." She trudged up the stairs in the manner of someone climbing a scaffolding.

Cassie trailed behind her. "Yes, but they might well be far more sympathetic to your, um—"

"To the mess I've made of my life?"

"I'm not certain I would phrase it precisely that way. . . . Come, now, Delia, you needn't be at all apprehensive about this." Cassie's tone was deceptively optimistic. "It's nothing more than your family wishing to—"

"It's the *Tribunal,* Cassie," Delia ground out between clenched teeth. How could she have been so stupid as to not realize it before now? She never would have come if she'd considered for a moment the fate awaiting her. "You know it as well as I."

"*Tribunal* is such a harsh word," Cassie murmured. "We should never have called it that in the first place. *Gathering* is a much more pleasant word. The gathering of the ladies. As if it were a social society. A club, or something of the sort. I know—the Society of Effington Ladies. Yes, indeed, I like that much better. It has a lovely ring to it."

"It can sing like a robin, for all the good it will do me." Delia heaved a heartfelt sigh. "I'm doomed."

Delia and Cassie had noted some years ago their grandmother gathered her daughters-in-law together whenever there was an issue of importance regarding a family member, usually a female member. Indeed, the Effington men were never included in the Tribunal and Delia imagined they were most grateful for that omission.

The sisters, influenced by their French studies, had privately named it the Tribunal, partially because it seemed rather forbidding, and partially because whatever went on in that room between their female relatives, and whoever might be summoned before them, stayed within that room. Neither their grandmother nor their mother nor their aunts had *ever* given so much of a hint as to the proceedings. Which made it all the more sinister, as secrecy among Effingtons, especially Effington women, was a rare commodity.

According to the sisters' observations, the Tribunal was called in cases of scandal, dire circumstances or to pronounce a prospective Effington spouse worthy. Before their marriage, Pandora's husband had been summoned before the women and had obviously taken a vow of secrecy, as he had apparently never told a soul what had transpired in the ladies' parlor at Effington Hall.

"*Doomed* is rather a harsh word as well." Cassie sighed. "If it eases your mind at all, you should know I will be right by your side. In truth, I insisted on it."

"Why?" Delia studied her sister suspiciously.

"Because I am your sister and your closest friend." Cassie raised her chin in a noble gesture. "Because, regardless of what you do, I will stand beside you. Because there is a bond between us nothing can ever sever. Because—"

"Because no one believes you had nothing to do with my scandalous behavior?" Delia said wryly.

"Yes, well, that too." Cassie shrugged. "At any rate, we have both long expected that if either of us did anything serious enough for the Tribunal, it would be me. As you did promise to be by my side, I can do no less for you."

At once, Delia's apprehension lessened. She and her sister had always been a team of sorts, partners in chaos or crime, allies forever. With Cassie by her side she could indeed face anything. Even the Tribunal. Impulsively, she gave her sister a quick hug. "I can't tell you how much that means to me."

"Besides"—Cassie grinned—"this is my only opportunity to find out what truly goes on in that parlor without having to earn the privilege."

Delia stared for a moment, then laughed. "I should have known as much."

"You know as well that I'm teasing, although, I suppose, as I did think I would be in this position one day, I am better prepared to face it than you. I have always thought it was inevitable for me, whereas for you—"

"Yes, yes." Delia sighed. "I am the one no one ever expected to stray from propriety."

The women reached the top of the stairs and turned toward the family wing, down a long corridor lined with the portraits of generations of Effingtons. When they were very young, Delia and Cassie had thought the faces staring down at them were forbidding, even condemning, as if they were sitting in judgment of their descendents and finding them wanting.

But as the girls grew older, they'd noticed a hint of a

smile here, an amused look in an eye there. They'd paid more attention to the stories of those who had gone before them, about this particular duchess and that certain lord. About triumphs and tragedies, success and scandals. And they'd learned, because it was their lot to do so but more because it became a pleasure, of the heritage and tradition that made the Effingtons who and what they were today. That made Delia and Cassie who and what they were and, more, who they could become.

And if once these faces staring down at her had proven daunting, today they gave her an odd sort of strength. As if they were no longer critical but encouraging. As if to say certainly she had made mistakes, but indeed hadn't they all? It was a ridiculous idea, of course. Still . . . she smiled up at her ancestors.

"However, now that I have joined the ranks of Effingtons who did not live their lives entirely as expected"—Delia squared her shoulders and met her sister's gaze—"the first step toward the grand adventure of my new life is to summon the courage to face whatever consequences that mistake may bring."

Cassie studied her warily. "Grand adventure?"

Delia grinned and linked her arm through her sister's. "I have done a great deal of thinking in my solitude and I will explain it all to you later. For now, I would like to freshen up and then I shall face the Tribunal."

"*We* shall face the Tribunal," Cassie said firmly.

Delia squeezed her sister's arm affectionately. "As you were aware of this before I was, I don't suppose you have any plan of defense? Any suggestions or words of wisdom?"

"Not really. Although I have always heard, when confronting adversity, one should never show fear. Beyond that, I suspect it might be wise to avoid any mention of the term"—Cassie grinned—"*Tribunal.*"

* * *

Delia and Cassie traded cautious glances. They sat side by side on a small settee facing the rest of the female members of the family. If one didn't know better, one would think the arrangement of the seating was for nothing more sinister than purposes of casual conversation.

In truth, it didn't seem all that forbidding at the moment. On the contrary, it was much more on the order of a ladies' society than a tribunal with the power of a figurative guillotine in its hands.

Grandmother sat as regally as ever on the damask sofa, Aunt Katherine, the duchess, on her right, Aunt Abigail, Lady Edward, on her left. Aunt Grace, Lady Harold, perched on the arm of the sofa and their mother stood behind the rest, obviously too overwrought to sit. Cousin Thomas's wife, Marianne, Lady Helmsley; cousin Gillian, Lady Shelbrooke; and cousin Pandora, Lady Trent, sat off to one side. Pandora caught Delia's eye and winked in support.

Still, a man-eating tiger didn't seem all that forbidding either until it opened its mouth.

"You needn't look so nervous, you know," Aunt Katherine said with a pleasant smile. "As if you were about to be judged. This isn't at all what we are about."

"What are we about?" Delia said without thinking.

"Your life, Philadelphia," Grandmother said firmly.

"I suspected as much, Grandmother, and I am sorry about the scandal and—"

"Nonsense." Grandmother waved away the comment. "As scandals go, it scarcely signifies."

"It was certainly more impressive than anything I was ever involved in," Pandora said in a low aside to Gillian. Gillian shot her a quelling glance.

Grandmother ignored the exchange. "While our approval of your choice in husband is, at this time, neither here nor there since the poor man is dead, the manner in which you wed and the behavior that brought you to that point is most distressing."

"I know, Grandmother, I never meant—"

"However," Grandmother continued, "there is not one of us here who has not, at some time or another in our youth, displayed behavior that was inappropriate or ill-advised or, indeed, scandalous."

"Even Aunt Katherine?" Cassie asked.

Grandmother nodded. "Especially Aunt Katherine."

"I don't know that I'd use the word *especially*," Aunt Katherine murmured, looking more like a chastised schoolgirl than the current Duchess of Roxborough.

"Surely, *you* never—" Delia said without thinking. "What I mean to say is—"

"My dear Philadelphia, while it is perhaps difficult to realize now, I was not always as wise and ancient and perfect as I appear today." A wicked twinkle sparked in Grandmother's eye. "I myself had my share of, oh, shall we say, adventures in my youth. I survived and so shall you."

Delia studied the elderly woman for a moment. She chose her words carefully. "I'm afraid I don't understand, Grandmother. If you are not angry with me—"

"Oh, we would never be angry with you, Delia," Aunt Abigail said quickly. "We well understand the impulsiveness of youth."

"Mother doesn't," Cassie said pointedly.

As if of one mind, all gazes in the room, save the dowager duchess's, turned to Georgina, who huffed and crossed her arms over her chest.

"Of course she does," Grandmother said serenely. "As well, if not better than, the rest of us."

"Really?" Delia stared at her mother.

"Perhaps," Mother said loftily.

Aunt Grace choked back a laugh. Aunts Katherine and Abigail exchanged knowing glances. Grandmother looked innocent and it was obvious that the younger women hadn't the slightest idea what the older women were talking about. And Delia wasn't entirely certain she wished to learn just what possible indiscretions her aunts had committed in their youth or what adventures her grandmother had had as a young woman, and the very idea of knowing possible transgressions her mother had long ago put behind her brought an odd wave of unease to her stomach. Still, it was somewhat comforting to know whatever strange madness had brought Delia to this point might well be in her blood.

"Apparently your misbehavior was no more than the carrying on of a family tradition," Cassie said under her breath to her sister. "And obviously inevitable."

"Nothing is inevitable, Cassandra, save death." Grandmother pinned Cassie with a firm look. Cassie had the good grace to look appropriately chagrined. "Do not take what you hear today as sanction for inappropriate behavior. The mere fact that youthful high spirit is understood among all of us here does not also mean that it is approved."

"No, ma'am," Cassie murmured, her cheeks flushed. Delia squeezed her hand in silent support. Poor Cassie. Her biggest fault, and what got her into trouble more often than not, was her inability to hold her tongue and keep her thoughts to herself.

"My dearest Cassandra, I don't know what you have to worry about. I have never particularly worried about your future." Grandmother leaned forward slightly, as if she and Cassie were quite alone, her manner distinctly confidential. "It is always the quiet ones, you know, who surprise us. You have never been the least bit quiet. You are honest and straightforward as well as intelligent. In truth, you've always reminded me a great deal of myself." She straightened and flashed her granddaughter a conspiratorial smile. "Perhaps there is something to worry about after all.

"However, it is not your behavior nor your future that is the topic of concern today." Grandmother's gaze slid to Delia. "Philadelphia, have you given any thought to your future?"

Delia firmly pushed her plan to become an experienced woman to the back of her mind. Regardless of her grandmother's tolerance of the mistakes of youth, Delia was fairly confident she would not be especially pleased by Delia's thoughts for the future. "Not really, Grandmother."

"I see. Well, that's to be expected. Your life has changed a great deal in a short time." Grandmother studied her for a long moment and it was all Delia could do to sit still. At last, Grandmother nodded as if she had determined something only she would note. "Should you need advice or assistance in any way, do understand each and every one of us is available to you for whatever reason. We are your family and you must feel free to call on us.

"While we all feel your marriage was foolish and if you had had the foresight to confide in any of us beforehand we no doubt would have attempted to dissuade you from marrying Lord Wilmont, what's done cannot now be undone. However"—Grandmother's voice was firm—"I do believe an apology is in order."

"Of course." Delia drew a deep breath. "You have my abject—"

"No, no, dear," Grandmother said. "Not *your* apology."

Once again, all eyes turned to Georgina.

"Very well." Delia's mother cast her gaze heavenward

as if asking the stars for help, straightened her shoulders and met her daughter's gaze. "I . . . that is to say . . ."

Delia jumped to her feet, flew across the room and into her mother's arms. "Mother, I am so sorry."

"No, dearest, I am to blame." A sob sounded in her mother's voice. "I should have stood beside you instead of abandoning you—"

"But I deserved every bit of it. I misled you and deceived—"

"You are my child, and regardless of what you might do, you will always be my child." Helplessness rang in her mother's voice. "I was just so concerned that you had defied the course the stars had laid—"

"Superstitious nonsense," Grandmother muttered.

"Not at all," Georgina said with a long-suffering sigh. "Some of the most advanced thinkers of our time acknowledge the influence of the stars on our lives."

"Utter poppycock," Grandmother said.

Georgina glared at her mother-in-law. Georgina's superstitious nature, particularly her dependence on astrology, had always been a bone of contention between her and the rest of the family. Delia's father humored his wife, as did her children, but Grandmother and the other Effingtons thought Georgina's passion for astrology and various other forms of foretelling the future absurd. Especially as Madame Prusha, Georgina's astrologer, was not at all what anyone would think of as a seer. She was a friendly, apple-cheeked woman who lived in a pleasant cottage in a quiet village just outside of London.

"The fault, dear Brutus, is not in our stars but in ourselves," Aunt Grace murmured.

"Perhaps, but the stars have a great deal to do with those faults," Georgina snapped.

"Nonetheless," Grandmother's voice rang in the room,

"we do not allow scandal, dishonor, nor all the heavens above to come between family."

Georgina nodded at the dowager. "You're right, of course, but then you always are."

Grandmother cast her an affectionate smile. "I know, my dear."

The room released a collective sigh of relief.

"Now then." Grandmother gestured at the gathering. "If you would all be so good as to take your leave, I have a few things I should like to discuss with my granddaughter."

The ladies hesitated for the length of a heartbeat or two, the inevitable reluctance of natural curiosity to miss something that might be quite interesting, then stood, murmured their resigned good-byes and filed out, snippets of conversation trailing behind them.

"I must say, I'm rather disappointed," Pandora said to Marianne. "This is the first time I've been included in this particular gathering and I was expecting something a bit more exciting."

Marianne shrugged. "Perhaps the next scandal will be more impressive."

"There is always Cassie to give us hope." Gillian grinned at her cousin.

"I shall try to live up to your expectations," Cassie said wryly.

Georgina hugged Delia once again. "We shall talk later, dear heart." She nodded at her mother-in-law, then followed the other women. Aunt Katherine was the last out and closed the door firmly in her wake.

"You have made a mess of things, haven't you?" Grandmother nodded for Delia to be seated.

Delia returned to the settee and sank into it. "You could say that."

The older woman raised a brow.

"Yes." Delia heaved a heavy sigh. "I have made a mess of it."

"Thanks to your sister's efforts, your impulsive behavior is now being seen as quite romantic. And you as a rather tragic heroine."

"Yes, well . . ." Delia plucked at the fabric of the love seat. She wasn't at all sure she liked the idea of the rest of the world thinking she was something she was not.

"Such a shame, really, to go through all of this. The scandal and mourning and all."

"Perhaps," Delia murmured. It was a sort of penance and she probably deserved it. Still, Grandmother was right: It was a shame and it did seem to last forever.

"It would be different if you had loved the man."

Delia's gaze jerked to her grandmother's.

The older woman continued without pause. "Because then, of course, you'd be devastated."

Delia chose her words with care. "What makes you think I'm not devastated?"

"My dear child, you may well be able to fool the rest of the world with this story of irresistible love, but you cannot fool me. I know you too well." Grandmother folded her hands primly in her lap. "First of all, your eyes are not reddened, therefore any tears you have shed are long since past."

"I did cry for him," Delia said indignantly. *Or perhaps for what we might have had.*

"Of course you did, my dear, I would have been surprised if you had not. The death of anyone we know diminishes each of us in some way. But when one loses a love, there is an empty, lost area in one's soul and grief does not ease in—how long has he been dead?"

"More than six months now." Even as she said the words, Delia realized how little time had passed.

"That long?" her grandmother murmured, saying without words that six months was scarcely any time at all when one had lost a love. "Second, I know your mother well and she is a good person, if a little peculiar when it comes to fate and the stars and whatnot. A mother knows when her child's heart is engaged. She would never have been so unyielding had she thought you were truly in pain.

"And third, while you are willing to admit to your mistake you have never once blamed your actions on love. You have never so much as mentioned the word."

"Perhaps I simply do not care to flaunt my emotions?"

Grandmother smiled in a tolerant manner.

Delia sighed. "Very well, I admit it: I wasn't devastated by Charles's death, although I would not have had it happen." She rose to her feet and paced the room. "He probably deserved better than a wife who can't seem to find it in her heart to truly mourn him. I feel quite horrible about it all."

"That you didn't love him?"

"Yes." Delia wrapped her arms around herself. "I didn't even know him. Not really."

"Many people start marriages barely knowing their spouse, without love. It comes in time."

"That's what I was hoping, but we had no time, and . . ." She shook her head. "I don't really know what happened, Grandmother, one thing led to another, and . . ." She met her grandmother's gaze directly. "It's difficult to explain."

"And it has been a very long time since I was two-and-twenty and courted by very proper young men without so much as a glimmer of excitement in their eyes or a touch of adventure in their souls," Grandmother said in a matter-of-fact manner as if indeed she spoke from memory.

Delia stared.

"You needn't look so surprised. Young people always think they, and their circumstances, are unique. That no one in the world has ever experienced what they have. You are perhaps unusual in that you have not confused lust for love but you are not the first young woman to long for excitement or look for adventure in the arms of a handsome rake."

"Grandmother!" Delia gasped.

"Surely I haven't shocked you." Grandmother narrowed her eyes and studied her carefully. "But perhaps it wasn't like that at all?"

"No, no, it was exactly like that," Delia blurted. Heat flashed up her cheeks. "It just sounds so very odd to hear a discussion of such things from you."

"I am old, dear child, but not yet dead. Often, I remember the days of my youth better than I remember last week." She fell silent, obviously remembering days long passed, then grinned in a most ungrandmotherly manner. "I had a very good time."

Delia laughed and sank down on the sofa beside her grandmother. "I made a dreadful mistake."

"Of course you did, my dear. But you did marry him, and in this world, one can make no end of mistakes and will be forgiven as long as one rectifies them by conforming to the rules society lays down for such things. Young women who seek illicit adventures—"

"Grandmother," Delia murmured, again feeling the heat of a blush on her cheeks.

"—must pay with marriage. In point of fact, it is one rule that serves women better than men, so we cannot protest too loudly." She patted her granddaughter's cheek. "As for the scandal, even at the time it wasn't nearly as big as it may have seemed to you. And there are all sorts of juicier bits of gossip popping up like spring flowers. Why, just today Abigail told me of an incident in London involving that poor, dear Lord Bromfield and the widowed Lady Forester, who has far too much wealth for her own good and no idea what to do with it. Which reminds me." Grandmother stopped and her brow furrowed. "From what I have ascertained, Wilmont left you quite well off."

Delia nodded.

"I see." Her grandmother considered her for a long, thoughtful moment. "You have wealth, you have independence and you have youth. It is a potent combination. One fraught with all manner of danger and temptations."

"Grandmother, I—"

"I would encourage you to use the intelligence that is your birthright in navigating the waters that lie ahead. Do be careful, my dear." Grandmother's gaze searched hers and she smiled wisely. "Although you won't be, of course."

"Have you joined Mother in foretelling the future?" Delia teased. "Why would you say such a thing?"

"Because you remind me a great deal of myself."

"I thought Cassie reminded you of yourself."

"Whether you realize it or not, your likeness to your sister goes well beyond your appearance. Cassandra has always had a sense of her own spirit. It has just taken you longer to find yours. I see myself in both of you."

Grandmother smiled ruefully. "And heaven help us all."

Chapter 7

Tony had never particularly given much attention to the question of conscience; he'd never particularly considered that he had one. Yet, at the moment, it was that annoying facet of mind or soul that nagged at the edge of his thoughts day and night.

He adjusted the intricately tied cravat an Effington valet had arranged for him and grimaced at his reflection in the mirror in the room he'd been assigned to at Effington Hall. He had long ago given up the services of a valet as both unnecessary and intrusive. Still, if he were going to move about in society, he had best conform to its edicts. It struck him that this world, which he'd had no interest in up till now, went hand in hand with the inheritance of the title he'd also had no interest in. But at some inevitable point, it would *be* his world.

This was, in truth, the first public appearance of the new Viscount St. Stephens. An odd frisson of nerves skated up his spine. Ridiculous, of course. He had faced any number of perilous situations in the past in which one wrong word could cost him his life and had never experienced so much as a twinge of apprehension. This was nothing more than a mere country ball.

Oh, certainly, *she* would be there. *Delia*. No matter how he tried, he could no longer think of her as Lady Wilmont. They might well come face-to-face tonight without disguise or pretense between them. Well, not as much pretense.

He'd missed yesterday's famous Roxborough Ride. It had taken far longer than he'd anticipated to make certain all the arrangements for his absence were taken care of. The department had had no difficulties arranging for men to follow Delia's coach and infiltrate the ranks of Effington servants at the hall. Indeed, Lord Kimberly had managed to procure for Tony not only entrée to the dowager's ball, but a personal invitation to stay in the guest wing at Effington Hall as well.

With the apparent ease Lord Kimberly had displayed, Tony couldn't help but wonder why he simply hadn't done the same thing with Wilmont and circumvented any need to court Delia in the first place. Why, this whole nasty marriage mess could have been avoided. The woman could have been left alone to pursue whatever life she had pursued up to Wilmont's intrusion in it.

His jaw clenched. She hadn't deserved the hand she'd been dealt. And she deserved far better now than his deceit. At some point she would learn the truth and he refused to even consider her reaction.

At least the truth would not come out tonight. He studied his image in the mirror. If one knew what to look for, one might well think Lord St. Stephens and the butler Gordon bore a vague resemblance, particularly around the eyes. But the mustache he wore as Gordon well concealed his upper lip, the cotton jammed in front of his back upper teeth distorted his jaw, the powder in his hair effectively hid its natural dark color and the eyebrows and spectacles obscured his eyes. In addition, it was his experience that people rarely looked for that which they did not already expect to see. No, Delia would never recognize him.

Not that he planned to go anywhere near her. He would observe, nothing more.

He drew a deep breath, adjusted the cuffs of his coat and started toward the door.

Tony had had a long discussion with Lord Kimberly and suggested perhaps the time had come to give up the ruse. Or at the very least inform the lady in question as to Tony's true identity and his real purpose for being in her household. He'd pointed out that save for the ransacking of her house, there was no indication of anything further, nor was there any sign she was indeed in danger. To his credit, Lord Kimberly had listened and admitted Tony might well be right. But for now, Tony was ordered to stay precisely where he was, as a precaution if nothing else.

At this point, Tony was certain Delia had no knowledge of Wilmont's work, the Effington Papers or the missing notebook. She was an innocent in this whole affair. Still, that alone would not cause conscience to rear its ugly head. No, it was the woman herself who made him question his duty.

She was so bloody nice. She treated him, her butler—*a servant*, for God's sake—as if he had worth beyond the service he provided. As if he were a valued member of her family. As if she cared about him. What kind of woman cared about those in her employ for less than a month? She was either a complete fool or the kindest creature he had ever met. And she was no fool.

He started down the long corridor toward the main

section of the house. Another guest might well feel the need of a guide, but Tony had noted every turn and doorway and landmark when he was first shown to his rooms.

How would she feel when she knew the truth? About her husband? About her butler? And about Viscount St. Stephens?

She would hate him and he could not blame her. Not that it really mattered. When all this was resolved, she would go on with her life, her grand adventure, in whatever form it might take, and he would go on with his. Their paths might well never cross again.

Until, of course, the time came when he left the department and took up the responsibilities that went along with his title. That too was something he preferred not to think about. Still, the idea of meeting Delia in the future without a fabric of lies between them was surprisingly appealing. Not that anything could ever come of it. If he told her the truth, she would never forgive him—why should she?

He descended a flight of steps, joined the crowd already milling before the entry into the ballroom, then deftly sidestepped a servant announcing names of guests and slipped into the ballroom. He had no desire to have his name announced publicly. Oh, he was certain someone in the family knew of his presence; he would not be here otherwise. He simply didn't want to make a grand entrance. It would not suit his purpose. Besides, he was not altogether comfortable with his new title. It seemed as much a masquerade as his role as Gordon.

He accepted a glass of champagne from a passing waiter and casually circled the room, making note of the entrances and exits, sweeping the crowd for familiar or suspicious faces. His gaze connected with several of the department's men positioned around the room. The chances were excellent that nothing would happen here tonight. Still, it was prudent to be prepared.

He spotted Delia almost at once. She stood beside a seated elderly woman, probably the dowager duchess, and wore a black lace gown in what even he could see was the height of fashion. Damnation, she was a vision in black. Her skin glowed and her hair drifted about her head in a pale, ethereal manner. She looked fragile and delicate and just a touch uneasy. She wanted a grand adventure, yet she was obviously ill at ease in this setting. Still, there was a slight smile on her face and her chin was held high in a gesture he recognized. His heart twisted. It took a great deal of courage to defy the rules of mourning and appear in public, even if this was her family's home and the country. It took a great deal of courage as well to admit your mistakes and forge ahead regardless. No, she certainly deserved better than she had received thus far. From Wilmont or from him.

He watched her sister approach her and a moment later both women laughed. They made a striking picture. One in a pale greenish, frothy confection, the other dark and vaguely exotic.

"My lord?" A voice sounded behind him.

Tony turned. "Yes?"

An Effington footman nodded a bow. "His Grace has requested that you join him in the library."

The Duke of Roxborough? His stomach clenched, but he did not allow his surprise to show on his face. "Very well."

"If you would follow me, my lord." The footman turned and expertly made his way through the crowd, not once looking back to see if Tony did indeed follow. And why should he? A summons from a duke was second only to the command of the king.

The footman circled the edge of the room and opened a door that at first appeared to be yet another of the ornate panels that decorated the walls. Neither hidden nor obvious, this entry could best be called circumspect and Tony cursed himself that he hadn't already noticed it. He followed the servant down the corridor to a door Tony assumed led into the library. The footman opened the door, stepped aside to allow Tony to enter, then pulled the door closed behind him.

Tony paused. His gaze swept the huge, book-lined room. The Effington Hall library made the library at St. Stephens Court look like an afterthought. It was beautifully appointed. Tall windows filled the far end. Portraits of generations of Effingtons stared down at him disapprovingly.

"Surveying for assassins, St. Stephens?"

Tony's gaze snapped to the tall gentleman standing before an imposing mahogany desk. He had never met him before, but he had no doubt this was the Duke of Roxborough. "One can never be too careful, Your Grace, particularly in a place in which nothing untoward is foreseen."

"Indeed." The duke chuckled. "I expected no less from you."

"Did you?"

"I am well aware of your work and your record. It is exemplary. Quite impressive."

"Thank you, Your Grace." Tony's mind raced. He knew without question this was not a social meeting.

"Do come in and take a seat." The duke nodded at a pair of chairs arranged before the desk. "I assure you I will not bite." He smiled pleasantly. "Yet."

Tony stepped to the chairs and cautiously sat down. The duke picked up a decanter from the desk, poured two glasses and handed Tony one.

"You look like the kind of man who appreciates good brandy."

"Yes, sir." Tony accepted the glass and took a sip. "It is excellent, sir."

"Of course it is." The duke propped a hip on the desk, drew a swallow and studied Tony over the rim of his glass. His position required Tony to look up to meet his gaze in a most disconcerting manner. Tony realized that was precisely the duke's intent. Still, he found it difficult to resist the urge to squirm in his seat. "Do you know the name of Lord Kimberly's superior? Or the man above him?"

The question was abrupt and unexpected. What did the duke know of Kimberly's work? Caution edged Tony's response. "No, sir."

"Nor should you." The duke's smile widened. "Although I am confident you understand the, shall we say, discreet nature of the Department of Domestic and International Affairs?"

"Of course, sir."

"I support this country and king with my very life, but the stupidity of those in power ofttimes leaves me speechless." The duke shook his head. "The idea that the gathering of intelligence is not necessary during times of peace is shortsighted at best and, to my way of thinking, quite imbecilic. You do know the Depot of Military Knowledge has become little more than a storage facility for maps manned by nothing more significant than a minor clerk?"

"Yes, sir."

The duke blew a frustrated breath. "England has enemies both within and without, my boy, and the best way to guard against them is to know precisely what they are about. I thank God for the foresight of those few in public service intelligent enough to realize this. This department of ours is this country's best defense against those who would undermine the very stability of the government itself."

"This department of *ours*, Your Grace?"

"I would have been quite disappointed if you hadn't caught that." The duke sipped his brandy and considered Tony for a long moment. "Indeed, we are on the same side, St. Stephens. As for where I fall in the hierarchy of it all, suffice it to say I have been involved since long before the beginning."

The Duke of Roxborough? Involved in the gathering of intelligence? Spying? Surely not. At least not now, but perhaps once?

"You have a remarkable mind for solving puzzles that do not on the surface appear to have a solution, but I warn you, do not try to work this one out. Accept, for the moment, that I know far more than you about the workings of this department. Its concerns, goals and investigations."

"Do you, sir?" Damnation. The duke's family was the subject of the very investigation that started all of this. Still, that did not necessarily prove innocence. He chose his words with care. "Then should I assume you are aware of the nature of my current assignment."

"I am aware of what led to it as well. There were allegedly papers— correspondence, I believe—that indicated someone in my family was giving support in some manner to the French in or about 1814. Lord Liverpool was prime minister then, as he is now.

"While I think he has handled current domestic affairs abominably, to the eventual detriment of the country, I also think he is, at the present time, the most suitable man for the job. Or, at least, the best we have right now. I had high hopes when Wellington joined the administration, but . . ." The duke shook his head. "Politics are exceedingly odd, St. Stephens. A man you consider to be of vision and intelligence more often than not proves to be narrow-minded, out of date and unwilling to accept that the world as we have always known it is changing rapidly.

"But the nature of the current government is not why we are here."

"Why are we here, sir?" Tony kept his voice level.

"I became aware of this nasty effort to sell these so-called incriminating documents after Wilmont's death. You see, St. Stephens"—the duke's steely blue gaze met Tony's—"even if my involvement in the department is not generally known, I consider myself responsible for the lives of every man in its service. From the beginning, when one was killed, I was to know of it. Lord Kimberly, and those positioned above him, have told me all that had transpired."

"And were you angry, sir?" Tony asked without thinking.

"Yes. And no." The duke paused to choose his words. "I am not pleased to know that I or anyone in my family could be suspected of consorting with enemies of England, and yet I am pleased that the integrity of this office is such that even I am not above suspicion."

It was obvious the duke was not merely involved in the department but head of it. Tony chose his words with care. "Then are you ending this entire episode, sir?"

"Not at all. I am convinced these documents, if they existed at all, are forgeries. I do not doubt for a moment the loyalties of my brothers, or myself, to this country. However, forgeries or not, because of the close ties of my family to the current administration and the prime minister himself, the revelation of this correspondence would cause immeasurable harm, a nasty scandal that might possibly lead to the toppling of the current government. The opposition would have a powerful tool in its hands. While I am not overly fond of this administration at the moment, stability, more than anything else, is what is desperately needed right now."

"Wilmont was charged with the purchase of them, sir."

"And we don't know if he accomplished that before his death."

"No, sir." Tony leaned forward. "In truth, we have no idea if the exchange was made, if the papers were in Wilmont's possession or if the money was stolen. Neither the documents nor the money he was to have purchased them with have been recovered. We assumed they were lost with Wilmont. Now it appears Wilmont never boarded the packet, and we have no idea where the Effington Papers might be. Although, thus far, they have not been offered for sale.

"*The Effington Papers?*" Disbelief sounded in the duke's voice. "Rather a bit dramatic, don't you think?"

Tony winced. "Yes, sir."

"And you have no information yet as to the significance of this mysterious notebook Wilmont allegedly discovered?"

"No, sir."

"I assume, given your masquerade as my niece's *butler* . . .*"

Tony tried not to cringe at the duke's tone.

". . . you have thoroughly searched his house."

"It was searched right after Wilmont's death, sir, and someone as yet unknown to us had searched it before Lady Wilmont's return. We are in hopes whoever is looking for the notebook will return under the belief that it is still in the house or even in Lady Wilmont's possession."

"Is it?"

"Not to our knowledge, sir, but she might well have it or have information about it and not know it."

The duke studied him carefully. "What's your assessment of the situation, St. Stephens?"

Tony pulled his thoughts together. "When we learned Wilmont was not on the packet we thought perhaps, for whatever reasons, he may have feigned his death. However, as it has been more than six months and he has not appeared, we discarded that idea."

"He could simply be waiting for an opportune moment."

"Possibly." Tony nodded. "Certainly he was reckless and somewhat unpredictable in his personal life, but I never noted those qualities in his professional behavior. While patience was never one of his virtues, he was quite good and always above reproach."

"I am well aware of that."

"However, he did not execute this assignment as planned." Tony braced himself. "His task was to court your niece with an eye toward becoming familiar with family members and thereby ascertaining whether or not these documents could indeed be legitimate."

"Damnably stupid idea, St. Stephens," the duke said bluntly.

"In hindsight, indeed it was, sir." Tony drew a deep breath. "I admit, I had qualms about it myself, but we saw no other options for uncovering the truth at the time and it was important to determine precisely what we were dealing with. It was never anyone's intention to cause harm to . . . Lady Wilmont."

"Giving you and Kimberly and whoever else was in on this scheme the benefit of the doubt, I assume marriage was not part of the plan."

"No, sir. Absolutely not." Tony shook his head firmly. "I have no idea how it came to that. I did not have the opportunity to speak to Wilmont at any length after his marriage. But I did note his behavior was exceedingly odd. He was not at all his usual self and seemed withdrawn, as if he had a great number of things on his mind. In addition, he was reticent to talk to me about what he was doing. That in itself was suspicious."

Tony paused to choose his words. "To be honest, sir, Wilmont was my friend, and if I believed he was alive, then I would have to believe as well his pretense at death was for a nefarious purpose. And that I cannot accept, therefore I am certain of his death."

"But if he is alive and he has the papers, will he make them public?"

"I would never have considered such a thing. However"—Tony forced the words out—"if indeed he is alive, then he is not the man I thought I knew and I have no idea what he might do."

"Let us pretend for a moment that your friend, a heretofore loyal agent, is indeed alive." The duke narrowed his eyes. "What purpose would possession of these Effington Papers serve him?"

"Power," Tony said without hesitation. "I know he has no need of money; his fortune is quite substantial. Therefore power is the only other answer. Perhaps in terms of a new administration?"

"I was afraid of that," the duke said soberly. "The man who could give the opposition the means to form a new government would indeed be welcome to play a significant role in it. Had Wilmont ever expressed any political ambitions to you?"

"Not that I can recall." Tony chose his words carefully. "I have given this a great deal of thought, sir, and I suspect marriage might well change a man, even a man like Wilmont. I can see no logical explanation why he would have married your niece unless his affections were engaged. And if we are dealing with emotions rather than logic"—Tony shook his head—"there is no predicting what may happen next."

"Do you think my niece is in danger?"

"Not from Wilmont, sir," Tony said staunchly. "I am confident if he were alive, he would have let us know by now. I would now, and have in the past, trust him with my life and would now wager my life that he is dead."

The duke studied him for a long moment. "You would rather believe him dead than disloyal?"

"I would rather not think him as either, sir, but yes."

"I see." The duke thought for a moment. "Then you think the danger to my niece stems from whatever was in this notebook Wilmont possessed?"

"I'm afraid so, sir."

"But you have no idea where it is or what it contains?"

"No, sir."

"For someone whose job is the gathering of information, you don't seem to know a great deal," His Grace said sharply.

"No, sir."

"I don't like this, any of it." The duke paced the room. "I don't like her having married this man who may or may not be dead. I don't like you living in her house as her butler or anything else. I don't like using her to lure whoever is looking for this notebook, obviously the same people who might well have killed her husband, if indeed he is dead. And I don't like this entire deception surrounding her."

"Sir." Tony stood. "I have suggested to Lord Kimberly that we tell Lady Wilmont everything. That we enlist her assistance."

The duke stared at him as if he'd lost his mind. "Do you know nothing at all about women, St. Stephens?"

"I daresay I know—"

"I doubt that. Do you honestly propose to tell my niece her husband was an agent of the British government who courted her as part of a plan to uncover the traitorous secrets of her father or her uncles?"

"When you put it that way, sir, it doesn't sound—"

"And furthermore inform her that her butler is not an aged, doddering old man—"

Tony grimaced. "You know about the disguise then, too, sir."

"I know everything there is to know about this," he snapped. "Or at least as much as you do."

"Yes, sir."

"And then the final blow will be to tell her her life might well be in danger because of a blasted notebook whose contents and whereabouts are unknown." The duke snorted in disdain. "You think this will provoke her cooperation?"

"Perhaps not." Of course not. Had Tony completely taken leave of his senses where Delia was concerned? Certainly the woman was nice, but such a revelation would push even the nicest of females beyond a point of reason.

"Beyond that, she is an Effington female born and bred. They are a stubborn lot, opinionated and prone to do exactly as they please." He drained the rest of his glass. "I don't know what madness possesses the men in this family, but not one of us has seen fit to wed a pleasant, biddable woman. It's the challenge, I suspect. An ongoing game, if you will, of evenly matched opponents." A reluctant smile quirked the corners of his lips. "There is nothing like it. Nonetheless"—his amusement vanished—"my niece will not take any of this well, and you know who will bear the brunt of her wrath, don't you?"

"You, sir?" Tony said hopefully.

The duke stared for a moment, then burst into laughter. "Most amusing, St. Stephens. Best laugh I've had in a long while." He sniffed back a chuckle. "My niece will not know that I have had even the slightest involvement in all of this, nor will anyone else in my family. No one is aware of my connection to the department, including my wife, my son and my brothers, and they never will. My wife thinks I am simply exceptionally knowledgeable. You, St. Stephens, are now one of a select few who do know of my work." His eyes narrowed slightly. "You do understand what I'm saying?"

It wasn't exactly a threat, but it was closer than Tony would ever like to come. "Yes, Your Grace."

"My niece will not be told anything for the time being. You will continue in your position as her butler, but the department will arrange for additional staff, all our people, of course. I want this blasted notebook found and whoever is searching for it apprehended." The duke met Tony's gaze directly. "I too would prefer to think Wilmont dead than a traitor, but if he is alive, I want him caught as well."

"Of course, sir."

"Understand that I am not pleased with these arrangements. I think your charade is as absurd as Wilmont's original plan. However, I can think of nothing better at the moment. When one is deeply mired in the muck of an untenable situation, one can do nothing more than to struggle onward. And understand as well, St. Stephens, I hold you personally responsible for Lady Wilmont's safety."

"I already hold myself responsible."

"You do realize if anyone learns of your true identity, her reputation will be shattered."

"Beg pardon, Your Grace, but isn't that redundant? Hasn't her reputation already been thoroughly shattered?"

"Has it?" He frowned. "I thought I had heard something about a love match. Reforming a rake, and all that. Quite romantic and tragic, I believe."

"Of course, sir."

"Regardless of the past, she will not be able to recover if it becomes known that the Viscount St. Stephens, under whatever guise, had resided in a house alone with her. I do not wish her to be the subject of scandal yet again. I assume, therefore, should it indeed become known, you will do the honorable thing."

"The honorable thing, sir?"

The duke lifted his glass. A smug smile curved his lips and an odd gleam shone in his eye, as much wicked amusement as warning. "Welcome, my boy, to the game."

Chapter 8

"I don't believe I have ever felt quite so awkward in my life," Delia said out of the corner of her mouth, keeping a pleasant smile affixed firmly on her face. "Everyone is staring at me."

"Don't be absurd," Cassie said, wearing the exact same smile. "Not everyone."

"I knew I shouldn't have come," Delia murmured. It had taken all of Delia's determination to don the gown Cassie and her grandmother had ordered for her and to appear at the dowager's ball. The black lace dress was modest but not overly so. Indeed, when she had looked in the mirror, she'd looked very much like, well, a woman of experience. Even the stark color didn't make her appear quite as ghostly as usual. However, now that she was in public for the first time, she wasn't entirely certain she had the courage required to start down that path to experience, beginning with the flouting of convention. It took all she had in her not to turn and flee from the room this very minute.

"Nonsense, my child, this is your family's home and you have every right to be here," her grandmother said firmly.

"I doubt that sentiment is widespread, Grandmother. I am officially still in mourning, with a husband dead barely half a year."

"It's not as if you are dancing on his grave. In truth, you have been a widow far longer than you were a wife. No one expects you to be a recluse as well." Her grandmother smiled in a smug manner. "Besides, no one here or in London either, I suspect, would dare to question the propriety of your presence as long as I have given it my blessing, as indeed I have. Your period of mourning is not at an end, but in my home, the only rules that matter are my own.

"Besides, I have often thought the rules of mourning we drape about ourselves were instituted by men simply to make certain their wives do not do them in."

"Grandmother!" Cassie's eyes were wide with stunned amusement. "I can't believe you would say such a thing."

"Have I shocked you, Cassandra? Excellent." Grandmother chuckled. "I quite like shocking young people. It makes me feel young. Or perhaps it simply makes me feel clever, which is every bit as nice. Now then, what was I saying?"

"Something about women doing in their husbands," Delia said weakly.

"Indeed." Grandmother nodded. "I think no woman in her right mind would eliminate a husband knowing she would be forced to wear black—not everyone wears it well, you know—and avoid any sort of enjoyable activity for a full year."

"Looking dreadful would certainly dissuade me from killing a husband," Cassie murmured.

"And I am certain somewhere there is a man who rests easier with that knowledge." Grandmother nodded toward the dancers on the floor. "Why aren't you dancing, Cassandra? You should be enjoying yourself rather than keeping us company."

"*I* would be dancing if I had the chance." Delia tried and failed to hide the wistful note in her voice. If she were truly intent on grand adventures and any scandalous behavior that might entail, dancing while still in mourning would be insignificant. Perhaps she wasn't cut out for a life of adventure after all.

"But I quite enjoy keeping you company, Grandmother." Cassie bent and brushed a kiss across her grandmother's cheek. "You have a way of looking at the world that is always most interesting."

"Indeed I do. And it is the reward for living as long as I have that I can say exactly what I think. It is the greatest, if not the only, benefit of advanced age."

"You may well be the youngest person I know." Delia cast her grandmother an affectionate smile.

"In spirit, my dear, I may well be."

"And for that, the rest of us are eternally grateful," Delia said. "However, I believe my own spirit has had more than enough for one night and I think I shall take my leave."

"It is far too early for you to beg off from your first foray back into society, Philadelphia," her grandmother said mildly. "Has your courage run out so soon?"

"Yes." Delia shrugged. "It is more difficult than I imagined to pretend life is as it has always been."

"It's wearing black that does it." Cassie's gaze skimmed over her sister. "Although that dress does become you more than anything else I've seen you wear, the color still does not suit you."

"She would look lovely in the color you're wearing, Cassandra." Grandmother looked at Cassie. "Don't you think so?"

"Indeed, I do," Cassie said firmly.

Cassie's gown was a delicate green, the color of warm, shallow seas and cut in the first stare of fashion. The fabric seemed to shimmer with a life of its own. Delia sighed. "Perhaps someday."

"If you'll excuse us, Grandmother, I think I shall accompany my sister to our rooms," Cassie said in an offhand manner. "I have just this minute remembered something I wished to show her."

"And do you plan on returning?" Grandmother asked.

Cassie answered without pause. "Most certainly. There is a great deal of the evening left and I have not yet had my fill. Why, there are any number of gentlemen here who have yet to ask me to dance." She grinned and her dimple flashed. "I would hate for their evening to be a disappointment."

"As would we all." Grandmother's assessing gaze shifted from Cassie to Delia and back.

"I shall bid you good night, then." Delia bent to kiss her grandmother's cheek and whispered in her ear. "Thank you for everything."

"My dear child, I wish I could do more. But perhaps your sister . . ." Grandmother glanced at Cassie, who smiled in a too-innocent manner. The older woman pointedly looked away. "I refuse to condone or condemn tonight."

"What on earth does that mean?" Delia drew her brows together in confusion.

"Never mind." Grandmother waved them off. "Go on now and sleep well."

The sisters murmured their farewells and made their way to the entry, nodding a greeting here, casting a smile of acknowledgment there. They left the ballroom and started up the stairs.

"What, exactly, do you wish to show me?" Delia slanted a glance at her sister.

"Patience, dear sister." Cassie smiled a secret smile that never boded well. She refused to say another word until they were in her room, with the door closed firmly behind them.

"Now." Delia crossed her arms over her chest. "What did you wish to show me?"

"Just this." Cassie waved at the bed and grinned.

Delia took a step toward the bed and caught her breath. She stared in disbelief. "What is this?"

"This"—Cassie carefully picked up the gown of shimmering, delicate, sea-foam-green, an exact copy of the one she wore—"is for you."

"What exactly do you mean?" Delia said slowly.

"You know full well exactly what I mean."

Delia shook her head. "I couldn't possibly.

"Oh"—Cassie held out the gown enticingly—"but you could."

"I would never—"

"Oh, but you will." Cassie moved closer as if offering a forbidden treat.

Delia reached out and tentatively touched the delicate fabric, soft and silken beneath her fingers. "It's definitely not black and I am still expected to wear black . . ."

"But I'm not." Cassie's voice was seductive.

Delia's gaze shot to her sister. "It would be something of an adventure, wouldn't it?

Cassie nodded. "And didn't you tell me that you wanted to live a life of grand adventure?"

"Yes, of course, but . . ." Delia's gaze drifted back to the gown. The blasted thing was calling her.

"No one would know, Delia."

"Even so . . ." Beckoning her.

"I shall stay right here until you return." With her sister's voice. "What would be—"

"Cassie."

"No, wait." Cassie's brow furrowed. "I shall slip into the library instead. That way, if you encounter any problems—"

"What kind of problems?"

"Well, I certainly have not been the subject of scandal, but I have made any number of new acquaintances recently and, of course, one always renews old friendships during the season, and—"

"Anyone in *particular* I should be aware of?"

"Not really. The gentlemen I mentioned last night, perhaps, but I have engaged in nothing more than mild flirtations, for the most part. At least as far as I can recall." Cassie thought for a moment, then shook her head. "No, I'm certain there is nothing to be concerned with."

"You've never been especially good at remembering details."

"Even so, I do tend to remember men. Of the two of us, I have always been the one more interested in marriage, and therefore the one more attuned to the relative merits and detriments of any particular gentleman. And if I don't remember a man, he is not worth remembering."

"Excellent point," Delia murmured.

"However, if you find yourself in an awkward situation, simply tilt your head, widen your eyes and say, 'Sir, you have me at a disadvantage.' "

"And this works?"

"Always."

"Why haven't you told me this before?"

"You've never needed it before. Remember, before your Lord Wilmont, your suitors were also eminently respectable—"

"Boring," Delia murmured.

"—and therefore you were never in an especially difficult position nor did you have the opportunity to develop the finer points of flirting. Now you are going to be me and you need to know how to proceed accordingly." Cassie grinned. "This should indeed be an adventure."

"I don't know." Delia shook her head. "This is so—"

"Honestly, Delia." Cassie glared. "It's been months since you wore anything but black or did anything that even remotely resembled fun. You've hidden yourself away and you've been the perfect little widow, but it's absurd that you should be married for a few days and have to pay for it forever. Why, Grandmother as much as said the same—"

"That's quite enough," Delia said firmly.

"Not it's not," Cassie snapped. "It's not nearly enough. And I daresay—"

"Cassie," Delia said in a cool, level tone that belied the fluttering in her stomach. "If you don't hold your tongue right now and help me into this gown"—Delia grinned—"I shall never get back to the ball."

Welcome to the game.

Tony returned to the ballroom, the phrase lingering ominously in his mind.

Welcome to the game.

It scarcely mattered, of course; no one would ever discover his masquerade as Gordon. Still, would it be so bad to be forced to do the honorable thing when it came to Delia? Or would be . . . delightful?

He smiled at the thought of just how delightful it might be, then stepped into the ballroom and nearly collided with Delia's sister.

"Oh, dear." Wide blue eyes, the exact shade of her sister's, stared up at him. How could two women possibly look so much alike? She even wore the same fragrance as Delia. "I do apologize. I fear I was not paying attention."

"It is of no consequence, Miss Effington," he said firmly. "Indeed, it is I who should apologize."

"Whatever for?"

"For not knowing where the loveliest woman here is at any given moment." He took her gloved hand and drew it to his lips.

She stared for a moment, then laughed. The sound rippled through his blood. "Your words are as polished as your manner, sir." She withdrew her hand. "Now then, if you will excuse me—"

"But surely you are not leaving before we have had our dance?" The words were out before he could stop himself. Although, why shouldn't he share a dance with Miss Effington? He might well learn something about her sister that could assist him.

"Our dance?" A touch of what might have been panic flashed in her eyes, replaced almost at once by a look of determination and a slight lift of her chin. "I would not dream of leaving before we have had our dance." She cast him a brilliant smile and her dimple flashed. "But you must forgive me, I seem to have forgotten your name."

"Anthony St. Stephens," he said slowly. Of course she wouldn't remember his name; they'd never met. "Or rather Viscount St. Stephens." He shook his head. There was something here . . .

"Now you must forgive me. I have only recently inherited my title and I fear I am not yet used to it."

"I have always thought titles a bit difficult myself. There are so many rules regarding who we are, or rather what we are, and what we should be called. Were we not born to it, we should never be able to understand it at all and even now"—again the dimple in her right cheek appeared with her smile—"it can be most confusing."

"Indeed it can, my la—" He caught himself, startled to note that somewhere in the back of his mind he had seen the truth. "*Miss* Effington."

Except this was not Miss Cassandra Effington. The dimple told him that, as did the look in her eyes, the tilt of her chin and probably her fragrance as well.

He should be shocked by her ruse, her blatant disregard for propriety. Instead, the oddest feeling of anticipation surged through him. The opening strains of a waltz filled the air and his blood quickened at the thought of taking her in his arms.

"And I believe this is our dance." He offered her his arm.

"So it is, my lord." She smiled and laid her hand softly on his arm.

They took their place among the dancers. She fit into his arms as if she were made for him, as if they were made for each other. He resisted the urge to pull her close against him.

They moved through the steps of the dance with a shocking ease. She was graceful and fluid; he had never been much more than adequate, or perhaps he had never had a partner as perfect for him until now. It was as if they had danced together before. As if they were meant to dance together. Tonight. Always.

She looked up at him with a curious smile. "You dance quite well, my lord."

"We dance well together, Miss Effington." He grinned down at her and couldn't resist calling her bluff. "But then, we always have."

Unease flickered in her eyes, but she didn't hesitate. "Have we?"

"Indeed we have. And I grow more certain of it every time we take to the floor. I thought so again last week when we danced at Lady Locksley's gala, and before that at Lord and Lady Chalmer's ball and, of course, at Mrs. Huntly's birthday celebration. In truth, I think we are fated to dance together."

"Do you really think so my, my lord? Why, I should attribute it more to"—she smiled innocently—"sheer practice."

He laughed. "You are as charming as ever, Miss Effington."

"And you are as forward as ever." There was a distinct challenge in her tone and abruptly he realized she enjoyed the charade. And why not? Didn't she deserve a few minutes of enjoyment?

Didn't he?

"It is entirely your fault, Miss Effington." He heaved an exaggerated sigh. "You bring out the worst in me. I am usually most proper, and indeed have even been called stuffy and narrow-minded upon occasion."

She laughed. "I can't imagine that."

"It's true." His gaze caught hers. "Although, I must say I quite like what you bring out in me."

Her brow rose. "Do you?"

"I do indeed." For a long moment they stared into each other's eyes. His heart thudded in his chest. The room around them seemed to dim and vanish. The world, and everything in it, was of no consequence. Nothing mattered beyond the two of them.

He barely noticed when the music stopped. Reluctantly he released her and stepped back.

"How very odd, I find it difficult to catch my breath," she murmured. "It has been such a long time since I've danced a waltz." She caught her mistake and cast him a teasing smile. "At least a quarter hour or so."

"Then perhaps you should like a breath of fresh air." He offered his arm. "Would you accompany me to the terrace?"

"I get in rather a lot of trouble on terraces," she said, more to herself than to him.

"It is a beautiful night," he said in a tempting manner.

"Indeed it is, my lord, but"—she leaned toward him confidentially—"surely you realize if you and I are seen leaving together it would quite ruin my reputation."

"Of course." He cast her a resigned smile and pushed aside his disappointment. He couldn't blame her. It wouldn't be her reputation at stake, after all, but her sister's.

"Still . . ." She paused and he could read a myriad of thoughts in her eyes. Indecision and temptation and, at last, a glimmer of resolve. His hopes rose.

"However"—she smiled in a too-innocent manner— "if you should feel the need for fresh air, I would encourage you to retire to the terrace." Her gaze met his and she waved her fan before her face in a slow, seductive manner that would scarcely move a breath of air but was doing rather remarkable things to his insides. "One never knows who else might feel a similar need."

"I see." He nodded thoughtfully. "And perhaps I should bring a glass of champagne with me?"

"Or two. To sustain you, of course, against the night air."

"Of course." He took her hand and lifted it to his lips, his gaze never leaving hers. He breathed in the scent he could recognize in his sleep, felt the warmth of her hand through her gloves, lost himself in the deep blue of her eyes. In the slight puzzlement, the touch of apprehension and the cautious anticipation he saw there.

Her gaze locked with his and, without warning, the moment between them changed, lengthened, stretched endlessly. He wanted to pull her into his arms right here, right now, taste her lips, feel the warmth of her flesh beneath his hands, mold her body against his. Right here, right now, and the rest of the world be damned. He didn't care about impropriety or her uncle or his work or her husband or his friend. And he knew, from the look in her eye and the slight intake of her breath and the heat that flashed between them, without question, without doubt, she felt the same shocking connection.

He held her hand a beat longer than he should have. She pulled away a moment later than she should have.

"I . . ." She shook her head slightly as though to clear it, and he resisted the need to do the same. "Perhaps we shall meet again, my lord."

"Sooner rather than later, I should hope."

She nodded, smiled and took her leave, leaving a distinct air of confusion in her wake. It would have been quite satisfying if he hadn't been more than a bit befuddled himself.

What exactly had just happened here? They were playing a game of sorts, flirtatious and entirely light-hearted. At least, it had started as a game. And a dangerous one at that.

Still, was it wrong to want to be with her as himself and not as an elderly servant? Wrong to wonder where things between the two of them might lead? What the end result would be between Lady Wilmont and Viscount St. Stephens? It was not especially wise, perhaps, but wrong? He had no idea. It might well be inevitable.

He strolled toward the terrace and grinned to himself, resisting the oddest urge to whistle.

Welcome to the game.

Chapter 9

"*I* wasn't entirely sure you'd meet me."

"I wasn't entirely sure I'd meet you either." Delia sipped her champagne and studied the viscount curiously. What game was this man playing? Not that she really cared. She was rather enjoying it all.

She had taken the time to find Cassie in the library and quiz her about the charming viscount. Cassie couldn't so much as remember his name and pointed out, once again, if she could not remember a gentleman he was not worth remembering.

In this particular case, Delia suspected Cassie was wrong.

They stood in the shadows in a far corner of the terrace, just out of the pool of light cast by chandeliers placed along the stone balustrade. Delia and Cassie had been aware of the benefits of this particular spot for years. It was discreet but not overly secluded, with a conveniently placed stone bench. If one wanted to cast caution aside, there were any number of spots in the garden, most notably the mazes, as well as a variety of other well-placed benches, that provided far more privacy. However, this spot on the terrace was the perfect location for a rendezvous one did not want to get out of hand. Especially when one was pretending to be one's sister and, thanks to said sister's poor memory, had no idea how far things had progressed with the gentleman in question.

St. Stephens chuckled, a rather nice sound that warmed her down to her toes. "I'm not certain if I'm relieved by your hesitation or disappointed."

"Relieved, my lord?" She raised a brow. "Because of that stuffy, narrow-minded nature of yours?"

"It is my greatest fault," he said with an exaggerated sigh.

"Somehow I doubt that," she said wryly. He couldn't possibly be as stuffy as he claimed. If he were, he would not be engaged in a private meeting with an unmarried woman.

In truth, he was rather amusing, this unknown lord who apparently was in the midst of an ongoing flirtation with her sister. Or at least thought he was. She and Cassie had talked well into the late hours last night and Cassie had spoken of any number of prospective suitors who may or may not come up to scratch this season, and may or may not be worth the effort at any rate, but she hadn't mentioned St. Stephens. Which meant Cassie's affections were not so much as mildly engaged. St. Stephens's intentions, however, were unknown.

"And your disappointment?"

Although how Cassie could fail to mention St. Stephens, even in passing, was something of a mystery. He was entirely too handsome to be overlooked, and wonderfully tall, with the most intriguing gleam in his eye, as if he could see right through her and knew all her secrets.

"The reason for that, my dear Miss Effington, is obvious."

And liked what he saw. "Is it?"

"I quite treasure the opportunity to be alone with you."

"Why?"

"Why?" His brows drew together as if her question were phrased in a language he didn't speak.

"Yes." She bit back a grin. She hadn't been at all forward with a man until she'd met Charles. Now it appeared to be an altogether natural way of dealing with situations like this. And extremely enjoyable. "Why do you treasure the opportunity to be alone with me?"

"Well." He thought for a moment, as if desperate to come up with a suitable reason for being alone with a woman in the shadows of a terrace short of stealing a kiss. Delia suspected, or perhaps hoped, that would be at least part of his answer. "You are lovely."

"*Tsk, tsk,* my lord." She shook her head in mock dismay. "Is that the best you can do? I expected something far more original from you than that."

"Did you? Very well. I should hate to disappoint you." He set his glass on the bench, leaned back against the balustrade and crossed his arms over his chest. "Let me think for a moment."

"My, that is flattering." Delia wrinkled her nose and sipped her champagne.

"It's not all that difficult. I do enjoy the pleasure of your company."

"I see. It's my stimulating conversation, then?" Cassie had always maintained the most successful way to flirt with a man was to provoke him to discuss his favorite subject, usually himself.

"Most certainly." St. Stephens nodded.

"Coupled with my knowledge of current affairs?" Cassie's interest in what was going on in the world extended no further than the latest gossip and the newest fashion.

"Absolutely."

"And my understanding of the workings of nature as well?"

"The workings of nature?" He frowned. "I'm not certain—"

"Oh, you know." She glanced upward. "The stars, the moon, that sort of thing."

"Not at all."

"No? I thought certainly you would leap at that particular reason."

"No." His voice was firm. "When I am on a terrace, on a night like this, with you, Miss Effington, I am scarcely aware of anything but you. I note the stars only in the way in which they reflect in your eyes."

"My eyes?"

"Indeed." He straightened and stepped closer. "I cannot see their color at the moment, but I know, because I have gazed into them before, your eyes are blue as an ocean. And here in the night, the stars shine in them like fairy lights upon the water."

"Fairy lights, you say?" It was nothing more than flirtatious banter, yet it was hard to resist the fanciful nature of his words. And harder still to resist the oddly serious note that underlaid them.

"I have always been quite fond of fairy lights," he murmured, moving nearer. He stared down at her. "And then there's the moon, of course. The way the moonlight touches your hair, a kiss, perhaps, of magic."

"Magic, you say?" He was very good at this. "But there is no moonlight tonight, my lord."

"And yet, I know." His voice was soft, seductive . . . irresistible.

He lowered his head toward hers. She strained upward to meet him.

Without warning, she realized she'd been in precisely this position before.

She drew a sharp breath, stepped back and downed the rest of her champagne. "Sir." She set her glass firmly on the balustrade. "I fear you have me at a disadvantage."

He narrowed his eyes in obvious confusion "What?"

"I said"—she swallowed hard—"sir, I fear you have me at a disadvantage." She fluttered her eyelashes for good measure.

He frowned. "Do you have something in your eye?" He stepped closer. "Can I be of help?"

"Of course I don't have something in my eye." She huffed in frustration and stepped away. "I shall try this once more." She squared her shoulders. "Sir, I fear you have me at a disadvantage."

"Blast it all, woman, what are you talking about?" He stared. "I certainly don't feel as though I have you at any disadvantage whatsoever. In truth, Miss Effington, I fear you have me at a disadvantage."

At once the absurdity of the situation struck her and she laughed. "Perhaps, I have, my lord. How does it feel?"

"Confusing. Annoying. Irritating." He smiled grudgingly. "Intriguing."

"If that intrigues you, you might appreciate this as well." She drew a deep breath. "I have a confession to make and I neither make them lightly nor well."

"Then I am honored you have chosen me to confide in."

"I hope you will continue to be honored rather than

insulted. You see, my lord, I fear my memory has failed me." She paused to gather her courage. It was bad enough that she was pretending to be someone she wasn't, but she preferred not to compound her sins with additional pretense. Besides, Cassie really didn't remember him. "You have my most sincere apologies, but I cannot recall meeting you."

His eyes widened in disbelief. "You do not remember our dances together?"

She shook her head. "I am sorry, but no."

"But surely you recall that this is not the first time we have retired to a terrace?"

"It isn't?"

"No indeed." He shook his head and sighed with disappointment. "I warn you, Miss Effington, I shall be shattered if you tell me you don't remember sharing a kiss on a terrace very much like this under stars very much like these."

"I'm afraid I don't." Or rather Cassie didn't. "Are you certain?"

"I most certainly am."

"You're not confusing me with someone else, perhaps?"

"Never," he said staunchly.

"I can't imagine anyone forgetting something like a kiss," she murmured.

"Nor can I. It's not at all flattering, you know. A man likes to think his kisses are memorable."

She would have to throttle her sister when she saw her. "I don't know what to say."

"Neither do I. I am crushed." His shoulders drooped in an exaggerated sigh, then he straightened. "Perhaps you just need something to refresh your memory." He took her hand in his and brought it to his lips. His gaze locked with hers and the odd drowning sensation she'd had when she'd first looked in his eyes tonight gripped her with a vengeance. His voice was low, intense, intimate. "I know I shall never forget."

For an instant, or perhaps forever, she stared into his eyes. She had made one horrible mistake with a man that had changed her entire life and no matter how appealing the idea of becoming an experienced woman was, she truly hated to make another mistake. A voice in the back of her head, the same voice that had warned her against involvement with Charles, screamed this man was every bit as dangerous. Possibly more. Yet, something somewhere deep inside, something perhaps nearer her heart, urged her onward, and she had the strangest feeling this was no mistake.

This was right.

His lips brushed against hers and her eyes closed. Her body melted at the mere suggestion of his lips near hers and she knew she was lost.

And didn't care.

He paused and she felt him sigh against her. "I fear I too have a confession to make, Miss Effington."

Her eyes snapped open. "Now, my lord?"

"I'm afraid so." Neither of them moved.

There was little more than a breath between them. "Are you certain?"

"Unfortunately, I am." Regret sounded in his voice.

If she reached upward the tiniest bit, she would be the one kissing him. Would he insist on confession then? "If you tell me I have you at a disadvantage, I will not believe you."

"It's not that, although I suppose I have, in truth, had you at a disadvantage all along."

She rested her hands on his jacket. His muscles tightened beneath her touch. "Wouldn't you rather kiss me first and then confess?"

"Good Lord, yes."

"Excellent." She pressed her lips against his.

He hesitated, then pulled away slightly. "But I can't. Your memory is not failing, Miss Effington." She felt his muscles tense against her and wondered if he was bracing himself. "We have never actually met before." He held his breath.

"I see," she said slowly. "Then why—"

"I don't know," he sighed. "It was rather amusing at first and I was curious as to how long it would take for you to admit that you didn't remember me. It did take rather a long time, you know."

"I was trying not to be rude," she said in a lofty manner.

"You were most polite. It was a silly game, but rather fun nonetheless." He smiled sheepishly. "I was carried away, and I do apologize."

She should be annoyed with his deception but instead was relieved and rather pleased. It was one thing to flirt with a man who had kissed your sister, and something else altogether to kiss a man who had never met your sister at all.

"Then we have never danced before tonight?"

"No."

Yet they did dance together with an ease born only of practice or nature. As if they were meant to dance together.

"Nor have we met on a terrace beneath the stars?"

He shook his head. "I am most sorry, but no."

Even so, it was a meeting lacking in the awkwardness of most first meetings. As if indeed they had met and talked before.

"And never shared a kiss?"

"No. To my everlasting regret, no."

"I see."

She could put an end to this. Now, this very minute. Turn and walk away, and not even he would blame her. Still, his sense of honesty would not allow him to kiss her under false pretenses. It was quite an honorable thing to do and really rather impressive. Why, the man should be rewarded. Or, at the very least, given an opportunity to atone for his sins.

"Then this, my lord"—she slipped her hands up and around his neck—"shall be our first." She met his lips with hers.

He hesitated for less than a heartbeat, then wrapped his arms around her and pulled her against him. His lips were warm and firm and tasted delightfully of champagne, or perhaps starlight. In spite of the forward nature of her actions and his obvious desire, the touch between them was light, tentative, cautious. The last time she'd been kissed it had led to passion and scandal. Now she wasn't sure where this would lead. His lips pressed harder against hers and she realized she didn't care. Desire and need swept through her and her restraint snapped. Regardless of what might happen between them, she wanted this, wanted him. Wanted his lips pressed against hers, his tongue meeting and mating with her own, his body firm and strong against hers.

His hand splayed across the small of her back and held her tight against him. Her hands clutched at the back of his neck and she clung to him as if he were the answer to her prayers. Or her life. He slanted his mouth harder over hers, and one kiss turned to another and another, until she thought she would surely swoon of the sheer bliss of his mouth on hers, of being in his arms.

At last, he slowly raised his head. "Well . . ."

"Good heavens." An odd note of awe sounded in her voice.

"I know I shall surely remember that," he said under his breath.

"As will I." She sighed and wanted nothing more than to remain in the warmth of his embrace. Forever.

He released her with a reluctance she shared. They stepped apart and she struggled to catch her breath.

Silence fell between them and stretched, long and awkward. She wasn't entirely sure what had just happened, but it was obviously much more than a kiss. Her legs were unsteady and her heart pounded in her ears. She had known passion and desire before, but this was different. This reached inside her, past mere passion and ordinary desire to something deeper, richer, terrifying. To her very soul, perhaps. Who was this man?

She stared at him and wondered if it was those same emotions she saw reflected his eyes. Or was it just the shadows? Did he too feel that what had just passed between them was far more significant than a stolen kiss under the stars. Or was it just another flirtatious moment?

There was obviously a great deal to say, a great deal she wanted to say or at least should say, and a great deal she was afraid to say. She drew a deep, steadying breath. Surely a woman of experience wouldn't be the least bit flustered, regardless of the impressive nature of a kiss or the weakness in her knees or the fluttering in her stomach. But perhaps she didn't have the kind of nature required to truly be a woman of experience.

"Well, I should probably . . ." She stepped toward the light.

"No doubt." He cleared his throat. "As should I. . . ."

She took another step. She wasn't sure if she wanted

him to stop her or let her go. She wasn't sure of anything at all. "I think it's . . . best . . ."

"I want to see you again," he blurted, and closed the distance between them. His gaze searched hers, and even in the dim light, she could see an intensity there far beyond a mere kiss shared in an impetuous moment.

An intensity that was at once exciting and shocking. And all the more so because it was shared.

She stepped back and forced a teasing, lighthearted note to her voice. "On a terrace, under the stars, perhaps?"

He drew a deep breath, his tone matching hers. "Or anywhere at all, Miss Effington."

A myriad of unsaid declarations or vows or questions hung between them.

What would a woman of experience do now?

"I refuse to make any promises beyond the moment. One never knows what tomorrow will bring." Her voice was surprisingly steady. "As for seeing you again"—she shrugged in an offhand manner—"we shall see, my lord." She cast him her most flirtatious smile, turned on her heel and headed back toward the ballroom.

His low laugh drifted after her. "Indeed we shall, Miss Effington, indeed we shall."

She resisted the urge to look back or, worse, to turn back. Certainly she wanted to turn back. To throw herself into his arms and kiss and be kissed until he picked her up and carried her off to his bed. And his life.

Odd, she had known a similar desire with Charles, but this was somehow different. She wasn't certain exactly what the difference was, but she knew it was different as surely as she knew her own name. Perhaps it was the difference between curiosity and excitement and something . . . more. Something deeper. Something better. Something special.

Ridiculous, of course. The man was a complete stranger even if he didn't quite seem like a stranger. Still, she'd had the strangest feeling that she had met him or spoken with him or even shared secrets with him before. It was an absurd sensation, of course. She certainly would have remembered St. Stephens.

Delia had barely met this viscount. He might well be nothing more to her than her means of becoming an experienced woman. Indeed, he could simply be another mistake. Exactly like Charles.

No. Sharing Charles's bed was not the mistake. Not the mistake she regretted. The mistake was in believing, if only for a moment, that there was more to what the two of them shared than mere lust and desire. That mistake she would not make again.

The problem wasn't in taking this particular man to her bed.

The problem was in taking him to her heart.

Chapter 10

Dearest Cassie,

I confess to being quite impatient and eager to learn if you have discovered anything of interest regarding my friend as per my request. I should very much like to renew our acquaintance as soon as possible.

Up to now, I have always considered myself a patient person. Apparently that is yet another virtue I have misplaced in recent months. . . .

"Salmon or butter cream?" Delia muttered to herself. She stood in the center of the parlor studying the walls that were, at this point, a nondescript dull greenish brown paper.

Salmon or butter cream, it was all the same to her. She sighed with frustration. Her mind simply wasn't on colors or fabrics or anything else that had seemed so interesting before her stay at Effington Hall. In the three days since she'd returned to London, she'd yet to make a decision on anything regarding her house. She had, however, made a decision regarding her life.

Lady Wilmont wanted Viscount St. Stephens.

She wasn't precisely sure what she wanted him for, whether her intentions could be considered honorable or quite disgraceful, but she definitely wanted him and definitely wanted to find out why she wanted him. Nor was she precisely sure how to go about getting him or even finding him. Cassie had promised to make subtle inquiries, but Delia had yet to hear from her.

Delia picked up a book of wallpaper samples, leafed through it for perhaps the hundredth time without seeing anything that caught her interest, then tossed it onto the sofa. The refurbishing of her house held no appeal at the moment. The only thing on her mind was the tall, dark-haired, all-too-mysterious viscount and her own idiotic behavior. Oh, not kissing him on the terrace, but fleeing afterward like a frightened fawn.

What on earth had gotten into her? It was a mere kiss. Nothing more significant than that. Even before Charles, she had been kissed. Not frequently and not indiscriminately and probably far less than Cassie had been kissed, but on occasion and more than once.

Charles's kisses had promised adventure and excitement. St. Stephens's kiss too held an offering of adventure and excitement, but promised something ethereal and elusive as well, something she could not quite put her finger on. Beyond that, this man she had barely met possessed an odd air of familiarity. In the timbre of his voice, perhaps, or the way he moved. As if they had met before. As if their meeting were fate or arranged by the stars. And wouldn't her mother love that?

"Whatever are you doing?" Cassie's voice sounded from the parlor door.

"I'm trying to decide between salmon"—Delia grimaced—"or butter cream."

Cassie wrinkled her nose. "For supper?"

"No, for the walls." Delia waved at a large book of paint samples precariously balanced on top of a stack of similar catalogues on a side table. "I was trying to decide on a color."

"Salmon is far too pink for this room and butter cream entirely too pale." Cassie strode into the center of the parlor, dropping yet another folio on the unsteady pile on the table as she passed, took off her hat, smoothed her hair and surveyed the room. "If pink or pale is what you've come to, dearest, I have arrived just in time." She pulled off a glove in a considering manner, her gaze moving from wall to wall. "The question of color is paramount, especially in this room. Indeed, that's precisely where we should begin."

Delia stared at her sister in surprise. "You have given this a great deal of thought, haven't you?"

"Someone should." Cassie removed the other glove absently. "Salmon or butter cream." She snorted in disgust.

"I rather like salmon," Delia murmured.

"As a fish course, perhaps, but not for a room. You are the mistress of this house and its rooms should complement you. Especially this one, as it is your most public room. You did say you wished to do a great deal of entertaining in the future, didn't you?"

"I look quite nice in salmon," Delia said loftily.

"Indeed you do. You also look far and away too, well"—Cassie smacked her gloves against her palm—"innocent."

Delia stared at her sister. "And we wouldn't want to mislead anyone, now, would we?"

"Come, now, Delia, that's not what I meant, or at least not entirely what I meant."

Delia crossed her arms over her chest. "What did you mean?"

"You needn't be so sensitive. I simply meant that you are an independent woman of means and your surroundings, the manner in which you live, should reflect that. Nothing pretentious, of course, but rather"—once again Cassie surveyed the room—"classic. Elegant. Here, let me show you."

She picked up the book she'd brought, ignoring the unsteady sway of those beneath it, and paged through it. "This is Mr. Hope's book of furniture designs. Some of it might be too extreme for your taste, and we really should do something about that in the future, but much of it is lovely. I thought it might give you some ideas as to the kinds of things you want."

"I may not act like it, but I do appreciate your help." Delia sighed and shook her head. "I must confess, though, I have had very little interest in the house since my return from the country."

Cassie narrowed her eyes. "Please do not tell me you are still thinking about that viscount."

"Very well. I won't." Delia met her sister's gaze and winced. "But I am."

"Delia!"

Delia ignored her. "Have you found out anything about him?"

Cassie's hesitation was so slight only someone who knew her as well as her sister knew her would notice. She shook her head firmly. "No."

Delia narrowed her eyes. "You most certainly have."

Cassie pressed her lips together stubbornly and hugged the book against her. "I most certainly have not."

"You cannot lie to me."

"Only because I haven't had as much practice lying to you as you have lying to me," Cassie snapped.

For a moment the sisters glared at each other. Finally, Delia drew a deep breath. "I didn't exactly lie to you—"

"Lies of omission are just as bad."

"Very well. From this moment forward, I shall try never to lie to you by omission again. I am sorry about it all, you do know that, don't you?"

"Of course I do. And I am sorry I brought it up. But I can't help thinking that if I had known about Wilmont, if you hadn't deceived me, everything might have turned out far differently. And now there is a new gentleman who has obviously turned your head on the basis of one single dance, one simple conversation and one mere kiss."

"It was an impressive kiss." Delia could deny it to herself all she wanted, but St. Stephens's *mere* kiss had lingered in her mind and in her dreams.

"It scarcely matters if it was the best kiss since Adam first kissed Eve. It was one kiss, Delia. You cannot change your life on the basis of one kiss."

"It wasn't just the kiss, although it was an excellent kiss." Delia wandered around the perimeter of the room trying to pull her thoughts together. "I don't know that I can explain this. When I was with him, when we talked or when he kissed me, I had the oddest sensation of . . . inevitability with him. Of fate, perhaps. And I had the strangest feeling we had met before, spoken before. That I had stared into his dark eyes before." She glanced at her sister. "Did I mention how dark his eyes were?"

"Several times."

"And how tall he was?"

"More than once."

"And how we danced together as perfectly as if we were fated to dance together?"

"Yes, yes, that's been mentioned as well."

"I know you think I'm being absurd. I have only just met this man and he could well be the greatest mistake of my life—"

"I should think Wilmont gets that particular honor," Cassie said under her breath.

"Such as it is." Delia shook her head. "But if he's not a mistake—St. Stephens, that is—and I pass him by, I shall never know if he and I are meant to be together. I could continue for the rest of my life not knowing if the one soul I am fated to be—"

"He inherited his title about two months ago when his brother died." Resignation colored Cassie's voice. "His brother was considerably older, oh, ten years or more, I think. St. Stephens served honorably in the army during the war, I don't know which regiment, that information is rather vague, but I believe he received several commendations."

"How on earth did you discover all this so quickly?" Delia stared at her sister with admiration.

"It wasn't overly difficult." Cassie shrugged. "He is an unmarried man and, from what you have told me, over and over again, not unattractive—"

"Not the least bit unattractive. With the most wonderfully wicked smile."

"I know." Cassie heaved a long-suffering sigh, then continued. "St. Stephens has not been active in society, nor was his brother, apparently; however, the simple fact that he exists—with a respectable fortune, I might add, and an estate in Surrey or Sussex or Hampshire, I really don't remember where—is more than enough to make every mother in England with an eligible daughter in tow sit up and take notice. Or take aim. Although he does seem to be extremely elusive," Cassie said thoughtfully. "Grandmother's ball is the first time anyone remembers actually seeing him, although *someone* in the family must know him rather well."

"Why?"

"He stayed in the guest wing at the hall."

"He was staying right down the corridor and I had no idea?" Disappointment washed through Delia.

"It wouldn't have done you any good had you known," Cassie said firmly. "I understand he left quite early the morning after the ball."

Delia drew her brows together. "How did you know that?"

"I found out much of this before we left Effington Hall. From Aunt Katherine, primarily."

"Why didn't you tell me then?"

"Because"—Cassie studied her sister, concern creasing her brow—"I am worried about you."

Delia eyed her warily. "Why?"

"Because I don't know what you're going to do next. First you tell me you've decided to become a woman of experience, which didn't seem at all worrisome initially. After all, I had to practically threaten you to get you to simply put on a decent gown and pretend to be me for a few minutes."

"Have I thanked you for that?" Delia cast her sister an overly innocent smile.

"Yes, but I should never have encouraged you," Cassie said sharply. "The next thing I know, you're dallying with some stranger on the terrace—"

Delia laughed. "I most certainly was not dallying."

"—and going on and on about this . . . this . . . this Lord Mysterious—"

"Lord Mysterious?" Delia laughed. "I rather like the sound of that."

Cassie ignored her. "And how wonderful he is—"

"He may well not be wonderful, Cassie, but I should very much like to find out."

"Delia." Cassie studied her sister carefully. "If you had known he was staying at the hall, you wouldn't have done anything ill-advised, would you?" A casual note sounded in her sister's voice. "Throw yourself into his bed or anything of that nature?" Cassie raised a brow. "Would you?"

"Of course not, I'd just met the man. I'm certainly not ready to throw myself into his bed or anyone else's. Although"—she cast her sister a wicked smile—"the thought of the bed of Lord Mysterious is extremely tempting."

"Dear Lord." Cassie sank onto the sofa and stared at her sister. "I do wish everyone who had thought I was the one on the path to ruin could hear you now."

Delia grinned. "Shocking, isn't it?"

"And dangerous as well."

"Why?" Delia plopped into a nearby chair. "If I am to become a woman of experience, St. Stephens would be the perfect place to start. I find him wildly attractive. He is apparently quite respectable when it comes to his family and title and that sort of thing. You said he has money, so he wouldn't be interested in me for mine. And anyone who kisses that well obviously has had a great deal of experience doing so."

Cassie groaned.

"I'm simply being practical. I could do far worse than to start with St. Stephens." Delia's voice was thoughtful. "I should think if one wants to become a woman of experience the best way to do that is with a man of experience. I could probably learn a great deal."

"Philadelphia Effington!" Cassie stared in stunned disbelief. "I can't imagine what is in your head. Obviously your ill-fated marriage, and the scandal, *and* your exile at the very ends of the earth have addled your brain. This entire woman-of-experience nonsense is absurd and ridiculous and . . . and . . ." She paused and her eyes widened as if she were suddenly struck by some hideous thought. "And I have never been so jealous of anyone in my entire life."

"What?"

"I just realized it." Shock rang in Cassie's voice. "I am entirely and completely envious of you."

"Really?" Delia grinned. "How lovely."

"No, it's not. You're on the road to scandal and ruin."

"I have already been ruined, and the center of scandal as well. Whatever I do now won't be of nearly as much interest as what I have done."

"It's not at all fair. You have independence and wealth and freedom." Cassie glared. "Hell and damnation, Delia, you have an entire herd of horses in your future and I suspect you intend to ride!"

Delia stared at her sister, then burst into laughter. Cassie buried her face in her hands. "I can't believe I said that."

"Nor can I."

Cassie lifted her head. "I didn't mean it precisely the way it sounded."

Delia wiped her eyes and sniffed. "Thank God."

"Are you really planning on . . ." Cassie gestured helplessly.

"Indiscriminate riding?" Delia forced an innocent note to her voice.

Cassie grimaced. "For lack of a better phrase."

Delia considered her sister for a moment, then sighed. "I don't know. As you have pointed out, it took rather a lot of encouragement simply to get me to pretend to be you. I'm not certain I have the courage to be a woman of experience."

Cassie breathed a sigh of relief, then frowned. "That is at once good to hear and rather disappointing."

Delia laughed. "I am sorry. If it makes you feel better, while indiscriminate riding is not in my plans at the moment"—she drew a deep breath—"I am intent upon . . . something with St. Stephens."

"Are you sure?"

"More than I've been sure of anything in a long time."

"Very well. Then you shall need this." Cassie flipped open her book and pulled out a folded note. "This came for me today, but it's really for you." I must tell you I debated over whether to give it to you at all. She handed it to her sister. "It's from your Lord Mysterious."

"He's not my Lord Mysterious." Delia took the note and unfolded it. "Yet." She scanned the message. "Did you read this?"

"It was addressed to me."

"Of course," Delia murmured, and read the brief lines again. She glanced at her sister. "Did you like the flowers?"

"They were lovely. I've always been fond of roses. I would have brought them along, but"—Cassie shrugged casually—"I thought I deserved something for all this."

"He wants to meet me at Lord and Lady Puget's reception tonight." She drew her brows together. "How on earth will I manage that?"

"The same way you managed the first time you met him." Cassie shook her head in disbelief. "You shall take my place."

Delia shook her head. "I don't think—"

"However, this will be the last time, and I have conditions."

"Doesn't everyone?" Delia muttered. "Well?"

"First, do not forget, dear sister, it is my reputation you hold in your hands. And regardless of how much I may envy your independence and everything else that goes along with it, I still have hopes of making a good match, preferably with a man I love. You may well wish to pursue experience, but I am still in pursuit of marriage. And right now I am far from ready to follow in your footsteps."

"I shall guard your reputation as if it were my own."

"Oh, please, do better than that."

"Is there more?"

"Yes." Cassie leaned forward, her tone abruptly serious. "I want you to consider your meeting with St. Stephens something of a test."

Delia frowned. "What kind of test?"

"A test of his nature, his character, as it were." Cassie thought for a moment. "He has no idea that you're a widow; he thinks you're me. A secluded meeting on a terrace, even a few kisses, are forgivable, but the kind of man who would continue the type of behavior that risks a lady's reputation and, indeed, skates perilously close to scandal is—"

"Precisely like Charles," Delia said simply.

Remorse colored Cassie's face. "Oh, dear, I didn't mean—"

"No, you're quite right." Delia chose her words carefully. "I knew of Charles's reputation from the beginning, but I quite enjoyed the secretive nature of our meetings. My adventure, if you recall. So, to a great extent, the fault for all that transpired was mine. The question is whether a truly honorable man would have let our clandestine adventures continue."

"But he did do the honorable thing in the end. He did marry you and, in doing so, redeemed you from ruin." Cassie paused. "Redeeming himself as well, perhaps?"

"Perhaps." And became cool and remote in the process. "Do you think marriage changes men, Cassie?"

"Grandmother would say that one can only hope."

Delia laughed.

Cassie considered her for a thoughtful moment. "There is much about you and Wilmont you have still not seen fit to tell me, isn't there?"

Delia shrugged. "Nothing of importance."

"You told me you didn't lo—"

"I didn't," Delia cut in, then sighed. "But I could have quite easily and probably would have eventually."

"And with St. Stephens?"

"I don't know. It's one of many things about the man I should like to find out.

Cassie paused. "You have to tell him who you really are, you know."

Delia raised a brow. "Is that another condition?"

"Absolutely." Cassie nodded. "If indeed he is an honorable man—and regardless of your intentions, I daresay you don't want to be involved with a man who isn't—the longer you let this deception continue, the greater his annoyance will be when he discovers the truth. You could lose him entirely."

"You're right. I hadn't thought of that. And I do intend on telling him the truth."

"When?"

"When the moment is right."

Cassie narrowed her eyes.

Delia sighed. "And I suspect that moment will come sooner rather than later."

"I shall hold you to that. Besides, I do not intend to sit at home while you take my place at balls and parties."

"Of course not, that wouldn't be at all fair. I do promise this will be the last time. Besides"—Delia cast her sister a knowing grin—"I can't very well become a woman of experience pretending to be you."

* * *

It was a complicated scheme involving torn dresses and two separate social events and God knows what else. Tony eased away from his discreet position beside the barely opened door to the parlor and tried not to grin. Still, what the women planned in order to change places for tonight should well work. Indeed, Delia and her sister were formidable and, under far different circumstances, the sisters would have done rather well in his own line of work.

He signaled to the footman who waited down the hall near the back stairs. At once the man assumed his position at the front door. The footman was one of a half dozen new servants Delia had returned to find in her house, although she seemed to pay them little heed.

There were now footmen and maids and an underbutler, as well as a cook's helper who only came in during the day. As per the duke's orders, all of the additions to the household were in the employ of the department and charged with Delia's protection—with the single exception of the cook's helper. She was hired for the protection of everyone's digestion, and Mrs. Miller was more than willing to let the other woman do the bulk of the work in the kitchen.

Life in Delia's house was busy, what with the new servants who weren't servants but played their parts well, and Delia's meetings with various merchants that she ultimately paid scant attention to. But overall it was positively dull compared to other assignments he had had. And he rather liked it that way for now. Nothing out of the ordinary had occurred and indeed there was no indication that Delia was in any kind of danger. Tony wondered if the department had been misled. Regardless, his assignment was to stay, and stay he would.

Delia had been preoccupied since her return from the country, which had actually worked in his favor. He'd returned to London only the day before she had. He'd had to scramble to meet the duke's orders regarding servants, as well as Delia's orders about appointments and meetings. The duke's commands were easily carried out. Delia's proved to be far more trying for himself and the department.

He stepped into the library, closed the door behind him and strode across the room to take a seat at the desk. Delia would be busy with her sister for at least the next half hour and he had personal correspondence to deal with. And decisions to make.

He spread out his correspondence and stared at it unseeing.

Whether he liked it or not, this would probably be his final job. Oh, certainly the Duke of Roxborough could head a secret department of the British government and still handle the responsibilities of his title. But the duke had resources well beyond Tony's, including the extensive Effington family and four loyal, competent brothers. Tony was alone in the world. The duke had grown up knowing full well someday the Roxborough title and the responsibilities that went with it would be his. He had been trained and taught and raised accordingly. Tony never imagined the brother he barely knew would succumb to a sudden illness and die without issue.

One of the letters before him forwarded from his estate was from the manager of his brother's—no, *his*— property asking questions Tony had no idea how to answer. He had always thought himself skilled, competent and up to any situation. He could slip into an enemy-held city unnoticed or take on a new identity so thoroughly even his own mother wouldn't know him, or, if necessary, kill a man without making a sound. But he hadn't the foggiest idea how to be an English lord.

He could not put it off much longer. He'd always

owed his complete allegiance and loyalty to his country and his king. Now there were people he'd never given a second thought to dependent on him. On his actions and decisions and patronage. Servants and tenant farmers and God only knew who else.

He blew a long breath and ran his hand through his hair. It was past time he learned precisely what was involved in being the Viscount St. Stephens. Exactly what his new responsibilities were to his family, or rather his heritage, his title and, well, the future. A future that required his ensuring his lineage and his title did not end with him. Like it or not, providing for the future meant one thing, and one thing only: a wife.

He'd not given much consideration to the idea of a wife up till now. In his nearly thirty years of life he really hadn't seen much use for one. He'd simply assumed someday at some point he would wed some pleasant, biddable woman who would spend her days taking care of his needs. But now his life had taken a turn he had not foreseen. Now he had responsibilities beyond himself. Now a wife was no longer a vague concept somewhere in the far-off distance but a very real possibility, if not a necessity.

Had Wilmont thought the same thing? Had he too realized the time had come for him to live up to the responsibilities of his position? Had he decided Delia was part of that?

Tony drummed his fingers thoughtfully on the desk. Why Wilmont had married Delia was still a mystery. But if he had decided she would make an excellent wife, not merely for an agent of the British crown but for a baron with wealth and responsibilities and possibly a need for a connection with a powerful family, their marriage made sense. And if Wilmont had come to that conclusion, perhaps he had made the same decision Tony had.

Had Wilmont felt he was working on his final job as well?

It was an interesting idea and possibly explained the man's odd, reticent behavior between the day of his wedding and the day of his death. How did it all get so twisted? Tony knew full well the initial plan did not involve marriage, yet marriage was the end result. Unless . . . Tony's fingers stilled.

Unless Wilmont found himself caught in his own trap?

At once, the myriad pieces that had floated in Tony's head for six months snapped into place.

Baron Wilmont, Charles, had fallen in love with Philadelphia Effington. It was the only thing that made sense. Tony probably hadn't realized it before now because he hadn't known her until now. Now he could well see how even the most jaded of men could fall under the spell of her charm and her laugh and the way she felt in his arms.

She was, in truth, all Tony had ever wanted in a woman. Bloody hell, she was all he'd ever wanted in a wife—except for that biddable business, and the challenge of marrying an Effington woman would likely make up for that. At least the duke thought so.

Whether she realized it or not, with all that independent widow nonsense she and her sister had spoken of, Delia—any woman, really—needed someone to take care of her. Why shouldn't it be him? If she had spent a great deal of time thinking about him since their meeting on the terrace, he had spent at least that much thinking about her. Dreaming about her.

Besides, Tony was her late husband's friend, and the least he could do for Wilmont was take care of his wife. Viewed that way, it didn't seem the least bit like betrayal, but rather a solemn duty. Beyond that, he could have as easily drawn the assignment to court her as Wilmont. Indeed, couldn't the dramatic upheaval in her life be at least partially blamed on Tony? And when seen in that light, it could well be considered his responsibility to . . . to what?

Marry her?

His stomach lurched at the thought. Marriage was a remarkably permanent institution. In spite of the changes in his own position, and his acknowledgment of the need for a wife, he still wasn't especially certain he was ready for marriage. Yet. However, he certainly was not about to allow the woman he might, or might not, marry to go off and become a woman of experience. Not without him. Why, it was practically his duty to protect her from herself and each and every unsavory male who lay in wait for a lovely, lonely, wealthy widow. The best way to protect her might well be to occupy her time himself and hopefully her thoughts and, if it came to it, her bed. He damn near owed her that.

As she had apparently selected him as her first stepping-stone down the path to experience, the least he could do was cooperate, starting this very night. Indeed, if she wanted an honorable man, he would make certain she got one. Regardless of his current deception, he was, in truth, a man of honor and had every intention of behaving as one tonight. And how would Delia respond to that? He grinned. He quite looked forward to this evening.

Besides, the simple truth was he wanted to be with her as himself. He'd quite enjoyed talking with her and dancing with her and, most of all, kissing her. They hadn't spent nearly enough time together and, as odd as it sounded, with every passing day he grew rather jealous of Gordon. Of *himself*. And with every passing day it grew more difficult not to take her in his arms.

She had the strangest effect on him, and had since the

first moment he'd looked into her blue eyes. He wanted her, of course, in the way men want women who are pretty and clever and amusing. He'd already acknowledged that. But there was more to it than mere desire. And what that more was might well be the most exciting thing he'd ever done. And the most dangerous.

If Wilmont had indeed loved her, that explained why he had married her. But even if Wilmont had married Delia for love, had she married him for the same reason? Had Delia loved her husband?

And worse, did she love him still?

Chapter 11

This might well be an enormous mistake. Or a truly grand adventure.

Delia slipped into the massive salon at Lady Puget's and adopted the distinct air of someone returning from the ladies' retiring room rather than someone who had just now arrived. She smiled Cassie's confident smile, joined the stream of guests circling the outer edges of the room, then slipped out of the flow of the crowd and stepped into a large, circular alcove. Floor-to-ceiling windows provided light for the cluster of potted palms and exotic plants positioned in the center of the alcove. During daylight hours, the windows provided a delightful panorama of Lady Puget's impressive gardens.

Delia had been to Lord and Lady Puget's fetes before and knew this spot was the perfect place from which to view the room. One could even have a private conversation while in full sight of the rest of the gathering, unless one chose to survey the gardens from the widows and was therefore forced to step behind the palms, which could be perfect as well for a bit of seclusion. After all, she did have Cassie's reputation to consider, even if it was surprising to learn Cassie was concerned about such things. And surprising as well to realize she did not know everything about her sister. However, this was most definitely a public sort of place and absolutely no one could chastise a young woman for speaking with a gentleman here. If, of course, one could find said gentleman.

Delia scanned the ballroom in search of a tall, dark-haired stranger. Lord Mysterious. She smiled to herself.

It was such a perfect name for St. Stephens. Oh, certainly Cassie had managed to find out the basic details of his life, but it appeared no one really knew the man. Delia wasn't entirely sure if that was a problem or a benefit. She rather liked the idea of a gentleman who did not drag the past along with him. She rather liked the idea of Lord Mysterious.

Of course, tonight a gentleman of mystery was most appropriate, given the machinations she and Cassie had gone through to get her to this point.

Cassie and their parents were to come to the Pugets' reception but planned on nothing more than making a brief appearance, for reasons of both society and politics, and then proceed on to another gathering elsewhere. At the last minute, Cassie claimed to have torn her gown, insisted her parents go on without her and promised to join them at the second location. Accompanied by her maid, she had then taken a carriage to Delia's, where Delia waited already wearing a gown she had earlier pulled from her nearly forgotten trunk. Cassie stayed behind and Delia proceeded to the reception, vowing to return within two hours.

Delia resisted the urge to laugh out loud. It had already been quite an exhilarating evening, and most definitely an adventure. She hadn't had so much fun since her secret meetings with Charles in what seemed a lifetime ago. But this was entirely different.

With Charles, from their first moment, she'd understood her feelings completely. Right or wrong, she'd seen him very much as her last chance for adventure and had entered into their liaison with her eyes wide open. When she considered it, she'd really been rather practical.

With St. Stephens, she had no idea exactly how she felt except for a sweet, awful yearning deep inside her. It wasn't simply a physical desire to know more of those things Charles had briefly introduced her to, although admittedly there was some of that. No, it was something more profound. Something exquisite and more than a little frightening. There was a danger inherent in involvement with St. Stephens that went well beyond the threat of scandal.

"Once again, I feared you would not come." St. Stephens's voice sounded from the other side of the palms and a shiver of anticipation tripped up her spine.

"And once again I have surprised you." She slanted him a quick glance and thought surely her very bones would dissolve at the simmering look in his eyes. Still, it would not do to let him know. She continued to study the crowd and forced a casual note to her voice. "How could I possibly resist such a charming invitation?"

"Did you like the flowers, then?"

"They were lovely." Indeed, had she ever seen a rose that wasn't lovely? "I am exceedingly fond of roses."

"I hoped you would like them." He stepped to her side. "I particularly thought that color would suit you."

She didn't allow her smile to so much as flicker. "It's long been my favorite."

"Really?" He studied her curiously. "I always thought red was the favorite of most women."

"Most, perhaps, but I assure you"—she adopted a breezy tone that belied the fact that she had no idea what color her flowers, no, *Cassie's* flowers, were; and she had no intention of wasting any of her precious time with him discussing them—"I am not like most women."

"I did not doubt it for a moment." He chuckled in a manner entirely too intimate and seductive to be proper.

She favored him with a knowing smile, then strolled toward the windows and gazed out into the garden, illuminated tonight with lanterns set strategically amid the plantings. "Look, my lord. Fairy lights in the garden."

"I have always been quite fond of fairy lights," he murmured.

She caught his gaze in the reflection of the window. "You haven't even looked."

"At the garden, no." He shook his head slowly. "Why should I, when I can gaze into your eyes?"

She stared for an endless moment, mesmerized by the meeting of their eyes in the dark reflection of the window with the lights of the ballroom and the crowd behind them, caught in a spell of something entirely too special. Something magic.

She forced herself to break free and turned toward him, a light note in her voice. "And how are you finding London, my lord?"

He raised an amused brow as if he knew precisely why she had changed the subject. Precisely what she'd been feeling. "I find London much the same as always."

"Do you spend a great deal of time here, then?"

"Some." He stepped closer, caught her hand and drew it to his lips. "I should like to spend a great deal more. There is much to be admired about the city."

"Oh?" A tremor of excitement ran up her arm at his touch, but she kept her voice cool. "And what is it you admire?"

"The sights, Miss Effington." His voice was low. "I find I quite appreciate the sights of London."

She reluctantly but firmly reclaimed her hand. "Any sights in particular?"

"One sight, in particular, has attracted my interest." He stared down at her.

"Has it?" There was an odd, breathless tone to her voice.

"Miss Effington, I have a question to ask you." His gaze searched hers and her heart caught in her throat.

"Yes?"

"I would very much like to . . ."

Take me into the gardens and make me yours right here? Right now?

"Yes?"

He straightened his shoulders slightly and for just an instant she had the distinct impression Lord Mysterious was apprehensive. "I should very much like to speak to your father and ask permission to call on you formally."

For a moment she could do nothing more than stare.

"Miss Effington?"

"Why?" she blurted.

"Why?" His brow furrowed. "Because that's what one does when one is in a situation like this."

She studied him suspiciously. "A situation like what?"

"A situation wherein"—he drew a deep breath, as if just that moment making up his mind—"a gentleman has met a lady he may well not be able to live without."

"Really?" She stared in delight.

"Really." He nodded in a no-nonsense manner and stepped closer. "Indeed, Miss Effington, I cannot seem to get you out of my head."

"You can't?" Without thinking, she took a backward step.

He moved toward her again with an eager, even enthusiastic step. "Day and night, all I can think about is you. You've even invaded my dreams. I can no longer get a decent night's rest. It's enough to drive a man mad."

"I rather like the idea of driving a man mad." She lifted a shoulder in a casual shrug and again stepped away. As much as she wanted more than a mere kiss with this man, it was perhaps too soon for more. "And are you mad, my lord?"

"Yes, blast it all, I am bloody well insane." He glanced around and she realized their odd dance had taken them behind the palms to a spot of relative privacy. "And you, Miss Effington"—he grabbed her shoulders—"are the reason why."

He yanked her to him and kissed her hard and long, until she thought her toes would curl and the rest of her pool into a lifeless heap at his feet. Perhaps it was not too soon for more after all.

Abruptly he released her and she caught their reflection in the windows, noting in the back of her mind that anyone in the gardens could have witnessed their kiss. Still, at the moment, Cassie's reputation was not foremost in her thoughts.

Delia gazed up at him, her voice breathless. "Am I?"

"Yes, you are." He adjusted the cuffs of his shirt as if they were of paramount importance, but she suspected he needed as much time to catch his breath as she. "And that, Miss Effington, is why I insist on meeting your parents."

"I don't believe they'd at all appreciate a kiss behind the palms," she murmured, still delightfully befuddled by his kiss. His second kiss, while far shorter than the first, was every bit as wonderful, and she quite looked forward to the third and the fourth and every kiss thereafter.

"Excellent, as I have no desire to kiss your parents behind the palms or anywhere else." He shook his head as if to clear away the absurd conversation. "I must confess, I had no intention of saying any of this tonight, but—"

"Is it the madness, my lord?" she said innocently.

"Quite." He grinned ruefully and took her hand. "And I fear it is a permanent affliction."

"What a charming thing to say. You do have a nice turn with a phrase."

"Thank you." He studied her carefully. "Now, about speaking to your father."

"I would prefer that you didn't." She shook her head. "But I do appreciate that you wish to. It says a great deal about your character. Why, I should give any man who has behaved as you have high marks indeed." She cast him a brilliant smile.

"I am glad I am up to your standards, Miss Effington, but I am interested in more than your approval. I want . . . that is, I'd prefer . . . or rather, I wish . . ." He glared in annoyance. "Blast it all, Miss Effington, I believe I may well want your hand."

"My hand? You mean in marriage?" There was an odd note of horror in her voice.

He looked as shocked by his declaration as she was. "Well, yes, I think I am talking about marriage." He shook his head in disbelief that he would say such a thing. "That too was not my intention."

She raised a brow.

"Well, not quite yet. You do tend to muddle a man's mind, Miss Effington."

"First I drive you mad, then I muddle your mind." She crossed her arms over her chest. "Is that really the kind of woman you wish to marry, my lord?"

"Not in the least. You are not at all the sort of woman I had planned to marry, but, well, I don't care." He looked her square in the eye and she could see he was most determined. "Damnation, Miss Effington, why not? It was probably inevitable. Fate and all that. I knew it the first time I met you. And I know as well that you feel precisely the same way."

He stepped toward her and again she stepped back. She needed a clear head for this particular conversation, and her head would be anything but clear if he so much as took her hand. "I will concede that possibly I may feel—"

"Hah." He snorted in disbelief. "There is no *possibly* about it. I can see it in the look in your eye. The tone of your voice." He lowered his voice. "The eagerness of your kiss."

"I should be as eager to kiss anyone who kisses as well as you," she snapped.

"Now, now, Miss Effington. Do not forget your reputation," he said in a smug and most annoying manner. "What would people think if they knew you would be as eager—"

Shock widened her eyes. "Surely you wouldn't—"

"Never," he said firmly, then grinned in a teasing manner, and all her annoyance with him fled. "But I am most appreciative of the compliment and, I promise, I intend to improve with practice. In point of fact, I intend a great deal of practice."

"Oh, my." She stared up at him, resisting the urge to tell him how very delightful a great deal of practice sounded. She summoned her resolve and lifted her chin. "As much as I do appreciate your determination, I must tell you, my lord, I am not particularly interested in marriage at the moment."

He scoffed. "Don't be absurd. Every woman is interested in marriage."

"I'm not," she said staunchly. "At least not now."

"Why not?"

"Because I . . ." She bit back the words just in time.

She couldn't possibly tell him she wasn't interested in marriage because her first marriage had lasted less than a week and her last husband had been dead barely half a year. Or that she wasn't interested in marriage with anyone she'd just met no matter how right, how natural it was to be with him. Or that she wasn't interested in marriage because marrying once had been the biggest mistake of her life and she wasn't eager to make another.

And she certainly couldn't tell him she wasn't interested in marriage because she had just begun the life of an independent widow and had yet to become an experienced woman. "I simply don't see the appeal of marriage, nor the benefits."

"The benefits of marriage? I should think that would be obvious for a woman. The protection of a man's name, at the very least. A respectable position in life. Children. Companionship. Affection." He studied her curiously. "Don't you wish for affection?"

"Most certainly, but—"

"Have you ever been in love, Miss Effington?"

She shook her head. "No."

He paused in surprise. "No?"

"No. Have you?"

"No, but I am confident I will know it when I see it."

"One moment, sir." She pulled up short and planted her hand on his chest to stop his forward progress. "Are you trying to say that you are in love with me?"

He thought for a moment. "I believe I might well be."

"But you're not sure?"

"Of course I'm not sure." His brow furrowed in annoyance. "How in the name of all that's holy can I possibly be sure? I've never felt this way before. But if I am not in love . . ." He grabbed her hand, pulled it to his lips and placed a kiss in the center of her palm. His gaze met hers. "Then I must truly be mad."

She ignored the urge to fall into his arms and snatched her hand away. "That is a distinct possibility and something of a problem, I should think."

"For you." A wicked gleam flashed in his eye.

"Not at all, I . . ." her gaze locked with his and her resistance eased. "Very well, then, yes, for me. For us both."

"It is nice to see we agree on something." He chuckled. "We shall suit well together, Miss Effington.

"A charming declaration, but you don't know me well enough to know whether we shall suit or not." As much as a part of her wanted to throw caution to the winds and leap headfirst into this man's life, up to and including marriage, she was not about to make another mistake. One she might well pay for with the rest of her life.

"Oh, but I do know you. I know the kindness of your nature and the clever way you have with words. I know you are thoughtful and generous and intelligent. I know the pleasure of hearing you laugh and admire the determined note that sounds in your voice. I know the . . ."

She stared and his voice faltered.

He shrugged, his smile apologetic. "Or perhaps I don't know at all. Perhaps I just imagine that I know."

"I am most impressed, my lord, and flattered, and . . ." Delia shook her head. She was not about to commit herself to marriage, but she dearly wanted to have him in her life. And who knew what might happen in the future? She'd never known a man who might be in love with her. Or mad. But regardless of whether he was truly in love or truly insane, she'd never known a man who made her feel as he did.

Of course, she could do nothing whatsoever until she told him the truth.

"My lord." She met his gaze firmly. "I have another confession to make."

"Oh?" He smiled in a teasing manner. "I understood you did not make them lightly or well."

"I don't, but I am getting better at it. Practice, no doubt," she muttered. She drew a breath and squared her shoulders. "I should tell you—"

"Cassandra?" A familiar voice sounded behind her.

Delia's heart plummeted. She cast St. Stephens an apologetic look and turned slowly. "Good evening, Mother."

William and Georgina Effington, Lord and Lady William, stood beside the palms. Delia's mother wore a look of distinct annoyance. Her father bore the long-suffering smile that typically accompanied his formal attire.

"I did not expect to see you here, my dear," Mother said, her considering gaze moving from Delia to St. Stephens and back. "Needless to say, when someone who had been wandering in the gardens claimed to have seen you through the windows in what might be a most compromising position, I said it couldn't possibly be you, as you weren't even here." She studied her daughter thoughtfully. "You can imagine my surprise to discover I was wrong."

"Indeed I can," Delia said weakly.

"Nonetheless, I—" Mother sucked in a sharp breath and her eyes widened. "Good Lord. Phil—"

"Lady William," St. Stephens said smoothly, stepping forward. "I can assure you nothing untoward happened here this evening. Your daughter and I have been having a most pleasant conversation and I suspect anyone who claims to have seen otherwise has, in truth, seen nothing more than an image distorted by the glass."

Delia released a breath she hadn't realized she'd held.

"Very good," Father murmured. "We'll stick with that then."

St. Stephens turned toward her father. "Sir, I am not sure if you remember me, but we met last week at Effington Hall."

Her father's eyes narrowed slightly, then he nodded. "Of course. St. Stephens, isn't it? My brother speaks quite highly of you."

"I am honored, sir. I had planned on calling on you at a later date, but this seems as good a time as any." St. Stephens cast Delia a quick smile. "I should like your permission to call on Miss Effington."

"*Miss* Effington? You mean Cassandra?" Her father's gaze shot to her and she smiled uneasily. For as long as she could remember, he could immediately tell one of his daughters from the other. He claimed it was something in their eyes. He choked back what might have been a cough but was more likely a laugh.

"Sir?" St. Stephens said. "Are you all right?"

"I haven't been all right in years." He eyed his daughter pointedly. "Not since I had children. Daughters in particular. Damned difficult creatures. Age a man before his time."

"Thank you, Father," Delia murmured.

"I shall remember that, sir," St. Stephens said. "Now, about this particular daughter—"

"I have nothing to say about this particular daughter at the moment." Her father fixed her with a steady stare. "I believe she has a great deal to say before I do."

"Or rather a great deal to explain." Her mother glared at her.

"And I understand there are cigars in the library, which is where I would much rather be right now. So if you will excuse me . . ." Her father took her hands and leaned close, his voice low and for her alone. "You do realize there will be hell to pay for this, and you are well aware of precisely what that hell is. Is he worth the trouble?"

"Honestly, Father, I don't know, but I should very much like to find out."

"Be careful, my dear." His gaze searched hers. "But then I'd wager you will be. You have learned hard lessons and I suspect you have learned them well."

She sighed. "I do hope so, Father."

He smiled and stepped back. "On further thought, as excellent as Lord Puget's cigars are, I fear I shall have to pass. We have another engagement this evening and should be on our way. Georgina?"

Her mother pinned Delia with a pointed look. "I assume you will be accompanying us?"

"Nonsense," her father said quickly. "She probably has a carriage waiting and can certainly return home the same way she arrived."

"Thank you, Father." Relief washed through her.

"Very well," her mother said with a sigh of resignation. "As it is getting late, we will discuss this tomorrow."

"Yes, of course." Delia forced a pleasant smile, and why not smile now? Tomorrow would hold nothing to smile about. "I shall quite look forward to it."

Her mother leaned closer and kissed Delia's cheek. "I wouldn't."

Her parents murmured their farewells, then headed toward the entry.

"Are your parents always that enigmatic?" St. Stephens asked.

"Usually they are quite direct, as I should be. However, my mother was right. It is far later than I realized and I must be off."

"But what of your confession? Surely you're not going to leave me hanging? You could not possibly tease me that way?"

"Oh, but I quite enjoy teasing you, my lord." Her manner was offhand in spite of the turmoil in her stomach.

It would have been a much simpler matter to tell him she was not actually *Miss* anything but rather *Lady* Wilmont before her parents arrived. And that was certainly her intention. But now that he had asked permission to call on her, confession would be most awkward. The man might well be horribly embarrassed, even humiliated. It was entirely possible he would not want to see her again after learning the truth. Oh, not because she was a widow with a touch of scandal in her past, but because she had lied to him. He was, from all she could determine, a man with a very definite sense of honor.

The least she could do was make certain he was spared any further embarrassment in public.

She thought for a moment. "My . . . my sister is having a few guests for dinner tomorrow night and I should quite like it if you could attend."

"On one condition."

"You too?" She sighed. Did everyone in the world have conditions for her? "Very well."

"I shall attend only if you promise to confess all, although I can't imagine any sins you may have committed that require more than a causal mention. Your last confession was simply that of a faulty memory, and in truth"—he smiled boyishly—"that was my doing. Unless, of course"—his gaze bored into hers—"you wish to confess that you have no feelings for me whatsoever."

"And if indeed that is my confession?"

"You shall quite break my heart, Miss Effington." He sighed in an overly dramatic manner. "And you shall leave me no recourse."

"Oh?"

He shook his head in feigned remorse. "I shall be forced to mount a campaign that will make any of Wellington's pale in comparison."

She laughed. "I should like to see that."

"Oh, if necessary, Miss Effington, you shall." He leaned closer, his dark eyes simmering. Her breath caught. "You see, Effingtons are not the only ones who refuse to lose."

Chapter 12

*I*f one was fortunate enough to have the resources of a department of the British government behind him and intelligent enough to have the foresight to leave a carriage and driver far enough away to avoid the jam of vehicles in front of the Puget mansion, one could easily manage to return home well before anyone else. Particularly necessary if one also needed a few extra moments to change from a young viscount to an elderly butler.

Tony glanced in the gilded mirror near the front entry and nodded with satisfaction. Not a hair on Gordon's head was out of place. He caught the eye of Mac stationed by the front door. The man gave an almost imperceptible nod of approval. Tony resisted the urge to grin. No, he resisted the urge to laugh out loud.

The evening with Delia had gone far better than he'd dreamed. She certainly hadn't recognized him, and it had been rather wonderful to be with her as himself. And that nonsense with her parents—he choked back a laugh. Well, she deserved it. Pretending to be her sister and defying all the conventions of society by going out in public. Oh, certainly she had done the same thing at Effington Hall, but if one looked at it through particularly narrowed eyes, one could say that was hardly public. It was her family's home, after all.

Mac opened the door and Delia swept into the entry.

"Good evening"—he paused for a heartbeat—"my lady."

"Good evening, Gordon." She nodded briskly. "Is my sister in the parlor?"

"Yes, ma'am."

"Excellent." She started toward the parlor. He reached the door a step ahead of her and pulled it open. She stepped over the threshold and stopped in midstride. "You know who I am?"

"Of course, Lady Wilmont."

She glared up at him suspiciously. "How?"

"The look in your eye, ma'am," he said in his best unruffled butler manner. "It is unmistakable."

"Charming," she muttered, and turned back into the room. He closed the door behind her, leaving it discreetly cracked open just enough to hear as much of the conversation as possible, then took up his position beside it.

"Well?" Miss Effington's voice sounded from the library. "Was it—"

"Some of it was quite wonderful, but the evening did not turn out precisely as I had planned." Delia sighed. "I encountered an unexpected problem."

He could well imagine the look on her sister's face.

"What kind of problem? You haven't ruined me entirely, have you?"

"Of course not, don't be silly." Delia paused, obviously gathering her courage. "Do sit down, Cassie, I have a great deal to tell you." Delia lowered her voice and, as much as Tony strained, he could not make out her words. He anticipated a shriek from her sister at any minute.

He certainly expected Miss Effington to be overset by the unexpected *problems* her sister had encountered, although certainly she was as much to blame as Delia herself. This should well be a lesson for them both about deception and impersonations.

He brushed aside the hypocritical nature of his criticism. After all, he was engaged in a far more extensive deception with an impersonation that had invaded Delia's own household, her privacy, even her confidence. He knew full well she would see her sins as much less significant than his own, although he could certainly argue that, while her masquerade was for distinctly personal reasons, his was for a higher purpose, primarily her own safety. Indeed, one could even say his ruse was undertaken for the very security of his country. Why, looking at it that way, it was his patriotic duty to lie to her.

Regardless, she would never forgive him.

A leaden weight settled in the pit of his stomach. She would, in all likelihood, despise him. And in truth, who could blame her? He had deceived her, lied to her, from the very moment he stepped into her house. He used said deception to work his way into her confidence, even her affections. And tonight, he simply compounded his sins.

A peal of laughter sounded from the parlor. Tony and Mac traded glances. Tony had no idea if the laughter was a good sign or very, very bad.

Tony hadn't intended to tell Delia he might well love her; he hadn't really yet admitted it to himself. And he certainly hadn't planned to bring up the possibility of marriage. The very thought of marriage, of permanence and commitment and confinement, brought a cold chill to his soul, although marriage, permanence, commitment and even confinement did not sound quite as bad with Delia. Indeed, it really had a rather intriguing appeal. Still, he wasn't at all sure why he had mentioned marriage, although it had certainly been on his mind of late. The easy and obvious answer was that he had simply been caught up in the moment. Playing out that bit about insisting on meeting her parents, asking her father for permission to call on her, all in the name of presenting himself as an honorable man. He cringed at the thought. He did indeed have a well defined sense of honor, but Delia would most definitely not see it that way.

He would be lucky if she allowed him to live after all of this. Tony had been in dangerous situations before now, but none as potentially lethal as the game he was caught up in with Delia.

Welcome to the game.

Was it the duke's fault, then? Had His Grace intentionally planted the idea of marriage in Tony's mind? He wouldn't put it at all past him, given his annoyance at having his niece involved in the first place. Probably his way of enacting revenge. The man was indeed diabolical.

No, it wasn't the duke's fault. Nor was it Delia's or her sister's or anyone's fault, really. Blame it all on fate, perhaps, and the strange sequence of events that had begun half a year ago with Wilmont and taken them all to this point. The plain and simple fact was that he had indeed fallen in love with the woman he was deceiving and, more, wanted to spend the rest of his life with her.

A life she might well cut short when she knew the truth. She was probably as diabolical as her uncle. Just look at the convoluted, and fairly successful, plan she and her sister had cooked up for tonight. Diabolical no doubt ran in their blood.

There was no good way out of this mess. Confession

on his part could well lead to murder on hers. The duke expected Tony to do the honorable thing if his ruse was made public, and while Tony was willing, he would wager his entire fortune Delia would not be. Now that she had wealth and independence, Tony didn't doubt for a moment she would not be at all inclined to do anything she didn't wish to do.

And she wished to become an experienced woman, not a wife.

Still, in spite of her intentions, he was confident she was not the sort of woman who could indulge in the carnal aspects of *experience* without involving her emotions as well. If he helped her achieve her objective, with a bit of luck, when the time came to tell her the truth she would be as in love with him as he was with her.

By God, that was the answer. He would mount a campaign for her heart that would indeed rival Wellington's quest to defeat Napoleon. As reluctant as he was to admit that she had worked her way into his heart, he did love her and he didn't want to lose her. He could easily see how Wilmont might have loved her as well.

Still . . . He straightened at the thought. She had not loved Wilmont. She had said as much tonight. If that was true, then it stood to reason she had not married him because she wanted to, but because she had to. Because Wilmont had ruined her and she saw no other choice. Tony had already concluded there was at the very least the possibility of affection on Wilmont's side, but now he wondered which had come first: the seduction or the emotion.

If Delia wasn't mourning the man she loved, there might well be room in her heart for Tony.

Abruptly, the murmur of voices in the library grew louder and Tony moved away from the door. A moment later the door opened and Delia and her sister stepped into the entry.

Miss Effington cast him a pleasant smile. "So nice to see you, Gordon. I trust you are feeling better?"

"I am, miss. Thank you for asking," Tony said politely.

Delia's brows drew together. "What are you talking about? Are you ill?"

"One of the other servants informed me Gordon was not feeling well and had taken to his bed. I didn't see him at all this evening." Miss Effington studied him carefully and he couldn't help but wonder if she believed his story or considered him some kind of slacker.

"Oh, dear." Delia turned a worried gaze toward him. "Are you all right? Should you be up and about?"

"I am quite well, ma'am. It was nothing at all." His voice was firm. "No doubt something I ate."

"I did think the food had vastly improved," she murmured, studying him far too closely for comfort. "Very well, then, if you're sure." Delia turned toward her sister. "Thank you again. If you need me—"

"Oh, I shan't need you." Miss Effington grinned. "I can handle Mother. In truth, I rather look forward to it. Besides, the thrill of being the good sister has worn rather thin."

"I thought it would," Delia said wryly.

A few moments later, Miss Effington took her leave.

"Did the"—he cleared his throat—"*evening* go well, ma'am?"

"The evening was not without its merits." Delia crossed her arms over her chest. "You don't approve, do you?"

"It's not my place to approve or disapprove, my lady."

"I see." Delia's voice was thoughtful. She turned and headed toward the library. "Would you care to join me for a brandy and a game, Gordon? I am far too restless to sleep. Brandy and losing a game or two to you should do the trick."

"As you wish." Tony stepped to the door, pulled it open an instant before she reached it, congratulated himself on his timing and followed her into the room. She headed toward the backgammon table, while he proceeded to the liquor cabinet. He poured them each a glass, then joined her at the table.

She sipped the brandy he'd handed her absently. They started the game in relative silence and continued through one long move after another. For a woman who claimed to be too restless to sleep, she was unusually subdued and it was damnably irritating. Indeed, she'd been uncharacteristically quiet ever since she'd returned to London. In his role as Gordon, Tony thought he had mastered the art of patience, and up to now he had not pressed her for her thoughts, but apparently his patience had a limit.

"Have I offended you in some way, Lady Wilmont?" He forced an offhand note to his voice.

"Other than the fact that you have thoroughly trounced me every night for the last three? Why, no." Delia studied the backgammon table. "Why do you ask?"

"You have been remarkably quiet since your return from the country, and remarkably quiet tonight as well."

"I thought you preferred silence when you played."

"Silence from you, my lady, is more disturbing than noise."

She glanced up at him. "Forgive me, Gordon, my mind has been occupied with other concerns of late."

"Forgive *me*, my lady, if I overstep my bounds."

"Not at all," she said firmly. "I have already given you leave to speak your mind. I do not intend to renege on that now simply because I am preoccupied."

"Might I be so forward as to ask if something happened while you were at Effington Hall? Or perhaps tonight?"

"Any number of things happened at Effington Hall." She sipped her drink thoughtfully. "I discovered my family was not nearly as upset with me over my marriage and the scandal it aroused as I was myself. Indeed, I discovered the scandal itself was not as great as I had believed. Odd, don't you think?"

"Not in the least. We are all the leading characters in our own dramas."

"I suppose we are. How terribly astute of you, Gordon."

"Thank you, my lady." He bit back a smile. "Astute is something I strive for."

She laughed, and it was good to hear.

"Gordon," she said slowly, still pondering her next move. "Do you recall when you said I should find a husband and I said I was not especially interested in finding a husband?"

"Quite clearly."

"To be perfectly honest, I don't know that I want another husband. I'm not ruling it out completely, but I'm not sure I want to leap into another marriage. At least not yet. However, I find it's dreadfully lonely to live by oneself. What I do think I want . . . well . . . that is . . ."

"Yes?" he prompted.

"A man, Gordon." She heaved a resigned sigh. "I should very much like a man in my life."

"A certain man in particular, ma'am, or will any man do?"

"I do have a man in mind. Most definitely." She laughed an odd, soft sort of laugh, as if she weren't sure if what she was about to say was amusing or upsetting. "And I think—no, I know he has me in mind as well."

"And this distresses you?"

Her gaze snapped to his. "No. It's really rather wonderful. He's really rather wonderful."

"I see." He nodded thoughtfully.

"Then would you be so good as to explain it to me?"

"You are troubled because you have feelings for this man and your husband has not yet been dead a year."

"Guilt, then, you think?" She sat back in her chair and stared. "That's very good, Gordon. Even, dare I say, astute? I may well be feeling a bit of guilt, but . . ." She paused for a long moment. "My marriage was a horrible mistake. I scarcely knew my husband."

"And you don't wish to make the same mistake again?"

"Good God, no." She downed the brandy in her glass, set it on the table with a thunk and leaned forward. "I absolutely will not make another such dreadful mistake. I refuse to. After all, marriage is a permanent state. And one cannot count on one's husband conveniently dying so soon after the wedding."

Her eyes widened and she gasped in shock at her own words.

"I didn't mean . . . that is, I never . . . oh, dear." She buried her face in her hands. "I am a loathsome person."

Tony stood, fetched the brandy decanter and returned to his seat. "I would say, ma'am, you are not unusual."

"Hah." She groaned, her face still hidden in her hands. "Then the world is full of loathsome people."

"I suspect everyone has some unpleasant qualities on occasion," he said mildly, refilling her glass. "And much of it is relative. What one thinks is, oh, say, dishonorable, someone else might see as a necessary evil. In service to one's country or something like that."

She raised her head and stared in confusion. "What are you talking about?"

"A random thought, my lady, nothing more." He handed her the glass.

"I've always thought of myself as a rather nice sort of person. It's most distressing to realize I was wrong." She shook her head and took a long, bracing sip. "I can't believe I said such a thing. I can't believe I even thought such a thing. What kind of woman thinks things like that?"

A woman who had not loved the man she'd married.

"A loathsome woman." She aimed her glass at him pointedly. "That's who."

"Not at all. A *young* woman says such things, my lady," he said firmly. "A young woman who finds herself in an untenable situation with no means of escape."

"But I certainly did not wish him dead!"

"Of course not." He studied her carefully. "However, it is the nature of mankind to see the benefits inherent in even the worst of circumstances."

She wrinkled her nose. "More astute philosophy, Gordon?"

"One does what one can." As informative as this discussion was, it was not precisely what he wanted. "Might I ask what all this has to do with the current gentleman in question?"

"The current gentleman in question is . . ." She paused for a long moment to choose her words or perhaps sort her thoughts. Tony held his breath. "As much as I fear making another mistake with my life, as much as I realize that, in truth, I don't know him even as much as I knew my husband when I went—when I married him, it feels as if I know him very well."

She rested her elbow on the table, disregarding the playing pieces, and propped her chin in her free hand. "I don't know what it is, Gordon, but he seems remarkably familiar. Something in the way he stands, perhaps—he is exceedingly tall."

Without thinking, Tony slumped slightly in his chair.

"It's the timbre of his voice, or maybe the intonation of his words."

"Indeed," he said, his voice a shade deeper than before.

"Or possibly the look in his eye. His eyes are the darkest shade of brown I've ever seen. Similar to yours," she said thoughtfully. "Although yours are difficult to see behind your spectacles."

"An unfortunate aspect of age, I'm afraid." Tony sent a silent prayer heavenward in thanks to whatever bit of foresight had had him add glasses to the rest of his ensemble.

She swirled the brandy in her glass. "And when we speak together, it feels strangely as though we have spoken before. Long, intimate conversations. I know we've never even met. Still . . ." She sighed. "It is both disconcerting and quite nice."

The last thing he wanted was for her to dwell on why he seemed so familiar and discover the truth on her own. It would be bad enough when he told her, but at least he would be in control of the situation. There was nothing worse in his experience than unexpected revelation.

"There are those in the world," he said thoughtfully, "who believe one's soul never dies. That it is reborn over and over and that we live our lives again and again."

"Reincarnation." She nodded. "My mother has spoken of it. It's one of the many things she believes in."

"It claims those we know in this life we have known before and will know again. It is said to be why people we have never met sometimes seem so familiar."

"Because we've known them in another life? I've never given it much consideration before, but it's a lovely idea. Then those we love in this life . . ."

"We have loved before."

"How terribly romantic. Fated to be together through

all eternity. Although I suppose you could also be destined to make the same mistakes over and over."

"As I understand it, in each new life, one has the opportunity to atone for the sins of the past."

"That certainly is good to hear." She flashed him a grin. "Still, it does take something of the fun out of it all, don't you think? I mean, if everyone we meet is someone we've met before, someone we are intended to meet, it takes a bit of adventure out of life."

"Adventure may well be what we make it, ma'am."

She laughed. "You do lift my spirits, Gordon."

"Then my work this evening is done," he said lightly. He quite liked lifting her spirits, even if he did so as her butler rather than himself. He liked the way she listened to him and the way she looked at him as if he had all the answers to all the questions of life. Once again, he felt the oddest twinge of jealously toward "Gordon."

"Now then, answer me one more thing."

"I shall do my best."

"Disregarding the whole idea that the gentleman and I might have met at a previous point here on earth, at this particular moment in time I need to find a way to explain to him . . . well . . ." She wrinkled her nose.

"That you are not your sister?"

She nodded.

"If I might be so bold as to make a rather shocking suggestion . . ."

"Shocking suggestions have long been my favorite kind. What do you propose?"

"Tell him the truth, my lady."

She grimaced. "That is shocking."

"You would be surprised how very much gentlemen prize honesty. If he is the man you hope he is, if he is at all worthy of your affections, he will be most gracious."

"Do you really think so?"

"My lady, I should stake a month's wages on it."

She considered him carefully for a long moment. "You're right, but then I'm beginning to believe you always are. I did try to explain tonight, but"—she shrugged—"nothing went quite as I had planned. In fact, I don't see any other way to proceed short of handing him over to my sister and allowing her to continue my masquerade. And I much prefer to avoid that.

"Very well, then." She sat back in her chair and lifted her chin in that determined way she had. "I shall bare my soul to him tomorrow night. I shall confess all and hope for the best."

"I am confident all will be well, my lady."

Indeed, he could guarantee it. He would do all he could to make it as easy for her as possible without revealing his own secrets. He would act surprised by her confession but not offended by her ruse. He'd be gracious, charming, even amused. They'd probably laugh about it. It would be a most beneficial and enjoyable evening.

"I seem to have disturbed the playing pieces." Delia surveyed the board, then smiled. "Somehow, I quite like the idea of disrupting the board. Now I suggest we start this game over. I find I am eager to play and, I must warn you, I intend to win. And furthermore"—a wicked twinkle sparked in her eye—"I don't intend to be the least bit quiet."

Chapter 13

My Dear Delia,

As much as I should like to say I am not at all surprised, I must confess to being more than a little shocked today. It is the behavior of our parents that has put me in such a state, an irony I am still unable to completely grasp.

I am not entirely sure exactly what transpired between them, but as I understand it Father has told Mother you are past the age of consent and have earned the right to make your own mistakes. Furthermore, even while I am as yet unwed and residing under their roof, Father has declared I too am old enough to make my own mistakes although I assure you I have no intention of doing so.

Mother took it with a serene demeanor I have rarely seen her exhibit. I can only suspect the stars have changed their alignment in the heavens or

Hades is remarkably chilly or swine shall soon take flight. . . .

"Crimson or eggshell," Delia said under her breath, pacing the parlor and twisting her hands together.

This was absurd. For one foolish moment she had thought focusing her attention on the consideration of a dominant color for the refurbishing of this room, or any room, would take her mind off the fact that St. Stephens would be here at any minute. She should have known better. Nothing short of a herd of rampaging horses in the front hall or the flying pigs her sister had referenced could ever take her mind off of St. Stephens's imminent arrival.

Delia was certainly as prepared as possible. She wore the black lace gown she'd worn to her grandmother's ball and knew she looked as good as she ever could in black. Indeed, her anticipation, or apprehension, of the forthcoming evening had brought a blush of color to her cheeks. In addition, she'd spent much of the day going over and over a dozen different versions of what she would say to him and how she would say it. Pity, at the moment she couldn't think of one.

"Crimson or eggshell."

What if he had decided not to come at all? Surely he would send a note if he was unable or unwilling to come. He was not the kind of man to accept an invitation and then fail to appear. St. Stephens considered himself far too stuffy for that. She smiled at the very thought. The man wasn't the least bit stuffy, and whoever had called him such was no doubt mad.

"Crimson or eggshell. Crimson or eggshell . . ."

Of course, if he had found out she was not *Miss* Effington, he might be too angry to come. Or humiliated. She could well understand how her deception might make him feel like a fool, particularly given his encounter with her parents. Why, he might even believe she was simply playing some sort of flirtatious game with him. Good heavens, the man had spoken of marriage and the possibility of love, no doubt difficult topics for a man to discuss aloud under any circumstances. Her throat tightened at the thought that she might well never see him again.

Lord Mysterious. It certainly suited him. He obviously had a few secrets of his own. Knowing so little about him made him all the more interesting. He could well be the beginning of her new life of grand adventure. The thought was at once exciting and terrifying. Although she suspected St. Stephens would not be content with simply being the first step on her road to experience. And she suspected, as well, neither would she. Oddly enough, that thought was just as exciting.

"My lady." MacPherson stepped into the parlor. "Lord St. Stephens has arrived."

"Excellent," she said with a sigh of relief. "Please show him in."

The footman turned toward the door. Delia moved to one side of the fireplace, a position previously determined to provide her with the most fetching setting, clasped her hands together, affixed the smile she'd practiced in the mirror several times today and realized something was missing.

"Just a moment. Where's Mr. Gordon?"

"Indisposed, my lady," MacPherson said smoothly.

She drew her brows together. "Is it serious?"

"I don't believe so, ma'am. He should be—" MacPherson choked back a cough. "Beg pardon, ma'am. Mr. Gordon expects to be *himself* in the morning."

"Thank you."

MacPherson nodded and left.

Still, Delia should have someone check on Gordon later tonight. She would do it herself, but going to his room might well be going too far. She had already crossed the boundaries between servant and mistress in any number of ways, but she suspected even dear Gordon would consider her appearance at his room entirely too much. No, his dignity would not permit such a thing.

He had become her closest friend of late. Oh, certainly, now that she was back in her family's good graces, she had Cassie to talk to and other relatives would no doubt call. But Cassie and the rest of the family did not live in this house with her, and as lovely as it was to have guests, inevitably they returned to their own homes. It struck her that she was nearly as much in exile here as she had been in the Lake District. And struck her as well that both exiles were self-imposed.

Perhaps her venture last night was far more important than simply a desire to see St. Stephens again. And perhaps St. Stephens was more than her first adventure. Perhaps he was indeed the start of a new life.

"Lady Wilmont?" St. Stephens strode into the room with a smile that reached into her very soul.

"Lord St. Stephens." She drew a deep breath and favored him with her most welcoming smile. "I'm delighted you were able to accept my invitation."

"How could I refuse an invitation from such a lovely hostess?" He took her hand and raised it to his lips, his gaze never leaving hers.

"You do have a way with words, my lord. You shall quite turn my head." She forced a light laugh that belied the turmoil in her stomach.

He glanced around. "Am I the first to arrive, then?"

"Yes, well, about that . . ."

"Forgive me for staring, Lady Wilmont." He studied her carefully. "But the resemblance between you and your sister is quite remarkable."

This time her laugh was genuine. "I have heard that my entire life, my lord, but there are indeed differences between us. We are not exactly alike but rather reflections of each other. Mirror images, as it were. For example, my sister favors her left hand and I favor my right."

"Really?" His brows drew together. "I consider myself fairly observant, and I was certain it was Miss Effington who favors her right."

"You are indeed observant, but my sister favors her left," she said firmly, realizing that if he understood the import of her words, she might not actually have to confess. And confession grew no easier with practice. "It is I who favors my right."

"I'm afraid I'm a bit confused." He narrowed his eyes. "Or perhaps I should say: I fear you have me at a disadvantage."

"Well, it is my turn, isn't it?" she murmured, then drew a deep breath, squared her shoulders and met his gaze directly. "I have a confession to make, my lord."

"You too?"

She pulled her brows together. "Me too—what?"

"Your sister told me last night she had a confession to make."

She waved away his comment. "We are a family full of secrets." Delia turned and paced the room in an attempt to recall her courage. She should have blurted out the truth a moment ago. Should have just come right out and said it. It would all be over by now. She was doing entirely too much thinking about his reaction and her apology and any consequences and—

"Well?"

"Well what?"

"The confession?" he prompted.

"Indeed, the confession." She glanced at him. "Did I tell you I do not confess lightly nor well?"

"Your *sister* mentioned something of the sort." He crossed his arms over his chest and leaned against the mantel. "I must say, Lady Wilmont, I find this all most amusing.

"Oh?" She pulled up short and stared. "Precisely what do you find amusing?"

"You, my lady, are trying to work up your courage. It's really quite charming."

"I'm glad one of us is enjoying it." Her voice was a bit sharper than she'd intended and she realized irritation with him had quite swept away any anxiety. "Now then, my lord—"

"I should probably save you any further effort."

She narrowed her eyes. "As much as I appreciate your kind offer, how on earth can you possibly do that?"

He shrugged. "To start with, I could say there is no need for confession, as I know precisely what you are having such a difficult time saying."

"You do?" Her heart sank.

"Indeed I do." A knowing smile lifted the corners of his mouth. "You wish to tell me the woman I danced with at Effington Hall and met again last night, the woman I know as Miss Effington, Miss *Cassandra* Effington, was, in truth, Lady Wilmont, formerly Miss Philadelphia Effington. And that would be you."

She winced. "Well, yes, that is more or less the essence of it all. How long have you known?"

"Only since a moment ago when you insisted you were the sister who favors her right. I pride myself on my powers of observation, Lady Wilmont, and I know the woman I have been with favors her right hand."

She was at once relieved and the tiniest bit annoyed at the arrogance of his manner. "You have a great deal of confidence in yourself, my lord."

He flashed a wicked grin. "Indeed I do."

She considered him carefully. "You don't seem at all angry about this."

"Oh, I admit I had a twinge of annoyance when I realized your deception. But I am a rational man and there are far and away more benefits to pursuing a widow than a never married woman." He drew his brows together. "Unless, of course, this was all some kind of cruel game on the part of you and your sister."

"I assure you, I would never do such a thing," she said quickly. "In truth, at Effington Hall I was attempting to leave the ballroom when we met because I was not at all sure I had the courage to pretend to be someone I wasn't."

"I'm very glad you didn't." His tone was light, but an odd intensity underlaid his words and her heart fluttered.

"As am I." She smiled. "I must admit, I am most relived. I had no idea how you would take this, and—" She stopped and studied him. "What benefits?"

He laughed. "First of all, it's not necessary to ask your family's permission to call on you."

"Although you already have," she said primly.

"And was told by your father he had nothing to say about this particular daughter. I should have determined the truth of the matter then." He grimaced and shook his head. "You certainly could have saved me a great deal of trouble. I daresay my heart was lying somewhere in the vicinity of my stomach at that moment. Do you have any idea how difficult it is for a man to ask permission of a father to call on his daughter?"

She grinned. "But you did it extremely well."

"And I shall never do it again," he said pointedly. "Once was quite enough."

"It was probably good for you. Strengthened your character, and that sort of thing." She nodded at a decanter and glasses conveniently residing on a nearby window. "Would you care for a glass of sherry?"

"Yes, thank you."

"So, tell me, my lord, are there other benefits to pursuing a widow other than the avoidance of parental permission?" She poured a glass for him and another for herself. "And precisely how do you know?"

She handed him a glass and his fingers brushed hers. A shiver ran up her arm. She took a quick sip and choked. "Why, this is brandy."

St. Stephens drew a swallow and nodded. "Indeed it is, and excellent brandy at that."

She stared at the glass and frowned. "I distinctly told Gordon—Gordon is my butler—to place a decanter of sherry in here."

"Perhaps he simply realized men in general much prefer brandy."

"Perhaps." She shook her head. "He has not been feeling well of late, and even before that I have noticed confusion on his part as to his duties. He's getting on in years and I confess I am a bit worried about him."

"I'm confident he'll be fine," St. Stephens said firmly.

"Yes, of course." Still, she would make certain he was checked on later this evening.

"And when I see him I shall be sure to thank him for saving me from sherry." St. Stephens grinned, and she found it most contagious.

In a few mere moments he'd managed to dispel all her apprehensions. He'd taken her confession far better than she'd ever dreamed he would and brushed aside her deception as if it were of no real consequence. It was extremely gracious of him. She was not at all certain she would be so pleasant if the situation were reversed. Perhaps he was simply a better person than she was. His reaction tonight, coupled with his honorable behavior last night when he had insisted on speaking to her father, quite warmed her heart. He was, all in all, a very nice gentleman, this Lord Mysterious of hers.

She sipped her brandy and met his gaze over the rim of her glass. "What other benefits?"

"Of pursuing a widow?"

She nodded.

"Any widow, or one widow in particular?" His voice was cool, but his piercing gaze brought a flush of heat to her face and a recklessness to her manner.

"One widow in particular, I should think."

"Ah, the benefits to pursuing the lovely Lady Wilmont are far too numerous to mention, but I shall try." He sipped his brandy and considered her in an intimate way, as if he were seeing her without benefit of her black lace. She rather liked it. "As a widow, you have far more freedoms than other unmarried women. You are independent. You have your own house and no need for chaperones, for the most part. You can, in very many ways, live by your own rules."

"Still, there are rules of society one is bound by," she said loftily. "I would hate to court scandal."

He raised a brow. Obviously the man was aware of her past.

"Very well, then. I should hate to court *more* scandal."

"Given your recent deception, I find that difficult to believe."

"Nonsense. I was discreet and my performance was excellent." She cast him a smug smile. "You, my lord, had no idea of the truth."

"To my everlasting humiliation." He lifted his glass to her. "And you will probably never allow me to forget it."

"Never." She laughed. "I admit that I am not overly

concerned with scandal. I have tasted it and survived and come to the realization that no one's opinion of my actions is as important as my own. I fully intend to live my life for my own approval and no one else's."

"As well you should." Admiration colored his voice.

"However, I fear that is easier to say than to do. I'm not entirely sure I have the courage to completely flout the rules of society that I have lived by all my life."

"That too is good to hear."

"Why?"

"Well, I should hate for my future wife to be embroiled in one scandal after another." He shook his head in a somber manner she would have believed, were it not for the gleam of amusement in his eye. "Think of how poorly it will reflect on the children."

"The children?" She raised a brow. "I have not said I will marry you, nor, unless my memory has become as poor as my sister's, do I recall you asking me."

"Why, I believe you're right." He widened his eyes in feigned surprise. "I can't imagine I would have forgotten such a thing as asking you to marry me. Very well, then, I take it back."

"Take what back?"

"You may be as scandalous as you wish."

"Oh, thank you for your kind dispensation," she said dryly.

"Think nothing of it." He gestured graciously. "Indeed, I am quite looking forward to your scandalous behavior." He leaned forward until his lips were a scant inch or so from hers. Was he going to kiss her? "As long as you confine said scandalous behavior to me."

"To you, my lord?"

"Anthony," he said, his gaze shifting from her gaze to her lips and back. "My friends call me Tony."

"Will I be a friend, then?" She certainly wanted him to kiss her.

"Indeed you will." He leaned nearer, his lips a mere breath away from her own.

And this particular kiss would be vastly different from the last.

"Delia," she said, without thinking. "Or Philadelphia, really. But Delia is what my dearest friends and my family call me. If I am to call you Tony, you should call me Delia."

This kiss would be between Lady Wilmont and Lord Mysterious.

"Very well. Delia." He said her name as if it were a gift or the answer to a prayer.

Philadelphia and Anthony.

"Of course, that in itself is highly improper. Calling one another by our given names, that is."

Delia and Tony.

"You're rambling, Delia." His smile was slow and seductive.

"I never ramble." What was he waiting for?

"Perhaps it is time to do a great number of things you have never done." His voice was low and seductive.

"Perhaps." She gazed into his dark eyes and wanted everything they promised. "What do you suggest?"

"Well, just as a first step, you understand, I would suggest a kiss."

"Ah, but I have been kissed before. In fact, I have been kissed by you before."

"Indeed you have." He nodded thoughtfully. "But our kiss at Effington Hall scarcely counts because it was not you I believed I was kissing. Furthermore, it was a first kiss, after all, and you know how inconsequential they are."

"Inconsequential?" Her gaze slipped to his lips. "I would hardly call it inconsequential. I thought it quite significant."

"Its significance lies primarily in its position as first."

"Not as I remember it," she murmured.

"Nonetheless, I wouldn't say it was our best effort."

"I thought you did an excellent job of it."

"I'm flattered, but I can do much better."

"I'm certain you can." She laughed. "And I suspect the second kiss was far too quick to be at all worthy of the name?"

"Exactly. It's scarcely worth mentioning."

"Then that leaves us . . . ?"

"With nothing." He shrugged. "Not a thing."

"My, that is a shame."

"However, it does put kissing me on the list of those things you have never done." He set his glass down on a table, plucked hers from her hand and placed it beside his.

"Why, so it does." Her heart thudded with anticipation.

"And it is past time to remedy that."

He slipped his arms around her and pulled her close. His mouth met hers gently, firmly. His lips were warm and tasted of brandy and secrets and promises. She slid her arms around his neck and his kiss deepened. Her lips opened beneath his and his tongue met and mated with hers. The hot thrum of desire welled within her and she noted dimly it was different with him. It was somehow deeper, richer . . . more. She pressed hard against him, noting the beat of her heart in her ears, the beat of his in her blood. She wanted to lose herself in his embrace, in the excitement of his mouth joined with hers, of his body hard against hers. She wanted . . . everything.

He pulled his lips from hers and nuzzled the side of

her throat. "I daresay that more than makes up for any perceived inadequacies."

She struggled for breath. "I know I am pleased."

"What else have you never done, Delia?" he murmured against her neck.

"Aside from sharing your bed?" she said without thinking.

He raised his head and stared in surprise. "I thought I'd work my way up to that one." He wagged his eyebrows in a truly wicked manner. "Although I should like to put it on the list."

"Oh, you may certainly put it on the list." She pulled his lips back to hers. She wanted to taste of him, to drink of him, to drown herself in the sensation of touching him and being touched by him. She wanted to lose her soul to him. Now. Forever.

He wrenched his lips from hers and kissed the corner of her mouth. "Just out of idle curiosity, mind you"—he kissed the line of her jaw and a lovely spot just below the lobe of her ear—"how long is this list and where is that particular item?"

"I don't know." Her voice had an odd breathless quality. "But I suspect it is moving higher."

His hands roamed over her back and lower, to her derrière. "Surely there's more?"

Her fingers entwined in his hair and she angled her head to give him greater access. "Yes, well . . ." His mouth traveled to the base of her throat and she gasped. "I have always wanted to have . . . a life of grand adventures."

"Indeed." One hand splayed across the small of her back, his other moved slowly and deliberately up her side. "What kind of adventures?"

"Grand," she murmured.

"You said that. What specifically?"

"I should like to . . . um . . ." It was impossible to hold a rational thought and she said the first thing that popped into her head. "Ride a camel . . ." His hand caressed her breast and she caught her breath.

"How interesting." His breath was warm on her neck. "Anything else?"

"I . . ." Her nipples tightened beneath the fabric of her bodice. "Drift . . . down the Nile. . . ." And she wondered if he would rip her dress from her body.

"I've heard the Nile is nice this time of year."

And how she could encourage him to do so.

He cupped her breast and she thought her knees would buckle. "Is there more?"

"More?" Her breath was short and her mind was fogged. "Yes . . . well . . . there could be . . . I . . ." She drew his lips back to hers and pressed her body tighter against his. His arousal was evident between the layers of her clothes and his. And still she wanted . . .

He pulled his mouth from hers. "What else?" His voice was heavy against her ear. "What else have you never done?"

"What . . ." She could barely think. "I have never . . . never . . ." *I have never shared your bed.* Why was that the only thing she could think of?

He drew back and studied her. "What else?"

She shook her head and stared up at him. "Do you want a serious answer? Now? This moment?"

He grinned weakly. "God help me, I believe I do."

"Your powers of observation may not be as good as you think them," she said under her breath.

Didn't the man see he could certainly have his way with her at this very moment? Why, she was barely coherent, thanks to the rather remarkable sensations produced by his lips and his hands. Not only would she not protest, but she was willing and eager. It was to his credit that he did not press his advantage of her vulnerable state. He truly was an honorable man. What a pity.

"Well." She drew a deep breath and reluctantly stepped away from him. "Those things I have never done are far greater than those I have, although I suppose I have never given them any serious consideration before now."

He picked up her glass and handed it to her. "Then this is your opportunity to do so."

"I suppose. If you insist." She took a fast swallow of the brandy, noting the trembling of her hand and a far more intense trembling of unsatisfied need deep inside her. "I fear they may sound ridiculous."

"It's been my experience grand adventures always sound ridiculous in the saying of them."

"Oh? Have you had many grand adventures, then?"

He sipped his brandy in a decidedly wicked manner. "One or two."

"Tell me about them."

He laughed and shook his head. "I think not. Besides, at the moment we are discussing what you want."

"Very well." She thought for a moment. "I have never spouted Shakespeare from a stage."

"And?"

She grinned. "I have never dined with a sheikh."

"Surely there's more."

Now that she thought about it, there was a great deal more. "I have never left England's shores. I have never been sung to in public." The words came out faster of their own accord. "I have never seen my name in a book." She widened her eyes. "I have never written a book."

He grinned. "Is that all?"

"Why, no, I don't believe it is."

"Your list is becoming rather lengthy."

"It's entirely your fault for encouraging me." She

drew her brows together and tried to sort out the myriad of exciting ideas filling her head. "I have never posed for a painting alone, without my family or my sister. And I have never done it without benefit of clothing."

He laughed. "That's good to know."

"Why?"

He raised a brow.

"Never mind." She cast him a wicked smile. "I know why. Still"—she struck a classical pose—"I should think it would be quite exciting to be painted sans garments, like a Greek goddess."

"The Goddess of Love, perhaps?"

"Unless there is a Goddess of Grand Adventure." Laughter bubbled up inside her.

"And where would one hang such a portrait, I wonder," he murmured.

She leaned forward and brushed her lips across his. "In one's bedchamber, I should think."

He laughed and reached for her. She danced out of his way. "Now, now, my lord, you started this."

"And I should like to finish it," he growled in a manner at once threatening and terribly exciting. "Is there anything else you have never done that you should like to do?"

"Yes," she said firmly. "All manner of things, really."

He groaned and rolled his gaze toward the ceiling. "I fear I have opened Pandora's box."

"Indeed you have." She drank the last of her brandy, set the glass aside and ticked the items off on her fingers. "I never raced a carriage through the streets of London. I have never danced in a fountain—"

"With or without clothing?"

"Either. And regarding clothes, I've never dressed like a man and slipped into the sacred halls of a gentlemen's club."

"I know you have shocked me now," he said dryly. "Doesn't every woman have a secret desire to invade those places forbidden to her?"

"Probably, though it isn't something I personally particularly want to do; but, as it is something I've never done and would be a bit of an adventure, I thought I should mention it." She glanced at him. "Or should I limit this list not merely to what I haven't done, but what I want to do?"

"I should think so. One has to draw limits somewhere."

"Limits, my dear Lord St. Stephens—Tony—have no place on a list of grand adventures." She thought for a moment, then grinned. "For example, I should very much like to stand on the top of the world and see the sun rise or set or anything at all. Touch the stars, perhaps. Improbable if not impossible, but a desire nonetheless."

"So." He caught her arm and pulled her close against him. "Now that you've compiled your list of adventures—"

"Grand adventures, if you please."

"What precisely makes an adventure grand as opposed to ordinary?"

"I can't imagine any true adventure being ordinary. As for what makes it grand, I'm not entirely sure, but I'm certain I shall recognize it when it happens. I suppose never having done something before would make it grand." She considered him thoughtfully. "You do realize this is no more than a cursory list? I'm confident I can add many more adventures."

"Where does sharing my bed now fall?" He smiled down at her. "Have I moved up the list or have I been crowded completely off it?"

"That's difficult to say," she teased, and slipped her arms around his neck. "If I tell you you have moved to the top, that confident nature of yours will only make you more arrogant. Besides, you might think me too willing, and I daresay men do not value what comes too easily."

"In this case, such a man would be a fool."

"Yet, if I tell you you have fallen below a ride on a camel, you might be quite disappointed."

"I am disappointed every moment you are not in my arms." He kissed her again with a fierceness that took her breath away, then reluctantly released her.

"I should not want you to be disappointed," she murmured. He had the most devastating effect on her ability to breathe. "Fourth," she said abruptly.

"Fourth?" His brows pulled together in confusion.

"On my list." She grinned. "You're number four."

"Four? I see." He nodded thoughtfully. "That's manageable."

"What do you mean?"

"I should be going," he said firmly.

"Going? Now? Before . . ." She stared in disbelief. "Now I am disappointed. You cannot kiss me like that and then bid me a good night."

"Believe me, it is as difficult for me as for you. However"—he grinned— "it will strengthen your character."

"But we have not yet had . . ." *A glorious passionate encounter beneath the bedcovers.* "Dinner. Yes, of course, we have not yet had dinner. You were invited for dinner." She didn't want him to leave. Not now, not yet. Not ever.

"I find my appetite for"—he cleared his throat— "*dinner* has vanished. And I have plans to make."

"What kind of plans?" She studied him warily.

"Plans for grand adventures." He grabbed her hand and pulled it to his lips. "Part of the fun of adventure is the surprise inherent in it. I should not like to spoil it for you."

"I daresay you couldn't." Her gaze met his and the look in his dark eyes promised far more adventures than any mere list could provide.

"In three days—no, four—in four days I shall return and—"

"Four days?" She grabbed his jacket and glared. "Four full days? Are you insane?"

He smiled weakly. "Probably."

"Four days? It sounds more like a lifetime."

"Delia." He wrapped his arms around her and drew her close against him. "Your life has changed a great deal this past year. Whether you realize it or not, your desire for grand adventure, your intention to do precisely as you wish and the consequences be damned, could cause you irreparable harm."

"I don't care about my reputation or scandal or—"

"I care. I don't want you to blithely throw away what cannot be recovered. Beyond that . . ." His gaze searched hers. "Damnation, Delia, I want you more than I have ever wanted a woman before, and leaving you now, at this moment, is one of the most difficult things I have ever done. But I feel it is the right thing to do."

"You could be wrong," she said hopefully.

"I'm not." He shook his head. "I don't want you to regret anything that passes between us. You did not know your husband well when you married him. I want you to know me before you decide if you will marry me. I want you to be certain you want to spend the rest of your days with me, and I warn you, I plan on that being a very long time."

"Oh, my." She swallowed hard. "I don't know what to say."

"Bid me a good evening." He kissed the tip of her nose, then turned and started for the door.

"Sleep well," she said without so much as a modicum of sincerity.

"I doubt that's even remotely possible." He reached the door, then turned back to her. "I want to share your bed, Delia, but more, I want to share your adventures and your life."

He cast her a wicked grin. "And in four days I intend to do just that."

Chapter 14

Dearest Cassie,

I am in desperate need of your help. You must come to see me as soon as possible.
 Please do not delay. Time is of the essence. . . .

"This is all you wanted?" Cassie stared at her in disbelief. "Good Lord, I thought at the very least your life was in jeopardy."

"It is," Delia said firmly. "Well, perhaps not my life, but definitely my future."

Delia glanced around the large bedroom that had once been Charles's but was now hers. The windows were bare, as was the bed. All the draperies and linens she had ripped off had been removed while she was away by her new, and quite efficient, staff. Only a feather mattress lay on the bed. She noticed there was a tear in its side—more a cut, really—and wondered that she hadn't noticed it before. It was of no significance; the mattress had no doubt caught on something.

"We have to do something about this room and we have three days in which to accomplish it."

Cassie crossed her arms over her chest. "Why?"

"This was Charles's room and I am not entirely comfortable sleeping in here. But it's the largest bedchamber and it's my house now and my room and I need it to be mine." Indeed, even though she'd made the decision to make this room her own, she actually hadn't done so yet. The thought of sleeping in the bed she had so briefly shared with Charles was disquieting and she couldn't quite bring herself to do it.

"That makes a certain amount of sense, I suppose." Cassie studied her warily. "But why three days?"

"It seems like a good idea to simply get it over with." Even to her own ears, Delia's explanation sounded feeble.

Cassie narrowed her eyes and Delia breathed a sigh of resignation.

"Very well, in four days Tony—er, Lord St. Stephens—"

"Tony?" Cassie's brow raised with her voice. "You're calling him *Tony* now?"

"It seemed appropriate," Delia said under her breath.

Cassie stared and Delia resisted the urge to squirm under her scrutiny. After a moment, her sister's eyes widened and she sucked in a sharp breath. "Philadelphia Effington!"

"Lady Wilmont," Delia said quickly. "For whom the rules of behavior are entirely different."

Cassie ignored her. "This man, this *Tony,* he's your first . . . your next—"

"My next what?" Delia narrowed her eyes. "I would choose my words carefully, if I were you."

"Well, I am not you, although you have certainly been

me." Cassie gasped. "He doesn't still think you're me, does he?"

"No, of course not." Delia scoffed indignantly. "I would never risk your reputation."

"Forgive me, I lost my head for a moment. It was probably that incident when you kissed in the window at a party that made me forget how wonderfully cognizant of my reputation you are."

"You needn't be sarcastic."

"I daresay, dear sister, sarcastic is the very least I should be." Cassie paused dramatically and glared. "*Victim!*"

Delia drew her brows together. "What?"

"*Victim*. That's the word I was going to use. St. Stephens is your first *victim* on your path to experience."

"I'd scarcely call him a victim." Delia couldn't resist a satisfied grin. "And if so, he's a most willing victim."

"Delia!"

"Don't sound so shocked."

"I'm not shocked," Cassie snapped. "Well," she sighed, "I suppose I am a bit. I know you said you wished to become a woman of experience, but I didn't realize you meant immediately. With the first gentleman who came along."

"I didn't realize it either, and I certainly didn't plan it. It all just happened. Mother would call it fate."

"Mother would call this all sorts of things, but I doubt fate would be among them," Cassie muttered.

"Probably not, but with Mother one can never be sure. Why, if she believes fate is involved she might not even be shocked."

Cassie snorted.

"Admittedly that is unlikely." Delia cast her sister an apologetic glance. "I do understand your reactions. I would probably be shocked too if our positions were reversed."

"Yes, but you've always expected behavior like this from me, even if undeserved."

"I know it's terribly unfair." Delia hooked her arm through her sister's and led her to the center of the room. "But, as there is nothing we can do about that, let's discuss what to do in here."

Cassie surveyed the room. "I'm not entirely sure how one decorates for seduction."

"You're not decorating for seduction," Delia said firmly. "You're decorating for me. Seduction is secondary."

"Then you are planning on seducing him. Here." Cassie wrinkled her nose. "With my help."

"Oh, I scarcely think I shall need your help." Delia grinned.

Cassie ignored her. "Unless, of course, you already have."

"Don't be absurd." Delia shrugged off the comment. "I barely know the man."

"That scarcely—"

"I know, I know. But I shall not make that mistake again." She smiled at the memory. "He will not let me."

"Really?" Skepticism colored Cassie's face. "How lucky that your first victim is such a paragon."

"Perhaps he is," Delia said smugly. "Perhaps he's perfect."

"A perfect man?" Cassie scoffed. "There is no such thing."

"Perhaps. But he is quite wonderful."

"But you know nothing about him."

"I know enough. Father says Uncle Philip speaks well of him, and he is the duke, after all, and can be trusted. In addition, Tony did insist on meeting the family. All very good signs as to his character."

"I suppose." Cassie stepped to the bed, sat down and

changed the subject. "So, do you want to change the furniture, then? Replace it with something less threatening, I presume?"

"It is rather threatening, isn't it?" It was dark and masculine and harkened back to the days of the Tudors.

"It's very valuable, though." Cassie nodded toward the bed posts. "The carving on the posts is quite intricate."

"Charles had excellent taste."

"And extremely comfortable as well." Cassie patted the bed beside her.

Delia hesitated, then drew a deep breath and settled on the bed beside her sister.

"Rather a shame to get rid of it." Cassie plopped back on the bed. "I daresay it's seen a lot of history."

"I suppose." Delia followed her sister's lead and laid back, to stare upward at the coffered ceiling. "I just prefer not to relive *my* history in it, thank you."

It was really rather nice to lay here side by side with Cassie, staring up at nothing and talking, just as they had done in their youth. They'd spent long hours discussing their lives and their hopes and dreams, what might or might not happen to them in the future. It struck Delia that they had come full circle.

"Can you imagine the sheer number of seductions that have taken place in this bed through the last three hundred years or so?" Cassie said thoughtfully.

"Innocents ruined. Virgins deflowered," Delia added. "Marriages consummated, that sort of thing."

"I'm rather surprised it's in such good shape. It's an amazingly sturdy bed."

"I don't really plan on seducing him, you know," Delia said idly.

"No?"

"Not at all." Delia grinned up at the ceiling. "I plan on allowing him to seduce me."

There was a second of shocked silence, then Cassie's laugh rang out in the room. Delia joined her, and they filled the next few minutes with the kind of easy laughter they hadn't shared in quite some time. The kind of laughter one could only share with someone who knew you as well as you knew yourself. It had been a very long time since they had been together like this. Delia had so missed her twin.

"Delia." Cassie rolled over on her side, propped herself up on her elbow and studied her sister. "What was it like? Being seduced?"

"Cassie!" Delia covered her face with her hands. "You can't ask me that."

"Of course I can, and I really want to know. I think I should be prepared."

"Prepared for what?" Delia peeked at her from between her fingers. "You're not planning anything rash, are you?"

"Not at the moment, but one never knows." Cassie shrugged. "I am as old as you, and while I would dearly love to be married, there is no one of interest in sight. Do you realize, after your marriage, all those terribly dull men you were not interested in turned their attentions to me?"

Delia laughed and rolled to face her, propping her head in her hand, in mirror image of her sister's position. "I am truly sorry."

"As well you should be." Cassie sniffed indignantly. "The very least you can do is tell me what I am missing."

"It was exciting and a bit strange, really, but nice. It's very . . ." Delia groped for the right words. "*Odd,* I suppose is the only word I can think of, to be intimate with a man. But it was . . . pleasant."

"You told me it had a great deal of potential."

"I'm not sure I can explain that either." Delia plucked

absently at the feather mattress. "With Charles, I always knew it was more the desire for excitement than anything else that drew me to his bed. Oh, certainly I liked him, a great deal, really, but I never thought I would actually marry him." She glanced at her sister. "That's terribly scandalous, isn't it?"

Cassie nodded. "Absolutely. Go on."

Delia smiled. "Our surreptitious meetings and even sharing his bed were all part of a grand adventure. The only one I thought I would ever have. I knew by doing what I was doing I might well never marry and I didn't really care. I've always accepted that marriage was inevitable, but it never particularly intrigued me. Probably due to the quality of my suitors."

Cassie studied her curiously. "Why didn't you ever tell me about this deep desire of yours for adventure?"

"I don't believe I realized it myself until the opportunity presented itself."

"In the form of Wilmont?"

"Apparently." Delia shrugged. "I have had a great deal of time to examine my actions and decisions in the past six months. In truth, far too much time. I have come to know myself far better than I ever have. I've realized with every passing year I have grown more and more restless."

"As have I, but it has not led me to throw myself into the bed of the first rogue I meet."

"Perhaps because you have always had the opportunity, whereas I did have not." Delia smiled slowly. "I never thought of myself as particularly adventurous before all this, and now there is so much I wish to do and see and experience."

"Like Lord Mysterious."

Delia laughed. "He is on the list."

"Do you know what you're doing?"

"Not at all." Delia pulled her brows together and tried to find the right words. "It's different with him than it was with Charles. The very clandestine nature of it all, the idea that it was quite scandalous and absolutely forbidden, was what made it all so exciting. With Tony, there is little risk, yet it is somehow more exciting."

"You are still in mourning. Being seen with him would indeed be scandalous."

"Yes, but that scarcely matters at this point. I have weathered scandal and it no longer holds the threat it once did. And I believe he is worth it." Delia sat upright and searched for the right words. "With Tony, a mere conversation is exciting and a simple waltz is an adventure. I suspect even a walk in the park with him would be grand. My heart beats faster when I so much as see him. My stomach flutters and it's difficult to breathe and I want all sorts of things I can't quite put into words."

"He sounds far more dangerous than Wilmont," Cassie murmured.

"He may well be. Cassie." Delia's gaze met her sister's. "He may not be my first step."

"Victim," Cassie said with a grin.

"Step," she said firmly, and held her breath. "He may well be my last."

Cassie studied her for a long moment, then nodded thoughtfully. "Blue."

Delia frowned. "Blue what?"

"For the room, of course. A sea-blue, I should think. Deep but not too dark." Cassie slipped off the bed and moved to the center of the room, surveying the walls and furniture with a critical eye. "I don't know if we can do it all in three days, mind you." She glanced at her sister. "It will cost a great deal of money to do it so quickly."

Delia laughed. "I have a great deal of money."

"Yes, I know." Cassie flashed her a grin. "And I shall have a great deal of fun spending it. Now then, we have no time to waste, so I suggest we visit the shops and make some calls and begin arrangements. With luck and money, we can have workers in here by tomorrow."

"Excellent." Delia beamed. "I suspected as much, so I had Gordon tell your carriage driver he would be needed shortly." Delia scrambled to her feet and started toward the door. "Why blue?"

"It's a lovely color for a bedchamber. At once peaceful yet intense, I think. Besides, it goes well with your eyes." Cassie nodded at her sister, a satisfied smile on her face. "We shall have Lord Mysterious seducing you in no time."

Tony moved away from the door and composed his features to hide the too-satisfied grin that had spread across his face midway through the conversation between the sisters. The very idea that Delia was refurbishing this room with seduction in mind—and better yet, his—was perhaps the most delightful thing he'd ever heard. His plan to make Delia fall in love with him was working far better and far faster than he'd expected. He was good. He was very good.

"Gordon." Delia stepped into the hall, her sister trailing behind. "We shall be gone for a bit, probably until well into the afternoon."

"Very well, my lady."

"There will be a great deal of activity here for the next few days, but it shall all be quite, quite worth it." Delia fairly burst with enthusiasm. "Will that cause any problems, do you think?"

"Not at all, ma'am," he said in his most competent butler voice.

"Excellent." Delia leaned toward him in a confidential manner. "We have decided on blue as per your suggestion."

"I am grateful I could be of help, ma'am."

"Are you feeling better today, Gordon?" Miss Effington's gaze skimmed over him in a speculative manner and he realized she didn't trust him and realized as well she probably wasn't quite sure why. It was wise of her and most annoying.

"I am quite well. Thank you for asking, miss."

"Good. I should hate to have anything happen to you." Delia cast him an affectionate smile and his conscience twinged. He ignored it.

"Come along, Cassie." Delia took her sister's arm and practically pulled her down the hall to the stairs. "We have a great deal to do and we need to accomplish as much today as possible."

Miss Effington muttered something Tony couldn't quite hear, and he thought it for the best. Miss Effington's tone was not nearly as enthusiastic as Delia's.

Mac assisted the ladies in the front hall, and after a brief flurry of activity, the women took their leave. Tony breathed a sigh of relief. He had a great deal to accomplish and could do nothing until Delia was occupied. For one thing, he thought it best to speak to Lord Kimberly in person today rather than reply to his latest note by messenger. For another, he had a number of arrangements to make regarding Delia's *grand adventures* and no time to waste.

He wasn't entirely certain which of those adventures he'd provide her with, although he had some excellent ideas. It all depended on which he could pull off without putting her in a position of public scandal. In spite of her declared lack of concern about scandal, he didn't want to be the cause of any further difficulties.

He ignored the fact that his very presence, both as Gordon and St. Stephens, put her in constant threat of scandal.

"She doesn't like you, does she, sir?" Mac said mildly. "The sister, that is."

"No, I don't believe she does."

Miss Effington was a bit of a problem. She was definitely suspicious of Gordon and, from what he had overheard, was not particularly pleased with Delia's interest in St. Stephens either. It struck him that it might be exceedingly awkward when he became a member of their family.

Of course, with luck, Miss Effington would never know of his identity as Gordon.

"Sir." Mac's brow furrowed. "It's not my place to interfere—you are in charge of all this—but . . ."

"But what?"

"Well, the other men and I were wondering . . ." Mac paused for a moment. "Is it entirely wise to, well—"

"Court Lady Wilmont?"

Mac nodded. "That would be the question, sir."

"Probably not." Tony rubbed his hand across his eyes wearily. "If I were to justify it, I would say spending time with her, whether as her butler or as myself, was all part and parcel of keeping her safe."

"And?"

"And it would be a lie." Tony crossed his arms and leaned against the doorframe. "It started that way, you know. It was all quite innocent and indeed even necessary, but now . . ."

"Now?"

Tony grimaced. "Now I'm going to marry her."

Mac grinned. "Aren't you a bit old for her, sir?"

"Old?"

Mac nodded toward the mirror, and Tony caught a

glimpse of himself with his bushy eyebrows, mustache, white hair and spectacles. He laughed ruefully. "I see your point."

"If I might ask, what does Lord Kimberly think of this?"

"I haven't quite told him yet." Tony winced at the very thought. "I'm not sure I'm going to."

"Sir?" Mac raised a brow. "Is that wise?"

"I don't seem to be doing much that's especially wise at the moment." Tony shook his head. "Have you ever been in love, Mac?"

"Depends how you define it, sir."

"And how do you define it?"

"Well, I've had my share of the ladies. Even spent quite a lot of time with one or another, now and again. But I've never felt the need to shackle myself to a particular one for life." Mac shrugged. "I'd say that's the definition."

"You might be right. I have to admit the very idea of wedded bliss has always scared the hell out of me. But with her, it sounds, I don't know . . ." He straightened and heaved a sigh of surrender. "Grand."

"Sounds like love to me." Mac paused. "What are you going to do about Gordon, sir? She's become quite fond of him."

"That's a sticky problem, and I'm not sure what to do about it, although I shall have to do something soon. We've been here for more than a fortnight now and absolutely nothing has happened, nor has there been any indication that Lady Wilmont is indeed in any kind of danger." Still, there was an odd sense deep in his gut that danger to her was still a possibility, but he was no longer sure if it was born of that instinct he had counted on for much of his life or his love for Delia. "Lord Kimberly's last note indicated it may well be time to call a halt to all this. Neither you nor anyone else has noted anything of suspicion."

"Not a thing, sir."

"Mind you, I think we were wise to watch her in the first place, but at this point I have to reluctantly agree with him."

"How will you tell her?"

"The truth, you mean?" Tony shook his head. "I haven't the vaguest idea right now, but something will come to me. It always has in the past."

"Pardon me for saying it, but isn't this rather different than anything in the past?"

"Rather," Tony muttered, and met the other man's gaze directly. "Still, there's nothing to be done for it, is there? I'll tell Kimberly everything and hope he is a wiser man than I am and has a way out of this mess."

"You know, sir," Mac said thoughtfully, "it shouldn't be all that curious if her new staff was to resign. We have not been in her employ for very long. And Gordon could always claim a distant relative, an elderly aunt, say—"

"She'd have to be ancient."

"Perhaps living near Edinburgh—"

"Edinburgh?"

"Gordon is an old Scottish name, and I myself have an elderly aunt living near Edinburgh. You can use her." Mac grinned. "She's a nasty old thing at that."

"I appreciate your offer," Tony said with a wry chuckle. "But Gordon has already told her he has no family."

"Even so, the point I'm trying to make is, why tell her the truth at all? We resign. Gordon goes off to care for his poor old auntie, or whatever else you can come up with, and she's none the wiser."

"It's an interesting idea, but"—Tony shook his head—"it doesn't seem right. It seems—"

"As if you're lying to her, sir?"

Tony studied the man. "I know what you're trying to say, but I can't compound one lie with another. She deserves to know the truth."

"Beg pardon, sir, but if you don't mind my saying, that's, well, one of the stupidest things I've ever heard any man say." Mac shook his head, sympathy in his eyes. Obviously for Tony's lack of intelligence. "It's been my experience with women that the less of the truth they know, the less they can hold against you or over you. And quite frankly, sir, this particular woman has enough to make your life miserable for the rest of your days."

"Thank you, Mac, I hadn't thought of that," Tony said dryly. "You do put it in an interesting perspective."

"When it comes to women, there are times for honesty, sir, and times when the wisest course is to keep your mouth shut."

"You're probably right. I'll consider it. It's a better solution to all this than I have thus far."

Indeed, thus far his only solution was a vague, convoluted plan to get Delia to fall in love with him on the theory that she would then forgive all. A plan he still believed had some merit, although even he could see its potential for disaster. Still, he'd hate to start their lives together with a deception of this magnitude between them. And he did love her.

Perhaps Lord Kimberly would have a suggestion if, of course, he didn't have Tony shot for mucking everything up.

On the other hand, being shot might just be the best solution of all.

"Is she back yet?" Tony closed the front door behind him. He'd been gone the better part of the day. Mac, as always, was in his assigned spot.

"No, sir." Mac studied him curiously. "If I might ask, how did it go with his lordship?"

"Not well, not well at all," Tony said, and headed toward his room. He wanted nothing more at the moment than a bit of privacy to gather his thoughts and decide on a next step.

Indeed, saying Lord Kimberly had not taken Tony's confession well was something of an understatment. Even now, hours later, Tony was still blistering from his superior's dressing down. He well deserved it, of course. There was never a particular problem with involvement with a women, even bedding her, in the course of an investigation, especially if it provided needed information. But this was not any female. This was the niece of the Duke of Roxborough, who was not merely powerful but the ultimate head of the organization. A man who was already quite unhappy with the use of his niece in an investigation that had stretched on for more than half a year, cost the life of a good man, ruined a young woman's reputation, put her at risk of further scandal as well as real harm and occupied far more department resources than could be spared.

Tony had unwisely pointed out that that first part was not his fault.

Kimberly had taken that bit of information even worse, if possible. However, to give the man credit, he had had a modicum of sympathy for Tony's awkward position and thought a marriage with Lady Wilmont might well be the most graceful solution in the end. At least as far as the duke was concerned. Furthermore, he wanted Tony and the others to continue their masquerade. Kimberly had the same feeling Tony had that something was amiss, even though he too had nothing solid to base it on. Both men had long ago learned the value of listening to that vague instinct.

Nor had Kimberly been at all happy to hear Tony would be leaving the department when this episode was finished. All in all, it was not a particularly pleasant meeting.

Tony reached his room, stepped inside and shut the door behind him. It was small but adequate for his needs, or rather Gordon's, with a bed, chest of drawers and a writing desk. He leased rooms that weren't substantially bigger than this, but then he was scarcely ever there. It had only been recently that he'd spent more time in London than anywhere else. Indeed, he had a town house somewhere in the city, as part of his inheritance, that he'd never so much as stepped foot in. That too was something he needed to think about.

Still, Tony's day hadn't been a complete disaster. He had made arrangements to provide Delia with enough of her adventures to move sharing his bed to the top of her list. He smiled at the thought of what he had in store for her. She would have a day she would never forget. If all did not work out between them, he could at least give her that. A day to remember always.

He sat down at the desk, selected a piece of plain paper and a pen, thought for a moment, then penned a few lines. He folded the note and sealed it. That should do nicely.

Tony adjusted his mustache in the small mirror over the basin, checked to make certain his eyebrows were still straight, scratched his scalp, then dusted a bit more powder on it. He had become used to the cotton in his upper jaw and the spectacles and could even ignore them, but damnation, he hated the powder and the mustache and the eyebrows. At this point, he hated everything that made up Gordon. It would almost be worth it to confess all to Delia and take his chances.

Of course, those chances were slim at the moment, but

he loved Delia and he wanted to spend the rest of his life with her. He'd never given up on anything in his life without a fight, and he was not about to start now.

Tony returned to the front hall just in time for the arrival of Delia and her sister, accompanied by high spirits and a large number of oversized parcels.

"What a grand day we have had, Gordon." Delia's eyes sparkled with excitement. "We have made no end of interesting purchases of fabrics and linens and I can scarcely remember what else. Would you have these packages brought upstairs, please?"

"At once, my lady." He handed her the note. "This arrived while you were out."

Delia stared at it for a moment as if debating whether to read it now or wait until she was alone.

"Do open it now, Delia," Miss Effington said impatiently. "It's obviously from your Lord Mysterious."

Tony glanced at Mac, who was doing his best to hold back a grin.

"Very well." Delia unfolded the note and read it to herself, a slow, private smile spreading across her face.

"What does it say?" Miss Effington demanded.

"It's very brief," Delia murmured, still studying the note. "A carriage will arrive for me at dawn three days hence." Delia looked up. "It's signed 'St. Stephens' and that's all it says."

That wasn't entirely all it said, but Tony was rather glad she hadn't shared the rest with her sister.

"No indication of what he has in mind?" Miss Effington frowned in obvious disappointment. "I daresay that's rather annoying of him."

"I think it's quite exciting," Delia said staunchly. "Part of the fun of adventure is the surprise inherent in it."

"I suppose," Miss Effington muttered.

Delia stared at her sister. "I believe you're jealous."

"Good Lord, Delia, I've never been more jealous in my life." Miss Effington grinned. "You must promise to give me every detail afterwards."

"Every detail?" Delia's brow rose. She met her sister's gaze and the women laughed at some privately held joke.

Tony did hope Delia would not share *every* detail. It was difficult enough to try to win the heart of one woman without another scrutinizing his efforts. Particularly a woman who did not especially like him. No, if this was a sporting event, Miss Effington would no doubt be wholeheartedly cheering for the opposition.

"That's that, then. I must be off." Miss Effington gave her sister a quick hug. "I shall be back first thing in the morning with an entourage of workmen and a seamstress or two and whatever else I can think of."

"I do appreciate it all, you know," Delia said.

"As well you should." Miss Effington's voice rang with affectionate firmness.

The ladies said their farewells and Miss Effington took her leave. Mac and the other two footmen carried the packages upstairs.

"I am quite famished, Gordon, and should like dinner as soon as possible." She grinned. "Spending money takes a great deal of effort, you know."

"I can well imagine, ma'am."

She laughed and started up the stairs, then called back over her shoulder, "Backgammon after dinner, Gordon?"

"I quite look forward to it, ma'am."

"As do I." Abruptly, she stopped and turned back to him, her brow furrowed. "How are you feeling?"

He ignored a stab of guilt. "Quite well, thank you for asking."

"Good." She nodded with relief, started off again, then paused and turned back. "Life is really turning out quite better than I ever dared to hope." An expression akin to amazement or awe brightened her face and his heart twisted at the sight. "Who would have ever imagined?"

"I wish you every happiness, my lady," he said without thinking. "You truly deserve it."

"I doubt that, but thank you, Gordon." She laughed softly and continued up the stairs.

He stared after her for a long moment. She had the look of a woman falling in love. Odd, the realization didn't bring quite the same sense of smug satisfaction it had before.

His discussion with Mac hung in the back of his mind. Tony dreaded telling her the truth. Could she possibly ever love him or anyone enough to forgive a deception like this? Good God, he hoped so. Prayed so. He was betting his future on it. And his heart.

Still, there was a fine line between love and hate, and it was entirely possible knowing the truth might push Delia from one side to the other.

Chapter 15

My Dear Delia,

I left this note for you because I was not entirely certain you'd listen to me otherwise.

I know you are quite looking forward to whatever Lord Mysterious has planned for you, and as much as I wish you well, I urge you, dearest sister, to tread with caution. Your desire to be a woman of experience is one thing, but I fear you are in danger of losing your heart to this man. I suspect you weathered losing Wilmont as you did because love was not involved, and suspect as well you are perilously close to now finding love for the first time.

I freely confess you have surprised me any number of times in recent months, but still I know you well enough to know once your heart is engaged it can be easily broken. I fear my advice may well come too late, but take care, dear sister. Do not let your newfound passion for adventure lead you to heartbreak.

On other matters, I have all sorts of marvelous ideas for the refurbishing of the remainder of your house. I know you are as pleased as I with the result of our efforts in what I now think of affectionately as the blue room, although I prefer not to dwell on precisely what activities may take place there.

Curiosity kept Delia on the very edge of the carriage seat. She sat alone in the enclosed vehicle and had been a bit surprised when she realized Tony had not seen fit to accompany her. Still, his absence lent a delightful sense of heightened mystery to the proceedings. She smiled to herself. Not that the situation needed it. With every turn of the wheels, her anticipation and excitement grew.

It was good to get out of the house, although it was blissfully quiet this morning. The house had been filled with all manner of people in recent days: painters and paper hangers, movers and seamstress, all operating under Cassie's watchful eye.

Indeed, her sister had been not unlike a general commanding her forces in a battle waged with hammers and paint and fabric. It had seemed like a scene from Bedlam to Delia, although Cassie had constantly reassured her the chaos was entirely organized and proceeding nicely. Still, Delia had noted some of her things in the bedchamber she still used appeared to have been rearranged, although nothing was missing. It was probably no more than the work of the new maids, yet she had the oddest sense of something amiss.

Both sisters were surprised to discover Cassie had a true talent for decorating, a realization that spurred her enthusiasm and determination. Indeed the end result was a tasteful symphony in blues and golds, silks and satins. The perfect new bedchamber for a woman of independence. A woman bent on seduction.

Delia glanced out the window and noted they had turned into Hyde Park. The park was all but deserted at this early hour, no doubt exactly why this was her destination.

She'd been truly touched by Cassie's concern, but there was no need for it. Just as with Charles, she was keenly aware of what she was getting into. With Charles, she knew full well her reputation, the loss of her virtue and scandal were at stake. With Tony, quite simply, it was her heart. She knew the risk and was willing to take it for the adventures that went well beyond whatever he had planned for her. And what she had planned for him.

The carriage rolled to a stop. The door opened and Tony poked his head in.

"Beautiful morning for an adventure, Lady Wilmont." He grinned and helped her out of the carriage. This was a distant area of the park near the far end of the Serpentine that she'd never stepped foot in before. Almost like a foreign land. How very exciting. What was the man planning?

"Indeed it is, Lord St. Stephens." She held his hand a moment longer than was proper and gazed up at him. Her heart skipped a beat. "And where is my adventure?"

He tucked her hand into the crook of his arm. "Your grand adventure, don't you mean?"

"I daresay that's yet to be decided."

"I can see you are not going to make this easy." He led her around behind the carriage. "I believe your adventure—and I can confidently say it is in the category of *grand*—is about to begin."

She followed his gaze and stopped short. Delia widened her eyes in disbelief. "What is that?"

"Come, now, Delia, you know precisely what it is." A satisfied grin curled his lips.

"It's a camel," she said slowly.

A very large, pale brown beast stood beside the road chewing in what appeared a most contented manner, but Delia suspected it was a ruse. Nothing that large could truly be that docile. Besides, she'd read that the creatures were not at all pleasant. A grinning stableman held on to its reins and she hoped he had a firm grip. She'd only seen camels drawn in books or in an occasional painting depicting the mysteries of the desert. She'd never imagined they were quite so big, nor quite so threatening.

"Indeed it is." Tony stepped away and spread his arms in a wide flourish befitting grandness. "And he—actually, I believe it's a she—is your first grand adventure."

"Charming," she muttered.

"You said you wanted to ride a camel." He gestured again and she could have sworn she heard a trumpet fanfare in the far distance. "And here it is."

"I see that." Good heavens, one couldn't help but see it. It was enormous. "Might I speak to you for a moment? Privately?"

"Of course." He glanced at the stableman and lowered his voice confidentially. "She's quite excited by all this."

"I can see that, my lord," the man said, still grinning.

Delia stalked back to the other side of the carriage, Tony at her heels. This was absurd. Ridiculous. He was truly deranged if he thought for a moment she'd get on that thing.

She whirled toward him. "Are you mad?"

"Mad with desire, passion." He wagged his brows wickedly. "Possibly even love."

"Yes, well, love is the only thing that would get me on that . . . that . . . that animal!"

He folded his arms over his chest and leaned against the carriage. "Why, my dear Lady Wilmont, surely you're not afraid of a mere beast of burden?"

"I'm not afraid, exactly," she lied. "It's just most"—she searched for a word—"inappropriate."

He laughed. "There's scarcely anything on your list that isn't inappropriate. I daresay, inappropriateness is as much a part of adventure as surprise." He studied her for a moment. "You were surprised, weren't you?"

"Dear God, yes!"

"You said you wanted to ride on a camel. I distinctly remember. It was the very first thing you said. Therefore, I thought it was the adventure you wanted most."

She huffed. "It was the first thing that came to mind, not what I wanted most. And I'm certain I meant ride a camel in the desert, in some exotic country far, far away, not ride a camel in Hyde Park. One is an adventure; the other is a . . . a . . . a joke. You should have realized that."

"But you didn't say desert," he said pointedly.

"As I recall, I had difficulties saying or thinking much of anything at all at that particular moment." She wrung her hands together. "I can scarcely be accountable for what I might have gasped, *unthinking*, in the throes of—"

He grinned knowingly.

She absolutely refused to give him the satisfaction of saying *passion*. "In the throes of whatever I was in the throes of. I barely remember what I said."

"Fortunately for us both, I do."

"Oh, that is fortunate." She glared at him. "You are a truly wicked man, St. Stephens."

"Not at all." His grin widened, if possible. "I am a wonderful man."

"You have entirely too much confidence and you are quite, quite arrogant."

He shrugged in a humble manner she didn't believe for a moment. "I know."

Of course, his arrogance might have been the tiniest bit amusing. His confidence a tad admirable. His grin just a touch infectious. She struggled to keep a smile from her face and crossed her arms over her chest. "I am not getting on that creature."

"As you wish," he said mildly. "Although I must say I am surprised an Effington would be afraid of a mere camel. Why, a fair portion of the world rides camels every day. Men, children, even"—he paused for emphasis—"women."

He was good.

Tony shook his head. "I had always heard Effington women were a distinctly different breed from other women, but apparently that assessment was inaccurate. It's probably just those dangerous rules of society that Effington women flout. Something that, in truth, carries no real risk of actual danger or even . . . grand adventure."

He was very good.

Delia fisted her hands by her side and started back toward the camel. "If I do not survive this, St. Stephens, I shall haunt you for the rest of your days."

His laughter sounded behind her.

She approached the animal and stopped short. "He's shedding."

"She."

"Very well, *she's* shedding. Her coat looks positively moth-eaten. Is she all right? She doesn't have some sort of disease, does she?"

"It's perfectly normal." Tony's voice was casual. "I understand they molt at this time of year."

"Oh, that's lovely." Delia gritted her teeth and continued toward the beast. "You've provided me a molting camel."

"One takes what one can get. It's not especially easy to find a camel in London on short notice." Tony addressed the other man. "Does she have a name?"

"Bess, my lord."

"Bess," Tony said formally, "allow me to introduce Lady Wilmont."

Bess ignored him. As did Delia.

"And Lady Wilmont, this is Mr. Thomason, an excellent bloke. Quite skilled in the management of camels."

Mr. Thomason tipped his hat respectfully. "Pleased to make your acquaintance, ma'am."

Delia smiled weakly, her attention firmly on Bess. It seemed best to keep an eye on the creature at all times.

Tony nodded at Mr. Thomason, who immediately barked an unintelligible order to the camel. For all Delia could tell, he might have been saying sit or stand or kill. Bess reluctantly knelt, bringing her enormous head on a level with Delia's.

Delia cautiously stepped closer. Bess had the loveliest eyes, huge, of course, deep brown and rimmed with long, curled lashes. She looked rather affectionate and even a touch coquettish. Delia was not fooled.

Mr. Thomason placed a set of wooden steps by the animal's side. A small carpet had been thrown over her back and lay underneath an odd but sturdy-looking saddle of leather and wood.

At once, salvation struck Delia. "I wish I had known about this. You should have prepared me, my lord. I would have worn a riding habit." She shook her head regretfully and backed away. "What a pity, I can't possibly ride Bess in this gown."

Delia wore a deep green walking dress, another remnant of her unmarried days. She had no intention of wearing black today and didn't care in the least about the consequences of violating the rules of mourning, one of those dangerous rules of society Tony was so smug about.

"It is indeed a lovely dress," Tony said thoughtfully. "But I think you can still have your adventure."

"Oh, but the thought was really quite en—"

Without warning he scooped her up in his arms and, before she could protest, climbed the mounting steps and deposited her on Bess's saddle. The man was surprisingly swift. "Now then, you sit on it very much as you do a sidesaddle. You do know how to ride, don't you?"

"No," she snapped, then sighed. "Of course I know how to ride."

"Excellent."

He helped her get into the proper position, assistance that brought him into close proximity that would have been quite exciting were she not about to expire of sheer terror. Still, at this point, she was both committed and determined. She would not allow St. Stephens to get the better of her, nor would she allow his camel to do so either.

Mr. Thomason passed her the reins but thankfully kept a grip on the camel's bit. "If you would hold on to the front of the saddle, my lady, I'll get her to her feet."

Delia lifted her chin and forced a light note to her voice. "I am quite looking forward to it."

She heard Tony snort in disbelief but was not about to turn around to give him the scathing glare he deserved. She resolved to do something vile to him, if she survived.

Without warning, the beast lurched to her feet. Delia pitched forward toward the ground, held on for dear life, squeezed her eyes closed tight and resisted the urge to scream. Bess accompanied this movement with a most distressing snorting sound that did not inspire confidence.

"There, now, that wasn't at all bad," Tony said from somewhere off to her side.

Delia opened her eyes cautiously. Tony sat astride a horse beside and a bit below her. "Where did that horse come from?"

He chuckled. "It's been here all the time. You obviously didn't notice."

"I was occupied," she said in a lofty manner.

She wasn't entirely certain why this was so terrifying. She wasn't much higher than she would be on a horse. Of course, a horse's neck was substantially closer. Bess's neck seemed miles away and there was a distinctly uncomfortable feeling of openness. Perhaps it was the foreign nature of the beast that scared her. Or perhaps she wasn't cut out for adventures involving animals.

"All right, then." Tony nodded. "We're off."

"What do you mean, *off*?"

"Well the adventure was the ride, wasn't it? You wished to *ride* a camel, not merely *sit* a camel." He grinned. "The adventure is just beginning."

"Wonderful." She drew a deep breath. She had gone this far, she could certainly make it through a brief ride.

The stableman led the beast forward and she was at once grateful he had not abandoned her and a touch embarrassed. She was an excellent rider. On a horse, at any rate. Still, how much different could a camel be?

"I feel like a small child on a pony," she muttered.

The difference was immediately apparent. A camel did not move at all like a horse. There was an odd sway to her motion, akin to the feel of being on a boat. Not at all unpleasant, really. Delia's tension eased. She might well be able to get used to camel-riding. Might possibly even enjoy it.

"I say, isn't that interesting," Tony murmured.

Delia started. "What's wrong?"

He laughed. "Not a thing. I just noticed she moves both feet on one side of her body and then both feet on the other. Nothing like a horse. It's fascinating."

"No doubt."

A few minutes later, Delia realized it was not the least bit fascinating. Indeed, the rolling motion of Bess's walk, the rhythmic sway to and fro, triggered a most uneasy sensation in Delia's stomach.

"My lord. Tony." She took a slow, measured breath in an effort to calm her queasy insides. "I should like to get down now."

"Why? You look extremely impressive up there. Quite like a desert queen."

"Nonetheless, I have had enough."

"But you've barely gone a few feet."

"Therefore I have now ridden a camel." Delia hated to admit she did not feel at all well and forced a laugh that sounded more like an odd sort of squeak. "And quite an adventure it was. Truly grand. I am most grateful. Now—"

"I don't know," Tony said, shaking his head somberly. "I'm not certain if this counts as a true adventure, as brief as it is. I had planned on a nice brisk walk. Perhaps even a canter or whatever passes for a canter for a camel."

"I do appreciate the offer, but—"

"I did go to a great deal of trouble and it seems a shame—"

"Tony," she snapped, "get me off of this beast! This minute!"

"Come, now, Delia . . ." He studied her for a moment. "Do you know you look rather green?"

"I *feel* rather green."

Tony signaled to Mr. Thomason and Bess shuffled to a stop, then dropped to her knees. At once, Tony dismounted and hurried to help Delia off of the camel.

The moment her feet touched solid ground, her knees buckled.

"Damnation." Tony scooped her up in his arms. "Good Lord, Delia, I am sorry."

She moaned and sent a prayer of thanks heavenward that she had not eaten yet today.

He sat her down firmly on the mounting steps and knelt before her.

"Put your head down and breathe deeply."

"My head is not the problem." Even so, she followed his instructions. After a few deep breaths, her stomach calmed and she felt considerably better.

"Delia?" His hand rested gently on the back of her neck.

She raised her head and looked at him.

His expression was contrite, apologetic and almost worried enough to cause her to forgive him immediately. Almost.

He shook his head. "I am truly sorry. I never imagined you would . . . well . . ."

She narrowed her eyes.

"I thought your color was simply some sort of reflection from your dress." There was a helpless note in his voice that was almost endearing. Almost.

"I do hope . . ." He paused, indecision on his face. "That is to say . . ."

"Yes?"

"You won't hold this against me, will you?" His brow furrowed. "I did arrange it in good faith. I merely wanted the day to be one you would never forget."

"Thus far, you are succeeding admirably. I will certainly never forget this."

His expression brightened. "Then you're not angry?"

She considered him for a long moment. It was extremely tempting to let him suffer. At least until her stomach had fully recovered. Still, she had said she wanted to ride on a camel. He had no way of knowing it was no more than an impulsive comment, the first thing that had come to mind, and certainly no way of knowing the ramifications on her constitution of such a ride. Why, she'd had no idea herself.

"No, of course not." She favored him with a grudging smile. "You obviously went to a great deal of trouble. It was really rather thoughtful."

He raised a brow. "And grand?"

She couldn't hold back a laugh. "Perhaps."

"Are you feeling better?"

"Much."

"Excellent." He leaned forward, braced his hands on the step on either side of her and trapped her gaze with his, his voice low and intimate. "Then have I moved up your list? Am I now number three?"

His lips were a bare few inches from hers. If she shifted forward the tiniest bit, she could kiss him. She could wrap her arms around him and tumble off her perch to the ground with him here and now. Right in front of Mr. Thomason and Bess and anyone else who might happen along. Now, that would indeed be quite an adventure, and most definitely make this a day to remember. Perhaps she needed to revise her list.

"That would depend, my lord." She reached forward and brushed her lips across his in a teasing manner.

"On what?" His tone, his eyes, the very line of his body were entirely too seductive for such an early hour. The man obviously had no sense of decency. How delightful.

She smiled in an inviting manner that mirrored his. "On precisely what adventures you have planned for the rest of the day."

He laughed and pulled her to her feet. "I fear it is entirely too early for your next adventure."

"Is it?" She gazed up at him and quite regretted that it might be too early for any number of adventures that came to mind. "Whatever shall we do?"

"Delia"—his gaze roamed over her hungrily—"you are a temptress."

Or perhaps it wasn't too early at all. She grinned wickedly. "I know."

He stared at her for a moment, then shook his head as if to clear it and turned toward Mr. Thomason. "You have my undying gratitude, sir."

"Happy to have been of service, my lord. My lady." He touched his hat in a casual salute. "If you ever need a camel again, sir—"

"He won't," Delia said firmly, "but you have my thanks as well."

Tony laughed, bade Mr. Thomason a good day, then tucked Delia's hand in the crook of his arm. "I daresay a walk will be good for us." His voice was cool, but there was a definite twinkle in his eye. "After the exertion of our lengthy ride, that is."

"I have forgiven you, Tony, allotted you an adventure that does indeed move you up my list, but I shouldn't continue this topic if I were you," she said coolly.

He chuckled. "Perhaps not."

They strolled aimlessly, in the general direction of the trees near the Serpentine.

"Where did you find a camel?" she said idly.

"Oh, I know a gentleman who knows a gentleman who knows a gentleman."

"What if I had wanted to ride an elephant?"

"I know a gentleman who can arrange that too."

"That's not very specific."

"I should hate for you to know all my secrets." He

grinned down at her. "Where would be the adventure in that?"

"I told you my secret."

"I daresay the fact that you were not your sister was a secret only to me."

She laughed. "Perhaps."

It was delightful to be in his company like this. With a lovely sort of physical awareness between them that heightened her senses, coupled with a comfortable feeling that she knew him well. Perhaps, as Gordon had suggested, it was indeed in a past life. In this life, she barely knew him at all. "What are your secrets, my lord?"

"My secrets? Aside from where I find camels, you mean?" He shook his head with regret. "Because I can never reveal that."

"I understand," she said in a mock serious tone that matched his. "Actually, I was thinking of something a bit more mundane. Those ordinary details of your life you have yet to reveal."

"As my life is indeed both mundane and ordinary, I should hate to bore you."

"At the moment, boredom would be a welcome respite." She cast him a teasing smile. "Perhaps I have overestimated the value of adventure."

"Perhaps we should not have started with a camel." He laughed. "What do you want to know?"

"Everything." Her voice was firm. "I may well end up marrying you, and you yourself pointed out I should know you before I make such a decision."

"How very wise of me," he murmured.

"I do not plan to marry another man I know nothing about."

"Not even if you find me irresistible?"

"Especially if I find you irresistible."

"How very wise of *you*." He leaned back against the trunk of a tree, crossed his arms over his chest and grinned. "I am all yours, my lady. Ask what you will."

"Excellent. Now, as for the questions . . ." She clasped her hands behind her back and paced in front of him in the manner of a scholar. "My uncle speaks well of you, so your character and family are not in question." She glanced at him. "I understand you were in the war? What did you do?"

He paused for a moment as if deciding exactly what to say, then blew a reluctant breath. "I was involved in the gathering of information."

She stopped in midstride and stared. "You were a spy?"

"You could call it that."

"I've never met a spy before."

"Do you find it irresistible?" A wicked gleam showed in his eyes.

She laughed. It was rather irresistible, or at least intriguing, but she certainly was not going to tell him that. "Are you still a spy?"

"Alas, the days of spies in the service of the British military ended with the war."

"What does a retired spy do with his time, then?"

"Whatever one can, really, although admittedly there is not much call for former spies. At least not in this country." He shrugged. "I have traveled a bit since the end of the war and occupied my days with various endeavors. Now I find myself in the odd position of taking up a title I am not prepared for."

"You inherited from your brother, I understand."

"Half-brother. My father married my mother late in life. She did not survive my birth. My brother is, or rather was, some sixteen years older than I. My father died while I was away at school, and shortly thereafter my brother bought my commission. It was exceedingly generous of him." Tony's voice was matter-of-fact, as if this narrative were not the story of his life but that of someone else he scarcely knew. As if the facts he detailed were nothing more than facts, with no more emotion attached to them than if he were reciting the tables of multiplication or listing the memorized continents of the world. "My brother's wife died a few years ago. As they never had children, I was his only heir."

"Were you fond of one another?"

"There was no particular fondness between us, nor was there any particular animosity." Tony shook his head. "My brother and I were not close. In truth, we were never much of anything beyond a connection by blood. I was sorry when he died, of course, but I barely knew him."

"How very sad," she murmured.

"Why?" The question was offhand, but there was a curious look in his eye. "It doesn't strike me as being especially sad. It's simply how life is."

"It must be terribly lonely."

"I've never considered it such."

"Really? How odd." She considered him curiously. "I can't imagine not having family to share your life with. I have always had someone to talk to, someone to share my troubles or my—"

"Adventures?" he teased.

"Most definitely adventures." She smiled and shook her head. "I must admit, I have found it rather daunting not to have people, family, about to share my thoughts with. After my husband's death I spent months with a relative of my mother's in the Lake District. Granted, she was a most private person and not nearly as gregarious as I was used to. Still, she was present should I need her."

"And did you?"

"No. Oddly enough, I wished for nothing more than to be by myself. I had a great deal to consider. My actions—"

"You mean your marriage to Lord Wilmont?"

She nodded. "And beyond that, the reasons I did as I did."

"Love makes fools of us all."

"Yes, I suppose it does."

She bit back the urge to tell him it wasn't love with Charles but a longing for excitement, the lure of newly discovered lust and a desire for passion that decent, respectable, properly bred young women were not suppose to know about or, God forbid, want. What would he think of her? A widow, an experienced woman, could well know all sorts of things and have all sorts of desires it was not acceptable for a never-married woman to have. The fact that she was really no different now than she was before her marriage, save for that she now knew precisely what to expect and was, God willing, at least a bit smarter, was not information she thought it wise to reveal.

Still, she wanted him to know the feelings she had for him were unique in her experience. A strange mix of tenderness and desire she was not yet willing to call love, though she suspected that was precisely what it was nonetheless.

"I feel a bit of a fool myself." He reached for her in a lazy manner and pulled her into his arms.

"Someone might see us here, my lord."

"No one will see us here." He lowered his head and trailed his lips along the side of her neck. A shiver shot up her spine. "No one who is anyone would dare to be seen in the park at this obscene hour of the morning."

"Precisely why you selected it." She sighed, reveling in the nearness of him, the heat of him . . . the promise.

"Exactly," he murmured, his lips producing the most delightful sensations on her neck.

"Tony." She drew back and met his gaze head-on. "I think of the months I spent in the Lake District as a sort of self-imposed exile. Punishment, if you will. I didn't sleep well there and I didn't sleep well when I returned."

"Continued punishment?" The corners of his mouth quirked upward.

"Probably. It wasn't until I thrashed it all out with Charles—"

"What?" His brow furrowed in confusion.

She shook her head. "It's silly and of no real significance, but the point I'm trying to make is that I decided I would live my life by my own rules."

"I believe you've mentioned that."

Delia drew a deep breath for courage. If she meant what she said about living her life as she wished and this man was to be a part of her life, he would have to accept that. And if he couldn't, it was best to find out now. "That includes becoming"—she tried not to choke on the words—"a woman of experience."

His eyes widened and a brow shot upward. "Does it?"

"It does indeed." She lifted her chin, stared into his dark eyes and favored him with her most seductive smile. "As it is too early for my next adventure, I am living by my own rules and moving the sharing of your bed, or rather my bed, up on my list."

A slow grin broke across his face. "I knew the camel was an outstanding idea."

"Indeed, it was the camel that convinced me." She rolled her gaze toward the heavens. "However, there are conditions."

He groaned but kept his arms firmly locked around her. "There are always conditions."

"The first"—she leaned close and brushed her lips

across his—"is that I still receive whatever remaining adventures you have planned for today."

"Agreed."

"And second, it has occurred to me there is something else I failed to mention that I have never done. A failure you may easily remedy."

"And will it count as a grand adventure?"

"Once again, my dear Lord St. Stephens, that will depend entirely on you. You see"—she wrapped her arms around his neck and drew his lips to hers—"I have never been seduced in a carriage."

Chapter 16

Delia was taking him to her bed. Right now, this minute. Tony shifted uncomfortably on the carriage seat.

It was what he wanted, of course, what he had wanted almost from the beginning. Still, he felt rather, well, pursued, and he wasn't at all sure he liked it.

Delia turned from the window and favored him with a smile and an unspoken promise.

Although he could probably learn to like it.

She shifted on the seat to face him. "Well?"

"Well, what?"

"Well . . ." She gestured aimlessly. "Aren't you going to . . . that is . . . shouldn't you . . ."

At once he realized she was not quite as confident as her forthright manner would indicate. His own discomfort vanished.

"Seduce you?" he said with a knowing smile.

She breathed a sigh of relief and nodded.

His gaze met hers. "Seduction, my dear Delia, is not something one does on command." His voice was casual; his gaze never left hers. He took her hand and peeled off her glove in a slow, deliberate manner. "Seduction is, well, an art."

"Is it?"

"Indeed it is." He drew the glove off and traced slow, light circles in her palm. "As such it cannot be hurried."

Anticipation pulsed in the air between them.

"It can't?" There was a sweet longing in her voice that nearly undid him. Tony steeled himself against it.

"No." He kept his voice low, his tone suggestive. He outlined her fingers one by one, his touch barely more than a whisper.

Her breathing was short. "Not even a bit?"

"Not even a bit." Tony drew her hand to his lips and kissed her palm. She shivered slightly beneath his touch. "There is a natural progression."

"Is there?" Her words were barely more than a sigh.

"Indeed there is." He moved to kiss her wrist.

Her voice was shaky. "And next in this progression?"

"I can feel the beat of your heart against my lips," he murmured.

"Can you?" She swallowed hard.

He pulled her hand to the center of his chest and flattened it against him, covering her hand with his. "Can you feel mine?"

She nodded, her eyes wide with . . . what? Not fear, surely. Wonder, perhaps? Love?

"Tony," she said breathlessly. "I think, in the natural progression of seduction, it would be quite right for you to kiss me now."

"Do you think so?" He brought her hand back to his lips and kissed each finger.

She shuddered and licked her lips. "Oh, my, yes."

He slipped his arm around her back and drew her slowly across the seat to press against him. He cupped her chin in his hand and met her lips with his. Her eyes closed and her lips parted and her breath mingled with his. He kissed her gently, easily, savoring her as one might savor a fine treat, resisting his own need to devour and consume. She moaned and wrapped her arms around him and he angled his mouth over hers, tasting of her, drinking of her.

He dropped his hand to run his fingers down her side to her hip. She tensed beneath the fabric of her dress and her arms tightened around him. He shifted and pulled her closer, half onto his lap, and he hardened with her nearness. His hand skimmed down the length of her leg and he gathered the material of her gown in his hand until his fingers touched her stocking-covered leg. She gasped and her mouth grew more demanding.

His hand moved higher, over her shapely leg to her garter. He teased the bare skin just above the ribbon and she held her breath in anticipation. He resisted the urge, the need to take her right here, right now, and forced himself to proceed with a slow, even pace. To heighten her desire and no doubt drive himself mad. Besides, a carriage was far and away too risky.

He skimmed his hand lightly up her leg to the curve of her buttock and pulled her more firmly into his lap. Her hip pressed next to his swollen erection straining against the fabric of his trousers. With each rock of the carriage, she rubbed against him, and he struggled to keep himself in check.

He trailed his fingers over her hip, to the top of her leg and around to the juncture of her thighs and the coarse patch of hair that contrasted with the silk of her skin. She sucked in a sharp breath and wrenched her lips from his. Her head fell back and her bosom heaved and strained against the fabric of her dress. Good God, he wanted to rip it from her body, tear the fabric away and reveal her porcelain skin. Touch and taste and revel in her breasts and feel the soft fire of her body against his. Damn it to hell, why did she have so many clothes on?

He supported her back with one arm and bent to kiss the column of her neck. His other hand cupped her, his fingers sliding over her, wet and slick and wanting. She moaned and his fingers explored the soft folds of flesh swollen with desire and found the small, hard point he knew was the center of her pleasure. He flicked it gently and she cried out and arched upward and he clasped his mouth over hers to muffle her voice. His thumb caressed the point of her pleasure and he slid one finger and then another into her. She was tight and hot and her muscles clenched around him. She clutched at him, and writhed under his touch and rubbed herself against his arousal until his moans matched her own.

Wasn't risk as much an element of adventure as surprise?

He pushed her skirts up to her waist, then pulled her to sit upright and positioned her to straddle his lap. He started to unbutton his trousers, but she pushed away his hands to replace them with her own.

Her gaze caught his and he read excitement and desire and a touch of trepidation in her eyes. She smiled slightly and pressed her lips against his, then laid her hands over the bulge in his trousers. He throbbed against her. She raked her fingernails lightly over the fabric and he gasped. He felt the release of one button, then another, then—

The carriage rolled to a stop. The abrupt cessation of the sound of hooves on brick and the rattle of the vehicle was as startling as any noise.

Delia jerked back and her startled gaze meshed with his. "What on earth shall we do now?"

"Move quickly, my love, move quickly." He drew a deep, steadying breath. "Apparently we've arrived."

"I'm not sure *arrived* is the appropriate term," she muttered, and scrambled off his lap.

He laughed in spite of his discomfort and buttoned his trousers.

Delia grinned and brushed back her hair. "I believe I had a hat when we started."

He glanced around, grabbed it off the floor, started to offer it to her and paused. Her hair was tousled and her face flushed, her eyes dark, her lips swollen. She was the most enticing creature he'd ever seen. Mesmerizing and enchanting and everything any man could ever want. Perhaps he should tell the driver to go on.

"My hat?" she said with an amused smile.

"Of course." He shook his head to clear it, handed her the hat, then grabbed the door handle, as much to secure it against anyone opening it from the outside as to open it himself. "Are you ready?"

She adjusted her hat, drew a steadying breath and nodded. "Yes."

"Good." He cast her an encouraging smile and started to open the door.

She grabbed his arm. "Tony."

"Yes?"

She smiled the slow smile of a woman confident in her actions and confident as well of those of the man by her side. "That was indeed grand."

"Not entirely." He leaned forward and kissed her quickly. "But it will be. I promise."

"I shall hold you to that, my lord."

"I quite imagine you will."

Tony climbed out of the carriage and assisted Delia to the ground. It was surprisingly difficult to release her and he realized this woman had become such a part of him he could not conceive of ever letting her go. Ever living without her. Still, now was not the time to consider the future.

They started toward the house and she hesitated. "Tony." Her brow furrowed with concern. "I'm not quite sure how we're going to accomplish this."

He chuckled. "I thought we were well on the way to accomplishing it in the carriage."

"Not that." A charming blush washed up her face. "I have an excellent idea how we'll accomplish that, but, well, I should hate to scandalize Gordon. He really is rather stuffy and narrow-minded about what women should or should not do. And I daresay bringing a gentleman to my bedchamber before noon—"

"And I'm certain it's the time of day he will object to."

Delia ignored him. "I would hate for him to think poorly of me."

"Delia, I am sure the old gentleman is fond of you, but, well, frankly, my dear, he is a servant and you are the mistress of the house. This is your house and your life and Gordon will just have to accept that you are an adult woman and can make your own decisions."

"He's become my friend, Tony," she said staunchly. "In many ways, my confidant. I trust his advice."

"And he has advised you to do what?"

"He thinks I should marry again."

"We may well have something in common." He started toward the door and realized Delia had not moved. He looked back.

She stared at him with an odd mix of annoyance and exasperation on her face. He wasn't sure what he had done, but it was more than obvious he had done something. Something vile.

"That's quite enough, my lord."

He had no idea what she was talking about. "What's quite enough?"

"You have gone on and on and on about how you *might* wish to marry me or you could *possibly* want my hand in marriage or—"

He stepped closer and lowered his voice. "Are you certain you want to discuss this now? Here on the street?"

She lowered her voice to match his. "I had no intention of discussing this at all, but—yes! Right here, right now."

Tony had been in dangerous, even deadly situations in the past, and instinct warned him that right here, right now might well be the most treacherous of his life. And the most important.

"It is time, my lord, to stop mincing about the subject and tell me, one way or another: Do you or do you not wish to marry me?"

He chose his words carefully. "You said you were not interested in marriage at this time."

She waved away his words. "I am not the topic of discussion. You are."

"I have more than indicated my interest in marriage. I have said I wanted to share your life, your adventures"—he lowered his voice a notch and leaned closer—"your bed."

"Yes, well, now we've come to it, haven't we?"

"Come to what?" Tony considered himself an intelligent man, but Delia made no sense whatsoever. Were all women this insane, or was this sort of madness unique to Delia?

"We're about to blithely waltz into my house and scandalize poor, dear Gordon—"

"He'll survive," Tony said firmly.

"And I want to know what your intentions are."

He shook his head in confusion. "Those are my intentions." He ticked them off on his fingers. "Share your life, your adventures, your bed—"

"Shh!"

He lowered his voice. "And, at this very moment, my intention is to finish what we started in the carriage."

"My dear Lord St. Stephens, it has dawned on me—quite unexpectedly, I might add—that, while my plan was to become a woman of experience and have a life of grand adventure, I am no longer certain I wish to gain that experience or have those adventures with anyone but you."

"And that's bad?" he said slowly.

"Yes! No. Not really, but you have mucked up my plans for my life and I'm not at all pleased because I have no idea what your plans for my life are."

"I thought I was planning on marriage? I thought I had mentioned that?" He wasn't sure why everything he said was coming out as a question. "With you?"

"Do you care to make that somewhat more definitive?"

He had no idea what to say and suspected anything he might say to this lovely lunatic, the lunatic who had captured his heart, would be wrong. "I'm not sure?"

"Very well, St. Stephens. Obviously, the next move is mine." She clenched her fists by her sides. Fire flashed from her eyes. "Will you do me the great honor of becoming my husband?"

Shock hung between them. Delia was obviously as surprised by her impulsive words as he was.

He crossed his arms over his chest and considered her, resisting the urge to laugh out loud with relief and something suspiciously like joy. "I don't know."

Her eyes widened. "You don't know? What do you mean, *you don't know*?"

"Will you take care of me in the manner to which I am accustomed?"

"Most certainly not." She glared. "But I will allow you to take care of me."

"I see. But if I am to accept your gracious proposal"—he paused—"there are conditions."

"I expected as much," she muttered.

"First, all of your *experience* from this moment forward shall be with me." He forced a stern note to his voice and bit back a grin.

She thought for a moment. "Agreed."

"Second, all of your adventures from this moment forth shall be with me."

"I don't—"

"And in return I guarantee there shall indeed be adventures." He smiled slowly. "I shall endeavor to make every day an adventure."

"Grand?" Grudging amusement sounded in her voice.

"That, my dear, will be entirely up to you."

"I see," she said thoughtfully. "Then I find your conditions acceptable."

"Then you, my dear Lady Wilmont, should consider yourself a betrothed woman." He leaned closer. "I would pull you into my arms right here on the street and kiss you until the blue of your eyes darkens to the color of a storm at sea, as I have noted it tends to do in rather delightful moments, but that might create a ripple of scandal, and I suspect you and I might cause any number of scandals in the future. In the pursuit of adventure, of course."

"Of course." She gazed up at him with a desire in her eyes that reflected his own.

"Therefore, it might be best if we resist the urge to begin courting scandal now."

"In the interest of the children?"

"Exactly. Which is precisely why we must go in at once."

"Agreed."

She took his arm and they hurried up the front steps. Mac opened the door for them.

"Good day, my lady, my lord," Mac said. "Did you have a pleasant ride?"

"It was," Delia said with a laugh, pulling off her gloves and shawl and handing them to Mac, "quite unforgettable."

Tony chuckled.

Delia took off her hat and patted her hair, glancing around the entry. "Is Gordon about?"

"No, my lady he . . ." Mac's gaze slid from Delia to Tony and a determined gleam sparked in his eyes. He squared his shoulders. "He's gone, ma'am. Packed up and moved out."

"Gone?" Delia voice rose in dismay.

"Gone?" Tony's voice rose in shock.

"Yes, ma'am. Said something about an aunt."

"You must be mistaken. He told me he had no family."

Damnation. Why had he told her Gordon had no family? For one brief shining moment, he had seen a graceful means of escape that he'd had nothing to do with. Mac had handed it to him on a platter. And Tony was completely blameless.

"Perhaps you misunderstood," Tony said hopefully.

"I most certainly did not. I remember it distinctly. Besides, he would never leave without saying good-bye." Genuine hurt shone in her eyes.

It was Tony's undoing. He shook his head reluctantly. "I doubt that he's gone."

"Oh, no, sir." Mac nodded firmly. "He's definitely gone."

"I'm *certain* he isn't." Tony gritted his teeth. "In point of fact, I'd wager on it."

"No?" Mac met his gaze. "You've no doubt at all, then?"

"No."

Delia cast him a curious glance. "How can you be so sure?"

Tony chose his words carefully. "You said you and he have become friends. Therefore the man would not have left without notice."

"He's right, ma'am." Mac sighed. "I must have mistaken Gordon for someone else. Sorry, my lady."

"How on earth could you—Never mind." She stared in confusion. "Is he in his room, then?"

"No," Tony said quickly. Delia's gaze snapped to him. "Well, the man just said he'd gone out."

Delia drew her brows together. "He said he packed up and left because of an aunt."

"Hat, ma'am," Mac said quickly. "He packed up a hat. That's what he did. To bring it somewhere for . . . for . . ."

"Repairs?" Tony suggested.

"That's it. Repairs." Mac breathed a sigh of relief. "Mr. Gordon packed up a hat to bring it for repairs, and he's gone now, but he'll be back."

"I see," Delia said slowly. "I think."

"I confused *aunt* with *hat,* ma'am. Actually, I confused *hat* with *Pat,* because that's my uncle's name, which naturally reminded me of my aunt." Mac shook his head regretfully. "I do that sort of thing on occasion. I was wounded in the war and, well, you know."

"I think we can overlook it, Lady Wilmont. The man's a veteran, after all." Tony slapped Mac on the back, a shade harder than was necessary. "Probably been through a lot, haven't you, old man?"

"More than I care to say, sir."

Delia glanced from one man to the other. "Then Gordon is coming back?"

"As far as I know, my lady." A distinct note of regret sounded in Mac's voice.

"Good." She studied Mac closely. "I do hope you feel better, MacPherson."

"As do I, ma'am," Mac murmured.

Delia paused as if debating her next words. She straightened her shoulders slightly, in defiance or determination. "Lord St. Stephens has expressed an interest in seeing the refurbishment my sister and I have just completed."

She nodded at Tony, excitement mingling with hesitation in her eyes. She was not as sure of herself, as sure of what she wanted from him, or with him, as she would have him believe. As perhaps she herself would like to believe. There was an innocent, honest charm about that look that caught at his heart. She might well want to be a woman of experience with no concern for rules or propriety, but it did not come naturally to her and therefore took rather a lot of courage. She was quite remarkable.

"My lord?" She raised a brow.

"I shall be along shortly. I wish to speak to MacPherson for a moment. To make certain he's recovered from the effects of his"—Tony tried not to choke on the words—"war injury."

"How very thoughtful." She smiled at them both and sailed up the stairs, her hips swaying with every step, her hat dangling from her hand. The very essence of sensual innocence.

Both men watched until she disappeared at the top of the stairs.

"I believe you have already seen the refurbishment, sir," Mac observed mildly.

"Not like this," Tony murmured. "Regarding that." He drew a steadying breath and pulled his thoughts away from what awaited in Delia's redecorated bed- chamber. "While I tried to keep an eye on the virtual army that invaded this house in recent days, now that they are gone, have you recalled seeing anything of an unusual nature?"

Tony, Mac and Mrs. Miller, along with the other "ser- vants," had made it a point to keep those working on the house under surveillance at all times. If someone wished to find something hidden here, there could be no better guise than that of a painter or other workman.

"Nothing of note, sir, although Mrs. Miller did find a hidden niche in the paneling around the parlor fireplace today while you were out, where Wilmont might have kept valuables. It was empty."

"Mrs. Miller found it?"

"Cleaning, sir." Mac grimaced. "Or that's what she calls it."

"Of course." Tony bit back a grin. "And what of the women involved in the refurbishing?"

The workers had included several women charged with stitching all manner of fabric, coverlets, and cur- tains, and whatever else Miss Effington had decreed nec- essary for the room.

"Again, sir, they did not behave suspiciously, although I must say, that sister of Lady Wilmont's rules with something of an iron fist." Mac grinned. "We could have used her during the war. Probably would have beaten the French that much sooner with more like her."

"The flower of British womanhood. They are a force to be reckoned with." Tony laughed and started toward the stairs.

"Sir?" Mac's brow furrowed disapprovingly. "It's probably not my place—"

"Probably." Tony studied the other man. Obviously Delia's nonexistent butler was not the only one who was fond of Lady Wilmont. Even protective.

"Nonetheless . . ." Mac paused. "We've been talking, the other men and I, and we think Lady Wilmont has been dealt with poorly."

"You do?"

"Between that business with Wilmont and the scandal, and it was in truth the department's fault and we all feel somewhat responsible, and now our deception, your deception—"

"And I do appreciate your attempt to extricate me from that."

"Think nothing of it." Mac met his gaze directly. "We're concerned about Lady Wilmont."

"Oh?" Tony raised a brow.

"She thinks we're servants, sir, but still she's treated each and every one of us kindly. Not at all what any of us expected, and we should hate to see her hurt."

"Yes?"

"We've all agreed, sir, and we well know we might go to the gallows for it, but we're a crafty lot and it's possible no one would ever know. No body found, and all that."

"Your point, Mac?"

"We wouldn't want to do it, sir, but should you hurt her, cause another scandal or break her heart"—Mac squared his shoulders—"we would have to kill you."

"I see." Tony considered the other man. He had no doubt Mac and the others could carry out their threat. Of course, there would be a certain amount of remorse, not an especially comforting thought at the moment. "And if she should break my heart?"

"We would help you drown your sorrows." Mac grinned. "For as long as it took, no matter how many of us should fall in the process."

"I appreciate that." Tony could scarcely chastise Mac. He quite understood the men's attitude toward Delia. Tony would indeed rather forfeit his life than hurt her, although he preferred to live a long and happy life *with* her. "Does it ease your mind to know that she has agreed to become my wife?"

"It does indeed, sir." Mac heaved a sigh of relief. "We should hate to have to kill you."

"Always good to hear."

"When?"

"When what?"

"When will you marry her?"

"As soon as this is settled," Tony said firmly. "As soon as I have figured out how to gracefully end our deception."

"We will, of course, go along with whatever you decide, but have you given any further thought to—"

"Your suggestion of not telling her at all?" The idea still lingered in the back of his mind. But keeping this secret, this lie, forever was, well, wrong. "I have thought about it, but if she is to be my wife, if I love her, how can I keep something like this from her?"

"It seems to me, sir"—Mac's voice was firm—"if you love her, you have to keep it from her."

Tony ran his hand through his hair. "I just don't know, Mac."

Mac studied him for a moment. "I do wish you all the best, sir." He glanced at the upper stairs. "And good luck as well."

"Thank you. I'll take all the luck I can get." Tony started up the stairs. "And a prayer or two would be in order as well."

"Indeed, sir." Mac's voice trailed after him. "I suspect you'll need it."

Chapter 17

"I feel compelled to be honest with you." Delia paced the room, wringing her hands. A rather annoying habit she would have to do something about. "I think honesty is important when one is beginning an endeavor as serious, as permanent, as marriage. Don't you?"

There was no answer, of course. Tony wasn't even in the room. Whatever stories of war he and MacPherson were swapping were obviously going on a bit. Not that she minded. She could well use this time alone. She was rather surprisingly nervous.

Delia hadn't changed her mind about what she and Tony were about to do. The very thought of sharing her bed with him made her ache deep inside with longing and desire and, God help her, love. It had to be love. Nothing else explained why she had asked him to marry her. Why she was willing—no, wanted—to give up the life of independence she'd barely tasted. Give up the adventures she longed for to spend the rest of her days as his wife. She never would have imagined that marriage would seem like an adventure in and of itself. But she'd never imagined marriage to the man she loved before either.

"I should tell you . . . that is . . . explain to you . . ."

Good heavens, even to herself she sounded absurd. Exactly what was she going to say?

Tony, I didn't love Charles and only shared his bed because I felt my life was doomed to boredom and he was an exciting, dangerous and forbidden adventure.

Oh, that would certainly make her appear to be a woman of loose morals. A tart, at the very least. At best, it sounded stupid and naive. Tony had described himself as stuffy and narrow-minded, and while he certainly hadn't shown much of that side of himself— indeed, there was nothing the least bit stuffy about their carriage ride—he might well be stuffy and narrow-minded when it came to the woman he planned to marry.

Of course, he hadn't so much as flinched when she'd said she planned on becoming a woman of experience. She drew her brows together thoughtfully. How odd. Still, he no doubt assumed she already had a fair amount of experience. And how on earth was she going to explain that?

"Explain what?"

Delia whirled around. Tony lounged in the open doorway, arms folded over his chest, annoyingly knowing smile on his face.

"How long have you been there?"

"Long enough to hear you say something about how you should explain something to me. Do go on."

"It's nothing of significance, really." She cast him her brightest smile and opened her arms wide. "What do you think of the room?"

"It's blue." He stepped into the room, closed the door

firmly behind him and started toward her, loosening his cravat. "It matches your eyes."

"Exactly." She tried to ignore the fact that he continued toward her. Or the fact that he had pulled his cravat free and dropped it on the lone chair in the room. The oddest feeling of panic welled up inside her. "I quite like the fabric Cassie picked out, although I certainly helped in the selection, mind you, as well as the paper on the walls, and—"

"You're rambling, Delia." There was an intimate tone to his words. As if he were really saying something altogether different.

You want me, Delia.

He slipped off his jacket and tossed it onto the back of the chair.

"I never ramble," she murmured, stepping out of his reach. She did want him, wanted this, more than she had ever wanted anything, but couldn't quite quell a shaky sort of trepidation. And the certainty that this, that Tony, was much more important than anything ever before.

"You are rambling now." He sat on the edge of the chair and pulled off his boots.

You want me to touch you, caress you.

She ignored him. "I particularly like the touches of gold here and there. Not too much, mind you, but just enough to give it all a certain ambiance. A sense of—"

"Seduction?" He stood, pulled off his shirt and let it drop to the floor. His shoulders were rather impressively broad, his arms and chest firmly muscled, his waist nicely narrow. She swallowed hard.

Make you feel what you have never felt before.

Delia continued as if she hadn't noticed he was only half dressed. "Still, even with all that we've done, the room does seem exceedingly large and quite bare. Of course, it's not completely finished. Much of the furniture has still not arrived."

"With the exception"—his smile was entirely too wicked—"of the bed. It's quite impressive."

"Impressive?" She turned toward the bed and at once realized her mistake.

The bed was indeed impressive. Delia hadn't realized how imposing the French-styled piece was, with its deep blue and gold canopy and silken hangings, until now. Compared to Charles's bed it hadn't seemed at all massive, but at this very moment it was enormous, immense, endless. An undulating sea of froth and satin beckoning the unsuspecting to a voyage of carnal delights. It was an apparition of indecency. A vision of decadence. A setting for seduction.

"*Quite* impressive." His voice sounded close behind her.

"Really? I hadn't noticed."

So close she swore she could feel the heat of his body radiating from him in waves designed to melt her very bones. So close she could feel the movement of his chest with every breath. So close if she turned, she'd be pressed right against him.

"It creates an illusion." He rested his hands lightly on her shoulders.

"An illusion?" She could barely get out the words. His fingers drifted down her arms and back to her shoulders, in a slow, dreamlike way that was at odds with the strong morning light streaming in the windows.

"Of perfection, perhaps." He brushed his lips lightly across the back of her neck. She closed her eyes and let her head fall forward.

"Blue and gold are perfect?" she whispered, holding her breath, reveling in the feel of his mouth on her skin.

"Your eyes are blue." There was a slight tug at the

neckline of her dress and she knew he had untied the top tape. He unfastened the line of buttons running from neck to waistline so smoothly she felt nothing more than the loosening of her bodice, then he expertly pulled free the bottom tape. He had obviously done this before. "And your hair is gold."

He pushed the dress open and a slight breeze from the window whispered across her back. She shivered, as much with delight as with the waft of air.

He kissed the back of her neck and trailed his lips to nibble on one exposed shoulder. He pushed her dress lower down her arms until she impatiently shrugged it free, and it drifted to a puddle at her feet, leaving her clad in nothing but shift and stockings and shoes.

Gently, he drew her back against him. His naked chest was hot and firm against her bare skin and she could feel his arousal pressed hard against her. She rested her head on his chest, tilting it to the side, and he obligingly kissed the crook of her neck and tasted the curve of her shoulder. He slipped his hands under her arms to wrap around her waist and pulled her closer to him. She was aware of nothing save the feel of his body next to hers and the touch of his mouth on her skin and the broad span of his hands splayed across her stomach.

He moved his hands upward slowly to lightly cup her breasts, his fingers warm through the insubstantial fabric of her shift. She held her breath. His thumbs circled her nipples and they tightened under his touch.

For a moment, or forever, they stood, her back pressed against his chest, his hands in a gentle exploration. Every nerve in her body was alive with the remarkable sensations he produced. His touch was light, tender, almost reverent and quite, quite expert. Her senses soared. She could feel the beat of her heart and the beat of his against her. She could hear the slight rasp of her breath and the controlled evenness of his. With eyes closed, she saw, in her mind's eye, shades of billowing blues and golds, a visual accompaniment to his caress. Glorious. And not nearly enough.

He stepped back and turned her around. She opened her eyes to meet his gaze and her breath caught. His eyes simmered dark and deep with desire and emotion. He opened his arms and she stepped into his embrace, reveling in the feel of her body at last pressed against his. She lifted her head and her lips met his in a kiss long and intimate and as intoxicating as brandy.

He picked her up and carried her to the bed, laid her down, then slowly removed her shoes. She never imagined such a simple thing could be quite so intense. Or intimate. He untied her garters and rolled her stockings off one by one in the same slow, sensual manner he had removed her glove in the carriage. She drew a deep shuddering breath.

He started unbuttoning his trousers and she realized if she was to say anything at all, now was the time.

"Tony?"

His dark gaze met hers. "Delia."

She propped herself up on her elbows and drew a deep breath. "I fear the moment has come for complete honesty."

His hands stilled on his buttons. "Now?"

"It's more of a confession, really, and you know I don't do them well."

"Now?" His voice rose

"It's best, I think," she said weakly. "I don't want you to be, well, disappointed."

He snorted in disbelief. "I could not possibly, ever be disappointed with you. With us."

"I'm not quite as"—she sat up and studied him—"experienced as you might think."

"You were married," he said slowly.

"Yes, well, not for very long or very"—she winced—"often."

"But you have . . . that is you did . . ."

"Of course I have, and yes I did. I don't know how to explain this," she said under her breath.

"Quickly would be nice," he muttered.

Delia glared at him. "This is rather difficult for me, and more than a little embarrassing, and that is rather selfish of you."

"I feel rather selfish at the moment. You can scarcely blame me. I had no idea we would be talking at this point. Frankly, that was not my intention."

"It was not my intention either, but I do want to be honest with you." Her gaze searched his. "I fully plan on you being my last husband, and it doesn't seem right to start a marriage or anything else without a certain amount of honesty."

"A certain amount of honesty has its merits, perhaps," he said grudgingly.

"I think so. And I think you should know"—she drew a deep breath— "Charles and I, well, we didn't—"

"You didn't?" Shock colored his face.

"Do be quiet and listen to me. We did, but"—she held her breath—"it was only once."

"Once?" His voice rose. "What do you mean, *once*?"

"I mean once. I think once is rather self-explanatory. Once. One time. One night. One, um, adventure." She waved helplessly at the bed. "Once."

"But you were married for, what? Nearly a week?"

"Fours days, actually, before he died."

"And he didn't . . . you didn't . . ." His brow furrowed in complete confusion, as if this were a concept he could not fully grasp. "Once?"

She nodded.

"Good God, when we've been married for four days,

you can be assured we will have done it more than once. In truth, I should think by our fourth day of marriage we will have lost count of precisely how many times we have done it."

She smiled in spite of her embarrassment. "What a terribly sweet thing for you to say."

"Perhaps, but it's no more than the truth."

"But"—she drew a deep breath—"I don't think I'm very good at it. You might not like it. Or, rather, like me."

He stared at her in disbelief, then burst into laughter.

She slipped off the bed to her feet, planted her hands on her hips and glared. "This is not funny!"

"Oh, but, my love, it is." He sniffed back a laugh. "It may well be the funniest thing I have ever heard."

"Tony!"

"Not like you?" He shook his head. "If that's true, Wilmont was either insane or an idiot or both."

"That too is a very nice thing to say, but—"

He laughed. "It's not just nice, it's a fact." He reached out and pulled her into his arms. "Now, as much as I would prefer to put off discussion of anything short of how intriguing I find the curve of your neck or how inviting I think it is that you hold your breath when I touch you in a certain way—"

"Tony!" She laughed in spite of herself.

"And despite the fact that I want nothing more than to carry you to that bed and disprove your fears that I shall not like you"—he nuzzled the side of her neck—"over and over again, I suspect we cannot continue until you tell me everything."

"There really isn't much to tell." Although it was surprisingly easy to talk with his arms around her. "I shared Charles's bed, we were married—"

"Afterwards?" His brow rose.

"Yes." She lifted her chin and stared into his eyes.

"Afterwards," she said firmly. "I assume you will not comment on that, as you and I are not yet wed and in our situation too, marriage will be afterwards."

"I wasn't going to say a word." He widened his eyes in an expression of innocence. "And I'm offended that you think I would."

"My apologies." She pulled out of his arms. "As I was saying . . ." She paused to gather her thoughts and her courage, wrapped her arms around herself and paced. She had not admitted this to anyone, not even to her sister. "After we wed, he no longer seemed at all interested in me. He was preoccupied, brusque in his manner, even somewhat cold. He was away more than he was home."

"And you thought it was because your night together was disappointing."

"Yes. No. I don't know." She heaved a heartfelt sigh and looked at him. "It sounds absurd, I know, but I did think that at first, and while sharing his bed was not as, um, glorious as I'd assumed it would be, it was not . . . unpleasant."

Tony bit back a grin. "How interesting."

"I did think it had a great deal of potential," she murmured.

"Indeed it does," he said under his breath.

"I thought perhaps it was because there was no love between us—"

"You did not love him, then?" His voice was matter-of-fact, but there was an intense gleam in his eye.

"I know it's dreadful of me, and you shall think me terribly shallow, but no." Delia squared her shoulders and met his gaze. "I did not. Nor did he love me, although I did think we liked one another. At least at first." She shook her head. "It was all such a dreadful mistake, and every day of our marriage that passed I knew it more and more, but . . ."

"You would not have wished him dead," he said quietly.

"Never." She sighed. "And for a long time I blamed myself. As if his death were a direct result of something I had done. Some sort of punishment, a dire fate, perhaps, for not being what he wanted. Or driving him away. Or marrying him at all. Or not loving him."

"It wasn't your fault. Not his manner, nor his death."

"I know," she said firmly. "But it took me months to accept that, and I'm not sure I fully did until I returned to this house. His house and now my house."

"I see." His voice was thoughtful.

"So." She studied him carefully. "Do you still want to marry me?"

"I don't know."

Her heart caught. "Very well, I—"

"I prefer to withhold judgment until . . . afterwards." His voice was cool, but there was a teasing gleam in his eye. "Just in case you are indeed a dis—"

"Tony!"

"I would certainly hate to agree to marriage, only to find out—"

"You are a wicked, wicked man, Lord St. Stephens."

"You've mentioned that, and you should be careful, because I'm beginning to believe it."

"As well you should believe it," she snapped. "I have poured out my heart to you. Told you all sorts of things I've never told—"

"Did you know when you stand in that particular spot, with the light from the windows behind you, your shift, which is, I might add, exceedingly sheer, becomes essentially transparent?"

"Good heavens." She gasped and at once turned her back to him. "The least you can do is not look."

"Don't be absurd. I intend to do a great deal of looking. And I might add that view is nice as well."

"If you were a true gentleman you wouldn't look," she said over her shoulder.

"Damnably lucky for you I'm not." Before she could protest, he scooped her up in his arms and carried her back to the bed. "I am a newly titled lord without the vaguest idea how to be a newly titled lord, therefore the phrase 'true gentleman' is probably questionable at best."

He tossed her on the bed. "Besides, you said it yourself." He leaned over the bed, bracing one hand on either side of her. "I am a wicked, wicked man."

"*You* said you were stuffy and narrow-minded."

He grinned. "I lied."

"I'm not certain if I believe you." She reached up, wrapped her hands around his neck and pulled him onto the bed. "Perhaps you should prove it."

"Perhaps I should."

He gathered her into his arms and drew her close until his lips met hers. Her lips parted and a sigh of sheer anticipation whispered through them. His mouth pressed against her harder and she responded in kind, the desire that had ignited between them in the carriage once more flaring to life. Need swept through her with an urgency she'd never known. She reveled in the feel of her mouth against his, demanding and greedy and insistent.

She ran her hand over the curve of his shoulder, his flesh hot and firm and enticing. Delia dragged her lips from his and along his jaw to the strong line of his neck. He stilled beneath her touch and her excitement heightened. She tasted the hollow of his throat, trailed her tongue along his collarbone and nipped at his shoulder.

Her hand caressed the flat, hard planes of his chest and marveled at the strength of his body beneath her touch. His hands moved restlessly on her back. She traced a light circle with her fingertips around the slight ridge of his nipple, then shifted and leaned closer to flick it with her tongue, and he gasped.

She rained kisses on his chest and her hand drifted over his stomach and lower still to his trousers. She ran her fingernails lightly over the straining fabric. He drew a shuddering breath. She unbuttoned his trousers with a growing urgency. She wanted to feel him, see him, touch him.

"Wait." He gasped and pushed her away, then slid off the bed and removed his trousers.

For a moment, she could do nothing more than stare. The bedding with Charles had been in the dark of night.

Tony was rather magnificent and compared quite favorably with any statue of a Greek god she'd ever seen. His legs were long and lean, his shoulders broad, his stomach flat. And where his fig leaf would have been he was most impressive indeed.

"Delia?" His brow furrowed. "Are you all right?"

"I don't know." She should have been embarrassed, at least a little, but she felt nothing of the kind. Only a warm flush of anticipation and perhaps possession. She scrambled to her feet, pulled her shift off over her head, tossed it aside and cast him a tremulous smile. "Are you coming back?"

In less than a heartbeat she was in his arms, her body pressed tight against his, his arousal hard between them. They tumbled backward onto the bed and any restraint between them vanished in a frenzy of passion. She wanted to taste him, touch him, join her body with his. His hands, his mouth, his tongue were everywhere, seeking every part of her.

He took her breast in his mouth and her breath caught. With tongue and teeth he teased her, toyed with her, until her existence narrowed to nothing more than physical sensation. All she knew, all she wanted to know, was the feel of his mouth on flesh overly heated and far too susceptible to his touch. She wondered if anyone had ever died from pure pleasure. And doubted as well if they'd cared.

His hand caressed her stomach and drifted lower to the curls between her legs and she arched upward to meet his hand and urge him on. His fingers slipped over her and she moaned and reached down to find his arousal and grasped it in her hand. He drew a ragged breath. It was hot beneath her palm and hard as stone and covered in silk. His fingers moved over the too-sensitive spot he had discovered in the carriage and she gasped. He caressed her in an ever-increasing rhythm and her breath came short and fast. Without thinking, her hand moved over his erection, matching the rhythm he set. Tension wound tighter and tighter within her, as if she were straining toward something unreachable, yearning for something unobtainable. She noted an odd, whimpering sound and realized it was her.

Abruptly he stopped and, before she could protest, shifted to kneel over her, settling between her knees. He paused, poised above her and gazed into her eyes. "Delia, I—"

"Tony." She sighed with yearning and reached between them to guide him to her.

He slid into her with a slow, firm ease. Perfect and right. As if he were made just for her. Meant just for her. For a long moment he lay unmoving inside her and she marveled at the odd, lovely sensation of connection and fullness. Then he shifted, withdrew slightly and returned, pressing deeper. And again he slid back, then forward, and again and again, every stroke deeper, harder, more intense. She wrapped one leg around his and thrust upward to meet him.

His rhythm increased. She tightened around him. She matched his every move with a need of her own that surged from somewhere inside her. He thrust into her and she arched her hips upward to meet him. It was a dance of sorts, she acknowledged dimly. And in this dance too they moved together as perfectly as they had in the ballroom. As if they had joined together like this before or always or forever. He plunged into her harder and faster. His heat spread outward from his body to hers, surrounding her, engulfing her. She moaned with the unbearable joy of it and the unrelenting ache of desire.

He was pushing her, pulling her, dragging her unresisting to some point she wanted, she yearned for, she would die for but couldn't reach. The summit of an unknown peak, the top of a newfound world, the very stars above.

Without warning, the tension building ever higher and hotter within her shattered in glorious release. She cried out and her body jerked upward and waves of sheer sensation rushed from their joining to ignite every nerve in her body with an ecstasy that ripped away her breath and hammered at her heart and washed away her mind with colors of blue and gold. And clutched at her soul.

He gripped her tighter and thrust again and again until he groaned and his body shuddered and the warmth of his own release filled her. And she clung to him until he lay quiet on top of her and the trembling of her own body eased. And held him for long moments more.

At last he raised himself up and stared down at her, a bemused smile on his face. "Well . . ."

"Good heavens." She struggled to catch her breath. "That was indeed . . ."

He gently pulled out of her and she noted a moment of

regret at the loss of him. He shifted to her side and propped his head in his hand. "Yes?"

"Oh, my. It was . . ." She trailed a tentative finger over his chest.

"Glorious?"

She had the oddest desire to giggle. "If I tell you, it will simply go to your head."

"Probably." He grinned. "Have I told you that I like your bed and your room?"

"As well you should." She laughed. "It was decorated with your seduction in mind."

"It worked exceedingly well," he murmured.

"Then am I to assume you were not disappointed?"

"You can certainly assume that. And can I assume as well I—or, rather, this—lived up to its"—he cleared his throat—"*potential*?"

"Most definitely. Although . . ." She stared at him for a moment, then cast him a smile as wicked as any of his. "I suspect the potential might be far greater than I ever imagined." She drew his mouth back to hers. "And I think it's in the best interest of grand adventure to find out."

Chapter 18

"Don't you think a blindfold is a rather excessive measure?" Delia called upward, clinging to Tony's hand for both support and guidance. They were climbing what were apparently endless flights of stairs: some curved, some spiral, some winding. At least, that had been her impression so far. "I feel quite ridiculous."

"Nonsense, you look rather intriguing. To me, at any rate, although admittedly there might well be men who don't appreciate a woman in a blindfold," Tony said from somewhere slightly above her. "No, wait, I can't imagine any man not enjoying the illusion of a woman under his control. Not one as stubborn and opinionated as you anyway."

"I'm so glad one of us is enjoying this."

"Nonsense, Delia, you're enjoying it as well. Not knowing where you are is adding to the excitement." He squeezed her hand. "Besides, this particular adventure won't work if it's not a surprise."

"But surely people have noticed a man dragging along a woman in a blindfold. There can't possibly be that many women in blindfolds on the streets of London."

"You'd be surprised." Tony chuckled. "However, I did take precautions to limit the possibility of attracting undue attention. You are wearing an especially deep brimmed hat as per my request—"

"Anything for adventure," she murmured.

"And your blindfold resembles bandages; I was most solicitous, I might add; and we went directly from the carriage to—"

"To . . . what?" She adopted as innocent a manner now as she had the last dozen or so times she'd asked.

He laughed. "I will say this for you, you are a stubborn creature. Surely you didn't expect me to tell you this close to the end?"

"One never knows what to expect during an adventure," she said loftily.

"As I was saying, thanks to the lateness of the hour, we have not encountered many people at all, save for the excellent gentlemen I arranged this particular adventure with and the equally helpful gentleman who is guiding our way with a lantern even now. I have explained to them you have had something of an accident." He stopped, his voice lowered, and drew closer. "With a camel. Very tragic. You have their sympathy."

"I quite deserve their sympathy." She laughed.

All in all, his refusal to tell her what was afoot did indeed heighten her anticipation. Save for the fact that they were never going to reach the top of whatever they were climbing, not knowing and even not being able to see added to her excitement.

She smiled to herself. Not that he needed to put either of them through this kind of exertion for either excitement or adventure. He had already provided a great deal of both today.

"What are you grinning about?"

"You do realize, if I put my mind to it, I could determine exactly where we are by simply keeping track of the number of steps we've climbed and then proceed to eliminate structures that do not conform to my calculations?"

"I daresay you could. So have you been keeping track of the steps, then?"

"I didn't say I have, I said I could have."

Delia was, in fact, a touch confused and far too excited to do anything rational like keep count of endless numbers of steps. Besides, she hadn't thought of it until they'd already climbed a considerable distance. She had noted, though, that it wasn't a continuous climb. Their upward trek would stop briefly for progress on a level surface, then they'd head heavenward again. She was certain at one point they'd been on a spiral stair and right now negotiated a steep and winding stair. Still, it was difficult to give serious consideration to the question of where she was when she was intent on climbing without mishap while not panting for breath like an overexcited hound in the process.

By the curve and the climb, she at first suspected he might have taken her up in a lighthouse, but, even though they drove for a good hour before reaching their destination, she thought it was simply a ruse and was confident they had not left the city. Therefore, they had to be in a building within the confines of London. A very tall building. One conducive to never ending stairs, winding and twisting upward. Toward the heavens.

The heavens. Of course. The answer struck her and she was rather annoyed she hadn't thought of it before. It had to be St. Paul's. She was aware one could climb high up to a gallery on the outside of the dome, but she had never had occasion or the desire to do so. The only remaining question was why Tony was taking her here. For the life of her, she could not remember what adventures she had blurted out to him in the heat of passion. Although, in truth, it really didn't matter. Nor did this morning's encounter with Bess. The mere fact that the man was willing to go to such efforts to arrange for her to do things she had never done was the most wonderful thing anyone had ever done for her. The most wonderful thing she could ever imagine anyone doing for her. And quite obviously the act of a man in love.

"We're here." Tony's voice was light, but she suspected he was as relieved to at last reach their destination as she.

She heard the sound of a heavy door being pulled open and a cool breeze wafted over her.

"There you are, my lord," the guide said, his voice accompanied by a jingle of keys. "I'll stay behind here but will be right by the door if you need me." The man lowered his voice but not quite enough to prevent her from hearing. "Begging your pardon, sir, but is it wise, do you think, to take a lady who can't see to a spot like this?"

"It's something she's never done and I promised I would bring her here long before"—regret sounded in Tony's voice—"the accident."

"But it'd be my fault were she to fall, sir. And not being able to see and all, she could tumble right over the railing before you know it."

"Never fear, my good man, I shall make certain nothing of the kind happens." Tony wrapped his arm around her waist and escorted her forward.

Even without the sound of the door squeaking closed a bit behind them, she would have known they were outside. Perhaps it was a difference in the sound of Tony's voice or an immediate sense of openness, but she knew they were on the outside of the cathedral dome.

"Let me think." He paused, then turned her and shifted her over a few steps. "Excellent. Now stay still." He moved from her side to stand behind her, never completely letting her go, for which she was extremely grateful. She was not especially scared of heights, but the idea of standing where she thought she was standing, with a blindfold over her eyes, was the stuff panic was made of. Although, admittedly, it was quite exciting.

"First, the hat must go." He carefully untied the ribbons of her hat and pulled it off her head. His voice sounded beside her ear, an audible caress. "Are you ready?"

"I am indeed." Eagerness sounded in her voice and anticipation surged through her veins.

"Very well."

Delia felt his fingers work at the blindfold's knot at the back of her head, then the strip of fabric fell free. She opened her eyes and gasped.

The world stretched out at her feet.

"Oh, my."

He wrapped an arm firmly around her waist, anchoring her against him, and a warm sense of security and belonging washed through her. With his free hand, he gestured toward the west. "There, Delia, there's your sunset."

The sun had just dipped below the horizon, leaving in its wake slashes of light and color. A trail or a pathway or a memory of the day just ended. Brilliant white and blinding yellows, chased by rose, faded to blue and hung at the edge of the sky, the boundary between today and tonight.

"It's . . ." She could barely get the words out. "It's magnificent."

"You said you wanted to stand on the top of the world and watch the sun set."

"Of course," she murmured, vaguely remember saying something of the kind. Never imagining he could possibly make it come true. Never dreaming he would.

"You like it, then?" Tony said softly.

Something akin to awe gripped her. "I can see forever."

"Not quite forever."

"But almost." Excitement rose in her voice. "Look, Tony, there's the British Museum, and over there is Westminster Abbey, and oh, I can see the Thames, of course, and Buckingham House, I think." She stepped out of his embrace, grabbed his hand and started around the narrow gallery.

"Do be careful, Delia. Our guide would never forgive me if you should keel over the side."

"I have no intention of doing anything of the sort." She glanced at him over her shoulder. "You're not afraid of heights, are you?"

"I never have been before." He stepped nearer to the balustrade, peered over the side and shuddered. "Of course, I have never been at this great a height before. We are approximately two hundred and eighty feet up."

"And it's quite marvelous isn't it? Why, I feel as if I could do anything up here, even fly if I so wished."

"Only because nothing seems particularly real up here."

"Exactly. It feels as if anything is possible. As if we were in an entirely different world." She gazed out over the city. Lights were just beginning to twinkle on. "I would like to fly someday. I should really add it to my list."

"And I shall have to burn that list," Tony muttered. "Personally, I don't believe man was meant to fly. I think he was meant to keep his feet firmly on the ground."

"And I agree that man should keep his feet firmly on the ground, but only when it comes to camels." Delia laughed and linked her arm through his. The gallery walkway was no more than a yard in width, just wide enough to allow them to walk side by side.

"Oh, and do you see the Tower? I'm certain my house is too small to be seen from here, but I imagine we could probably find Effington House. I daresay, if it wasn't getting dark, we could probably see clear to the sea and beyond. Why, all the way to America, I should think."

"And, no doubt, to France on the other side."

Delia ignored the teasing note in his voice. "No doubt. Such a pity we're losing the light. There are so many things I should like to see while we're up here." She squeezed his arm. "This is indeed a grand adventure."

"There is one thing more I wish you to see." Tony led her to the east side of the gallery. In this direction, the horizon was already the darker blue of night and stars were just beginning to appear. He stepped behind her, pointed her toward the east, then wrapped his arms around her. "There you are."

She stared into the deepening darkness. "It's wonderful, Tony. Indeed, it's all wonderful, but I don't understand."

"The stars, Delia, you said you wanted to touch them. I fear this is as close as I could get you."

Her breath caught and the back of her throat ached. She resisted the immediate urge to cry. She'd never been so affected by a gift before. Of course, she'd never had a gift like this.

He'd laid London and the world at her feet and offered her the stars. It was indeed a grand adventure.

She swallowed hard. "It's perfect."

He laughed softly and rested his chin on her head. "I daresay everything looks perfect from up here. At the level of the heavens it's impossible to see the problems of those toiling on the streets. From up here, everything and everyone looks insignificant."

"Then at least until we return to the ground, everything is perfect," she said staunchly.

"Perfection is an illusion."

"Nonsense." She drew a deep breath. "At this very moment, my life is perfect, and that's not at all an illusion. It may well be something of a miracle. There was a time, you know, when I didn't think life could ever be so much as pleasant again. Now I am standing on the top of the world and have been given the chance to touch the stars by the man I love."

He pulled her tighter against him. "Do you love me, Delia?"

"Yes, Anthony St. Stephens, I believe I do." She waited for his response. "Tony?"

"Yes?"

"It's your turn."

"My turn for what?" he asked innocently.

"Tony!"

"I thought laying the world at your feet said far more than mere words could ever say."

"Sometimes words are a nice touch."

"Very well, then." He sighed dramatically and turned her around to face him. "Philadelphia Effington Wilmont, I do indeed love you." Tony took her hands in his. "I love your absurd desire for adventure and your equally fervent desire to break rules even if you find it difficult to do so. I love your kindness and your sense of responsibility toward those in your employ."

His gaze searched hers. "I love your curiosity and the way you raise your chin when you're determined and how you wring your hands together when you're nervous. I love your clever mind and your good heart. I love the way you admit your mistakes and continue on, and most of all, I love the courage I don't think you realize you have. And I cannot think of anything that would ever stop me from loving you."

She gazed up into his eyes and saw the stars, her stars, reflected there. "And there is nothing that would ever stop me from loving you."

"Are you certain of that?" A teasing smile lifted his lips, but his voice was oddly intense.

"I have never been more certain of anything in my life."

He raised a brow. "What if I were to do something truly vile?"

"I would forgive you," she said loftily.

"What if I have already done something truly vile? In the past, that is?"

"I would suspect former spies have any number of vile things in their past that I neither wish to hear about nor is it my business to hear about. However, short of confessing that you have a wife and seven children stowed away somewhere"—she lifted her shoulder in a gracious shrug—"I can't imagine anything you might have done that I could not forgive you for."

"Not anything?" He studied her for a long moment. Far too long. Unease fluttered in her stomach. "What if I were to have, oh, say . . ."

"Yes?" She held her breath.

"Something like, oh, a dozen children, not merely seven, and more than one wife? Would that be forgivable as well?"

"I don't know." She bit back a laugh of relief and shook her head solemnly.

"You don't like children, then? I was hoping we'd have a dozen of our own."

"Oh, I quite like children, although a dozen may be

about eight or so too many. It's the wives I would have difficulty with." She studied him curiously. "Do you have any wives or children lying about?"

"I don't believe so, but . . ." His brow furrowed in thought, then he shook his head. "No, no I'm fairly certain I have not misplaced either wives or children."

"Anything else I should know? This is probably an excellent moment and a rather appropriate place for confession."

He laughed. "I daresay I'm not any better at confession than you."

"Even so, this is your opportunity. Possibly the only one I shall ever give you." She slid her hands up to entwine behind his neck. "Reveal your sins, Lord St. Stephens, purge your soul, tell me everything."

Again he paused a shade longer than she deemed necessary. It was unnerving but probably nothing more than his past work that made him appear reluctant to divulge all. Perfectly understandable. This was a man who more than likely spent years unable to reveal anything whatsoever. Perhaps someday he could tell her his long-hidden secrets.

"I have nothing to confess save the fact that I shall love you forever." His arms tightened around her. "No matter what might happen from this moment forth, come what may, I shall always love you."

"And I shall always love you," she said with a fervency that welled up from somewhere deep within her.

His lips found hers in the dark and he kissed her with an intensity that quite took her breath away. As if this were a kiss to seal a promise. Or last forever.

At last he pulled his mouth from hers. "We should probably be on our way. I daresay our guide is getting somewhat impatient at this point."

She twisted in his arms for a last look over the city. The stars overhead shone down on the city lights below.

"I don't care, Tony, whether it's an illusion or not, I think, at this moment if no other, it's all quite, quite perfect. The city spread before us, this grand adventure and life itself. And I further think, while perfection may be an illusion or simply fleeting, we shall live quite happily for the rest of our days."

"And I think you're absolutely right, my love. At this moment, if no other, all is indeed perfect and just the beginning. It does strike me, though"—he nuzzled the side of her neck—"that the way your bedchamber matches your eyes is rather perfect as well."

"Are you certain?"

"No. In truth, I cannot remember the exact color of the room." He shook his head in feigned regret. "I'd have to compare the colors again to make sure. And it shall drive me mad until I am able to do so."

"Well, that's that, then." She tried not to laugh with the delicious anticipation bubbling up inside her. Apparently spending much of the day in her bed was not enough for him, which worked exceedingly well, as it was not enough for her either. "I should hate to see you mad."

"Mad with desire," he murmured against her neck.

She shivered with delight. "Pity we can't really fly. It shall take us forever to descend all those stairs."

"Then we should begin at once. Come on."

Tony grabbed her hand and they carefully made their way back to the door. It was fully dark now, but the stars cast enough light to guide them.

"So, my lord, how will you explain to the gentleman waiting to take us back down that I am no longer suffering from the effects of my dreadful camel accident?"

"Why, my dear Lady Wilmont, I shall be completely

honest with him." A grin sounded in Tony's voice. "I shall tell him it was a miracle."

Hours later, Tony lay with Delia curled against him. They were both in a state of weary, content satisfaction he had not suspected existed.

Tony had never especially believed in miracles or fate or magic, and he'd never considered love at all. But tonight, with Delia lying in his arms, he didn't doubt that something beyond rational explanation had led them to each other. They were together as the result of a series of unique and somewhat far-fetched incidents that, in truth, never should have happened at all. Fate, magic and miracles seemed no less probable than love, and love was very, very real.

"I believe the potential of this type of activity cannot be overestimated," Delia murmured, her eyes closed, already more than half asleep. Between the camel, the climb to the top of the cathedral and the other *activity* they had partaken of today, she was exhausted.

Tony chuckled. "I daresay the potential is limitless."

She opened her eyes and smiled up at him. "It strikes me that something else I have never done before, my lord, is to fall asleep in the arms of the man I love."

"Then we shall end the day with yet another grand adventure." He brushed a kiss across her forehead.

"Perfect," she murmured, and closed her eyes, snuggling closer.

He pulled her tighter against him and stroked her hair until her even breathing told him she was at last asleep.

Bloody hell, how had it all gotten so blasted convoluted? How could he ever tell her the truth about his masquerade now? He had toyed with the idea tonight at the cathedral. It was indeed an appropriate place for confession and asking forgiveness. She had given him the perfect opportunity, although two hundred and eighty feet above the ground was perhaps not the most prudent place to disclose something like this. Who knew how she might react? Oh, certainly she was not the type of woman to fling herself off the building, but she might well try to push him over the side. And who could blame her?

Worse, any admission on his part would not end with him. One truth would lead to another. His deception could not be revealed without further explanations about Wilmont. Even if a woman is not in love, she still does not want to know her courtship was nothing but part of an ill-advised government plan. It might well destroy her. He might well destroy her.

Tony had lived in the shadows wrought by the nature of his work much of his adult life and hadn't realized it until her. Until Delia brought him into the light.

Mac was right: Tony could not tell her the truth. And he would do whatever he had to make certain she never found out any of it. To make certain she was never hurt.

It would be easy to get rid of the other servants, but the butler was a more difficult problem. Delia would never accept Gordon simply leaving her employ. He was too old to find another position. Why, she'd probably insist on pensioning him off and, in some way, taking care of him for the rest of his life.

Unless . . .

There was only one thing to do. Only one way out. He could see no other solution.

Gordon would have to die.

Chapter 19

"And you have come to me for advice?" The Duke of Roxborough studied Tony curiously. "Or are you looking for approval?"

"Both, I think, Your Grace." Tony chose his words with care.

The two men sat in the impressive library at Effington House, each with a glass of brandy in hand. Tony had indeed come seeking the older man's counsel. He had nowhere else to turn. "There is no one else who knows everything about the situation, save for Lord Kimberly, of course."

"And as the lady in question is a member of my family, he is not as qualified as I to determine her fate. Is that it, St. Stephens?"

"Something like that, sir."

"Coming to me may well be the wisest move you've made since this debacle began." The duke blew a long breath. "Kimberly has made me aware of your feelings for her, of course."

"Of course." Tony should have known Kimberly would have made certain Delia's uncle was kept informed of any new development.

"Has she agreed to marry you?" The duke's eyes narrowed thoughtfully.

"Actually, sir, I have agreed to marry her."

His Grace's brow rose.

"It's a long story."

"And I should prefer not to hear it." The duke shook his head. "Effington women." He said something under his breath Tony could not make out and thought it was probably best. "Do you know what you're getting into with her? With this whole blasted family?"

"Not entirely, sir, but you yourself warned me of the challenge inherent in involvement with an Effington female."

"And are you up to that challenge?"

"I don't know, sir." Tony met the duke's gaze directly. "But I shall do my best."

"That's all we can ask for, then." The duke paused for a moment. "You've never truly been part of a family, St. Stephens. It's one of the things that has made you so good at the work you do. Nor, to my knowledge—and I do make it a point to know everything about those who work for me—have you ever been seriously involved with a woman. You have always been as solitary as Wilmont. Indeed, more so. He, at least, made his existence known in society—in a disreputable manner, mind you, but known nonetheless. You have never had a life outside your work." Roxborough studied him carefully. "Are you certain about this? About her?"

"I have never been more certain of anything in my

life." Tony raised a shoulder in a helpless shrug. "I love her, sir."

"God help us all." The duke threw back the rest of his brandy, got to his feet, strode across the room and promptly refilled his glass. "Then do it now."

"Do it—" Tony stood.

"Marry her. Now. As soon as possible."

"But she's not officially out of mourning, sir."

Roxborough snorted in disdain. "If she's like the rest of the women in this family, a little thing like disregarding the prescribed period of mourning won't stop her. Unless, of course . . ." His brow furrowed. "Did she love Wilmont?"

Tony paused. "No, sir."

"Does she love you?"

"Yes, sir."

"Good. I'll arrange for a special license and by this time tomorrow you will be wed."

"Do you think that's wise?"

"Do you think it's wise to be her betrothed and her butler at the same time? Even you cannot be in two places at once. Where is she now, by the way?"

"I drove her to call on her family before I came here. I thought it best for her to be out of the house if I was not there."

"Very good, but you cannot keep this up. It will all come to a head and then there will be the devil to pay." He narrowed his eyes. "I needn't remind you, regardless of what happens, she will never know of my part in any of this, do I?"

"No, sir."

The duke thought for a moment. "We'll have the wedding here."

"Here?" Tony stared in surprise. "Won't Lady Wilmont think that rather odd?"

"Everything about this is rather odd, my boy. But I'm her *uncle* and head of the family. Tell her I'm an old friend of your father's or your brother's. I did meet one of them on occasion, I believe." The duke pulled his brows together and paced the floor. "She already knows we're acquainted and you must be held in some favor, as you were a guest at Effington Hall. Tell her . . . you came to me for fatherly advice. Yes, that's good. And I encouraged an immediate marriage, even offering to have the wedding here, to . . . to . . ."

"What, sir?"

"To . . . get her life back in order. That's it. Put that whole business with Wilmont behind her and start her life over. With you. That sounds reasonable. Yes, I like it. Besides, having the ceremony here will give a stamp of family approval to it and minimize any scandal."

"But shouldn't I speak to her father? Ask for her hand?"

"Nobody bothered with that for her first marriage, I can't see that it's necessary for the second. You can talk to him at the wedding, if you wish. Indeed, I have already spoken favorably of you to her father. And I daresay, knowing my brother, he'll be pleased to see her finally settled with the right man." His Grace met Tony's gaze firmly. "And in spite of the way this has become so horribly mucked up, I do think you're the right man, St. Stephens."

"I appreciate that, sir, but isn't this rather too fast?"

The duke's brow rose. "Changing your mind, are you?"

"Not at all," Tony said staunchly.

Indeed, making Delia his wife as soon as possible was not merely a solution, but a heartfelt desire. He couldn't imagine his life without her. He simply wasn't entirely sure he wanted to marry her so soon. Tomorrow. Less than twenty-four hours from this very minute. Why, a scant month ago he hadn't considered marrying at all. Now he stood at the very edge of that yawning abyss prepared to fling himself into it.

"Good. It's been my experience that the faster events progress, the less time people have to think about silly questions like why. Of course, there may be speculation that she is with child. There isn't any chance of that, is there?"

"I wouldn't think so, sir." Of course, there was, but the timing would be a matter of days and scarcely worth noting.

"Indeed." The duke huffed skeptically. "No, in this case the answer to why is simply love. As ridiculous as it sounds, no one questions love." His Grace chuckled ruefully. "It's a powerful weapon.

"Now then, my wife will arrange everything regarding the wedding. She'll be in a frenzy and she'll make life hell for anyone who dares to cross her path between today and tomorrow, but she'll love every moment of it. The duchess is excellent at things like this."

"Pardon me for saying so, sir, but should we make an event out of it? Given the circumstances, I mean. Perhaps it would be better to just marry without any particular fuss."

"You obviously know nothing about women, St. Stephens. A wedding requires a certain amount of fuss for females. It's part of their nature. Some sort of primeval ritual. But it won't be an event per se. Simply whatever family members are in town and can be located, although I suppose that is a fair number at this time of year."

"I'm not sure an immediate marriage solves anything, sir."

"It solves everything, and quite nicely too. You'll take her away for a long wedding trip. To avoid the scandal,

of course. By the time you return, all will have been forgotten and forgiven. I hear Greece is nice at this time of
year. My brother Harry and his wife are traveling there
next month to dig about at some ruin or other. Or even
better, take her to Italy. For some reason, women love
Italy. Probably that rascal Byron's influence."

"She would like to travel," Tony said thoughtfully.

"Of course she would. And while you're gone, you'll
receive a letter informing you that her dear friend the
butler"—he rolled his gaze toward the ceiling—"has
passed on. You'll be right there to comfort her and take
her mind off his"—he cleared his throat—"*death*. It's
hard to mourn when you're blissfully happy. And I suspect you can make her such."

"That is my intent."

"In addition, should she ever learn the truth—and
with each passing day this ruse continues, that is indeed
a possibility—she will be wed to you. Bound to you for
the rest of her days. In truth, trapped."

"You make it sound so appealing," Tony murmured.

"What I'm trying to say is marriage keeps her by your
side. With luck she will never know the truth, but if she
does, she will have to forgive you at some point. Certainly in this case it could take years, but eventually
she'll have no choice."

"Because she's trapped." The word didn't have nearly
as bad a ring to it when used in respect to Delia as opposed to him. In truth, he rather liked the idea of her being trapped with him. For better or worse. For the rest of
their days.

"I have to admit, St. Stephens, I'm really rather
pleased with how this whole thing has turned out. As
you well know, I was not at all happy to learn it was my
department's fault, my government's fault, that my niece
was the center of scandal. That her life was irrevocably

altered. All you have to do now to make everything turn out well is convince her to marry you immediately."

"I shall do my best."

"Kimberly has told me you plan to leave the department after this is concluded."

Tony nodded. "I have responsibilities now that I did not have before. I see no other choice."

"Indeed, you *have* no other choice. It's a wise man who understands that." The duke considered him for a moment, then favored him with a slight smile of approval. "The department will be the poorer without you, but I suspect my country's loss will be my family's gain."

"Thank you, Your Grace."

"In the meantime, we shall hope for the best. The British government got you and my niece into this mess, and by God, I, as a representative of the British government, will bloody well get you out."

"I appreciate that, sir."

"Marry the girl. Kill the butler." The duke raised his glass. "And we'll all sleep better at night."

Was her history repeating itself?

Delia paced the short width of the library, absently wringing her hands.

Was she doomed to once again make an enormous mistake? And would this be so much worse because her heart was involved?

She had no idea, and God help her, she wasn't sure she cared.

"Did you wish to speak with me, my lady?" Gordon said from the doorway.

"Yes, please, do come in." She waved him into the room.

"You seem distraught, ma'am." Gordon moved to the

cabinet and poured two glasses of brandy. She bit back a smile. Brandy and backgammon had become something of a ritual with them, and she rather liked that Gordon took it upon himself to fetch the brandy without waiting for her request. She would miss these evenings.

"Thank you." She accepted the glass he offered and took a long sip. "*Distraught* is perhaps not the right word. I am . . . I don't know what I am exactly." She took her usual seat at the backgammon table and waved him to the other chair.

He sat down and studied her. "Are we to play, then, ma'am?"

"Not tonight, Gordon, I simply need to talk." She stared at the brandy in her glass as if it had the answers she searched for, then looked up at him. "I am going to marry Lord St. Stephens. Tomorrow."

"My congratulations, ma'am."

She raised a brow. "You don't think it's too soon? It's been barely seven months since my husband died. Don't you think it's terribly improper to marry so quickly? Before the required period of mourning, that is?"

"It is indeed quite improper, and scandalous as well. However . . ." the butler paused as if considering his words.

"Go on."

"Well, my lady, you told me you wished to live by no one's standards but your own. If indeed you meant those words—"

"I did."

"Then this is the perfect opportunity to do just that. As I understand it, Lord Wilmont has no family, so there could be no censure from that quarter. In addition, your family is both powerful and wealthy. It's been my experience that the indiscretions of those with wealth and power are forgiven far faster than those of anyone else. As scandals go, I doubt this will be that significant.

"Lady Wilmont, I suspect you must follow where your heart leads." His eyes behind his spectacles met hers. "Is St. Stephens where your heart leads?"

"Yes." She pulled her gaze from his and stared unseeing into the dim shadows of the room. "I love him, Gordon. It sounds so odd to admit it aloud. I have had a great deal of doubt about the very existence of love, but nothing else explains it. The way I feel when I'm with him and, as well, the way I feel when I'm not."

"Pardon me for pointing this out, ma'am, but you did not know your first husband well. Do you know this man any better?"

"I do, or at least I think I do." She laughed softly. "My uncle, the Duke of Roxborough, has given his approval. Indeed, he has invited us to marry at Effington House, so I daresay St. Stephens's credentials are more than acceptable. I am not overly close to my uncle, but I do trust his judgment. And"—she blew a long breath—"I suppose I should trust my heart as well. St. Stephens is the most wonderful . . . and he makes me feel . . ."

"Yes?"

"As if I am the most important thing in the world." The wonder of it all sounded in her voice. "As if nothing matters to him but me. As if I am unique and special."

"My dear Lady Wilmont, you are both unique and special."

Her gaze met his and she smiled with affection. "What a very nice thing to say."

"It's true," he said staunchly.

She laughed. "It's not precisely true when your sister looks exactly like you. When you're used to being referred to as 'one of the Effington twins.' It wasn't until I married that I became, well, an individual." She thought for a moment. "Perhaps that's part of why I've made the decisions I have. Neither Wilmont nor St. Stephens has ever seen me as one of a pair. Indeed, St. Stephens has never even met my sister."

"He's seems a decent sort of chap, ma'am."

She raised a brow. "I wasn't aware you'd met him."

"Only in passing, my lady." Gordon cleared his throat. "He has been in the house a great deal and somewhat impossible to avoid."

Heat flushed up her face, but she ignored it. After all, she had wanted to become a woman of experience, and if that effort had lasted no more than a day, regardless of whether she was now going to marry the gentleman in question or not, she had nothing to be embarrassed about. Still, it was difficult to disregard a lifetime of expectations of proper behavior.

"After we marry, St. Stephens is taking me to Italy." She wrinkled her nose. "In part, I think, to avoid whatever scandal might be caused by our hasty nuptials, but also because he knows it will be a grand adventure."

"You have always planned to travel."

"It will be glorious, Gordon, every bit of it. Travel and marriage to a man who loves me as I love him, and eventually children and growing old by his side. A lifetime of adventures. Grand, all of them." She brushed a strand of hair away from her face and noticed her hand trembled with emotion. "It's all quite perfect. In truth, I think it's something of a miracle." She shook her head.

"And it scares you," he said softly.

"A great deal, actually. I am at once so happy and so afraid it will all be taken away." She sipped her brandy and thought for a long moment. "I have not made especially wise decisions when it has come to men and marriage. This is the second time I will have married hastily."

"But you are marrying now for far different reasons, aren't you?"

She nodded. "I married Lord Wilmont because it seemed like an excellent idea given the circumstances. My choices were rather limited once I had . . ." She shook her head. Delia was fairly certain Gordon had long ago realized that she had shared Charles's bed before marriage, but she preferred not to say it aloud.

"Yet you have any number of choices now. You have a residence of your own, you are wealthy in your own right and you have independence as a widow you did not have before. The mere fact that you and his lordship have become"—Gordon cleared his throat—"*close* does not mandate marriage. It seems to me that the one fact that is present now that was not present in your first marriage is the one factor that should indicate future happiness."

"Love?"

"Love." Gordon nodded. "I confess, I am not an expert in that elusive emotion, but I have seen enough to know that when it is present, there is nothing on earth that is more powerful."

"Your wisdom continues to amaze me, Gordon," she said with a laugh.

"Then might I add, ma'am, that life, even in moments like this, is rarely perfect. Men in particular are, by their very nature, imperfect creatures." Gordon paused to choose his words. "All men, even those who are in the throes of love, or perhaps especially those who are in the throes of love, make mistakes. Sometimes dire, tragic mistakes, often when they truly believe they are doing what is right for their family or business or country. Such errors in judgment may seem unforgivable at first but rarely are."

"And obviously all men think alike." She shook her head. "Lord St. Stephens and I have had a very similar discussion about forgiveness."

"Indeed? Well, it's no doubt a good thing to keep in mind," he murmured. "Probably can't be mentioned often enough."

"Probably." She paused for a moment. "There is something else I wish to speak to you about. When St. Stephens and I return from Italy there shall be a great many changes."

"I thought as much, ma'am."

"He has a house in town he has never seen, although I don't quite understand that, but it all has to do with the recent death of his brother and the inheritance of his title and property. In addition, he has an estate somewhere. What I am trying to say is I doubt that I, or we, shall continue to live here."

"I am certain the rest of the staff and I can find suitable employment elsewhere, ma'am," Gordon said with the oddest note of what might be relief in his voice.

"Don't be absurd." She stared at him in disbelief. "You can't think I would turn you and MacPherson and Mrs. Miller and the others out on the streets?"

"I didn't—"

"I have no intention of letting any of you go. Good heavens, you especially have become like a member of my own family. Gordon, I fully intend on your being in my employ for however long you want. And when the time comes that you wish to retire from service, I also intend to find a cottage on one of the estates, my family's or my husband's, where you may live out the remainder of your days in comfort."

He stared in silence.

"What? Nothing to say, Gordon? No astute observations? No words of wisdom? Have I shocked you into silence?" She grinned. "I rather like that. It's as good as beating you in backgammon."

He shook his head slowly. "I simply don't know what to say, my lady. I am touched by your kindness."

"Nonsense, Gordon, you have been far more than an employee to me." She placed her hand over his. "You have been a friend when I truly needed one. I can never repay you for that."

"Thank you, my lady." He gently pulled his hand away and she tried not to smile. The dear old man would share a brandy with her but would only go so far past that ever-present barrier of mistress and servant. "I am most grateful."

"However, I am not entirely certain our games can continue." She searched for the right words. "St. Stephens has declared himself to be stuffy and narrow-minded and I daresay he would think our sharing brandy and playing backgammon was not entirely proper."

"Then perhaps marriage is not a good idea," Gordon said loftily.

"Come, now, I should think you of all people would understand that attitude," she teased. "Indeed, haven't I heard you refer to yourself as stuffy and narrow-minded?"

"In my case it's entirely different."

She laughed. "Why?"

"It's my place to be stuffy and narrow-minded." He paused. "Might I suggest, my lady, we play once more, in defiance of the stuffy and narrow-minded?"

"Excellent idea."

He opened the drawer on the side of the table and removed the game pieces, placing them on the board. His gaze was on what he was doing and the tone of his voice was offhand. "Are you happy, then, my lady?"

"I would not have thought it possible a few months ago. . . ." She shook her head, still not able to fully grasp all that had changed in her life. "I have been given something of a second chance, I think. My mother would say my stars have realigned themselves. As odd as it sounds, I might well believe her right. I do feel as if something, some unknown hand, has guided me to this point."

"Fate, you mean?"

"I suppose. I really don't know and I don't especially care." She shrugged. "Regardless of whether it was fate or the stars or something entirely different that brought me to this point and St. Stephens into my life, I shall be forever grateful.

"So, to answer your question"—she met his gaze firmly—"I am indeed happy. You see, I have found a man who loves me in spite of my faults and my mistakes. I suspect such a thing is exceeding rare in this world.

"Given that, I can't imagine being anything but happy for the rest of my days."

Chapter 20

The muscles in the back of his neck tensed the moment Tony stepped over the threshold of the library at Effington House. Instinct told him he'd just stepped into a well-laid trap. His very life might well be at stake, or at least his future.

"Don't just stand there, St. Stephens, come in." The duke leaned on the edge of his desk, Delia's father at his side, both with a glass in hand. A trio of younger gentlemen stood a few feet away. "I daresay, no one's armed." Roxborough sipped his drink. "At the moment."

Tony adopted an air of relaxed confidence and strode into the room. It would not do to show fear to this particular gathering.

"Whiskey or brandy?" The duke gestured at a footman standing beside a tray of decanters and glasses. "Or whatever else you might like. It's probably the right moment for it."

"I'll have whatever they're having," Tony said smoothly.

"Very good." The duke chuckled. "I don't know if you've met anyone here, with the exception of my brother, Delia's father, Lord William Effington."

"Indeed, we met under rather unusual circumstances." Lord William studied him in an assessing but not unfriendly manner.

Tony sent a silent prayer of thanks heavenward that he'd been listening when Delia's test was proposed and had asked her father if he might call on her. Or rather call on Miss Effington.

"St. Stephens, allow me to introduce my sons." Lord William nodded at the younger men, who had shifted their position to form what could well be described as a united front. A suspicious, threatening, formidable united front. "This is Leopold, Christian and Andrew."

The brothers shared a distinct family resemblance with their sisters, although none were quite as fair. They did have Delia's blue eyes, even if hers were not nearly as steely and cold. All three were of a like height and build to Tony's, and a single look told him they were the kind of men one wanted to have by one's side in a battle. Loyal and fierce and steadfast. He suspected a match between him and any one of them might well result in a draw.

"Gentlemen," Tony said coolly. His gaze shifted from brother to brother. "Your sister has told me a great deal about you all."

"Has she?" Leopold's eyes narrowed. "How intriguing, as I cannot recall her speaking of you."

"Really?" Tony accepted a glass from the footman and sipped thoughtfully. Whiskey. Scottish, and of an excellent quality. He suspected he would need it. "My name has never come up, then, when you've called on her?"

The men exchanged uneasy glances.

"I spoke with her at Effington Hall," Christian said staunchly. "And she did not mention you then."

"Of course not." Tony smiled pleasantly. "We had just met."

"Then perhaps it's far too soon to marry." Andrew crossed his arms over his chest. "Don't you think it would be prudent to wait at least until her period of mourning is at an end? It's only a few months more."

"No, in truth, I don't." Tony hardened his voice. "I understand your concern is born of affection for your sister. However, Delia is of age, highly intelligent and knows her own mind. I wish to marry her and she wishes to marry me. It's really quite simple."

Christian glowered. "We would hate to see her involved in another scandal."

"We would feel it necessary to do something, should that occur," Andrew added, a definite warning in his voice.

"I do hope that is not an idle threat, as there is bound to be some scandal simply because this is her second marriage in a year," Tony said mildly. "She is aware of that and prepared for it, as am I."

"My brothers are a bit more"—Leopold's gaze locked with Tony's—"*vehement* than is perhaps necessary at this point. You must understand we knew nothing of Delia's involvement with Wilmont until after the fact. We certainly would have taken matters in hand or, at the very least, discussed her welfare with him in advance of their nuptials had we been aware of their intentions. Do you have sisters, my lord?"

"No." Tony would have wagered a great deal that Leopold and the rest already knew the answer to that question, as well as virtually every other detail there was to be found about the new Viscount St. Stephens. He resisted the urge to smile at the knowledge that there was not a great deal of information available.

"Then you cannot understand how, oh, *responsible* we felt when Delia ran off with Wilmont," Leopold said.

"We should have kept a closer eye on her," Christian muttered.

"Or any eye on her." Andrew snorted in self-disdain. "We were too busy watching Cassie."

"And we have no intention of allowing her to make yet another mistake." Leopold smiled. "Do you understand?"

"No, I'm afraid I don't." Tony sipped his whiskey thoughtfully. "I fully intend to marry Delia within the hour. If you consider that a mistake"—he shrugged— "so be it."

Leopold looked at his father.

Lord William shook his head. "Don't turn to me for assistance on this. We are not of one mind. I think marrying St. Stephens might well be the best thing your sister could do. I'm really quite pleased."

Christian's brow furrowed. "Why?"

"First of all, my brother has vouched for St. Stephens's character, as well as his family and the respectability of his title and his fortune." Lord William glanced at his brother with an odd look of respect and curiosity. "I have no idea how he does it, but in my experience, his information is never wrong. Furthermore, when Delia impersonated her sister—"

"What?" Andrew stared.

Leopold rolled his gaze toward the ceiling.

"We were definitely watching the wrong sister," Christian muttered.

"As I was saying, when Delia attended a party pretending to be her sister, St. Stephens asked me for permission to call on her. I was, quite frankly, impressed.

And impressed as well that he has obviously forgiven her for her masquerade." Lord William cast him a rueful smile.

Tony smiled weakly and resisted the urge to meet the duke's eyes.

"Beyond that, I have always felt that my children, upon reaching a certain age, should be responsible for their own actions, for good or ill, and should be allowed to make their own decisions."

"Still, Father"—Leopold shook his head—"her decisions, especially regarding men, have not been particularly astute."

"It seems to me your own decisions have not been particularly astute when it comes to women," Lord William said casually.

Christian and Andrew traded glances and grins.

"That's an entirely different thing." Leopold lifted his chin in a gesture exactly like Delia's. "After all, I'm a man. Therefore my mistaken judgments regarding women are forgivable. Society judges the mistakes of females far more harshly. Indeed, it is up to men to protect women from the frailties of their own judgments, as they are ruled more often by emotion than intelligence."

"I'd like to hear him say that to Grandmother," Andrew said in a low aside to Christian.

"You do understand, my lord"—Leopold turned his attention back to Tony— "we have nothing more than our sister's best interests at heart."

Tony met his gaze directly. "It's a bit late for that, don't you think?"

"Of course not," Christian said with a frown. "We may well have failed her once, but we shall not fail her again."

"When you say once"—Tony chose his words with care—"are you speaking of Wilmont?"

Andrew huffed. "Of course."

"How interesting." Tony considered the brothers for a moment. "I thought perhaps you were speaking of the time following Wilmont's death, especially since her return to London, because, to my knowledge, not one of you has called on her. Nor have you sent her a note or gone out of your way whatsoever to assure yourselves that she was well. As touching as your worry about your sister is now, I find it rather hypocritical."

"We understood she was fine." Leopold glared. "We assumed she would let us know if she needed anything. Indeed, we expected her to call on us should she require assistance of any sort."

"What you *expected* was that she would sit in her dead husband's house for a full year and reflect on her sins." An anger he hadn't realized he had toward these men welled up inside him. "What you *assumed* was that Delia was safely set aside and you needn't give her a second thought. And what you so conveniently *understood* was in error. She was as much in exile in that house of hers as she was in the Lake District."

"I say, that's not fair." Indignation sounded in Christian's voice. "Each of us went up to see her while she was gone."

"How very thoughtful of you." Sarcasm dripped from Tony's words. "Yet now that she is but a few minutes away, none of you have had the time nor the inclination to call. Do you have any idea how alone she has been? Save for her sister and myself, she has seen no one but her servants. Good God, her closest friend these days, her confidant, is a bloody butler!"

Tony glared with disgust. "She speaks with pride of all of you, of all the endless numbers of Effingtons and how close you all are. Family is extremely important to her, yet her family, particularly her overly protective brothers, have as much as abandoned her.

"I have no family to speak of and I have, up until this moment, been a bit apprehensive about joining yours. It seemed a great responsibility to be an Effington, even by marriage. Now I see that I am well up to the job, because it appears all I really need to do is make an occasional threat, squawk a bit like a peacock and ignore anyone who inconveniences my well-ordered life."

"Well said," the duke murmured.

Lord William bit back a smile.

Delia's brothers stared in stunned silence.

"I don't think that's quite fair," Christian said in a defensive manner.

"Although," Andrew said slowly, "it is more accurate than I would care to admit. We haven't been as attentive as we could have."

"We haven't paid her any attention at all since she returned to London. We've left her to be entirely on her own." Leopold blew a long breath. "He's right. We've shirked our responsibility to her now as we did before." He considered Tony carefully. "We shall not do so again."

Tony met his gaze firmly. "Nor shall I."

They stared at each other for a long moment. Tony had the oddest sensation that this was a man he could call friend, given the right circumstances. Possibly even, someday, perhaps, brother.

"You love her, don't you," Leopold said, his words more statement than question.

Tony nodded. "Yes."

Leopold nodded. "And you do intend to go through with this wedding?"

"I do indeed."

"Then there is nothing more to say. However, before we welcome you to the family, you should understand that my brothers and I have decided"—Leopold smiled a pleasant sort of smile; Tony didn't trust it for a moment—"should Delia bear a child in less than nine months from now—"

"We shall be compelled to throttle you." Andrew grinned.

Leopold's eyes narrowed. "And should you ever hurt her, we will—"

"Have to kill you," Christian said in a cheery manner that quite belied his words. Or perhaps emphasized them.

"Why am I not surprised?" Tony murmured.

"Now that that's settled, I suggest we join the others." The duke started toward the door, followed by Delia's brothers.

Lord William lingered behind and moved to Tony's side. "It's Anthony, isn't it, my boy?"

"Tony, sir."

"Well, then, Tony, welcome to the family." Lord William leaned toward him and spoke low into his ear. "You do understand, *Tony*, we all feel responsible for Delia's previous disastrous marriage, and regardless of my words here, should you indeed hurt my daughter I shall join my sons in making you regret the day you ever saw her. Do keep that in mind. Now then"—Lord William slapped him on the back and beamed at his soon-to-be son-in-law—"I believe we have a wedding to attend.

"Do you think I have made a mistake?" Delia sipped her champagne and surveyed the group milling about the Effington House parlor in advance of dinner.

It was a simple event, with mostly family present, and probably did not seem at all simple to anyone not used to a family the size and close-knit nature of the Effingtons'. There were perhaps twenty people present, including her brothers, the duke and duchess, uncles and

aunts, and a varied assortment of cousins and their respective spouses. It was a pity Grandmother could not
be here as well, but there was neither time to contact her
nor time for her to travel to London. Besides, she rarely
left Effington Hall these days. The only one here not a
relation of some sort was a Lord Kimberly, who was apparently an acquaintance of both Tony's and the duke's.
Given Tony's lack of family and even friends, no doubt
the result of the clandestine nature of his past profession,
she wondered how her new husband would adjust to the
boisterous, overwhelming and more than a bit intimidating Effingtons.

Cassie shrugged. "It's not for me to say. I am simply
glad to be included." She paused to add emphasis. "*This
time.*"

"And I am quite glad you are." Delia grinned. "*This
time.*"

In word and length, the ceremony had been precisely
like her first wedding. Indeed, Delia thought the clergy-
man in attendance looked eerily familiar and wondered
if he had also presided over her marriage to Charles, although it could well be nothing more than the nerves ca-
vorting in her stomach, an overactive imagination and
the fact that she thought all clergymen had the same appearance about them.

But the tone of the event had been entirely different.
Certainly she'd been excited when she'd married Charles,
but she'd had few expectations of the future and more
than a few qualms regarding the reaction of her family as
well as that of society as a whole. Now she didn't care
whatsoever about society. Her family was by her side and
her expectations for the future were boundless.

Today, when she'd promised to cherish Tony for the
rest of her days and he'd vowed the same, she was
gripped with an awesome sense of joy. Today, the man

she'd married was the man she loved. Today, she was happy and knew in her heart she would be happy tomorrow as well.

Across the room, Tony was engaged in a conversation with Leo and both men presented the appearance of cordiality. It was a good sign. She hadn't spoken to any of her brothers before the ceremony—indeed, she hadn't spoken to any of them since she'd returned from Effington Hall—but was fairly certain they had, each and every one, placed Tony on a sort of masculine probation.

"Come, now, Cassie, you have an opinion. I should like to hear it."

"I don't know why, I daresay you'd pay no attention to it. And at any rate, it's too late now. You are married. Again." Cassie studied Tony for a moment. "And he doesn't look like he'd be the type to conveniently die on you."

"Cassie!"

"If you don't want my honest opinion, you shouldn't ask for it. Oh, very well." Cassie sighed. "I don't know if this is another mistake or not. I do know you love him, which raises the stakes considerably." She met her sister's gaze directly. "And if he loves you as well—and I rather suspect he does, given how quickly he wanted to marry you when he certainly could have continued to share your bed without benefit of marriage—"

"Cassie!" Delia hissed. "Do keep your voice down."

"This from the same person who declared she wanted to become a woman of experience?" Cassie snorted. "Obviously, such a thing was not in your nature. That said, it's probably for the best that you married the first man you—"

"Cassie," Delia warned.

"Fell in love with." Cassie smiled sweetly, then sobered. "I simply want you to be happy. And if St.

Stephens can make you happy, then he has my approval." She glanced at Tony and a wicked gleam sparked in her eye. "He certainly is handsome enough."

"Isn't he, though?" Their mother stepped up from behind and linked her arm through Delia's. "Looks aren't everything, but I've always thought it wiser to spend one's days with a handsome man than one you would prefer not to gaze on in the light of day."

"Mother!" Delia laughed.

"I'm simply being practical, dear. Spending your entire life with an ugly man would, no doubt, grow wearisome if he was the tiniest bit imperfect in other ways, as most men are. The Effington men, as a whole, are a handsome lot." Her gaze settled on her husband and she smiled with satisfaction. "Your father is still exceptionally attractive. Why, I find even his increasing lack of hair only adds an air of distinction to his appearance."

"Perhaps you're seeing him through the eyes of love, Mother." Cassie studied her father. "Although he does seem to have aged well."

"Indeed he has, and I expect St. Stephens will age as well." Georgina considered Tony with an assessing eye. "He should produce lovely children, Delia. Blood will tell, you know." She squeezed Delia's arm affectionately. "Beyond that, I find him to be of a pleasant and courteous nature."

"You approve, then?" Cassie said.

"I do indeed." Georgina nodded. "Even if I didn't, your father does, and more importantly, the stars do."

Delia groaned. "Mother."

Georgina ignored her. "The moment I learned of this wedding yesterday, I sent for Madame Prusha. We consulted together the first thing this morning. She studied your stars, Delia, and says this marriage to this man was foretold. Furthermore, she agrees with me that her previous readings of the stars for you have been entirely accurate thus far. You should marry a man of mystery—"

"Obviously, St. Stephens," Cassie murmured.

"—and suffer a great loss, which you needn't worry about, as Madame and I have agreed it refers to Wilmont's death," Georgina said firmly.

"Of course, Wilmont was a bit of a mystery as well," Cassie pointed out.

"And you should live the rest of your days in great happiness." Georgina beamed at her daughter.

Tony caught her eye from the other side of the room and smiled a private smile meant for her alone. Even from here she could see desire and indeed love in his dark gaze that quite took her breath away.

"We're sailing for Italy tomorrow," Delia said, never taking her gaze from his. Tony said something to her brother, then started across the room toward her.

"I am quite, quite jealous," Cassie said.

"Your time will come, dearest," Georgina said firmly. "Madame had a few things to say about your life as well."

"I'm not sure I want to hear them." Cassie paused, then sighed in resignation. "Were they good?"

Georgina laughed and Delia moved toward her husband.

They met halfway across the parlor. She gazed up at him and the room and all its inhabitants faded away.

"How are you faring, Lady St. Stephens?" Tony's voice was low and intimate.

"Why, Lord St. Stephens, how thoughtful of you to ask." She drew a tremulous breath. "I am happy."

He raised a brow. "Just happy?"

She laughed. "There is no *just* about happy, but if you prefer, I am insanely, gloriously, unbelievably happy. I can scarcely breathe with the joy of it."

"And I shall keep you happy for the rest of your days." He took her hands. "Indeed, if I do not, your brothers have promised to kill me."

"Have they? How very thoughtful of them." She pulled her brows together. "But what if I do not make you happy? Do I face no consequences if you are unhappy?"

"There is no chance of that." His voice was light, but his gaze searched hers. "Your very presence in my life is enough for my happiness. Even if, for some reason, you should ever despise me, I shall still be content knowing you are my wife. My love. Forever."

"Oh, my." Her words were little more than a sigh.

"Can we take our leave now? Have we fulfilled our responsibility to this vast family of yours to assure them we are well and truly wed? We have a great deal to do before we sail tomorrow." He squeezed her hands and his dark eyes simmered with promise. "And a great deal to do tonight."

"I'm afraid not." She shook her head with genuine regret. "There is a supper planned and my aunt has gone to a considerable amount of trouble. I fear she'll be offended if we leave before then."

"I'd wager the duchess will understand."

"Probably, but"—she shrugged helplessly—"we can't go yet. My parents and my brothers and even—"

"Never mind. I understand, and you're right, of course. It would not be a wise move to abandon my first family occasion. I suspect these Effingtons are a demanding lot."

"They can be." She laughed with relief. "And you are among their number now."

"I am a lucky man," he said wryly. "However, if inclusion in your family is the price I have to pay for having you in my life"—he grinned—"it is a small price indeed."

"I believe I can make it worth your while." Delia smiled slowly. "When this is over and we have retired to my house."

"Oh?"

"You see, Lady St. Stephens has never made love to her husband, Viscount St. Stephens, before." She gazed into his eyes with all the desire he, and only he, could provoke. "It should be an exceptionally grand adventure."

Chapter 21

Tony closed the door of her bedchamber—their bedchamber—firmly behind him and shook his head. "This was an exceedingly long day."

"Endless." Delia waltzed to the center of the room and twirled around. "But lovely nonetheless. It was surprisingly nice to have my family around me. I have missed that."

"I know you have." Tony slipped off his jacket and tossed it on the chair.

"Did you find them too overwhelming?"

"They are a rather intimidating force of nature." He sat down and pulled off his boots. "Do you realize each and every male member of your family below the age of forty glared at me before, during and after the ceremony? If looks could kill, I should be quite dead."

"And that would be a great pity, my lord *husband*."

"I know I should regret it, my lady"—he stood and untied his cravat—"*wife*."

"Tony?" She absently twisted the new ring on her finger.

"Yes?"

"Will you take me to bed now?"

He grinned. "That was my plan."

This was extraordinarily hard to say. She didn't want him to think she hadn't enjoyed every wonderful moment with him thus far. Their lovemaking was so much more than she'd ever expected. Still . . . "Are you planning on being, well, civilized about it?"

His brows drew together. "What do you mean, *civilized*?"

"What I mean to say is . . ." She wandered to the other side of the room, placing the blue sea of the bed between them. "Well, as you know I had planned on becoming a woman of experience."

"Yes?"

"But thus far, that experience has only consisted of, well, you."

"Thus far and forever," he growled.

"That goes without saying, but I had expected this part of my life"—she waved at the bed—"to be a bit more . . ."

"A bit more *what*?" He crossed his arms over his chest. "If you say *exciting*, that does not bode well for the rest of our lives together."

"I wasn't going to say *exciting*. Being with you, every moment has been more than merely exciting. It's been more than I ever imagined. It has well lived up to its potential. I just want tonight, our first wedded night together, to be . . . unique."

"Should I dress like a highwayman? You could be a runaway princess." He wagged his brows wickedly. "I could take you at gunpoint."

"Gunpoint?" It wasn't precisely what she had in mind. "Not tonight."

He laughed. "Then what do you want?"

"I want you . . ." she drew a deep breath. "I want you to stop acting as if I were going to break. I want you to stop being so gentle and considerate and careful. Stop being so blasted nice."

"Wait just a moment." His brow furrowed. "I'm not sure I would call our lovemaking thus far especially *nice*. *Remarkable* is a better word. Indeed, I thought it was all exceedingly passionate and somewhat frenzied."

"It was remarkable, but—"

"You seemed to enjoy it." Indignation sounded in his voice.

"Oh, I have. More than I can say but . . . Oh, this is not coming out right. I want you to . . ." She thought for a moment, "Lose control of yourself."

He snorted. "I have lost control. Several times. And with a great deal of enthusiasm."

"I want you to *take* me. I want you to be carried away with desire. I want you to be dangerous and wicked and"—she leaned forward and planted her hands on the bed—"I want you to rip my clothes off. I want to rip your clothes off."

He looked down at his shirt. "But this is my favorite shirt."

"And I am exceedingly fond of this dress, but . . ." She straightened. "You think I'm a tart now, don't you?"

"Not at all."

"But you're offended."

"No." He studied her thoughtfully. "Actually, I'm quite intrigued."

"It's just that you've been such a . . . a . . . viscount. And I think, just for tonight, mind you, what I'd really rather like is"—she held her breath—"a spy."

"A spy," he said slowly.

"Good heavens." Embarrassment burned her cheeks.

She whirled away from him and buried her face in her hands. "I can't believe I said all that."

"You should be able to say anything to me."

"Even so. What you must think of me . . ."

"I think"—his words were measured—"you're the most exciting woman I've ever known."

She raised her head. "You do?"

"And I think I am an exceptionally lucky man."

Without warning, the room plunged into darkness.

"Tony?"

"Spies operate best under cover of darkness."

"Do they?"

"And this particular spy has been remiss in his duties." His voice drew closer.

She held her breath. "Has he?"

"Apparently he has not fully shown you how much he wants you."

He grabbed her from behind and spun her into his arms. His lips crushed hers and for a moment she wondered if she had made a mistake. She started to throw her arms around him, but he caught her hands and held them tight.

"Now, now, none of that." His tone was mild, but there was an undercurrent that was decidedly wicked. And extremely exciting.

Before she could protest, he wrapped something around her hands, binding them together. His cravat?

"Tony?"

"Quiet." He picked her up and tossed her on the bed. She tried to scramble off, but he grabbed her and pulled her back, straddling her and pinning her to the bed. He drew her bound hands up over her head and tied them to the bed. A tremor of delicious fear shivered through her.

"Tony?"

"You wanted a spy." His voice was low, almost a

growl. "You wanted me to be dangerous and wicked. Well, you shall have it."

"Perhaps I was mistaken?"

"We shall see."

He heard him leave the bed and heard the distinct sounds of him disrobing. Her heart thudded in her chest and she realized she did indeed want a bit of danger. At least once. And realized, as well, this man who had done so much to please her would never hurt her. She held her breath in anticipation.

A moment later he was back on the bed. Again he straddled her, looming over her, nothing more than a dark silhouette in the night.

"Tony, are you—"

"I shall do precisely what I please, when I please."

He bent to kiss the hollow at the base of her neck and she stilled. He trailed his mouth up her throat and along the edge of her jaw to a spot right below her ear, then he nibbled the lobe of her ear. With her arms tied over her head, her breasts were thrust upward and outward like a pagan offering. He cupped them firmly and caressed them through the fabric of her gown. His tongue trailed down the length of her throat and lower to her cleavage, deepened by her position. He ran kisses along the top of her bodice and she squirmed slightly with her rising desire. Without warning, his hands moved to the neckline of her gown and ripped her dress and the chemise beneath it down to her waist. She gasped in shock and excitement. Cool air wafted over her. She was thoroughly exposed and altogether thrilled. His hands cradled her breasts and he took one in his mouth and it tightened with his touch. He held her nipple with his teeth and flicked his tongue to and fro until she moaned and strained upward. He turned his attention from one breast to the other and back until she writhed with pleasure, breathless with need.

He moved downward to place his knees on either side of hers and clamp her legs together. Tony grabbed the remainder of her dress, her underclothing, and ripped them apart, exposing her fully. He bent and kissed the valley between her breasts and trailed his mouth lower and lower still, tasting her, drinking her. He sat up and slipped his hand between her legs and she whimpered at the loss of his mouth on her skin, hot and sensitive and aching for his touch. He slipped his hand between her legs and she wanted to open them for him, but he held her fast. His hand and fingers stroked her, caressed her and carried her to a place of irrational, sightless need.

Abruptly he moved, spread her thighs apart and knelt between her legs. He lowered his head, his tongue tracing patterns on her stomach and moving slowly, inexorably downward. He spread her open with his fingers and his tongue flicked over that most sensitive part of her. Shocking pleasure, intense and primitive, shot through her, and she cried out and a rational, thoroughly proper part of her mind noted this wasn't the least bit proper and she should tell him to stop. She ignored it. Never had she imagined such delicious sin, at once terrible and magnificent, that pulsed and throbbed from his mouth on her. Fire pooled deep inside her and flared and burned, a mindless fever that grew and roared hotter and hotter until she thought surely she would burst into flames.

Without warning, he stopped and she arched upward instinctively, seeking his touch. He planted his hands on either side of her and plunged into her, taking her as she had wanted. A declaration of possession and power and passion. She called out his name and pulled at her bonds and wanted to embrace him, but was unable to do more than revel in the power of his body joining with hers. She was helpless and he did as he wished with her and it was glorious.

She moved her hips with his. Met his thrusts with a wanton eagerness that had nothing to do with her position or this wedding night game and everything to do with her heart. He was a part of her that had nothing to do with the joining of their bodies and everything to do with the merging of their souls. She no longer knew where he left off and she began, and no longer cared. Pure passion, sheer pleasure carried her higher with his every stroke, every thrust, until she thought she could bear it no longer, and still she would not have it stop. Until he moaned and thrust yet again and glorious release seized her and she exploded around him, with him, in wave after wave of magnificent sensation and sheer joy and absolute delight.

He collapsed on top of her, his labored breathing against her ear. And she fought to find her own breath. His heart beat hard next to hers and it was as intimate as their coupling—no, more. His heart beat in time to her own. And she knew, with a deep certainly that came from her very soul, it always would.

He raised his head and she couldn't make out his features in the dark, but she could hear the grin in his voice. "Was that wicked and dangerous enough for you?"

"Indeed, I think it was quite . . . quite . . ." Laughter bubbled up from deep inside her. "Quite."

"Not *nice*, then?"

She laughed. "No, no, definitely not nice."

"Excellent." He rolled over to lay by her side.

"I believe you can untie me now."

"I don't know if that would be wise." He trailed his finger over her breast.

"Tony!"

"I rather like having you tied up. Think of it as an adventure."

"It was an adventure." She giggled. "And I rather liked being tied up as well. Being completely helpless."

"You, my love, will never be completely helpless."

"Perhaps I am a tart after all."

"Perhaps you are."

"But I'm your tart."

"Indeed you are, for now and always." He kissed her firmly.

"Perhaps someday I shall tie you up."

"Perhaps." He laughed, reached over her head and untied his cravat.

She wrapped her arms around him. "Or perhaps I can be the highwayman and you can be a runaway prince." She pulled him close and nibbled at his ear. "You did say something about gunpoint."

Tony awoke abruptly and sat upright in bed. For an instant he struggled to get his bearings, then recognized what had jerked him out of a sound, satisfied sleep.

The distinct acrid odor of wood smoke hung in the air.

"Bloody hell." He leapt out of bed and felt for his trousers, discarded somewhere on the floor.

"What is it?" Delia's voice sounded groggily from the bed.

"The house is on fire. Get up!" He found the trousers and yanked them on. "Now, Delia!"

"What?"

"Clothes, do you know where your clothes are?" His voice rang loud and sharp to drag her to her senses.

"I have a wrapper somewhere, I don't—"

He groped at the foot of the bed and found the robe and thrust it at her. "Here!" The smoke was not overly heavy, but he had no idea how bad it might be. "Quickly, Delia!"

"Tony." Her voice rang with confusion and shock, but she got to her feet and slipped on her robe. "I can't go—"

"Quiet!" He grabbed her, threw her over his shoulder and carried her out of the room.

Angry voices sounded from the lower floor. Halfway down the stairway, he noted light from the parlor and realized it was from candles and not an inferno. He drew a deep breath of relief and set Delia down on the stairs.

"Stay here," he ordered.

She struggled to stand. "Why? This is my house and if it's on fire I want to see how bad it is. You can't leave me here."

"For the first time in our lives together, and very likely the last, do exactly as I say." He cupped her chin and gazed firmly into her eyes. "Do you understand? I want you to remain here until I've determined what's happened. Besides"—his voice softened—"I would prefer my wife not present herself in front of the servants so scandalously dressed."

She stared at him for a moment, then nodded grudgingly and sat down on the step. "I warn you, I will not wait long."

"No doubt." He gave her a quick kiss and hurried down the stairs and into the parlor.

The heavy smell of smoke lingered in the air. The far wall was charred and water puddled on the floor, but the fire itself was out. Damage from the blaze appeared minimal.

"We were lucky, sir." Mac wiped a grimy hand wearily across his forehead. "We found it right after it started."

Mrs. Miller stood glowering between two of the other men.

"It was Mrs. Miller." Mac scowled at the woman. "We caught her trying to escape just after she started the fire. She still had a smell of lamp oil about her."

Mrs. Miller responded with a defiant glare.

"Is this true?" Tony said slowly, reluctant to believe that one of his own could be working against them.

"Sir, she had her bag with her and we found these." Mac handed Tony a packet of papers.

Tony untied the packet and leafed through the pages, then glanced at Mrs. Miller. "The Effington Papers, I presume?" He turned his attention back to the papers and his jaw clenched. As disappointed as he was in her, he was more so with himself. The threat to Delia had been right here under his nose all along and he hadn't seen it. "Where's the money?"

She shrugged.

"You have a great deal of explaining to do."

Mrs. Miller looked at him for a moment, then laughed. "Why should I explain anything to you?"

"Indeed. Why should you? The truth is evident." His gaze dropped to the papers. "They're forgeries, aren't they? And you had them all along, which means this is not what you've been looking for." At once the answer struck him. "It's the notebook, isn't it? That's what you were after."

"Come, now, St. Stephens, I know how this works. I've been in this position before. You think at this point I shall fall to pieces and confess all." Mrs. Miller snorted in disdain. "Not bloody likely."

"I've never laid a hand on a woman before, sir, but in this case," Mac said in a low, threatening voice, "I should be more than willing to—"

"It's not necessary, Mac." Tony studied Mrs. Miller for a long moment. "Whatever she's been trying to find is obviously still in the house, or at least she thinks it is.

But tonight was her last opportunity to do anything. Once my wife and I leave tomorrow, this operation is over and you will all have new assignments. As Mrs. Miller has apparently failed to find what she's been looking for in the house, her only option was to burn the place down." He narrowed his eyes. "With us in it."

"You have nothing of substance, St. Stephens." Mrs. Miller smiled in a smug manner. "The fire was scarcely more than an unfortunate accident. I simply dropped a lamp. Clumsy of me, but—"

"Accident, my ass," Mac said indignantly. "We caught her in the act, sir."

"On the contrary, Mrs. Miller, I'd say we have a great deal. Starting a fire and attempting to kill us all at the very least. Given your possession of the Effington Papers, I suspect we can add trying to extort money from the government, forgery and"—realization struck him and his stomach twisted—"the murder of Charles Wilmont. He is dead, isn't he?"

She raised a brow. "Did you doubt it? Did you ever truly think Wilmont would have betrayed you and that blasted department? He might have acted the scoundrel, but his loyalty to the crown and his sense of honor were far greater than I ever imagined. And if you've believed otherwise, even for a moment, you're not as good a friend as you thought you were."

"I—"

"You are not the one he betrayed." Her expression hardened. "He was never supposed to marry *her*. It shouldn't have happened. His purpose was to learn the truth about the papers and purchase them. Nothing more than that. It would have worked beautifully too if he had simply done as he was supposed to. He never would have known anything about me. I would have had the money and he and I . . ." Bitterness sounded in her voice. "He made promises and I believed them. I was a fool and he deserved what he got."

"You killed him?" Delia's disbelieving voice sounded from the doorway. "You killed Charles?"

"Yes," Mrs. Miller hissed. "And I quite enjoyed it."

"I don't understand." Delia stepped farther into the room, her gaze intent on Mrs. Miller. "Why?"

"Because of you." Mrs. Miller fairly spat the words. "Wilmont was supposed to be mine. You were nothing more than a—"

"Than a what?" Delia's voice rose.

"Mac," Tony said quickly. "Get her out of here."

"Wait," Delia snapped. "Than a what?"

Mrs. Miller smirked. "Ask your new husband. And while you're at it, ask him about your butler too."

"Mac," Tony growled.

"Yes, sir." Mac nodded at the other men, who hurried Mrs. Miller from the room.

"I don't understand." Delia shook her head. "My housekeeper killed my husband and now"—she looked around the room and her eyes widened—"has tried to set my house on fire?"

"I can explain," Tony said, stepping toward her.

She backed away. "And what was she saying about Gordon?" Delia glanced around the room. "He's not here. Where is he?"

"Delia." Again Tony started toward her.

She turned on her heel and started toward the hall.

Mac stepped in front on her, blocking her way. "My lady—"

"Let her go, Mac."

Delia cast him an odd look, full of doubt and confusion, then headed toward Gordon's room.

"She'll find out everything, sir," Mac said quietly.

"I know." Tony took a silver candlestick from a table

and lit it with a punk from the fireplace. Even to himself he seemed to move extraordinarily slowly, obviously reluctant to face what he knew was ahead. Still, it could not be put off. He drew a deep breath and started after her.

Delia stood in the center of the butler's room. "He's not here, Tony." Her gaze met his. "But you knew that, didn't you?"

"Delia." Tony set the candle on the desk.

"Where is he?"

Was it possible that she hadn't yet realized the truth? Could it be he still had a way to get out of this without telling her everything?

"Has he gone? Now, in the middle of the night? He's an old man, Tony. If that witch has hurt him . . ." She turned to the chest of drawers.

"Delia, don't!"

"If his things are here"—she yanked a drawer open—"then he's obviously in some sort of dire straits and . . ." She stared into the drawer for an endless moment.

"Delia." He stepped toward her.

With two fingers she pulled his mustache out of the drawer and stared at him. "What is this?"

"I can explain." He struggled to keep a note of desperation from his voice.

She dropped it on the top of the chest, then retrieved his eyebrows and spectacles, placing them next to the mustache. She stared at the articles of disguise for a long time. At last her gaze met his. Her voice was cold. "How could I have been such a fool?"

"It's not what you think," he said quickly.

"Who are you?"

"I am exactly who you think I am. Anthony St. Stephens, Viscount St. Stephens."

"Perhaps I did not phrase the question correctly," She said slowly. "What are you?"

He drew a deep breath. "I am an agent of His Majesty's government."

"A spy?"

"*Spy* really isn't the right term. *Agent* is more accurate. I work for a department of the government whose purpose it is to protect and investigate and . . ." She glared at him. "I suppose *spy* works as well as anything at this point."

"And Gordon, dear sweet old man that he was, my butler, my confidant, my *friend*, does not exist at all, does he?"

"No, I'm afraid not."

"You should be very afraid." Delia pushed past him and strode back to the parlor. Mac stood in the doorway. She stopped and cast a disgusted glance at him. "Are you a spy too?"

"I wouldn't use the word *spy*, my lady," Mac said. "I think *agent* is really—"

She uttered an odd sort of scream, and stalked into the room. Tony followed at her heels, disregarding Mac's halfhearted smile of encouragement.

"I'd tell you to shut the door, although I suspect your MacPherson out there would simply press his ear against it. Besides, we would both choke to death on the smell of smoke in here." She whirled toward him, clutching her robe tighter about her. "So what are you, in truth? An arrogant viscount? An incompetent butler? A spy?"

"Your husband." It was the first thing that came to mind, and he knew the moment the words left his mouth they were a dreadful mistake.

"That remains to be seen," she snapped. "I want the truth now. All of it."

"Perhaps if you would calm—"

"Calm? You wish me to be calm? Bloody hell, my housekeeper has killed my husband! I've married my butler, and all of my servants are spies! Spies!" Fury shot from her eyes. "I shall never be calm again!"

"Perhaps a glass of brandy will help—" He started toward the door. At once, a hand holding a decanter shot into view in the doorway and Tony grabbed it. Mac stayed discreetly out of sight. And range.

"Brandy? You think brandy will help? A bottle would not be enough to calm me down! I would have to be completely inebriated and unconscious, and even then my lifeless body would still be twitching in anger!"

Mac's disembodied hand offered two glasses. Tony took them gratefully, moved to a table and poured a glass. "It's been my experience, in times of great turmoil, brandy helps promote a certain amount of rational thinking, even clarity."

He cautiously held out a glass. She snatched it from his hand, downed it one swallow and clenched her teeth. "I am *rational*."

Tony carefully took her glass, refilled it and passed it back to her. He had never in his life deliberately tried to get a woman foxed before, but this seemed like a good time to start.

"I am rational," she said again, emphasizing each word. "And now, my lord viscount-butler-spy, I expect answers. Now!"

"Very well." He drew a deep breath. He should have rehearsed this, but he had hoped never to have to say it. "Perhaps you should sit down."

She narrowed her eyes.

"All right, then don't." The only way to get through it was just to begin at the beginning. "Last year, eight or so months ago now, my department was involved in an investigation regarding papers—correspondence, actually—that allegedly detailed dealings during the war between the French and members of an influential British family."

"I gather you're talking about my family?"

He nodded. "Specifically about the duke or your father or one of your uncles. At any rate, the papers were offered for purchase. We intended to buy them, but we also needed to learn if they were legitimate. It was decided that one way to do that was to become well acquainted with the family and thereby be welcomed at Effington Hall and elsewhere to be able to investigate without suspicion."

"This is the most inane thing I've ever heard of."

"Admittedly it was not our finest moment, but it did seem to make sense at the time."

Delia snorted and tossed back the rest of her brandy. "And by *acquainted,* do you mean flirt? Court? *Seduce?*"

"No! Not seduce. Good God, what do you take us for?"

Her eyes widened in outrage.

"Never mind," he said quickly. "That was a stupid question, but you should know Wilmont was never suppose to go as far as he did. We still don't know why he married you."

"Your flattery will quite turn my head, my lord." She gritted her teeth "Go on."

"When the packet wrecked, we assumed Wilmont was dead and the papers were lost with him. He was supposed to purchase them while on the boat."

"You *assumed* he was dead?" Her face paled and she sank down on the sofa. "You *assumed*? Is he then—"

"No, he is dead." Tony thought it best to omit the suspicion that had briefly arisen that Wilmont was alive. "Mrs. Miller killed him."

"I still don't—"

"Wilmont uncovered something else. We didn't learn of that until recently. We believe he was in possession of a notebook that had nothing to do with the Effington Papers." He drew his brows together. "I think now it might have led us to Mrs. Miller and God knows who else.

"Regardless, we believed both the Effington Papers and the notebook were lost in the wreck of the packet. Then we learned Wilmont had been seen with a woman on the docks before the packet sailed, and furthermore that woman had returned to London about the same time you did. We feared she might believe you to unknowingly or knowingly be in possession of the notebook and thought you might be in danger."

"So, to protect me, you became my butler and filled my house with spies." She eyed him coldly and a chill ran up his spine. "Of course, one of them killed my husband and was set, no doubt, to kill me as well."

"Yes, well, that was unfortunate." He cringed as he said the words. Even to his ears this whole thing sounded ill-conceived and completely bungled.

"Unfortunate? *Unfortunate?*" Delia laughed, a wrenching sort of mirthless sound. "Is there anything about this that was not unfortunate?"

"Well, yes, I think so," he said quietly.

"Do you, my Lord Mysterious?" She looked at him for a long moment. Disgust and betrayal shone in her eyes. His heart sank. "I trusted you. I confided in you. I took you into my home. No, I took a dear, sweet old man who doesn't bloody exist. What were you going to do about him anyway?"

"He was going to die while we were in Italy."

"How convenient."

"It seemed like a good idea," he murmured. "He'd

had a good, full life and was going to pass on peacefully, in his sleep."

"Damned decent of you. I'm surprised you didn't just throw him off the top of a blasted church." Delia shook her head. "I should have known. I should have figured this all out. There were all sorts of clues, weren't there?"

"Actually, I thought I was rather circumspect."

She ignored him. "But I did see it, although I disregarded it. I noted a similarity in your eyes despite your spectacles. Your hands were not the hands of an old man, I noticed that as well. And in both guises you referred to yourself as stuffy and narrow-minded. I thought it nothing more than a coincidence. All that should have given you away, but I failed to see it."

"People never look for what they don't expect to see."

"How very *astute* of you, my lord." Her voice was hard, her words more accusation than observation. "Have you any more words of wisdom you care to share? As viscount or butler or spy?"

"Yes." He sat down beside her and took her hand. She snatched it away. "I love you, Delia, and I would give my very life if all this had not happened to you. If it would change things, but it won't. You should know, as well, I have always intended that this be my final assignment. I have a position and responsibilities that I now have to attend to and I want you by my side. As Lady St. Stephens. As my wife."

"Do you really think that's possible?" She stared in disbelief. "You have just told me everything I have believed about Charles, about you, about *Gordon,* was a lie. How can I be your wife now? How can I trust you ever again? God help me, how can I trust myself?

"As for love . . ." She studied him for a moment, and he thought his heart would break at the pain that colored her blue eyes. "I fear it's as much an illusion as any other appearance of perfection." She thrust her glass into his hand, got to her feet and started toward the door.

He stood at once and followed her. "Delia."

"I know where your bloody notebook is."

Chapter 22

"Obviously, I am a better spy than you are." Disdain rang in Delia's voice. "But then, from what I've seen thus far, that would not take a great deal."

Delia crossed the hall, snatched an offered candlestick from Mac, gave him a scathing look and went into the library. She moved directly to a section of bookshelves, holding the candle close to scan the titles, then selected a book. She stepped to the desk, set the candle down and flipped the book open. She turned a page or two, then stilled.

"Delia?"

She stared at the book in her hand. "I had quite wanted to be wrong. I think I harbored an odd hope that if I was mistaken about this, then perhaps the rest of the night was a mistake as well and not . . . real, I suppose. Nothing more than a bad dream, and I could wake up and . . ." She snapped the book closed and tossed it on the desk. "Here. Take it."

He picked up the book. It was a volume of Byron's poems. "This is the book you gave me, isn't it?"

"No. If you recall, I told you I had another copy. This is *my* copy." She drew a deep breath. "Charles gave it to me."

Tony opened the book and paged through it. A few pages were indeed the works of Byron, but the center section of the volume had been carefully removed and replaced with pages covered with tight lines of handwriting.

"Charles obviously did that *after* we were married. I know it was simply a book of poetry when he gave it to me. I took it with me to the Lake District, but I never opened it again."

"It's definitely what Mrs. Miller was looking for," Tony murmured, his gaze skimming over the script. "I'm not entirely certain, but it appears to be a list of prominent lords and politicians with notations as to information that can be used to extort money from them or the crown. Apparently the Effingtons weren't the only targets of this scheme. It will be interesting to see how much of this is legitimate and how much is as fraudulent as the Effington Papers. Regardless, it's damnably clever."

"I put the book on the shelf when I came back to London."

"And as Mrs. Miller had already searched in here, she did not think to search again. Hopefully this will also lead us to whoever Mrs. Miller was working with as well."

"You have what you want, my lord, I suggest now—"

"Wait, Delia, there's something else here." Tony pulled free a folded piece of paper. He read it quickly and regretted doing so. "It's from Wilmont. Addressed to me, actually." His stomach clenched and he forced himself to meet her gaze. "In the case of his death."

"I don't really care at this point." Her voice was weary and resigned and caught at his soul.

"Nonetheless, you should hear this. He details Mrs. Miller's involvement and explains how he came by the notebook—"

"I said I don't care."

"And he talks about you."

She stared at him. "Do I really want to know this?"

"Yes." It was the hardest thing he'd ever had to say. He knew without question this admission of Wilmont's might well change everything between himself and the woman he loved. And knew as well she deserved to know what Wilmont had written.

Tony drew a steadying breath and read.

"'As for my wife, she was a mistake I should never have made but would make again. A grand mistake. Or in her words a grand adventure. All too brief and the best of my life. She touched something inside me I thought was long dead.'"

Tony forced himself to continue. "'I know you wondered why I married her, what had gone awry in our plans. The answer is overwhelming in its very simplicity. I loved her. Pity, I neither told her nor showed her. Indeed, I have not touched her since our first night together. I felt it was imperative to finish this last investigation so I might put this work behind me and start a new life with her, and my thoughts and time were fully occupied to that end. I could not be the husband she should have until then.

"'I leave her my fortune and I leave her you, my friend. See to it she is taken care of. She deserved far better than I gave her.'"

Delia stared, her eyes bright with unshed tears. Shock sounded in her voice. "He loved me?"

"So it would seem," Tony said softly, placing the letter and the book on the desk.

"And his actions were because of me?"

"Delia . . ." Tony moved toward her.

"Don't." She thrust out her hand and stepped back. "Don't come near me."

"You are not to blame for what happened to him."

"I am entirely to blame." Her voice rose. "He would not have been where he was if not for me. She would not have killed him if it were not for me."

"No. She killed him because he had found her out."

"She killed him because he had married me. Because he loved me." Her voice cracked. "And I did not love him."

"Delia . . ." A sense of helplessness swept over him. For the first time in his life he didn't know what to do.

"My God, he was so wrong. I did not deserve better than he." She bit back a sob. "He deserved better than me."

"Delia, it's over. The past cannot be undone. Wilmont's death was a tragedy, but it was not your fault. There was no need for him to finish what he'd been working on. He could have passed it off to someone else. To me, for that matter. He knew that and he knew as well the risks of his work. He died doing what he believed in."

"He would be alive if not for me."

"You don't know that."

"But I do. I know it here." She clasped her hand against her heart. "I have never known anything so much as I know this."

Tony wanted to take her in his arms and console her, assure her that all would be well, but he knew without question she wouldn't accept his offer of comfort. He feared she would never accept anything from him ever again.

"You have to go on with your life. We have to go on."

"We?" Anger rang in her voice. "There is no *we*! *We* are as much a masquerade, as much a deception, as . . . as Gordon!"

"I'm your husband."

"Charles was my husband too. And he was your friend." She clenched her fists by her side and drew a deep shuddering breath. At last she met his gaze. A cold hand squeezed his heart. Her voice was deceptively calm, her eyes cold. "It's nearly dawn. I want you, and your gang of spies or agents or henchmen or whatever you call them, out of my house with the sunrise."

His gaze searched hers. "What if I refuse to go?"

She shrugged. "Then I'll leave."

"I see," he said slowly. "For how long?"

"I never want to see you again." Her voice was steady, her gaze level. Not a touch of emotion showed in her blue eyes. "I want you out of my life."

"I will leave for now, but you are my wife, you are my soul and I shall not give you up."

"You have no choice."

"Not at the moment, perhaps." He kept his voice as cool as hers. "I understand you require time to come to grips with all of this, but I warn you, Delia, if it takes the rest of my days, I will win you back." He refused to allow the desperation in his heart to show in his voice. "I said I would love you forever."

"You said any number of things that weren't true." A weary note sounded in her voice and she sank down into the chair behind the desk.

"Nothing regarding my feelings about you was a lie." Anger born of fear welled up within him. He smacked his palms down firmly on the desk and leaned toward her. "And understand this, Lady St. Stephens, I revealed more of myself to you as Gordon than I have ever revealed to anyone. I was more honest with you while pretending to be someone else than I have ever been with anyone.

"I didn't pretend to be your friend, I *was* your friend, and I have not had many I could call friend in my life. And it was as your friend that I fell in love with you. I will not sacrifice that love because of actions I took to secure your safety. Actions that indeed were part of service to my country. Falling in love with you was not my intention, and once I had, I did everything in my power to keep you from being hurt. I hoped you would never know any of this."

"Not even about Charles?"

"I neither knew who killed him nor why until tonight. But yes, if I had known I would have kept it from you."

"And if you had known of his feelings for me? Would you have told me?"

He stared into her eyes. "No."

"I see." Her voice was cold and chilled his heart.

"It is not over between us, Delia, it will never be over. And not merely because I love you." He straightened. "But because you love me. And you know as well as I how difficult love is to find."

She folded her hands on top of the desk and gazed up at him as if they were discussing a matter of no more importance than the dinner menu. As if she were removed from the conversation. As if she didn't care. "Get out."

"For now."

"Forever."

An hour later, Tony was the last of the men left in the house. Delia still sat behind the desk in the library where he had left her, unseeing, unmoving.

He stood in the doorway for a long time and watched her. She paid him no heed, whether deliberately or otherwise, he didn't know. It scarcely mattered, he supposed.

Tony had never been seriously involved with a woman before. God knows, he'd never been in love. His heart had never broken before, but it was surely breaking now for her. She was wounded and hurt and in pain, and not all of it, but a great deal, could be laid at his feet. He ached for her and had no idea how to help.

He would make sure she was not alone, but he would give her time. As much as she needed, or maybe only as much as he could bear. In the meantime, he would take up his title. Learn what he needed to know to manage an estate, to be a viscount and a husband, even a member of a family.

He tried to memorize every curve of her face, the set of her chin, the tilt of her lips, and knew the effort was unnecessary. He already knew her face as well as he knew his own. She would linger in his mind and his heart until he was with her once again. And if he knew nothing else about his future, he knew that. He would not allow it to be otherwise.

"Farewell, Lady St. Stephens, my lady wife," he said quietly. "For now."

He left the house, closing the door firmly behind him, and vowed he would be back.

The sharp, hard sound of the front door closing echoed through the house. The empty house. She was completely alone and that was precisely how she wanted it.

Delia sat for a long time, unwilling, unable to move. Frozen, numb . . . dead.

At last she got to her feet and wandered into the parlor. The stench of smoke still hung over the room, but she barely noticed. She found the brandy decanter and her glass and started back toward the library. The charred wall caught her eye and she stopped and stared. The fire had obviously been extinguished before it could do much damage. Still, another few minutes and it would have caught the curtains and the carpet. The whole room would have gone from there, possibly the house. Certainly there was repair needed, but it could have been much worse.

They all could be dead.

She pushed the thought away and returned to the library. In the back of her mind, she noted even in the early morning light everything around her seemed blurred and unreal. Very much like a dream she moved through without conscious effort. It was an exceedingly curious sensation, as if all her senses and emotions had retreated or fled or escaped to a safe, protected spot far away. At the moment she didn't feel much of anything at all, but she knew she would, and it would be devastating. Brandy would numb the pain. Oh, not for long and not forever, but it seemed like a good idea at the moment.

She poured a glass and took a sip. Delia had lost track of the number of brandies she'd had in this room. The long, comfortable evenings. The games of backgammon. . . .

She collapsed back into the chair and ignored the liquor that splashed over the side of her glass and onto her fingers. A scant few hours ago she had been so blissfully happy. The future stretched before her, bright with promise and joy. The grandest adventure of her life.

How had it all gone so horribly wrong? Since the moment she'd met Charles, her life had been a lie. He'd wanted nothing from her but entrée into her circle of family. That in itself was difficult to face. The fact that he had married her because he loved her and was ultimately killed because of it was almost too unbearable to consider.

And what of Tony? He had become her friend when she was alone and had no one else to turn to. Was that part of his plan, or some odd quirk of fate? She well knew there were few other women of her acquaintance who would have shared their evenings with an elderly servant. If he had begun his impersonation with the intention of becoming her confidant, it was only luck that allowed him to succeed. There was a modicum of comfort in the thought.

As for the rest of it . . . she didn't know what to believe, what to think and had no idea what to do now.

Tony was indeed right about one thing: She did need time to sort all this out. Anger and hurt and guilt and pain all warred within her. She was furious with Tony for his deception and angry as well with Charles for his. Delia did indeed feel responsible for Charles's death and probably always would, to a degree. Still, if he had told her of his feelings, perhaps the outcome would have been different.

Charles would be alive and well and she would be his wife. And she never would have known Tony at all. The realization of how much she would regret that brought a fresh wave of guilt.

Delia heard the front door open and her heart leapt. *For now.*

Traitorous heart. No matter what Tony had vowed on his way out the door, her life with him was over.

"Good Lord!" Cassie's voice sounded from the hall. She murmured something Delia didn't hear and then appeared in the library doorway. "It reeks in there, although the damage doesn't seem too bad."

Delia sighed. The last thing she wanted at the moment

was to explain everything to her sister. Indeed, she wasn't entirely certain she *could* explain everything. "What are you doing here?"

"Your husband came to the house and demanded I be awakened. It's obscenely early, you know. He said there had been a fire or something like that and insisted I come over at once." Cassie pulled off her gloves and walked toward Delia, then paused. Her eyes narrowed. "You look dreadful." Her gaze slid to the decanter and back to Delia. "Are you drinking at this hour of the day? What's wrong?"

"I've done it again, Cassie. I've made another dreadful mistake in marriage."

"What on earth do you mean? Why, yesterday you were happier than I've ever seen you."

"Yesterday I didn't now what I know now." In spite of Delia's resolve, tears filled her eyes and a sob sounded in her voice. "My housekeeper killed my husband. I married my butler, and my house is full of spies."

Cassie stared. "What?"

Delia sniffed back a tear. "It's a long story."

Cassie pulled up a chair and settled into it. "Excellent, as I have a great deal of time. I am usually still abed at this hour."

"And it's a very odd story." Delia licked the brandy off her fingers. "Quite complicated."

"I assumed as much."

"Really rather fanciful, actually," Delia said thoughtfully. "I daresay I wouldn't have believed it at all if it had not—"

"Delia," Cassie snapped. "Tell me, right now. Every odd, fanciful, complicated detail."

"Very well." Delia paused. "But first I think you should probably swear never to reveal any of this to anyone."

"Why?"

"In the best interests of the crown, I should think," Delia said loftily. "Besides, I would prefer the rest of the world never know what a true fool I am."

"I can well understand that. And I promise not to reveal any of your odd, complicated, fanciful story."

"I wonder if I should make you take a blood oath or something of that sort," Delia murmured, more to herself than her sister.

"Delia!"

"Sorry." Delia thought for a moment, drew a deep breath and told Cassie everything, starting with Charles and ending with Mrs. Miller and the fire.

"Good Lord." Cassie slumped back in her chair and stared at her sister, wide-eyed with disbelief. "I don't know what to say. It certainly isn't . . . that is, I never . . . what I mean . . ."

Delia pushed the decanter of brandy across the desk at her.

"None for me, thank you. One of us should keep her wits about her."

"My wits are about me." Delia stared at her glass. "Tony said brandy promotes rational thinking and even clarity in times of great turmoil. I believe he's right."

"I knew that butler of yours was odd." Cassie shook her head. "There was something about him I didn't trust."

Delia heaved a heartfelt sigh. "I trusted him."

"Yes, I know." Cassie studied her sister thoughtfully. "I can certainly see why you might be a bit overset."

Delia snorted. "A bit?"

"So . . . when will you forgive him?"

"Tony?" Delia lifted her chin. "He's a lying beast and I shall never, never forgive him."

"Don't be absurd."

"I'm not being the least bit absurd. He lied to me. He used me. He became my friend under false pretenses. How can I ever forgive him?"

"How can you not? You love him. Beyond that"— Cassie's brows pulled together and Delia could practically see her twin's mind working— "it seems to me his deception initially was not of his making. And his solution was to marry you, sweep you away to Italy, provide you with the grand adventures and indeed the life you've always dreamed of and make you happy for the rest of your days. Would that I should find such a beast."

"You don't understand."

"I understand that two different men, both working for the crown, fell in love with you. And both men married you, such action having nothing whatsoever to do with their work. Poor, poor Delia."

"But Tony deceived me."

Cassie scoffed. "Men deceive women all the time. Usually with other women. Given that the only other woman concerned in this was a murderous housekeeper who I gather worked for your current husband but was not, well, *involved* with him beyond that . . ." She shook her head as if to clear it. "This is terribly confusing, but I am right on that point, aren't I?"

Delia tapped the decanter pointedly. "Clarity."

"I think it's best if one of us remains somewhat less than clear," Cassie said wryly. "I hate to say this, because I suspect you don't particularly want to hear it at the moment, but St. Stephens's crimes don't seem all that horrible to me."

"I poured my heart out to him. I talked to him about . . . him. I asked him for advice and I told him how I felt about him. He took unfair advantage of me." Delia huffed indignantly. "I told him things I never would have told him had I known who he was. About my life and about my feelings. He knows me as well as you do."

"So much the better. Once this little matter is cleared up, there should be no more secrets between you."

"But . . . but . . ." Delia glared in disbelief. "What about Charles?" A note of triumph sounded in her voice. "Don't I owe him something?"

"Absolutely not."

"Cassie!"

"Come, now, Delia. He did not turn you from his bed and he certainly could have, thus avoiding your marriage and everything that went with it. Then he never told you how he felt; in fact, he apparently treated you like he didn't care about you at all. And you were fully prepared to be a good wife to him. Indeed, didn't you tell me you thought love would come in time?"

"I might have said something like that," Delia admitted.

"You were not responsible for how he'd lived his life before he met you, nor were you responsible in any way for his death."

"Still . . ."

"There is no *still* about it."

"But . . . but . . ." Delia sat up straight and squared her shoulders. "Tony broke my heart. How can I possibly forgive him?"

"Nonsense." Cassie waved away the question. "He might have bruised your pride a bit. I feel rather foolish myself that I did not see the truth. As for your heart"— she leaned forward— "right now, this very moment, what brings you the most pain?"

"Actually, at this very moment, there is not a great deal of pain," Delia murmured.

"Clarity, Delia," Cassie snapped. "What makes you feel worse right now? The things that St. Stephens has done or the possibility that you will never be with him again?"

Delia had been so upset, so hurt, she hadn't truly considered that. What she might be giving up. Or tossing aside. Or losing forever. Her breath caught. "Good heavens, I told him I never wanted to see him again."

"And he told you he was a butler." Cassie shrugged.

"Perhaps he did not break my heart and perhaps I didn't really mean that I wanted him out of my life," Delia said slowly. "But I am angry at him. Furious, in fact."

"And you have every right to be. There's no reason why you have to forgive him today or even tomorrow. Indeed, I think you should make him suffer and expect a fair amount of groveling as well before you take him back."

Delia brightened. "That's exactly what I should do. Why, never seeing him again would only serve to make *me* miserable."

Cassie nodded. "If he were with you, you could make him miserable. At least a little, now and then. Why, think of the power you would wield over him for the rest of your lives. Whenever he did anything the tiniest bit annoying, you could . . ." Cassie thought for a moment, then grinned. "You could call him Gordon. You would scarcely have to do more than that."

"How perfectly brilliant." Delia lifted her glass to her sister. "That way of thinking is precisely why you're the sister everyone always expected—"

Cassie arched a brow.

"Perhaps that wasn't, given the circumstances . . ." Delia sighed and propped her chin in her hand. "I do so love him, Cassie. And aside from this butler-spy-viscount nonsense, he really is wonderful."

"You could certainly do worse."

"Indeed, and given the opportunity I probably would." Delia met her sister's gaze and both women grinned. "I must say, Cassie, I do feel much better."

"Good." Cassie rose to her feet. "Now, I think the very next thing we should do is send you back to your bed, because you look like you have had no sleep whatsoever."

Delia stood and yawned. "I am extremely tired."

"And extremely rational." Cassie hooked her arm through her sister's elbow and led her toward the door. "I'm going to send my carriage home with a note for Mother—"

Delia groaned

"I won't say anything about fraudulent butlers or spies, nor will I mention that you have thrown your new husband out. I will simply tell her there was a small problem and all of your servants have fled."

"That is true, after all."

"You should have a temporary staff by midafternoon. And I think we should simply tell the rest of the family that St. Stephens was called away unexpectedly. Some sort of crisis regarding his inheritance. I assume you don't want them to know about all of this."

"The last thing I want is for them to think I have made another mistake in marriage." Delia sighed.

"And when you awake, we shall discuss what we're going to do about your parlor."

"Scarlet or cream," Delia murmured, then looked at her sister. "How long, Cassie?"

"How long what?"

"How long should I make him suffer before I take him back?"

Cassie laughed. "How long can you bear being without him?"

"A month?" Delia shook her head. "No, perhaps only a fortnight. Yes, that's good. Two weeks. That's long enough for him to suffer." She cast her sister a wicked smile. "And long enough for me to suffer as well."

Scarcely a week later, Delia decided she was ready to graciously forgive her husband and welcome him back in her life and her bed.

Within a day of that momentous decision, she realized as well she had no idea where to find him.

Chapter 23

Two months later

My Dear Delia,

*Excellent news. I have just this morning learned St.
Stephens has returned to London, and furthermore
I have the location of his town house. There is
other news as well and I shall deliver that in person.*

*I should tell you this information is courtesy of
our brothers, although courtesy is perhaps not the
best term. Leo, Chris and Drew are in the foulest
of moods, which somewhat matches their appearance. It was they who located St. Stephens and, as
best I can determine, took it upon themselves to
call on him with the express purpose of doing him
bodily harm. They said St. Stephens was assisted
by a Scot and I believe they're referring to one of
your former footmen. Regardless of the fact that
your husband and his friend were outmanned, they
apparently gave as good as they got, as evidenced*

*by the bruised and battered faces of our brothers.
Apparently, the match was something of a draw
and ended in the consumption of a great deal of
liquor and the promise of all present to do whatever possible to encourage your forgiveness of
your husband. Extremely generous on the part of
our brothers indeed, as they still have no idea precisely what St. Stephens did.*

*To that end, I suspect Leo, Chris and Drew will
each bring up the subject of reconciliation with
your husband when next they call on you. Odd
how regularly they have been doing that of late . . .*

"I wonder when he is planning to call," Delia said,
more to herself than her sister.

Cassie sat on one of a pair of matching Grecian-style
settees and watched her sister with amusement. "I
suspect—"

"Or if indeed he is planning to call at all."

Delia paced the floor of her newly refurbished parlor,
redecorated in shades of wine and yellow. A bit out of
the ordinary, but quite striking nonetheless. Cassie had
done an excellent job in the parlor as she had in every
other room in Delia's house. Indeed, it was Cassie's determination to complete Delia's entire house as quickly
as possible, and her insistence that her sister be involved
in every detail, that had more than likely saved Delia's
sanity.

"I daresay he—"

"It's been two months, Cassie. In truth, it's been two
months and four days. Two very long months and four
endless days. He certainly could have returned long before now."

It had not been all that difficult to determine that Tony
had gone to his estate in the country, obviously to take

on the duties of his new title. It was both admirable that
he took his newfound responsibilities seriously and annoying. Delia never imagined he'd actually leave London. When she'd told him to get out, she'd only meant
her house, not her town. Given his declarations of undying love and his vow to return, she'd expected he'd wage
a concerted campaign to win her back. Instead, the man
had effectively vanished.

"How was he to know you'd welcome him back?"
Cassie's tone was deceptively idle. "Unless you wrote
him, of course."

"You know full well I didn't write him," Delia snapped.

For at least the last six weeks, Cassie had urged her
sister on a daily basis to write to Tony, quite logically
pointing out he would never know of the possibility of
forgiveness if she did not inform him. Delia absolutely
refused. It simply wasn't in the spirit of making him
grovel for her to approach him. Besides, he owed her abject apologies and he should make the first move. She
was the one wronged in all of this. Still, if she had
known it was going to take him so bloody long . . .

"What if he's decided I'm simply not worth the trouble?"

Cassie rolled her gaze toward the ceiling.

"I know, I know, I've probably mentioned this before," Delia said quickly. "But it preys on my mind. Even
you have to admit everything about our entire relationship from the very beginning was rather unique and indeed could be called quite odd, and I fear that—"

"That's quite enough," Cassie said firmly.

Delia collapsed on the other settee. "What am I going
to do now?"

"I wouldn't hazard a guess. However"—Cassie
flashed a knowing grin—"I'm fairly confident I know
what he is planning to do."

Delia sat up straight. "What?"

Cassie pulled a folded piece of paper from her reticule. "This"—she waved it temptingly before her sister—"is from St. Stephens."

"For me? Why on earth would he send you a note for me?" Delia reached for it.

"Not so fast, dear sister." Cassie jerked the note out of Delia's way and smirked. "It's not for you, it's for me."

"Oh?" Delia raised a brow. "And were there roses accompanying it?"

"Not this time." Cassie grinned and handed her the note. "You may read it, however."

"How very gracious of you." Delia skimmed the brief note. Her brows pulled together thoughtfully. "He says he wants your counsel on the refurbishing of his town house and requests you call on him this afternoon." She met her sister's gaze. "Don't you think this is rather odd?"

Cassie laughed. "My dear Delia, being in love and being without your husband has no doubt addled your mind."

"No doubt." Delia stared in confusion. "As I haven't the vaguest idea what you mean."

"Obviously the man is uncertain as to his reception from you and wishes to speak to me first to ascertain your feelings or possibly ask advice on how best to approach you."

"Do you really think so?" The very idea was delightful. "But why you?" Delia studied her sister. "You've barely met him. And I didn't think you particularly liked him."

"Who better than me? Leo, perhaps?" Cassie snorted with disdain. "Even a man who has completely lost his senses would be more astute than that. And it's not that I didn't like him. I scarcely know him; I was simply not overly fond of your involvement with him. However."

Cassie shrugged in surrender. "You love him, and everything he's done indicates he loves you as well. Besides, I think it's rather endearing that he hopes to find out from me how to get back into your good graces."

"It is endearing, isn't it?" Delia stared at his signature on the note, his hand firm and sure and strong. If she'd realized nothing else in these last two months without him, she'd realized how very much she missed him and how empty her life was without him.

"Is there anything in particular you wish me to tell him?"

"I'm not entirely sure I want you to tell him anything," Delia said thoughtfully. "But there are any number of things I should like to know."

"Very well. What should I ask him?"

"*You,* dear sister, shall not ask him anything."

Cassie stared for a moment, then smiled. "I see."

"I thought you would." Delia's smile mirrored her sister's. "Tony used *Gordon* to find out how I felt about him. It's only fair that I use the same ploy."

Tony glanced at the overly ornate bronze-cased clock on the mantel for perhaps the fifteenth time in as many minutes. In the back of his mind, he noted once again how the clock and damn near everything else in this house was not to his liking. Of course, it would be very much to his liking once it had a blue bedroom to match the blue eyes of its mistress.

Once it had a mistress.

Miss Effington was the first step toward that and the only way he could think of to approach Delia. He wanted to simply pound on Delia's door, but he had no idea if her attitude toward him had as yet softened. It had been two interminably endless months since he'd seen her, but if it took another two and another two after that and so on for the rest of his life, if necessary, he absolutely would not give up.

Where was Miss Effington anyway? Would she honor his request with her appearance? And if she did, would her attitude be like her brothers'?

Tony rubbed his jaw gingerly. Delia's brothers knew nothing of what had passed between Tony and Delia. They only knew their sister was upset and evasive and her husband, for whatever reason, was not in evidence. Without revealing most of the circumstances surrounding Tony and Delia's marriage, Tony managed to convince the men that his absence was not his choice but hers. Granted, the effort took persuasion both physical and verbal in nature, as well as the application of a great deal of liquor, but the end result was worth it. He now had the support, if somewhat begrudging, of Delia's brothers.

Still, that was not nearly as important as the backing of Delia's sister. Delia's twin sister.

As if on cue, he heard her arrival in the hall. In spite of himself, his heart skipped a beat. Cassandra Effington even sounded like her sister.

A moment later, Mac stepped into the room. "Sir, Miss Effington is here."

Tony drew a deep breath. "Excellent."

When Tony had left the department, Mac had come with him. He said he'd been with Tony so long he wasn't certain how to behave without him. Besides, he'd rather enjoyed helping Tony run Delia's household and thought he'd try his hand at running things on his own, pointing out he could certainly manage to do no worse a job than Tony had. Neither was especially certain what Mac's true position was: He was as much companion as servant. Indeed, both men thought of the Scot as essentially second in command in Tony's household, on the estate and probably in his life as well.

"Sir . . ." Mac hesitated, a puzzled look on his face.

Tony narrowed his eyes. "What is it?"

"I'm not quite sure." Mac shook his head thoughtfully. "It's probably simply nothing more than that it has been some time since I've seen Miss Effington. The resemblance to Lady St. Stephens is remarkable."

"Yes, well, let's hope both women have considerably softened their attitudes toward me. Show her in, Mac."

Mac stepped out of the room and a moment later reappeared, holding the door open for Delia's sister. Miss Effington swept into the parlor and his breath caught. He knew full well this wasn't his wife, but the resemblance was indeed remarkable.

"Good day, my lord." Her manner was brisk but not unpleasant.

"Miss Effington." Tony nodded, not entirely sure how one greeted the sister of an estranged spouse. "I am exceedingly grateful you could see your way clear to meet me."

"I wouldn't have missed it." A polite smile slightly lifted the corners of her mouth.

"Would you care for tea? I have an excellent cook."

"Really? And does she also"—Miss Effington paused for emphasis—"kill husbands?"

Mac choked back a cough.

"Not yet." Tony smiled and nodded at the Scot. "See to it, Mac."

"Tea would be lovely. If his war wounds allow for it," she said in an overly sweet manner.

"I'll manage, miss, thank you for asking," Mac said under his breath, and hurried from the room as if grateful to escape.

Miss Effington glanced around in a considering manner. "I can certainly see why you might need a bit of assistance."

"What?" Tony frowned in confusion. She knew what he wanted? "Oh, you're talking about the house. Of course. It is sadly out of date, or so I've been told. I've only been here for a few days and really haven't paid it much heed."

She raised a brow.

"Certainly even I can see . . ." He blew a resigned breath. "I fear you have found me out, Miss Effington."

"It wasn't especially difficult, my lord," she said mildly, cast a disparaging look at the well-worn sofa, then perched cautiously on its edge. "I assumed refurbishing was not uppermost in your mind these days."

"No." He sat down on a nearby chair and leaned forward. "Your sister is uppermost in my mind. Every hour of every day and every minute of every night. I consider myself an intelligent man, but I have no idea how to approach her and no idea if she'd as yet be receptive to even seeing me." He jumped to his feet and paced before her. "Good Lord, Miss Effington, it's been two long blasted months and four bloody days. I can't sleep, I can't eat, I can't concentrate, I can't think about anything but her. And I have a great deal to think about at the moment."

"The business of being a spy, perhaps?" she said pleasantly.

"*Agent* is the preferred term," he said without thinking, then narrowed his eyes. "You know?"

She nodded.

He should have realized the moment she mentioned murderous housekeepers that Delia had told her what had transpired. "Did she tell you everything?"

"Every horrid detail." Miss Effington's voice was

cool, but she was obviously holding back a grin. The woman, no doubt, enjoyed his discomfort. Her blue eyes glittered with amusement. *Delia's eyes.* He pushed the thought out of his head.

"You do understand the confidential nature of all this?"

Her eyes widened with indignation. "Do *you* understand that neither I nor anyone in my family would ever do anything that was not in the best interests of the crown?"

"Certainly, I simply—"

"And I should think revealing the comedy of errors that has taken place in my—my sister's house would certainly fall into that category."

"It was perhaps not our finest hour. Still, our intentions—"

"Intentions?" She snorted in a most unladylike manner.

He bit back a sharp reply. He wanted this woman on his side, after all. "Forgive me, Miss Effington." Tony ran his hand through his hair. "You're right, of course. It was all a disaster from beginning to end. Ill-advised, poorly planned and in many ways quite mad. I admit all of that. I further admit that I have a difficult time regretting most of it."

She stared in disbelief. "How can you possibly say that?"

"Because it's true." He sat down and met her gaze firmly. "While indeed my original purpose was primarily to protect Delia in the guise of her butler, I became her friend as well. And she became mine."

"But it was all a lie."

"Some of the details, perhaps, but not the feelings, the emotions, as it were." He struggled to choose the right words. "There was more truth in some of our discussions—on my part, at least—than I have ever known with anyone. It makes no sense, perhaps. I can't say I understand it myself. As for your sister . . ." He shook his head. "She was forthright and honest and caring. It's in those moments that we spent together playing backgammon and talking of matters of consequence or completely insignificant that I fell in love with her. It was as her servant, when I was pretending to be someone else, that I saw her with no pretense at all. And it was then she claimed my heart.

"No, Miss Effington." He shook his head. "Regardless of how it may seem to you, that I cannot regret. Nor do I regret loving her. I am, however, deeply sorry for the pain I have caused her, and I promise you I shall spend the rest of my days making it up to her."

"Will you?" Her voice was soft.

"You have my word." He caught her gaze. "Miss Effington, will you help me?"

"My lord, I . . ." She raised her chin. "I fear I have something of a confession—"

"Tea!" Mac strode into the room bearing a tray with the various and sundry items that comprised tea and a determined expression on his face. He set the tray down so hard the cups rattled and leaned toward Tony, lowering his voice confidentially. "Sir, I need to speak to you."

"Not now." Tony turned his attention back to Miss Effington. "You were—"

"Sir." Mac's voice rang a good two shades louder than necessary. "Perhaps Miss Effington would like to pour?"

"Of course." Tony smiled at her. "If you would be so kind."

Miss Effington started to reach out, then stopped. "I'd really rather not, if you don't mind. I find I'm a bit clumsy today."

A slight smile of triumph curved Mac's lips. What on earth did he have to feel smug about?

Mac handed Miss Effington a cup and their gazes met. The Scot's grin widened. Miss Effington appeared just the least bit flustered. It was all exceedingly odd, as though the two of them shared a secret Tony wasn't privy to.

"Sir, your cup." Mac thrust the cup at him and Tony could have sworn the man did it deliberately. Scalding liquid splashed onto Tony's lap.

"Yow!" Tony leapt to his feet which just resulted in the remaining tea splashing onto the front of his shirt, down the rest of him and onto the floor.

"Good heavens!" Miss Effington jumped up. "Are you all right?"

"Blast it all, man, what are you doing?" Tony glared at Mac.

"Sorry, sir." Mac's tone was contrite, but he was obviously trying not to grin. Tony grabbed a cloth off the tray and waved ineffectually at the wet spots on his clothes.

"Here." Miss Effington snatched the cloth from him. "Let me do that. You, MacPherson, go find something to clean up the mess on the floor." She proceeded to blot at the spill on Tony's chest.

"Really, Miss Effington, this is not necessary." Oh, this was certainly going well. She was dabbing a bit harder than necessary too. He stared down at her and his breath caught. Tony cast a quick glance over her head. Mac lounged in the doorway, a definite smirk on his face. Tony nodded almost imperceptively, stifling a grin of his own.

"Miss Effington." He caught her hand against his chest. *Her right hand.* His gaze trapped hers. "I have never noticed how like your sister you are."

"Well, there are some differences," she said uneasily, and tried to pull away.

He refused to let her go. "They're not apparent. In truth, they're insignificant. Your hair is her hair. Your eyes are her eyes." He jerked her into his arms. "You fit against me as perfectly as she does."

"My lord, release me at once!"

"I can't. Being without her has driven me mad. And you are so very much . . ." His gaze dropped to her mouth. "Do your lips taste like hers as well, I wonder?"

She gasped. "You wouldn't dare."

"Oh, but I would."

"You . . . you . . . I fear you have me at a disadvantage."

"I do hope so."

"My lord, I'm—"

"I'm going to kiss you, Miss Effington, and you are going to kiss me back." He tightened his embrace and leaned close to nuzzle the side of her neck. "Unless you would prefer to play highwayman and . . ."

She stilled.

". . . runaway princess."

Delia held her breath for a moment, then sighed. "You are a wicked, wicked man, St. Stephens."

"You have made me wicked."

"I have a confession to make," she said quickly.

"Why?" he murmured against her warm silken skin. "You don't make them well."

"You'll like this one." Delia drew a deep breath. "I have, more or less, decided to forgive you."

He drew back and stared down at her, into the blue eyes that had haunted his days and nights. "More or less?"

"Well, I certainly don't intend to ever let you forget all that has happened." She raised her chin in that way she had when she was taking on the world itself. Or right now, perhaps just the future. "I shall hold it over your head forever and use it to get whatever I want from you until the day I die."

"I see. You're saying that you will make me pay for my sins for the rest of my life."

"Absolutely." She nodded firmly.

He paused for a moment, then nodded. "I believe it's worth it."

"You were a charming old man." She slipped her arms around his neck and grinned up at him, the dimple in her right cheek flashing. "But you were a terrible butler, you know."

"And you, my love, were a most improper widow."

"Are you still a spy?"

"Agent," he said. "No. Simply a viscount. In dire need of a viscountess."

"Pity," she said with a grin.

"Why?"

"Well . . ." She sighed with exaggerated regret. "I didn't have the chance to become a woman of experience. And the last time I went to bed with a spy, I woke up to find my house in flames. It was really quite an adventure."

He laughed. "Grand?"

"Oh, most certainly grand." Her gaze met his and she sobered. "I have missed you more than I can say. And regardless of what has brought us to this point, I too cannot regret much of it because it led to you. To us. To a happiness I suspect will be the grandest adventure of all."

"And I have missed you. I . . ." He shook his head. He'd never been especially good with words, and words failed him now.

She laughed with joy that reflected his own. "I see I have you at a disadvantage."

"And I fear you will have me that way for the rest of our days."

He pulled her closer and bent to meet her lips with his, and knew she would always have him at a disadvantage. And knew as well she was his love, his life, and would be, for now and forever, for him and him alone, the only lady in question.